SAINTS

GENE LUEN YANG

COLOR BY
LARK PIEN

First Second

NEW YORK

First Second

Copyright © 2013 by Gene Luen Yang

Published by First Second
First Second is an imprint of Roaring Brook Press,
a division of Holtzbrinck Publishing Holdings Limited Partnership
175 Fifth Avenue, New York, New York 10010

Cataloging-in-Publication Data is on file at the Library of Congress.

ISBN 978-1-59643-689-3

First Second books may be purchased for business or promotional use. For information
on bulk purchases please contact Macmillan Corporate and Premium Sales Department
at (800) 221-7945 x5442 or by email at specialmarkets@macmillan.com.

FIRST
EDITION

First edition 2013
Book design by Rob Steen
Color by Lark Pien

Printed in China
10 9 8 7 6 5 4 3 2

BY ART
WE LIVE

Dedicated to the San Jose Chinese Catholic Community

第一章

Age 8

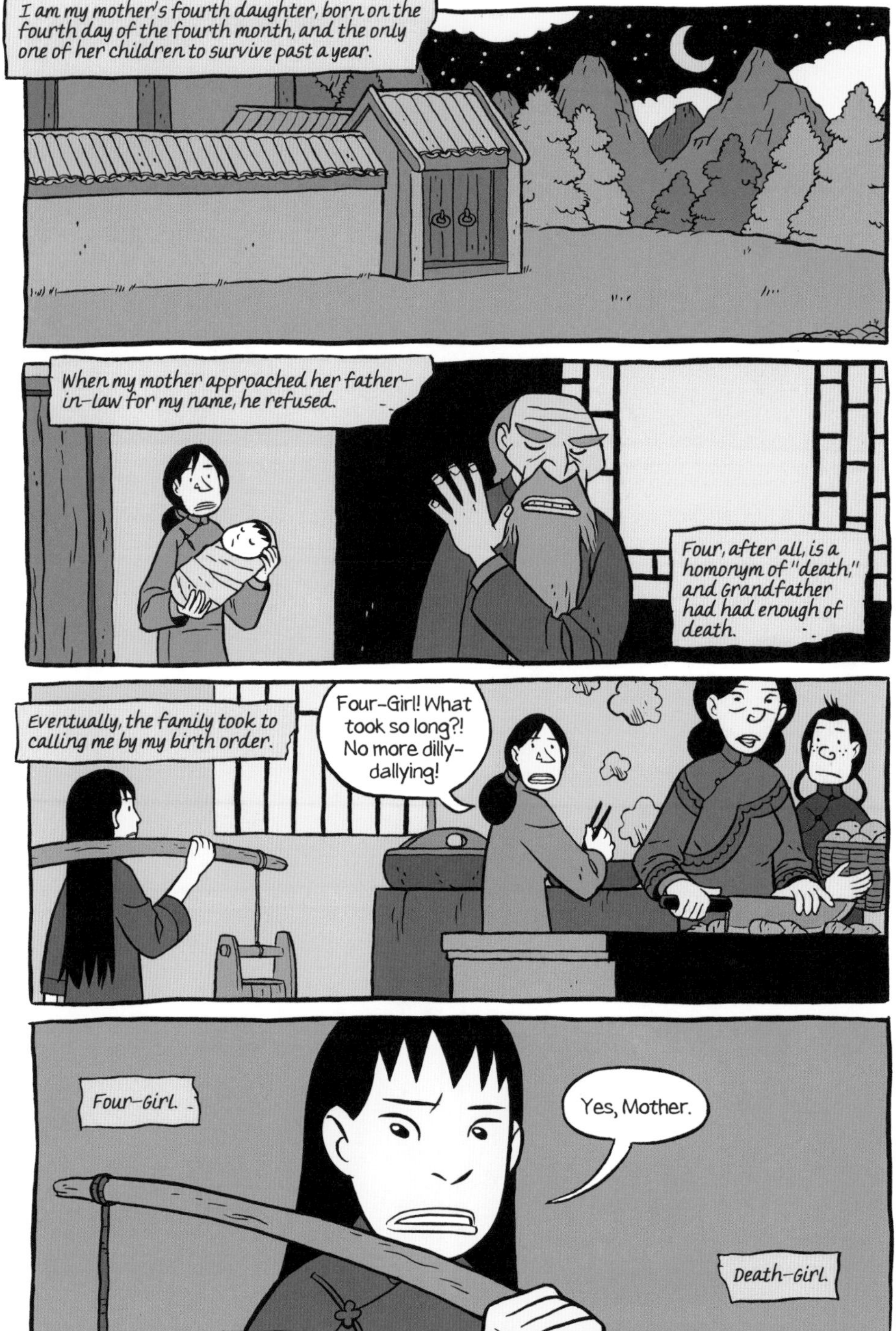
I am my mother's fourth daughter, born on the fourth day of the fourth month, and the only one of her children to survive past a year.
When my mother approached her father-in-law for my name, he refused.
Four, after all, is a homonym of "death," and Grandfather had had enough of death.
Eventually, the family took to calling me by my birth order.
Four-Girl! What took so long?! No more dilly-dallying!
Four-Girl.
Yes, Mother.
Death-Girl.

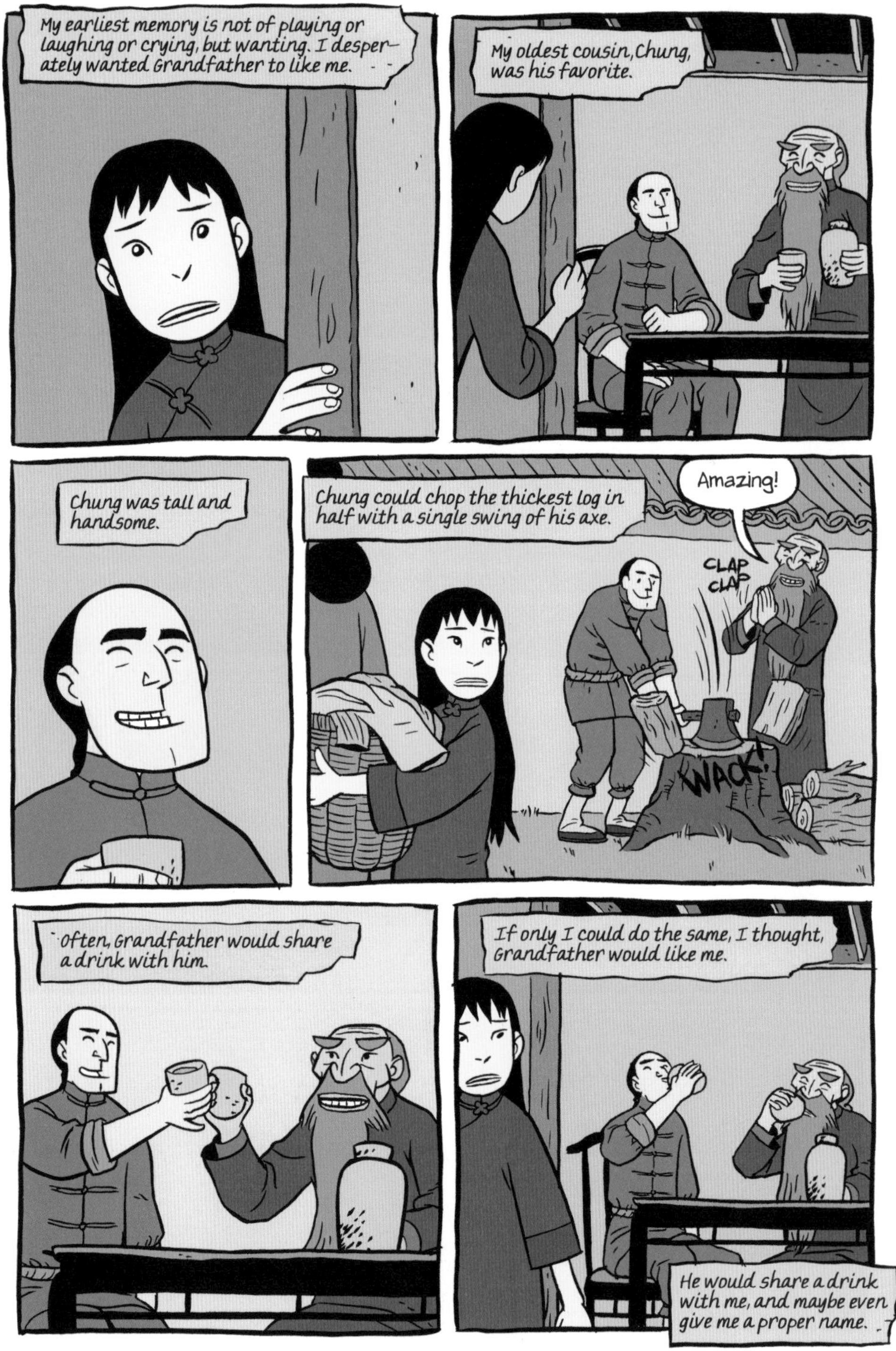
My earliest memory is not of playing or laughing or crying, but wanting. I desperately wanted Grandfather to like me.
My oldest cousin, Chung, was his favorite.
Chung was tall and handsome.
Chung could chop the thickest log in half with a single swing of his axe.
Amazing!
CLAP CLAP
WACK!
Often, Grandfather would share a drink with him.
If only I could do the same, I thought, Grandfather would like me.
He would share a drink with me, and maybe even give me a proper name.

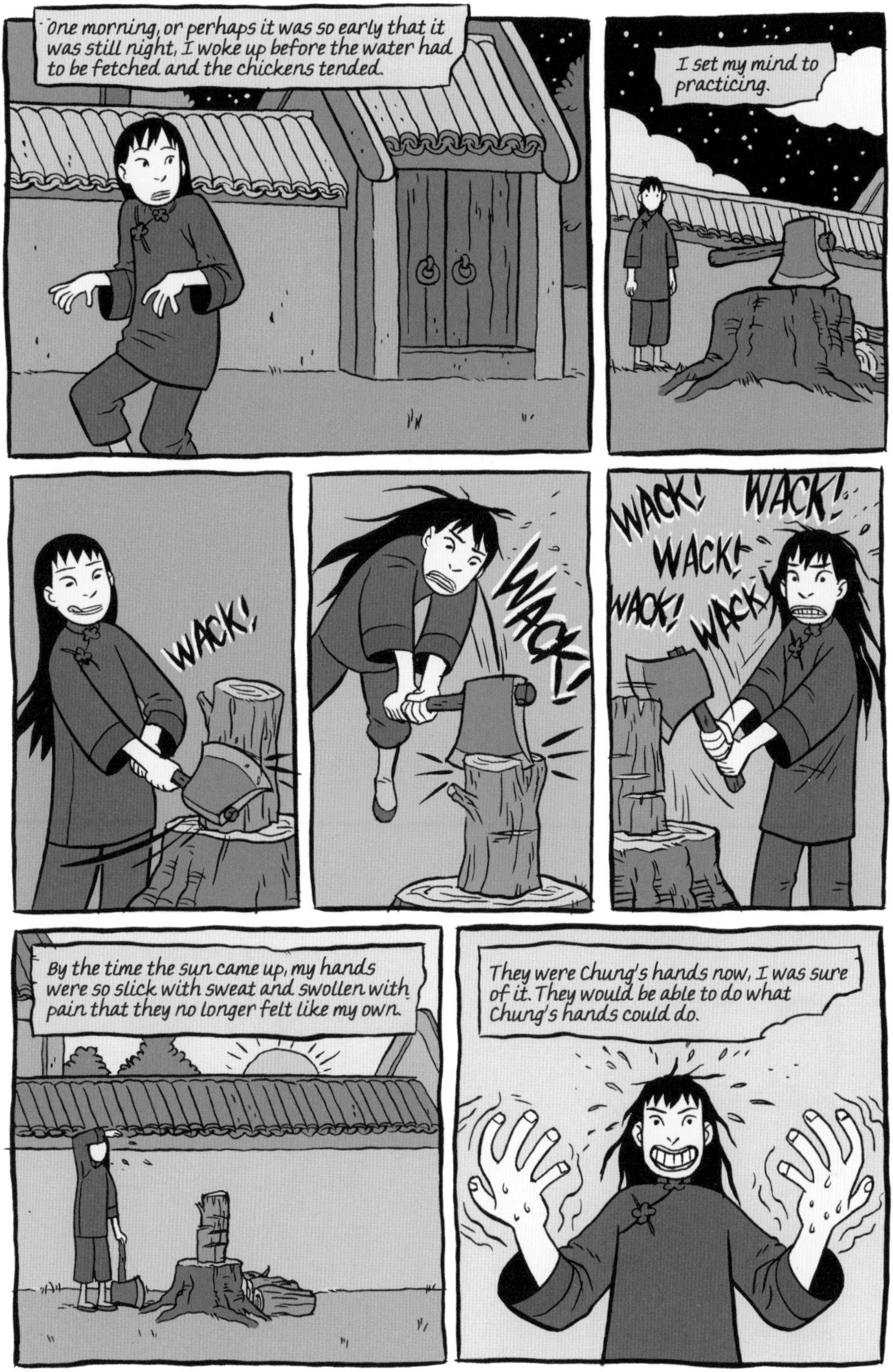

One morning, or perhaps it was so early that it was still night, I woke up before the water had to be fetched and the chickens tended.
I set my mind to practicing.
WACK!
WACK!
WACK!
WACK!
WACK!
WACK!
WACK!
By the time the sun came up, my hands were so slick with sweat and swollen with pain that they no longer felt like my own.
They were Chung's hands now, I was sure of it. They would be able to do what Chung's hands could do.

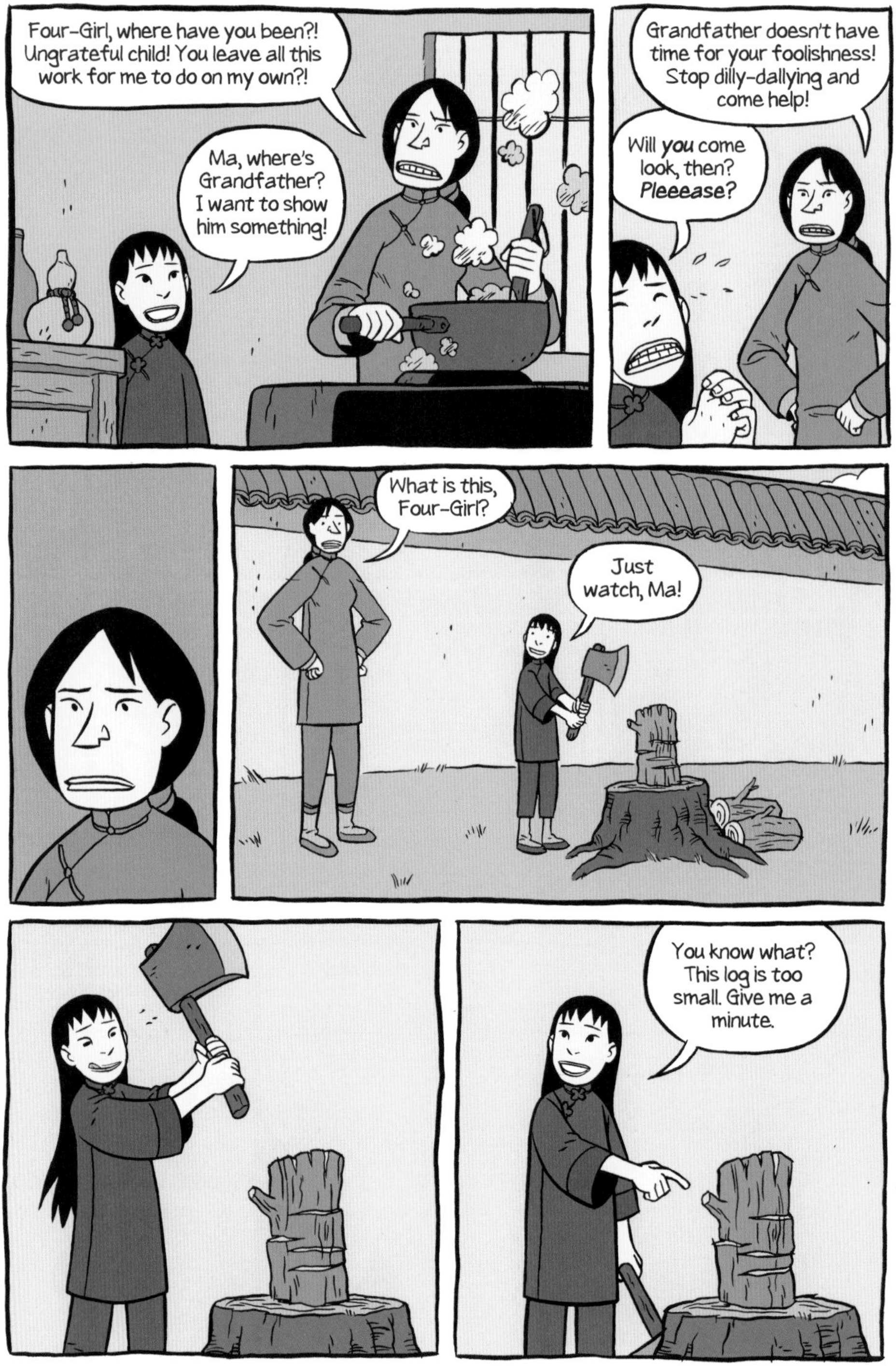
Four-Girl, where have you been?! Ungrateful child! You leave all this work for me to do on my own?!
Ma, where's Grandfather? I want to show him something!
Grandfather doesn't have time for your foolishness! Stop dilly-dallying and come help!
Will *you* come look, then? *Pleeease*?
What is this, Four-Girl?
Just watch, Ma!
You know what? This log is too small. Give me a minute.

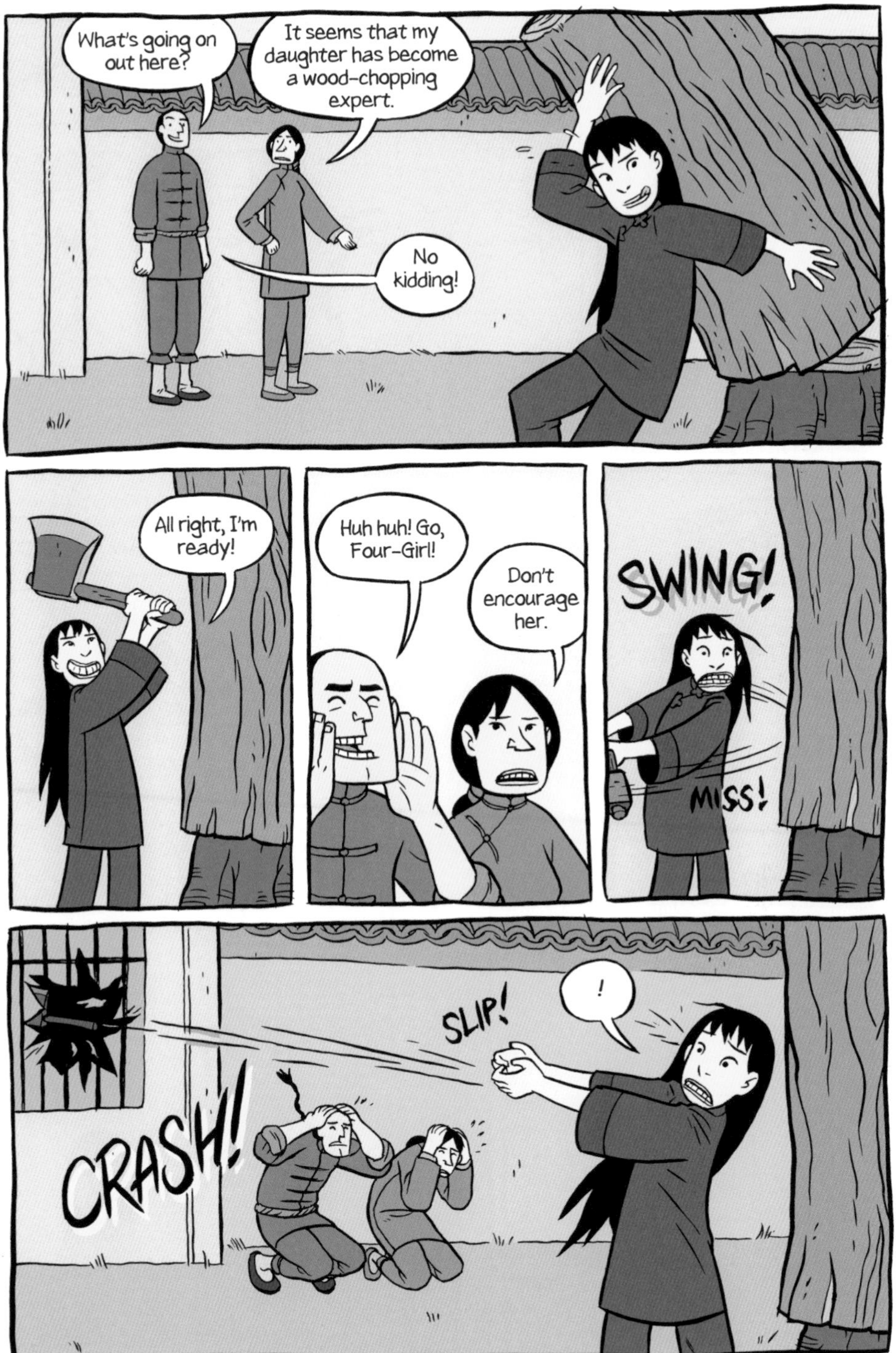
What's going on out here?
It seems that my daughter has become a wood-chopping expert.
No kidding!
All right, I'm ready!
Huh huh! Go, Four-Girl!
Don't encourage her.
SWING!
MISS!
!
SLIP!
CRASH!

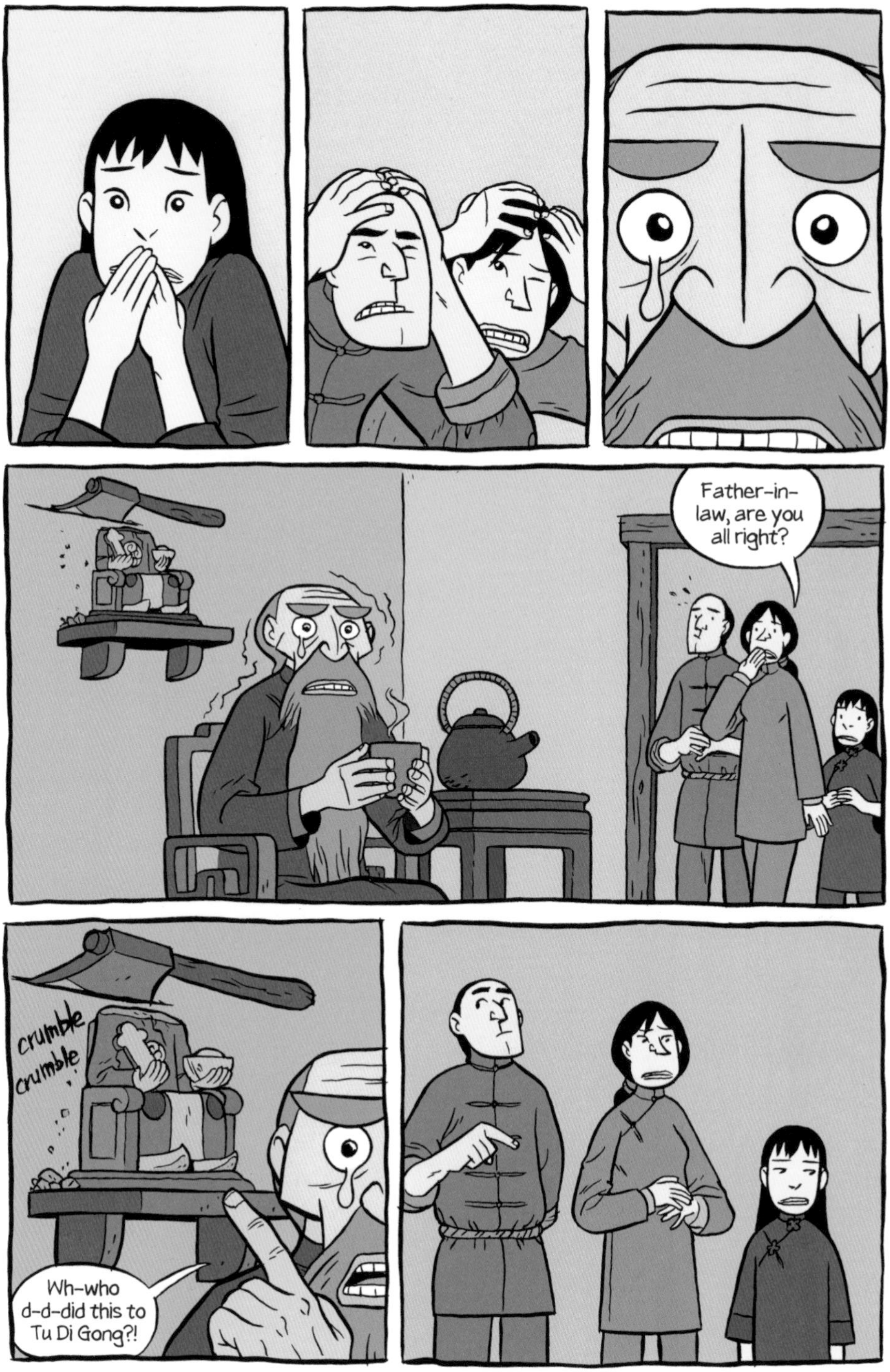
Father-in-law, are you all right?
crumble crumble
Wh-who d-d-did this to Tu Di Gong?!

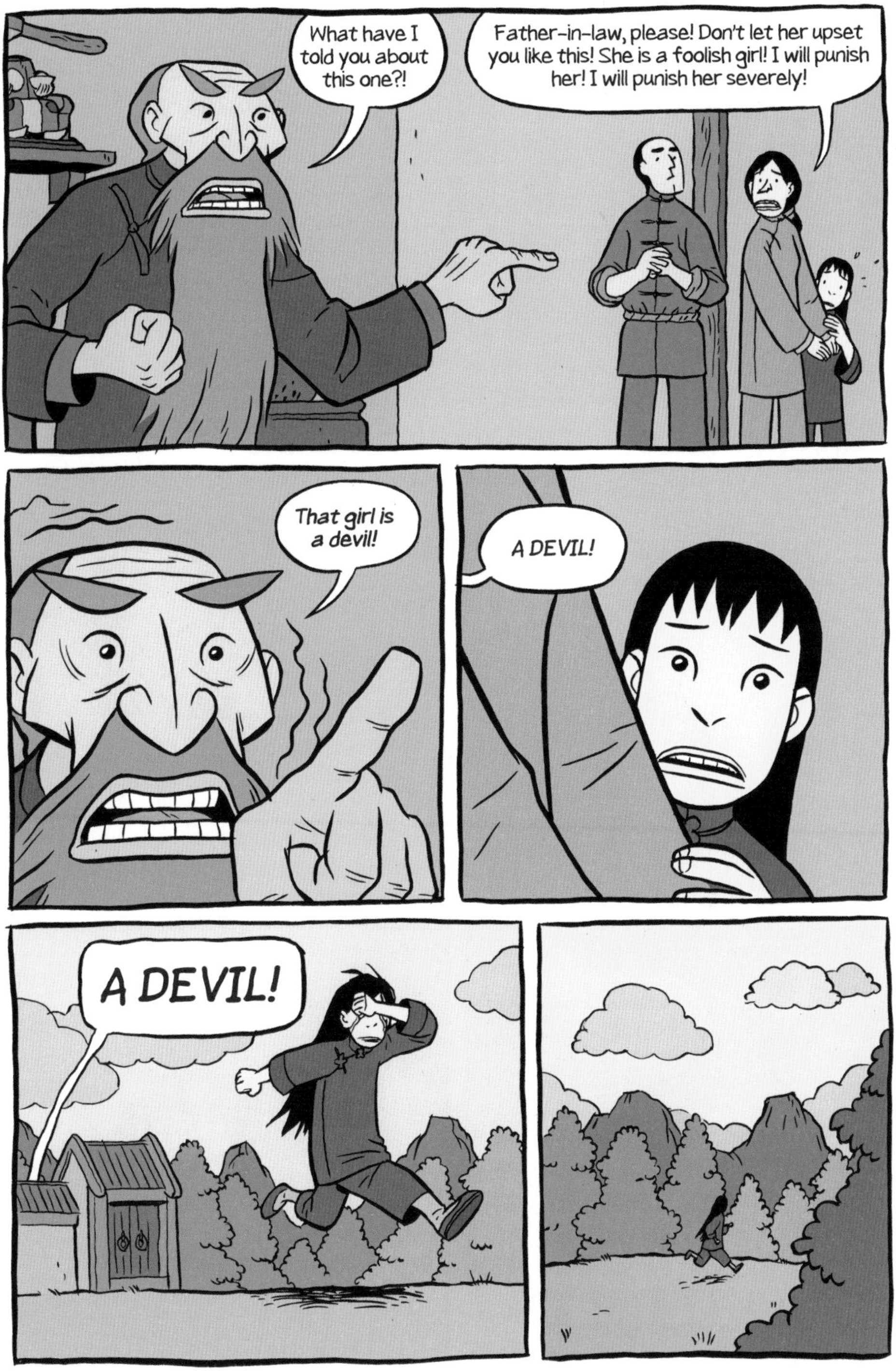
What have I told you about this one?!
Father-in-law, please! Don't let her upset you like this! She is a foolish girl! I will punish her! I will punish her severely!
That girl is a devil!
A DEVIL!
A DEVIL!

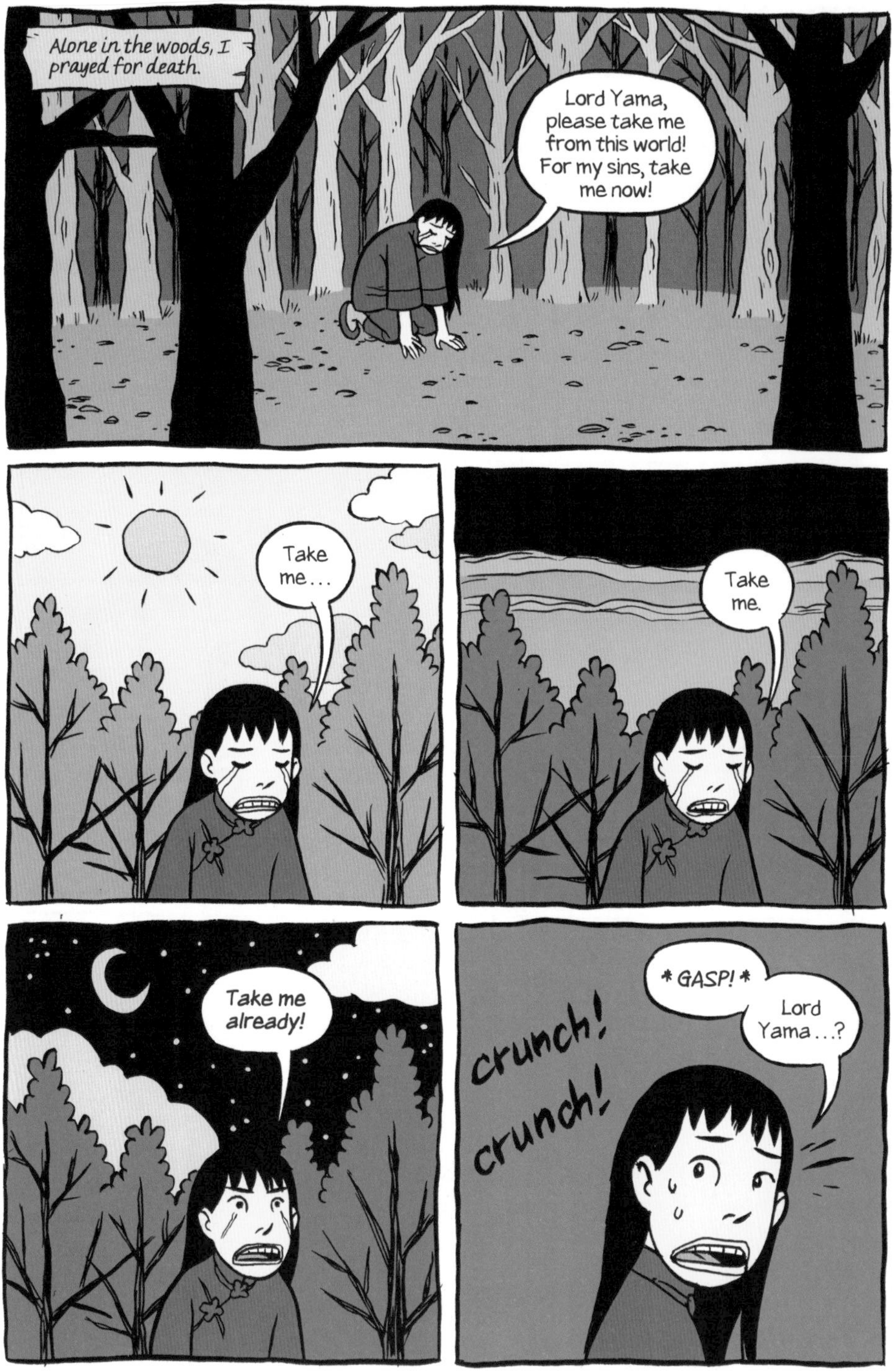
Alone in the woods, I prayed for death.
Lord Yama, please take me from this world! For my sins, take me now!
Take me...
Take me.
Take me already!
crunch! crunch!
GASP!
Lord Yama...?

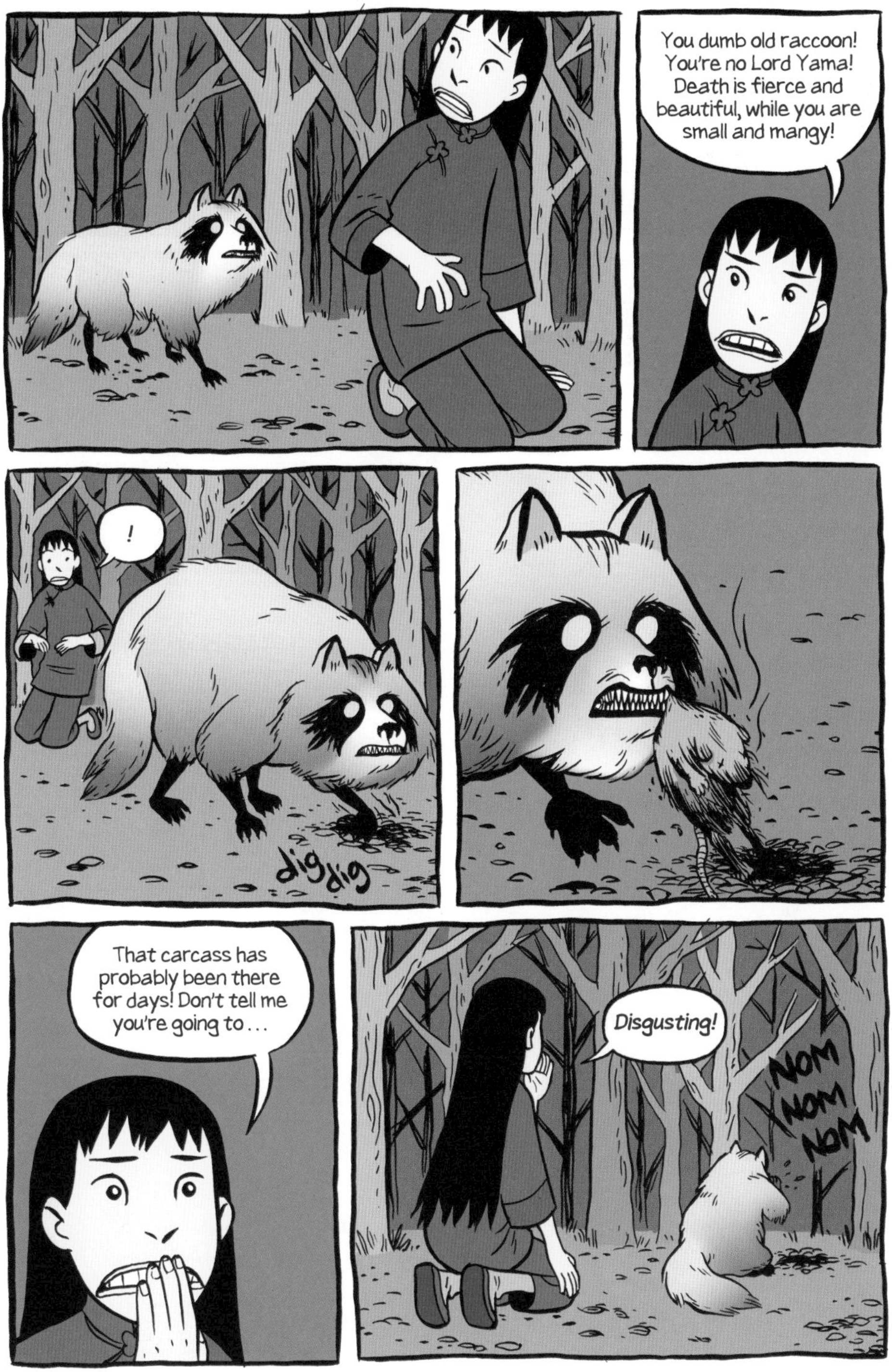
You dumb old raccoon! You're no Lord Yama! Death is fierce and beautiful, while you are small and mangy!
!
dig dig
That carcass has probably been there for days! Don't tell me you're going to . . .
Disgusting!
NOM NOM NOM

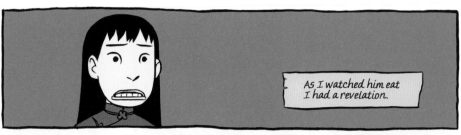

As I watched him eat I had a revelation.

Despite being the most wretched of animals, Old Raccoon didn't shed a tear.

He knew his place in the world and accepted it.

That night, I resolved to do the same.

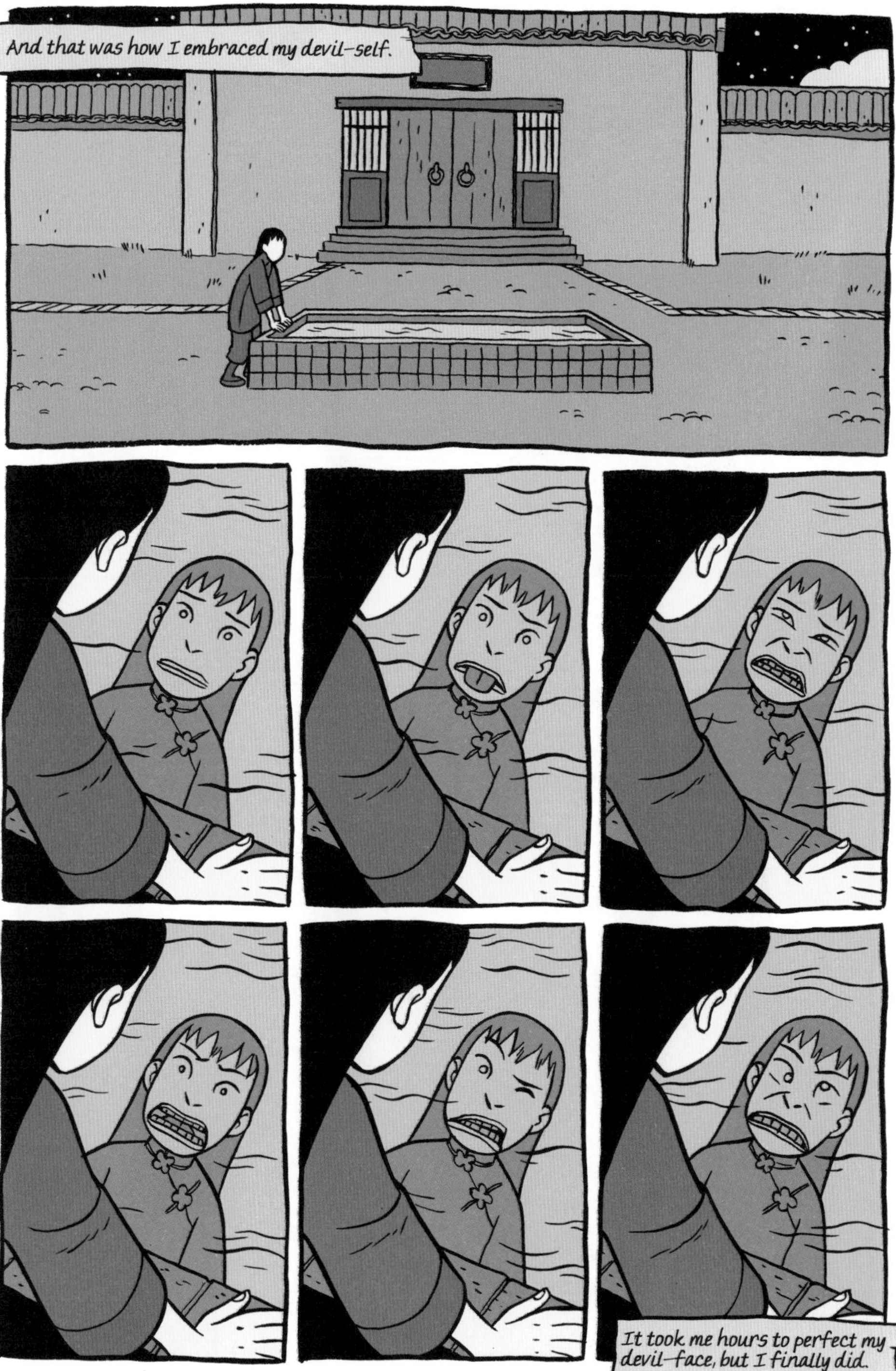
And that was how I embraced my devil-self.
It took me hours to perfect my devil-face, but I finally did.

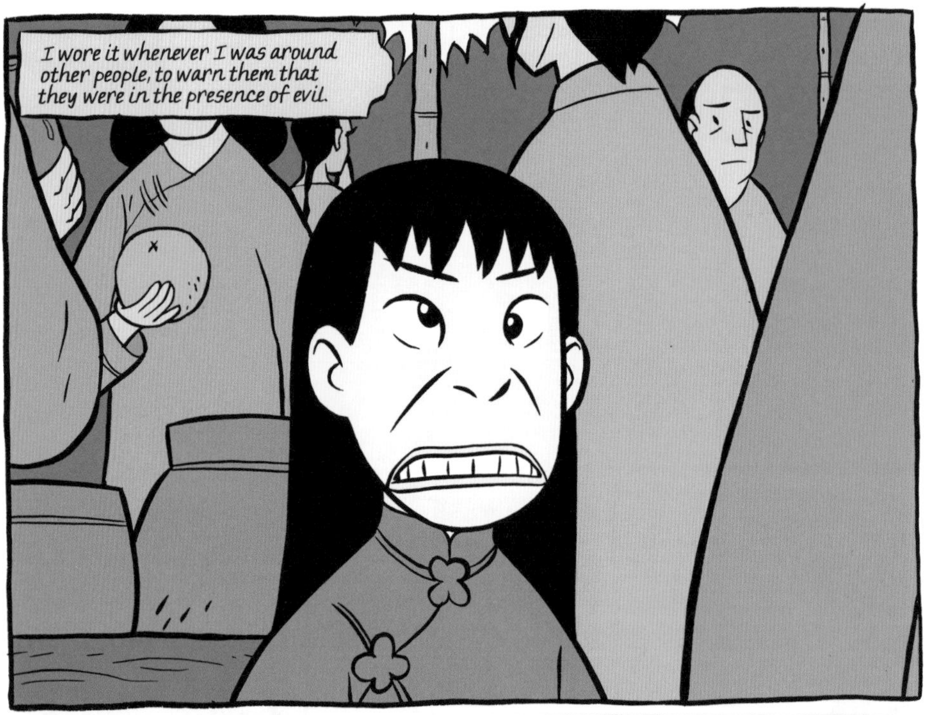
I wore it whenever I was around other people, to warn them that they were in the presence of evil.

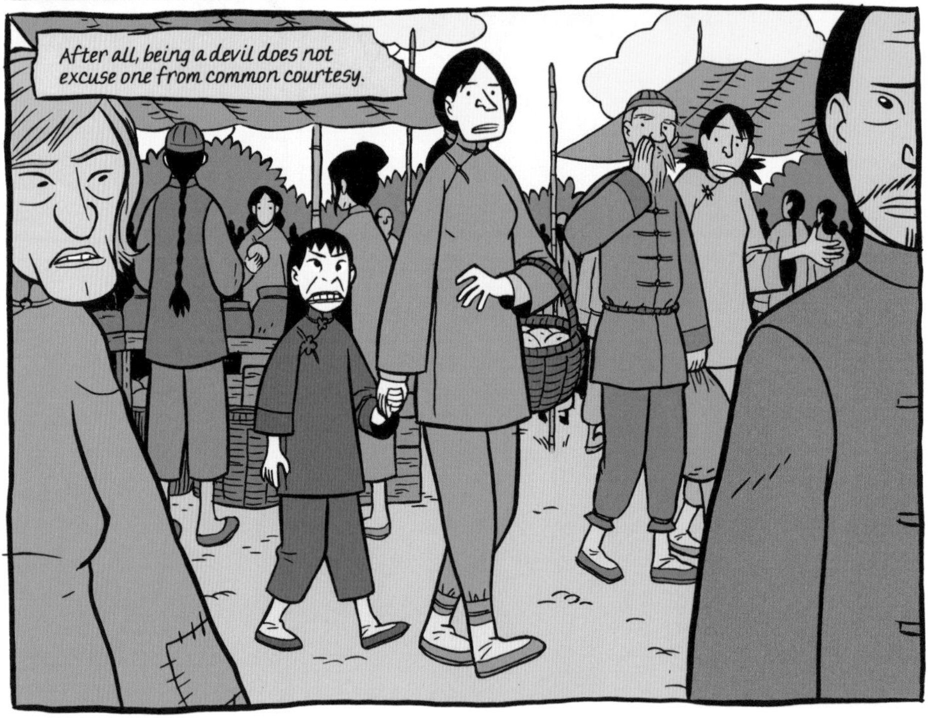
After all, being a devil does not excuse one from common courtesy.

第二章

Age 8

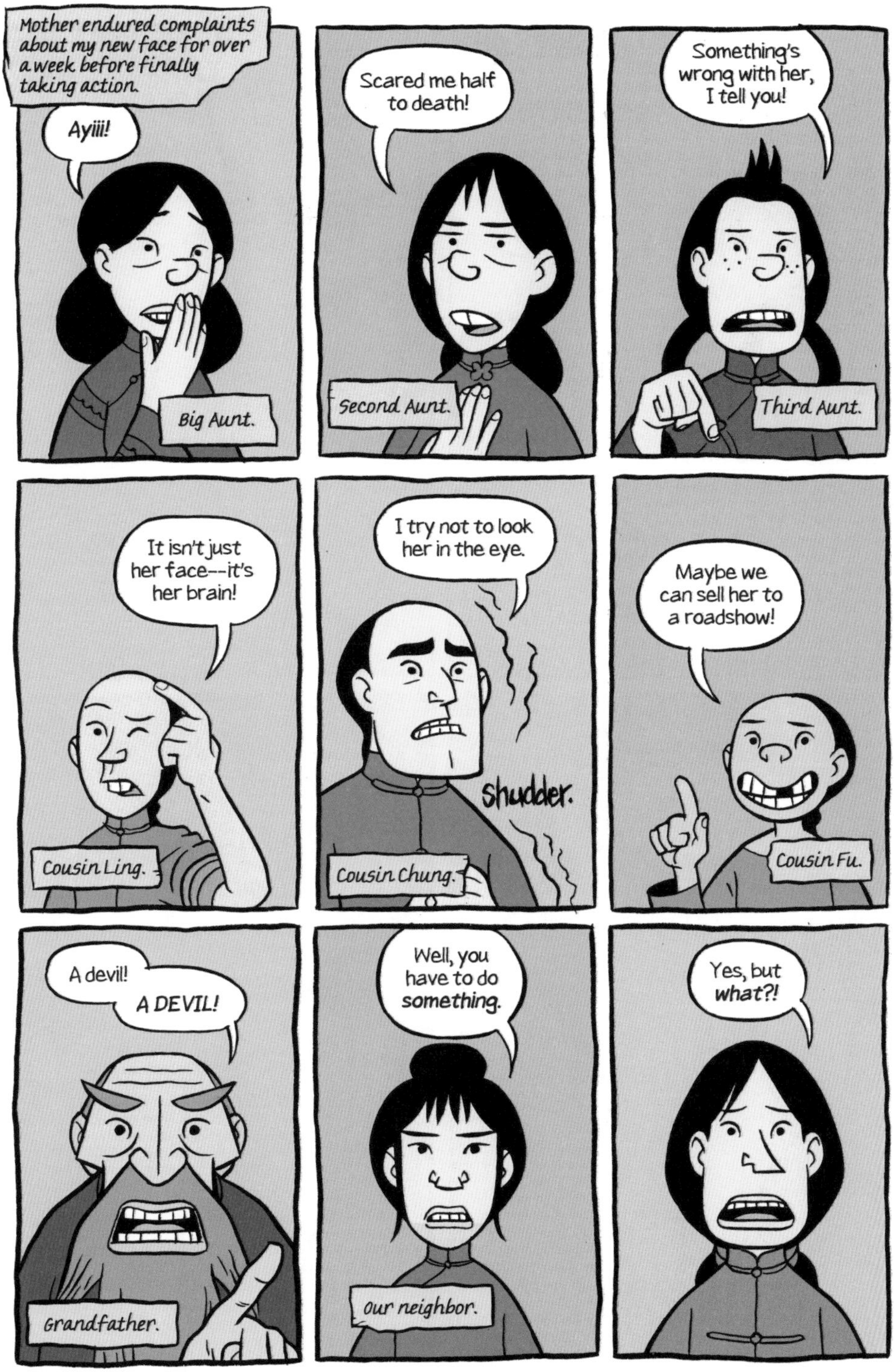
Mother endured complaints about my new face for over a week before finally taking action.
Ayiii!
Big Aunt.
Scared me half to death!
Second Aunt.
Something's wrong with her, I tell you!
Third Aunt.
It isn't just her face--it's her brain!
Cousin Ling.
I try not to look her in the eye.
shudder.
Cousin Chung.
Maybe we can sell her to a roadshow!
Cousin Fu.
A devil!
A DEVIL!
Grandfather.
Well, you have to do *something*.
Our neighbor.
Yes, but *what?!*

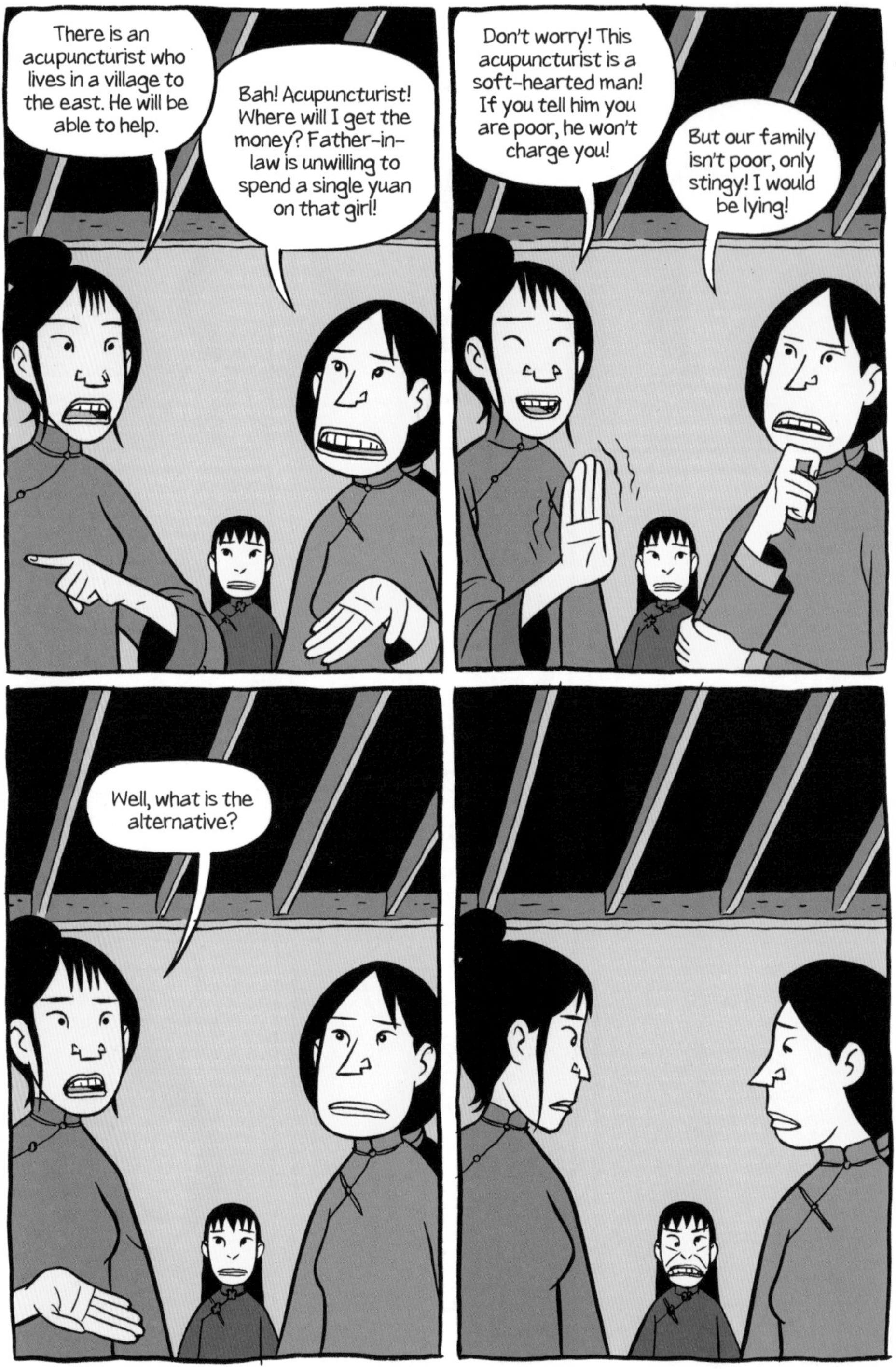
There is an acupuncturist who lives in a village to the east. He will be able to help.
Bah! Acupuncturist! Where will I get the money? Father-in-law is unwilling to spend a single yuan on that girl!
Don't worry! This acupuncturist is a soft-hearted man! If you tell him you are poor, he won't charge you!
But our family isn't poor, only stingy! I would be lying!
Well, what is the alternative?

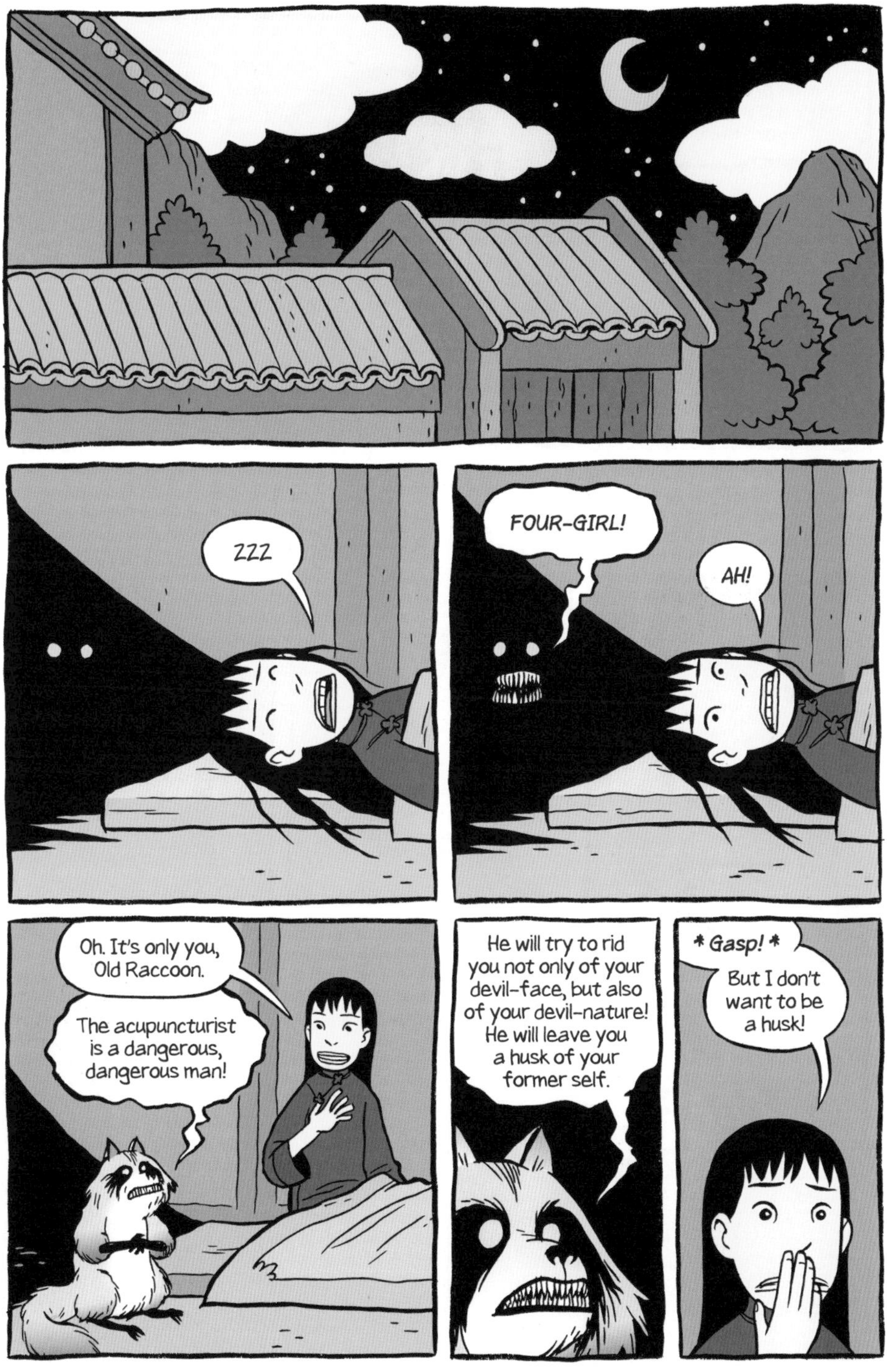
ZZZ
FOUR-GIRL!
AH!
Oh. It's only you, Old Raccoon.
The acupuncturist is a dangerous, dangerous man!
He will try to rid you not only of your devil-face, but also of your devil-nature! He will leave you a husk of your former self.
* Gasp! *
But I don't want to be a husk!

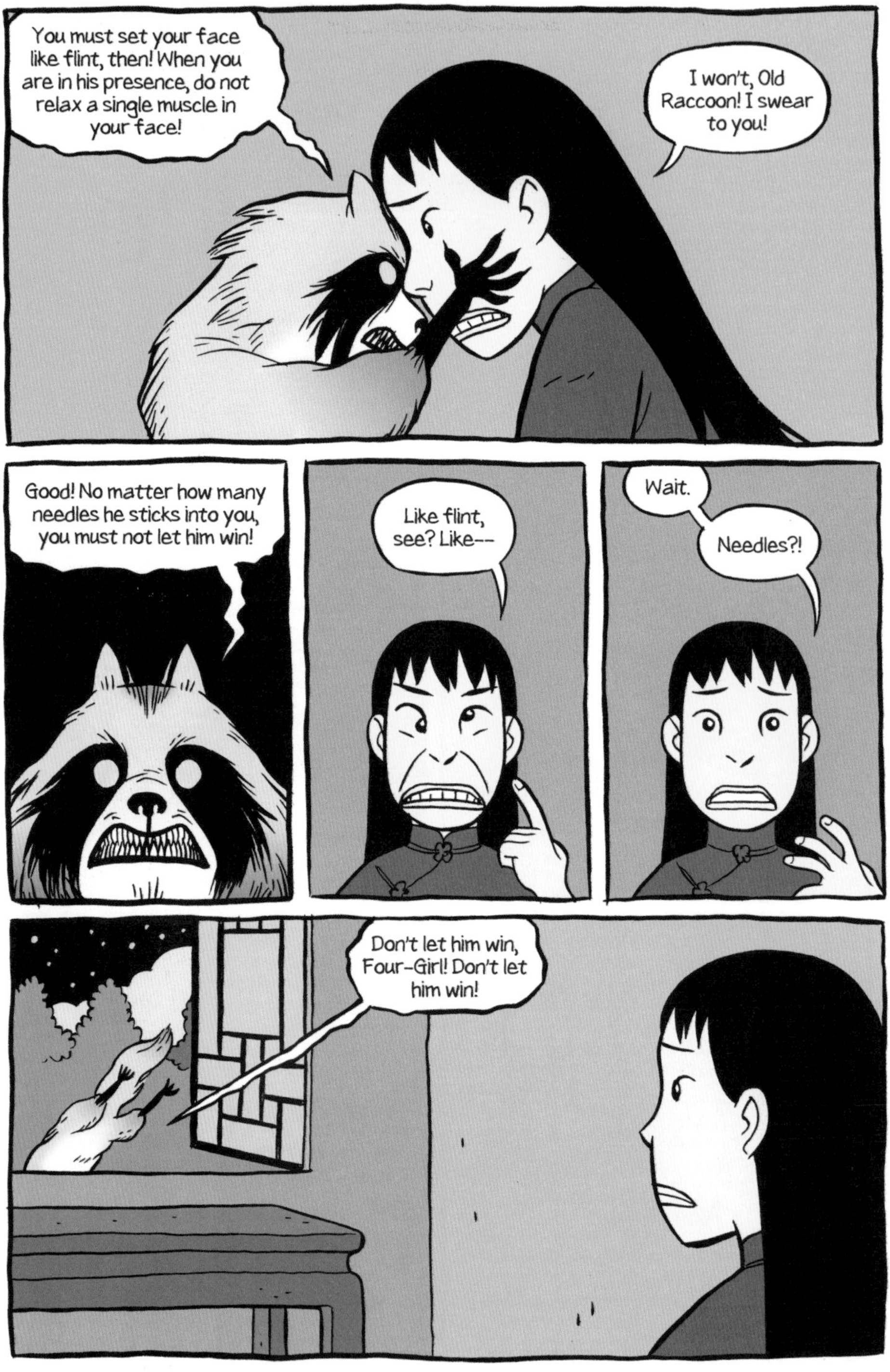
You must set your face like flint, then! When you are in his presence, do not relax a single muscle in your face!
I won't, Old Raccoon! I swear to you!
Good! No matter how many needles he sticks into you, you must not let him win!
Like flint, see? Like--
Wait.
Needles?!
Don't let him win, Four-Girl! Don't let him win!

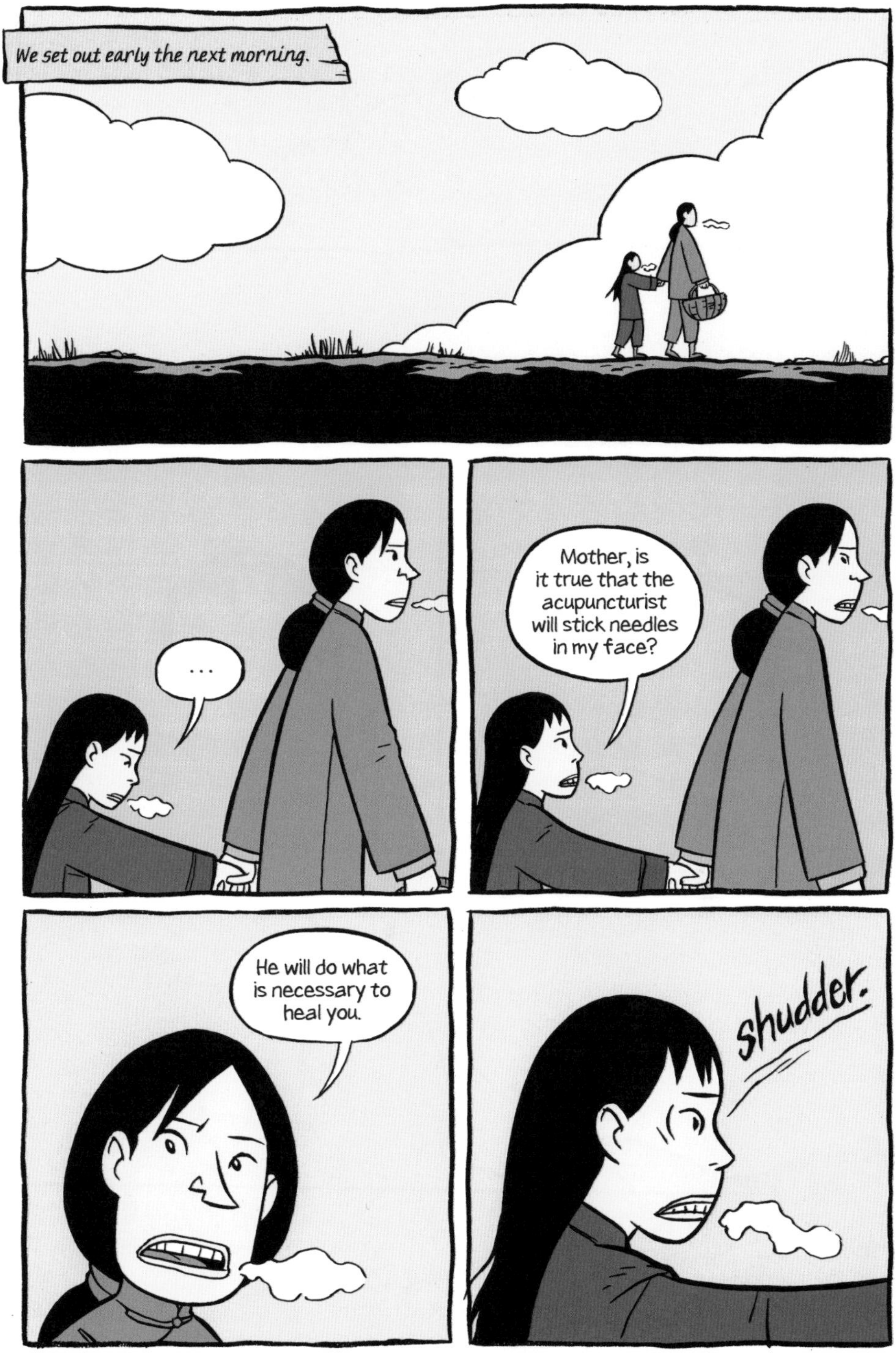
We set out early the next morning.
...
Mother, is it true that the acupuncturist will stick needles in my face?
He will do what is necessary to heal you.
shudder.

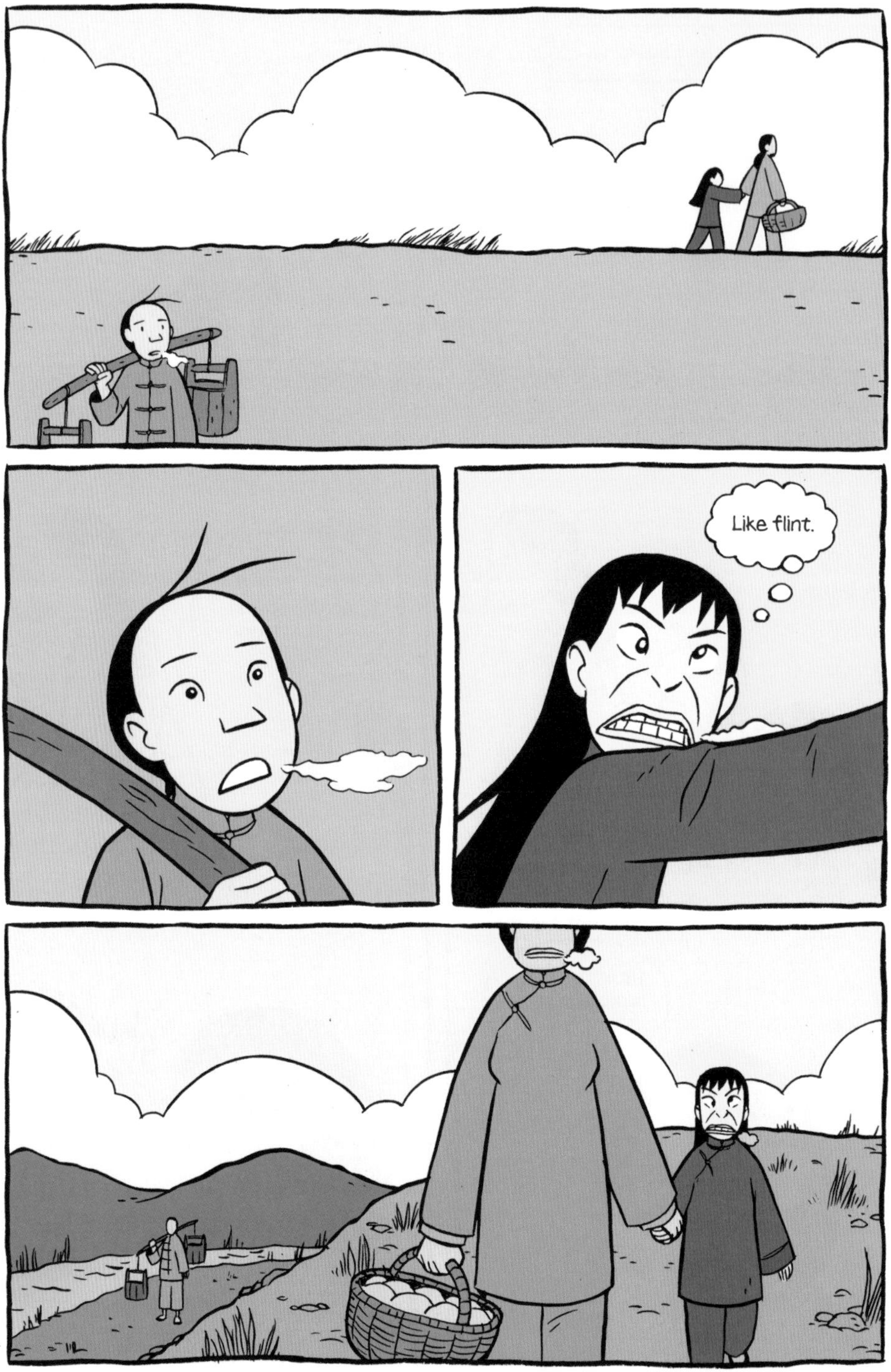
Like flint.

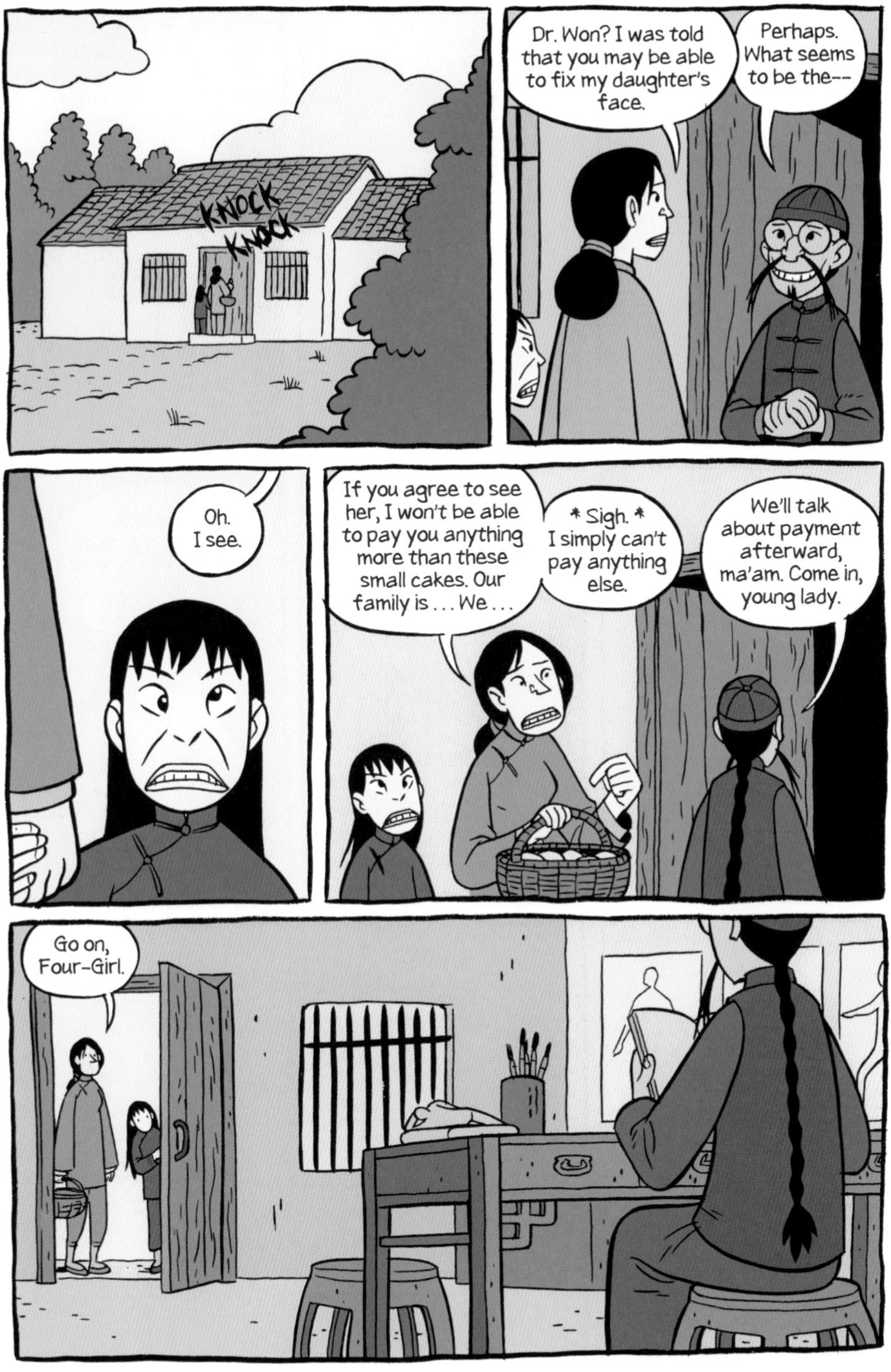
KNOCK
KNOCK
Dr. Won? I was told that you may be able to fix my daughter's face.
Perhaps. What seems to be the--
Oh. I see.
If you agree to see her, I won't be able to pay you anything more than these small cakes. Our family is . . . We . . .
* Sigh. * I simply can't pay anything else.
We'll talk about payment afterward, ma'am. Come in, young lady.
Go on, Four-Girl.

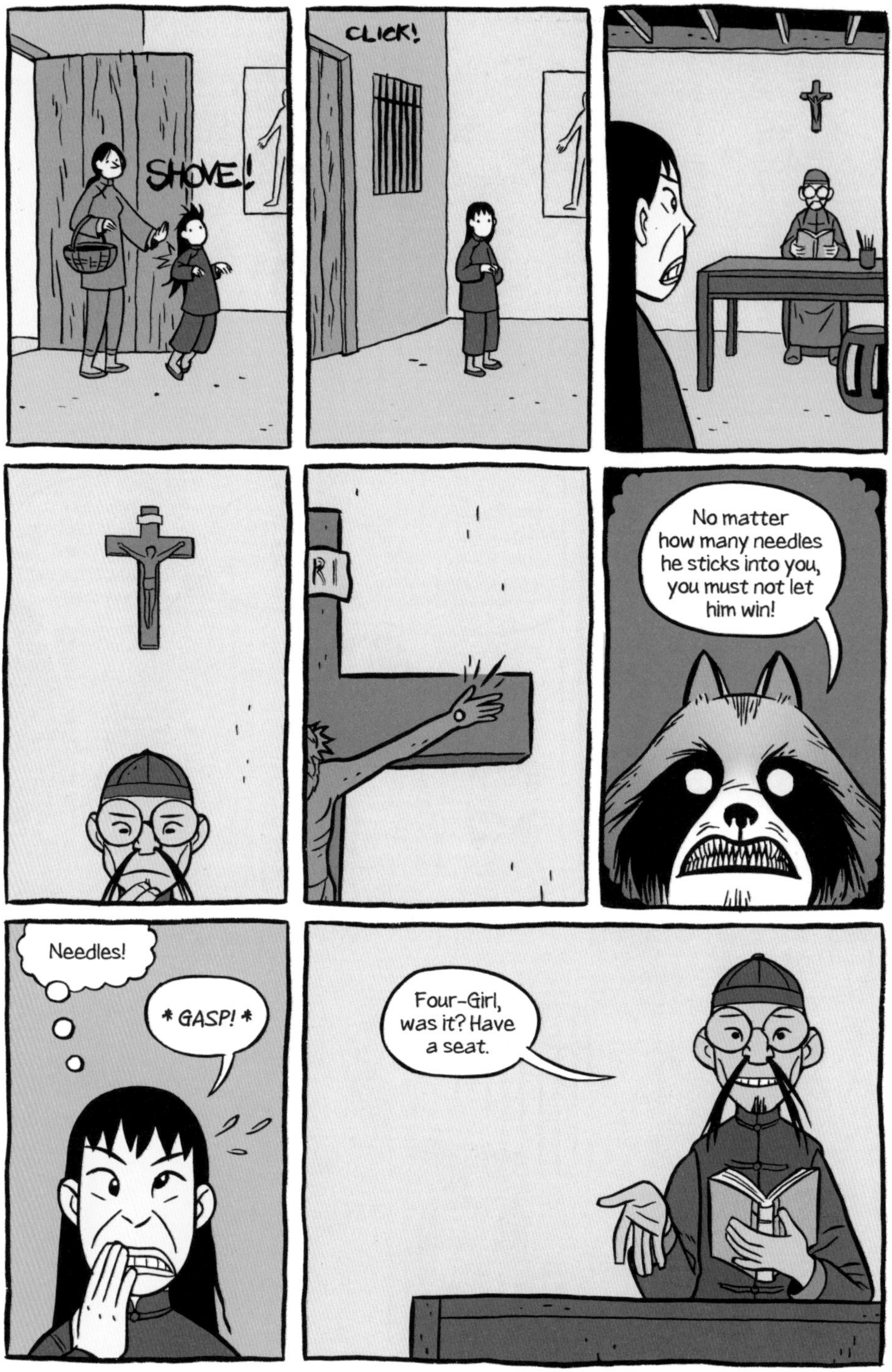
SHOVE!
CLICK!
No matter how many needles he sticks into you, you must not let him win!
Needles!
* GASP! *
Four-Girl, was it? Have a seat.

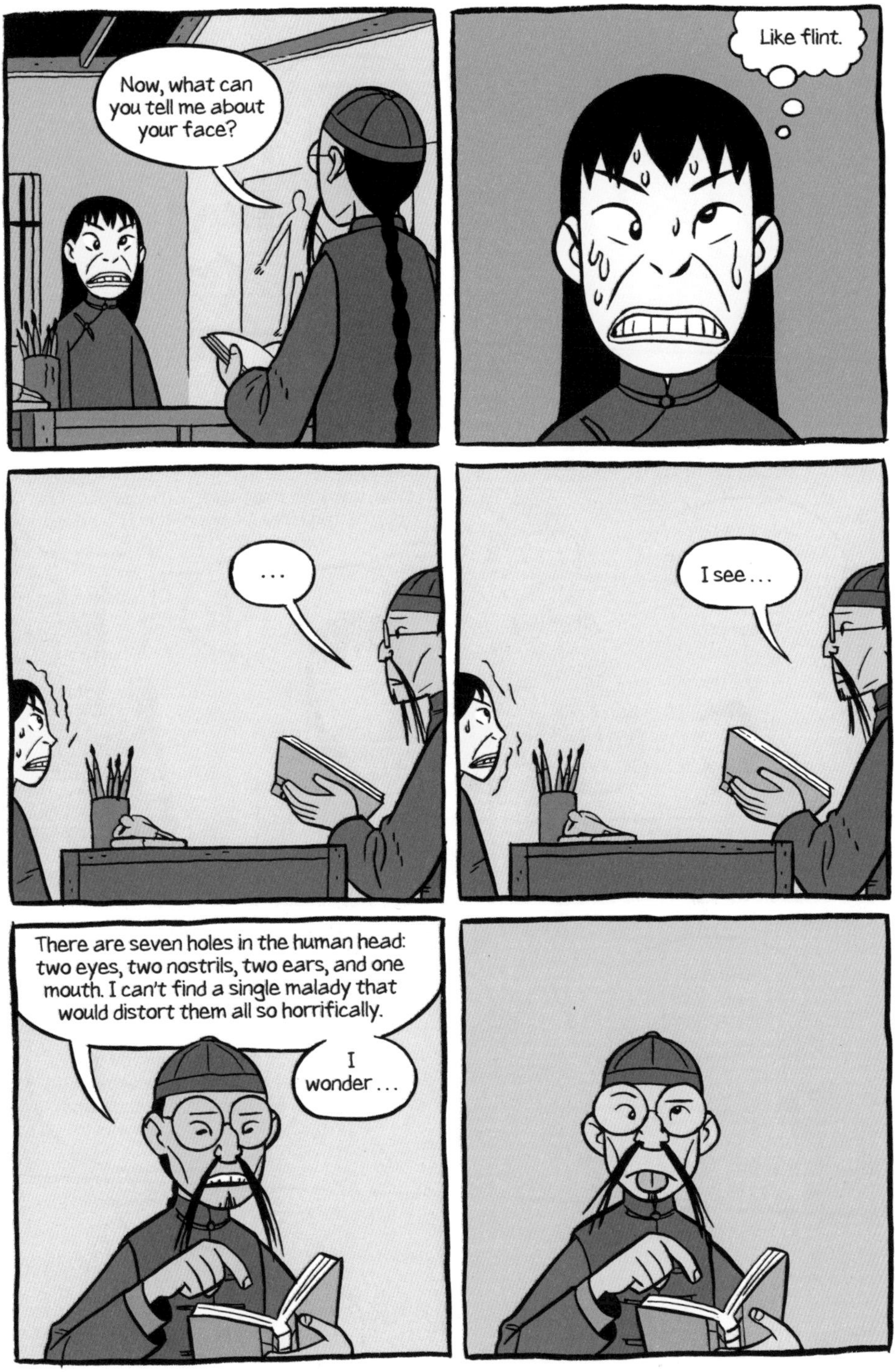
Now, what can you tell me about your face?
Like flint.
...
I see...
There are seven holes in the human head: two eyes, two nostrils, two ears, and one mouth. I can't find a single malady that would distort them all so horrifically.
I wonder...

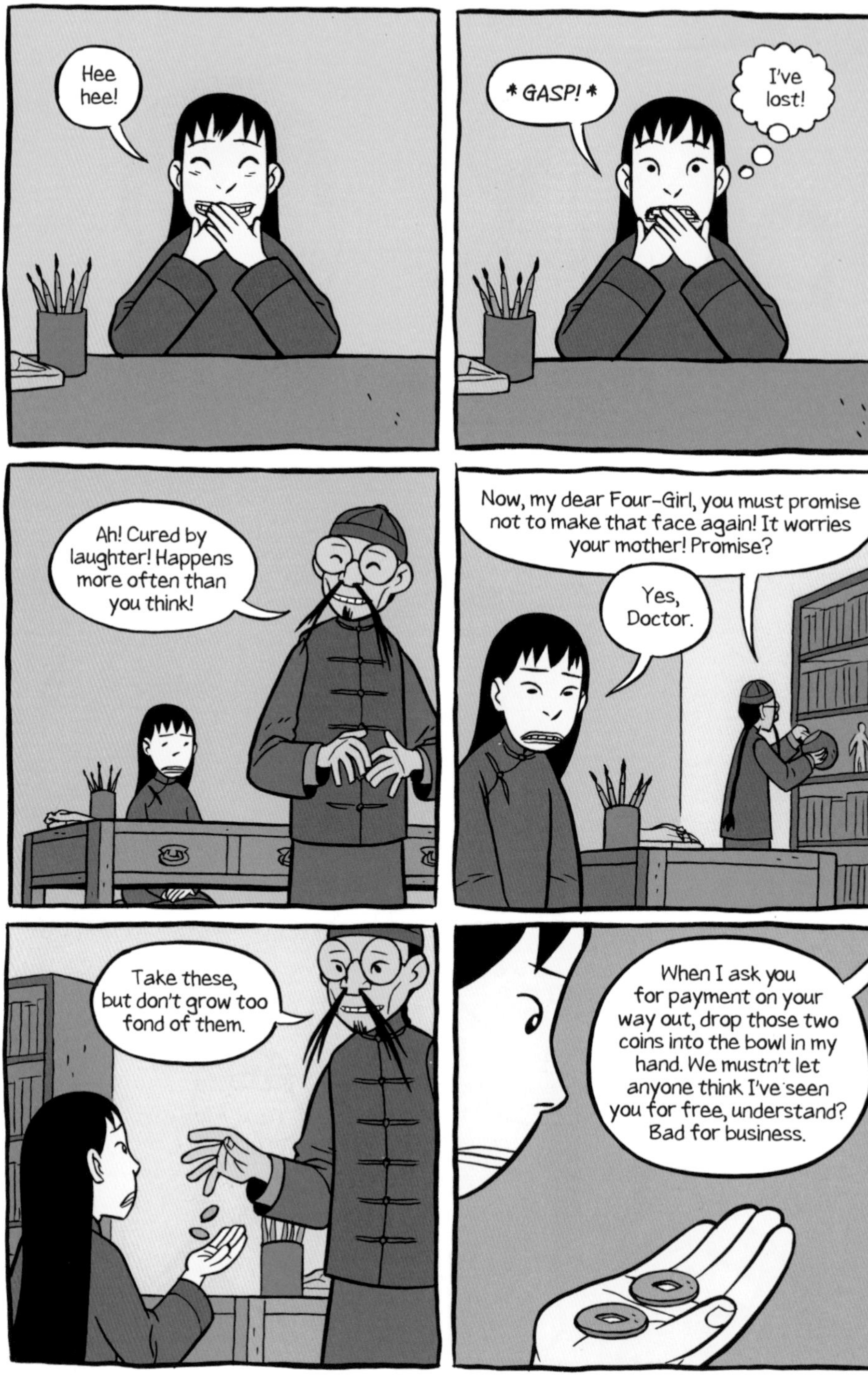
Hee hee!
* GASP! *
I've lost!
Ah! Cured by laughter! Happens more often than you think!
Now, my dear Four-Girl, you must promise not to make that face again! It worries your mother! Promise?
Yes, Doctor.
Take these, but don't grow too fond of them.
When I ask you for payment on your way out, drop those two coins into the bowl in my hand. We mustn't let anyone think I've seen you for free, understand? Bad for business.

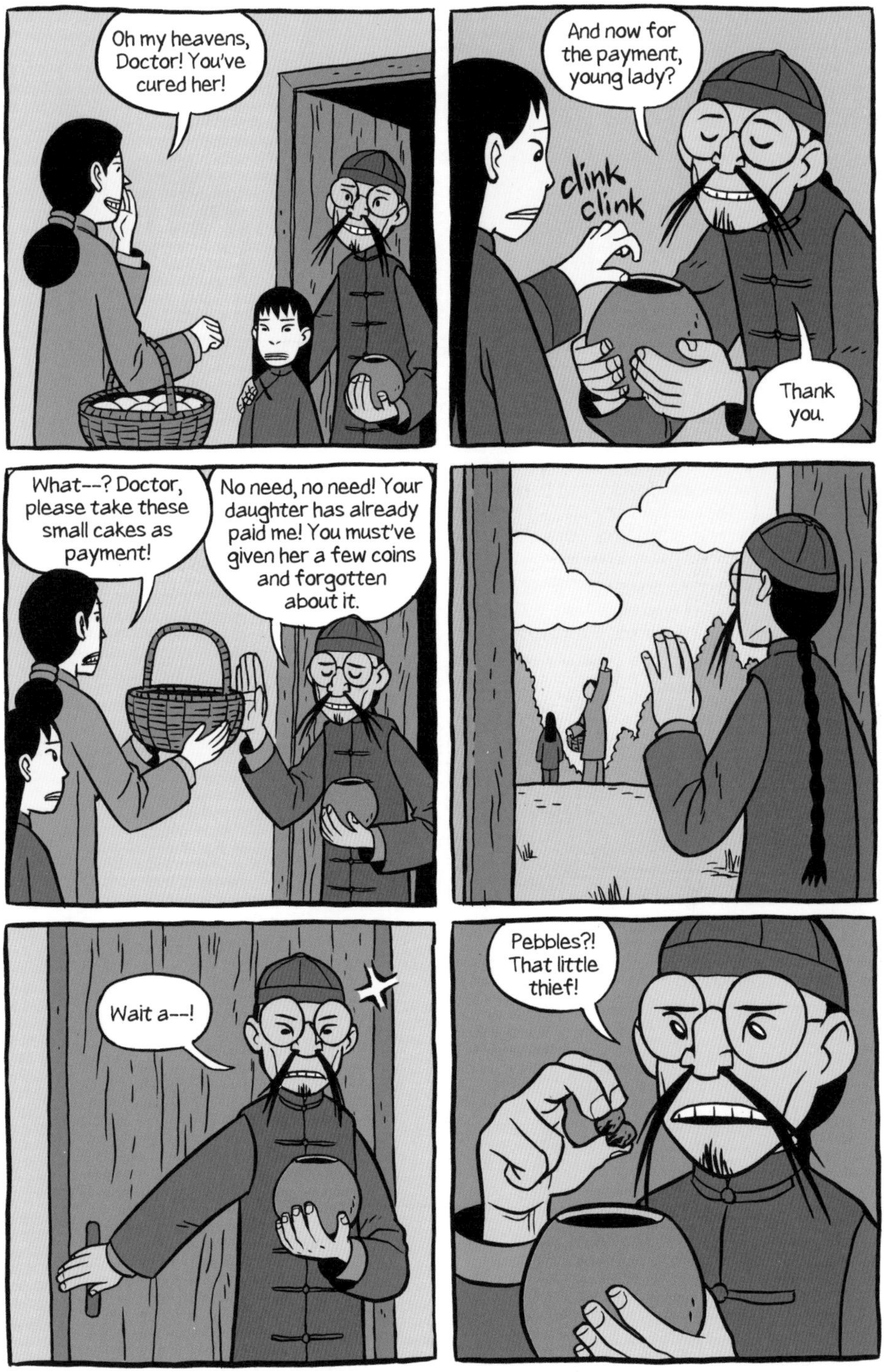
Oh my heavens, Doctor! You've cured her!
And now for the payment, young lady?
clink clink
Thank you.
What--? Doctor, please take these small cakes as payment!
No need, no need! Your daughter has already paid me! You must've given her a few coins and forgotten about it.
Wait a--!
Pebbles?! That little thief!

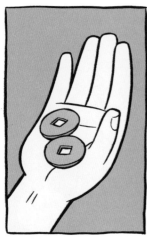

Sigh.

You swore to me, Four-Girl.

How was I supposed to resist? That acupuncturist had tricks, I tell you! *Tricks!*

You swore to me you would set your face like flint!

At least I stole some money from him! Look! You don't get much more devilish than thievery!

You are the most pathetic devil I've ever met.

I never made my devil-face again after that.

And soon, everyone stopped noticing me.

28

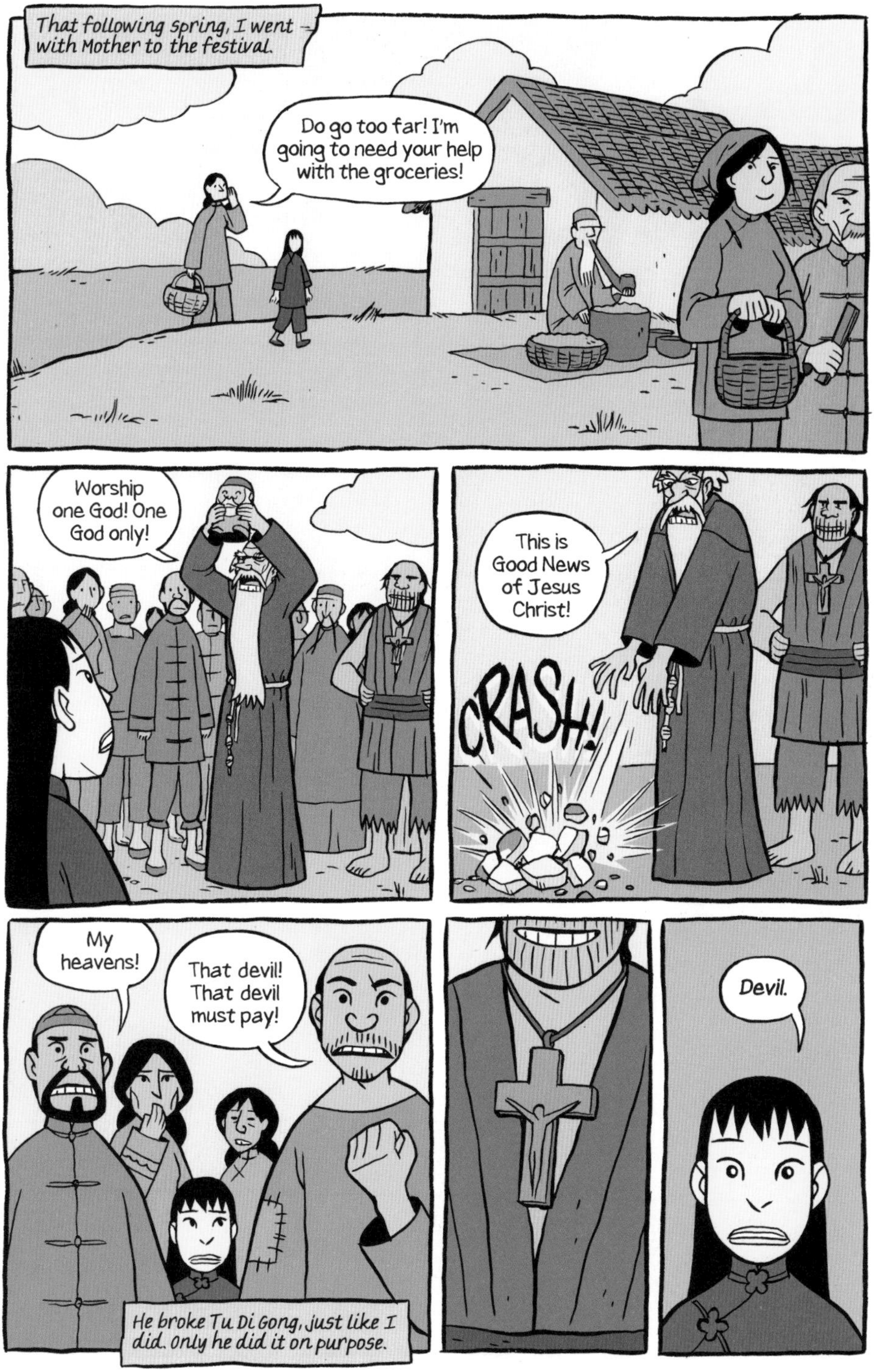
That following spring, I went with Mother to the festival.
Do go too far! I'm going to need your help with the groceries!
Worship one God! One God only!
This is Good News of Jesus Christ!
CRASH!
My heavens!
That devil! That devil must pay!
He broke Tu Di Gong, just like I did. Only he did it on purpose.
Devil.

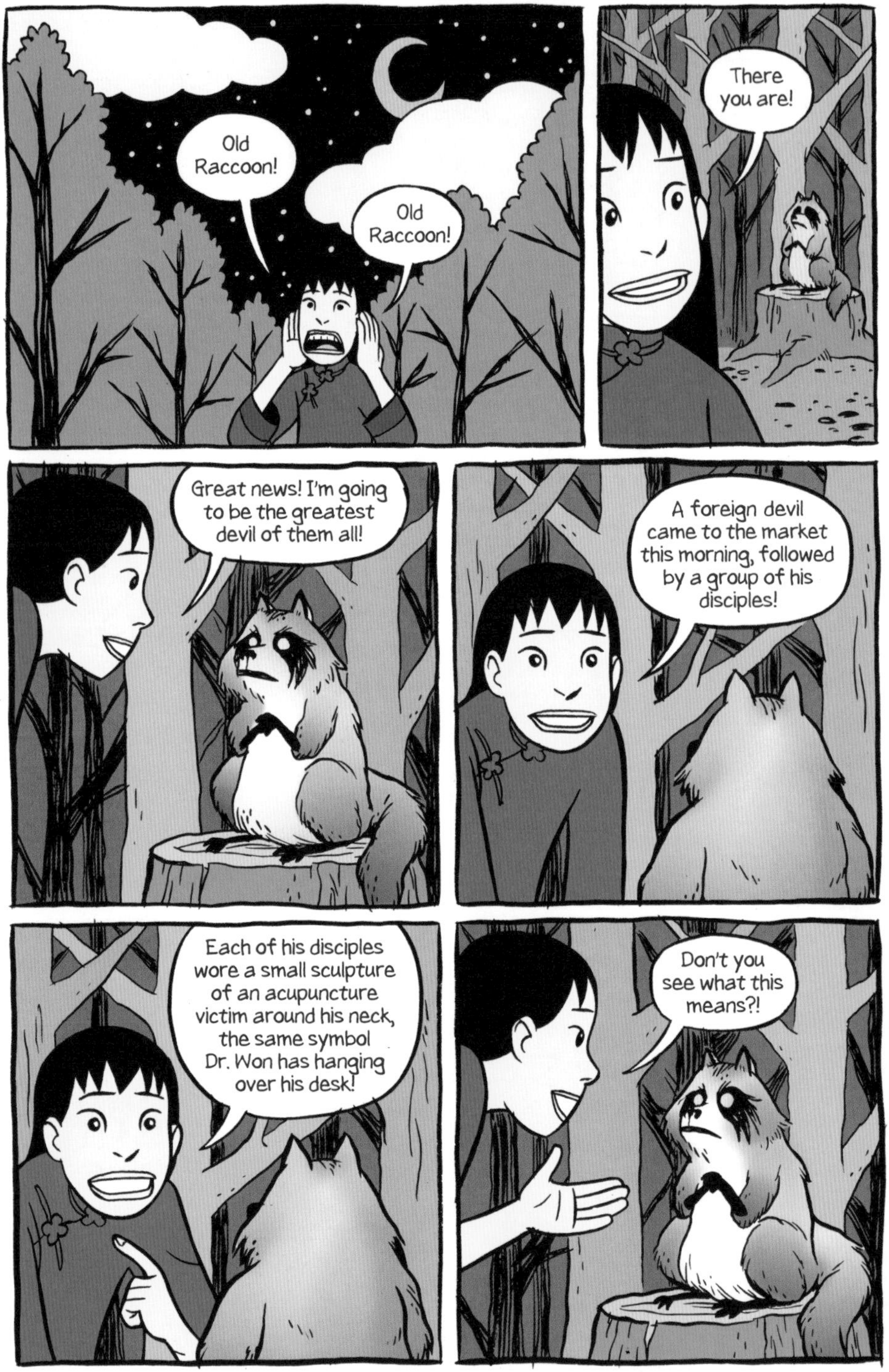
Old Raccoon!
Old Raccoon!
There you are!
Great news! I'm going to be the greatest devil of them all!
A foreign devil came to the market this morning, followed by a group of his disciples!
Each of his disciples wore a small sculpture of an acupuncture victim around his neck, the same symbol Dr. Won has hanging over his desk!
Don't you see what this means?!

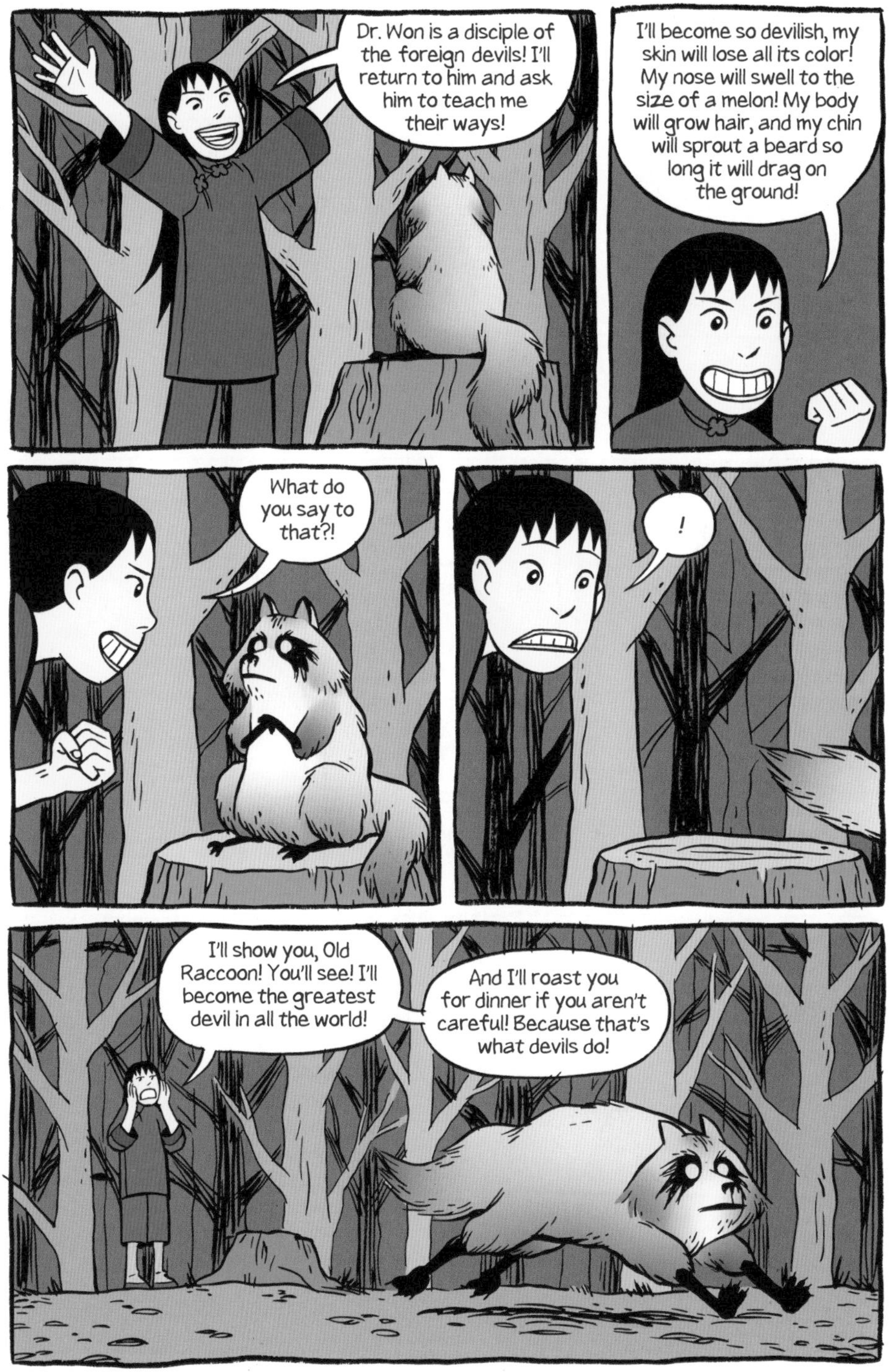
Dr. Won is a disciple of the foreign devils! I'll return to him and ask him to teach me their ways!
I'll become so devilish, my skin will lose all its color! My nose will swell to the size of a melon! My body will grow hair, and my chin will sprout a beard so long it will drag on the ground!
What do you say to that?!
!
I'll show you, Old Raccoon! You'll see! I'll become the greatest devil in all the world!
And I'll roast you for dinner if you aren't careful! Because that's what devils do!

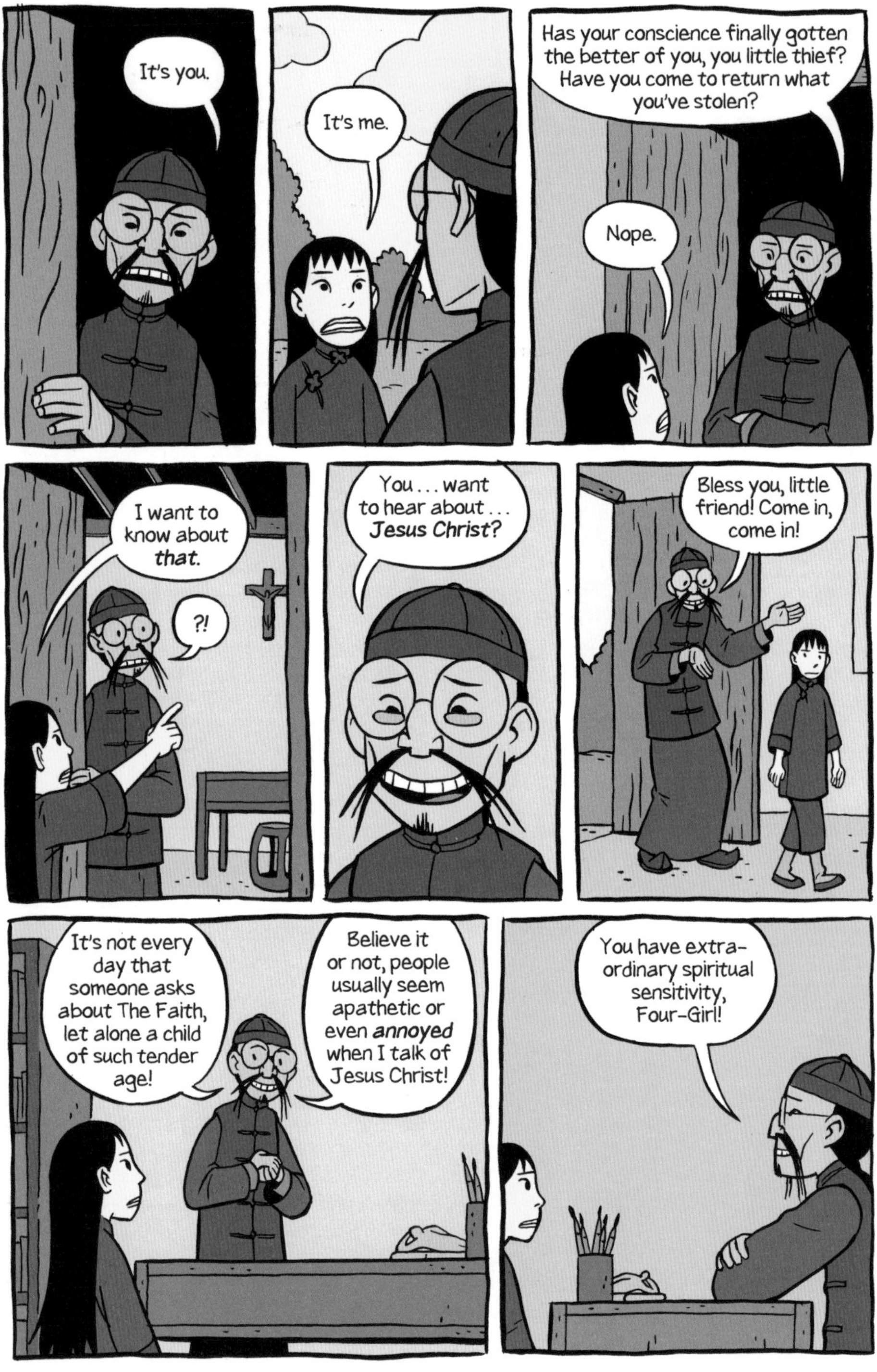
It's you.
It's me.
Has your conscience finally gotten the better of you, you little thief? Have you come to return what you've stolen?
Nope.
I want to know about *that*.
?!
You . . . want to hear about . . . *Jesus Christ*?
Bless you, little friend! Come in, come in!
It's not every day that someone asks about The Faith, let alone a child of such tender age!
Believe it or not, people usually seem apathetic or even *annoyed* when I talk of Jesus Christ!
You have extra-ordinary spiritual sensitivity, Four-Girl!

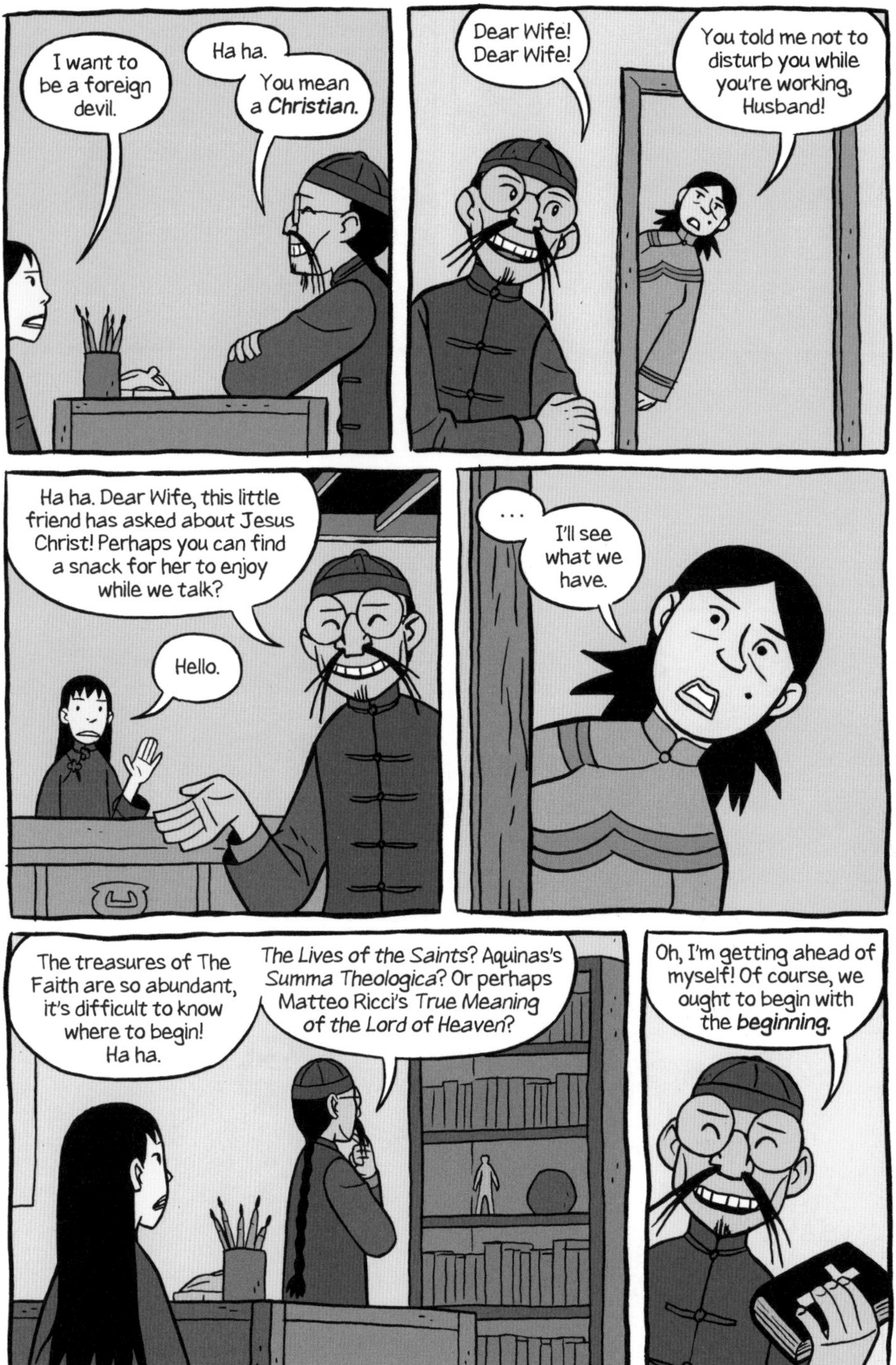
I want to be a foreign devil.
Ha ha.
You mean a **Christian.**
Dear Wife! Dear Wife!
You told me not to disturb you while you're working, Husband!
Ha ha. Dear Wife, this little friend has asked about Jesus Christ! Perhaps you can find a snack for her to enjoy while we talk?
Hello.
...
I'll see what we have.
The treasures of The Faith are so abundant, it's difficult to know where to begin! Ha ha.
The Lives of the Saints? Aquinas's *Summa Theologica*? Or perhaps Matteo Ricci's *True Meaning of the Lord of Heaven*?
Oh, I'm getting ahead of myself! Of course, we ought to begin with the ***beginning***.

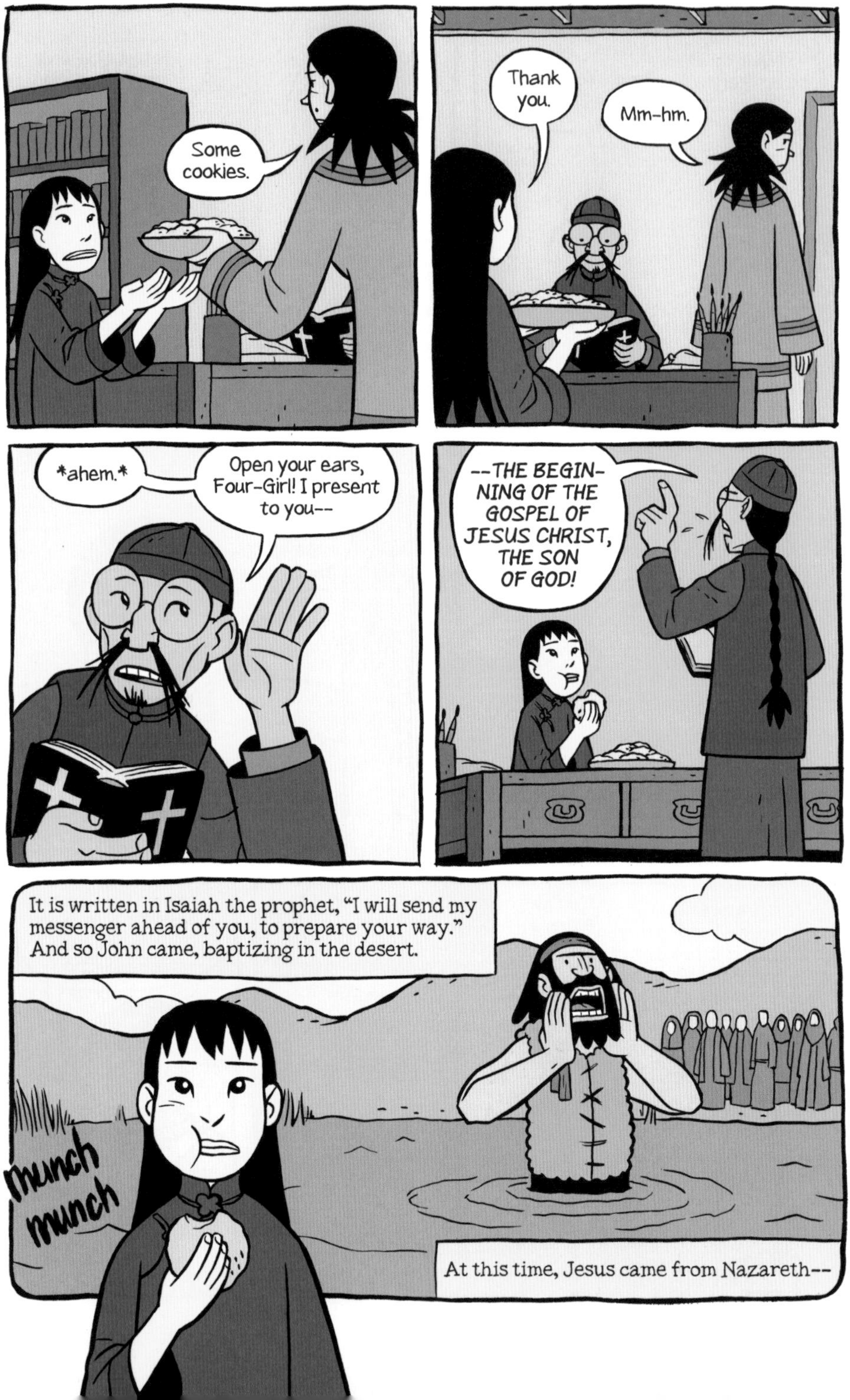
Some cookies.
Thank you.
Mm-hm.
ahem.
Open your ears, Four-Girl! I present to you--
--THE BEGINNING OF THE GOSPEL OF JESUS CHRIST, THE SON OF GOD!
It is written in Isaiah the prophet, "I will send my messenger ahead of you, to prepare your way." And so John came, baptizing in the desert.
munch munch
At this time, Jesus came from Nazareth--

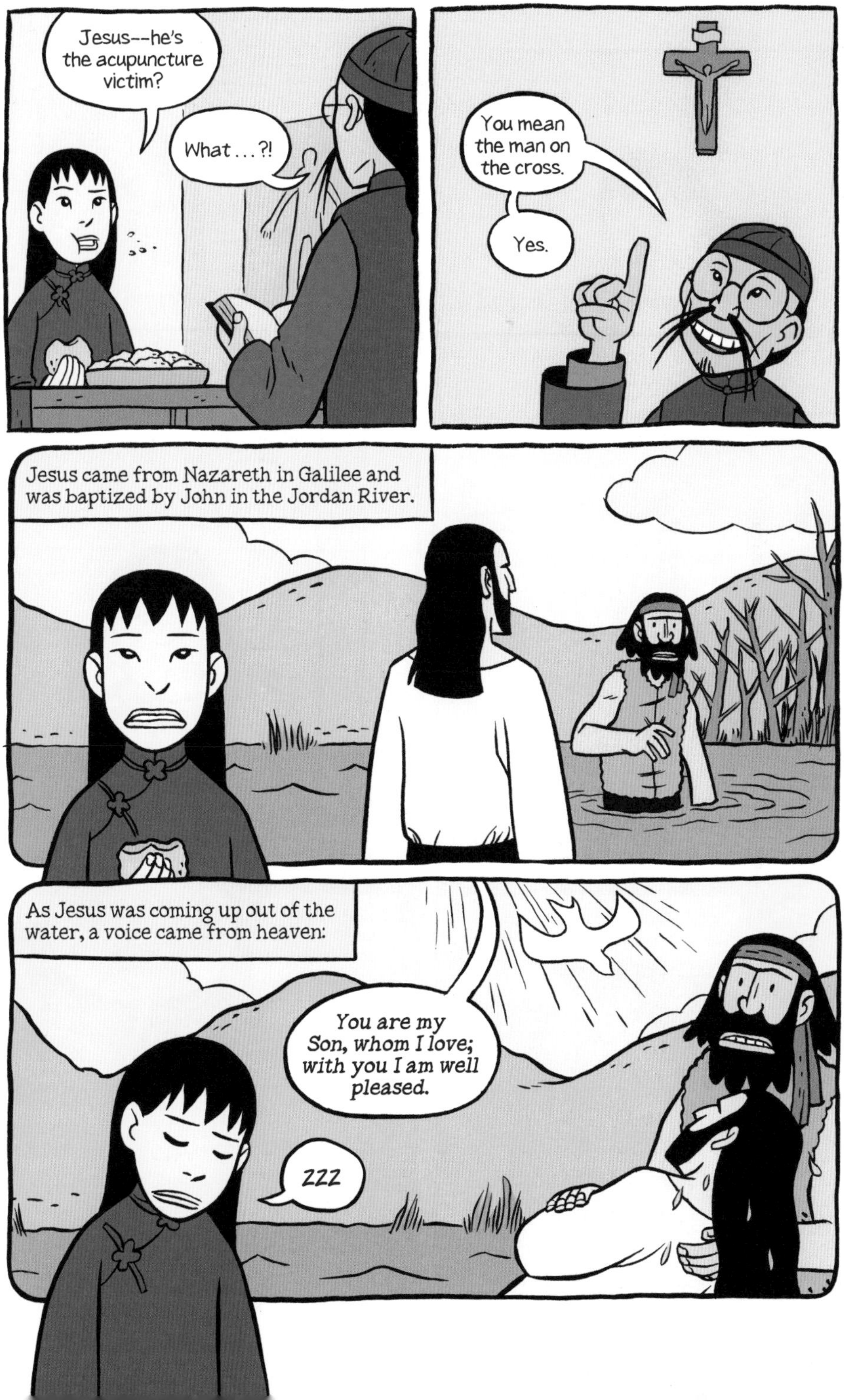
Jesus--he's the acupuncture victim?
What...?!
You mean the man on the cross.
Yes.
Jesus came from Nazareth in Galilee and was baptized by John in the Jordan River.
As Jesus was coming up out of the water, a voice came from heaven:
You are my Son, whom I love; with you I am well pleased.
ZZZ

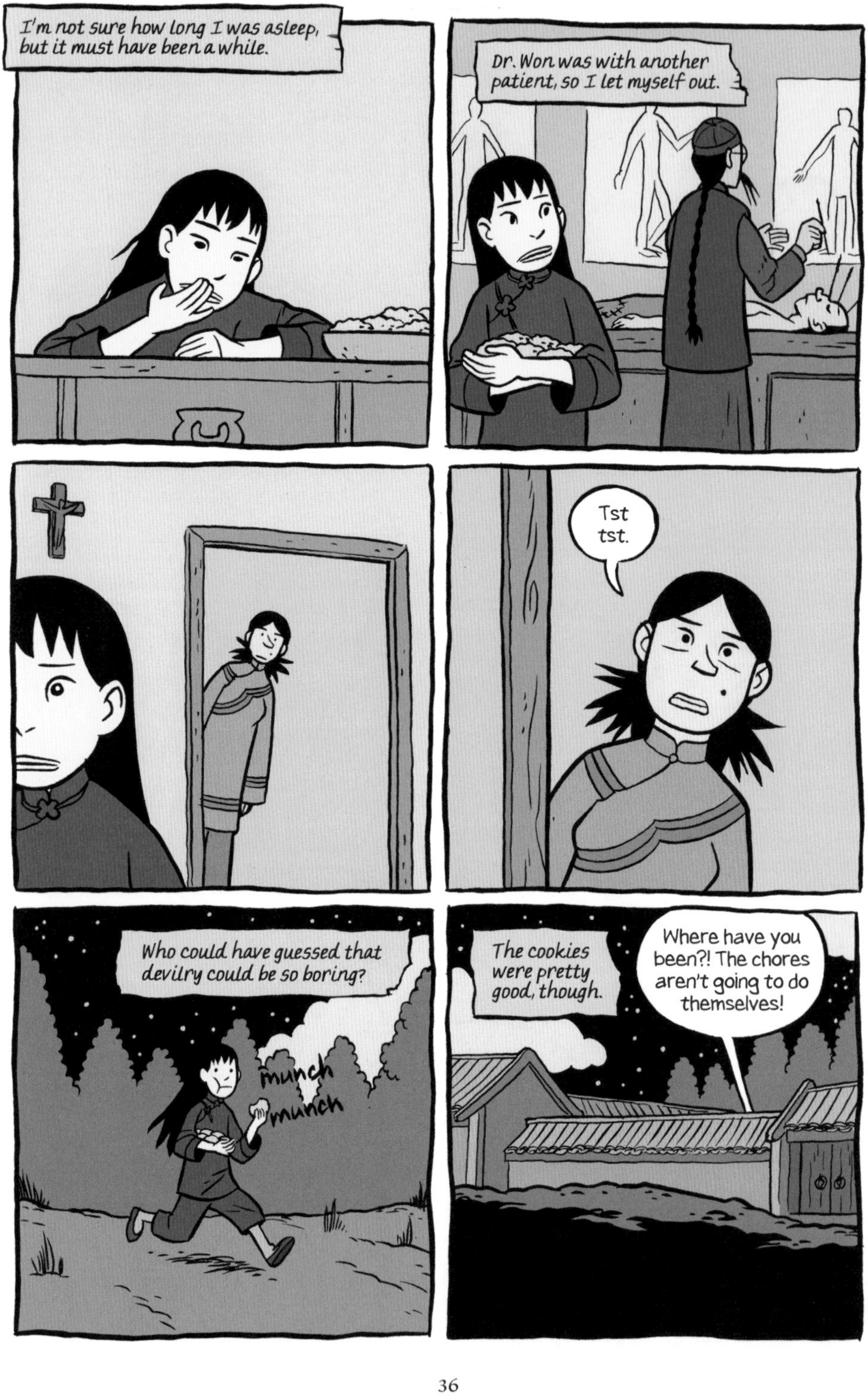
I'm not sure how long I was asleep, but it must have been a while.
Dr. Won was with another patient, so I let myself out.
Tst tst.
Who could have guessed that devilry could be so boring?
munch
munch
The cookies were pretty good, though.
Where have you been?! The chores aren't going to do themselves!

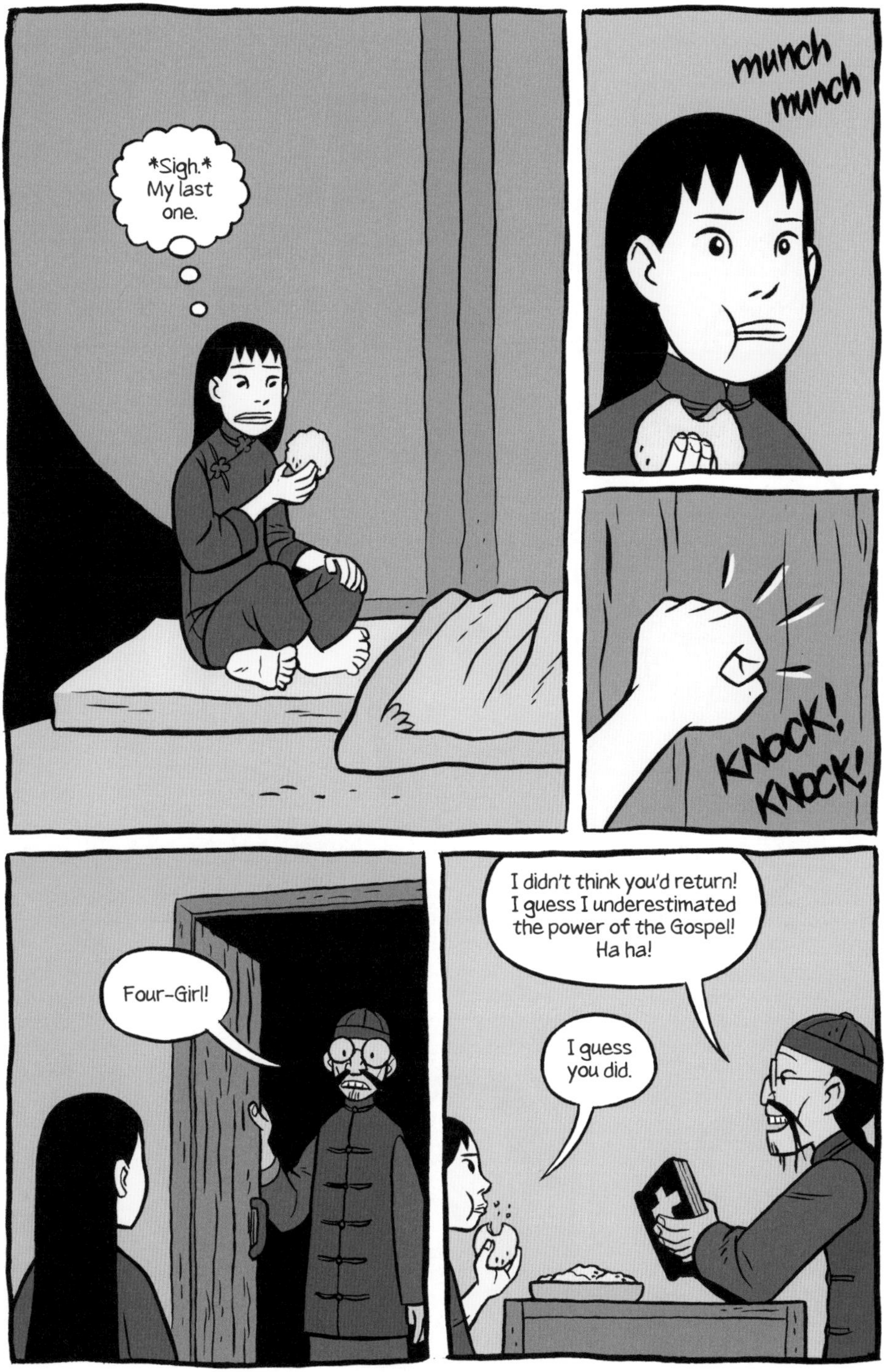
Sigh. My last one.
munch munch
KNOCK! KNOCK!
Four-Girl!
I didn't think you'd return! I guess I underestimated the power of the Gospel! Ha ha!
I guess you did.

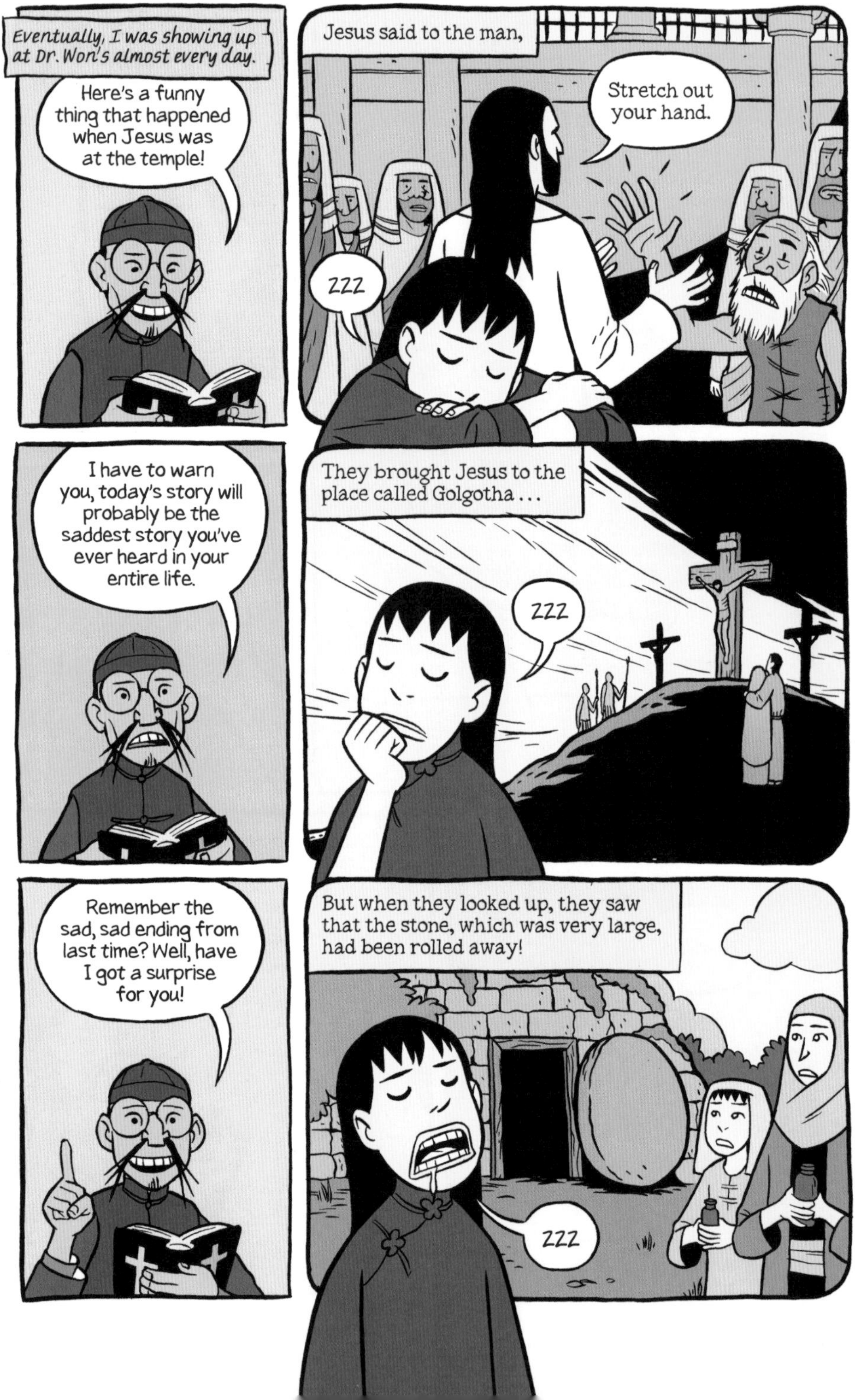
Eventually, I was showing up at Dr. Won's almost every day.
Here's a funny thing that happened when Jesus was at the temple!
Jesus said to the man,
Stretch out your hand.
ZZZ
I have to warn you, today's story will probably be the saddest story you've ever heard in your entire life.
They brought Jesus to the place called Golgotha . . .
ZZZ
Remember the sad, sad ending from last time? Well, have I got a surprise for you!
But when they looked up, they saw that the stone, which was very large, had been rolled away!
ZZZ

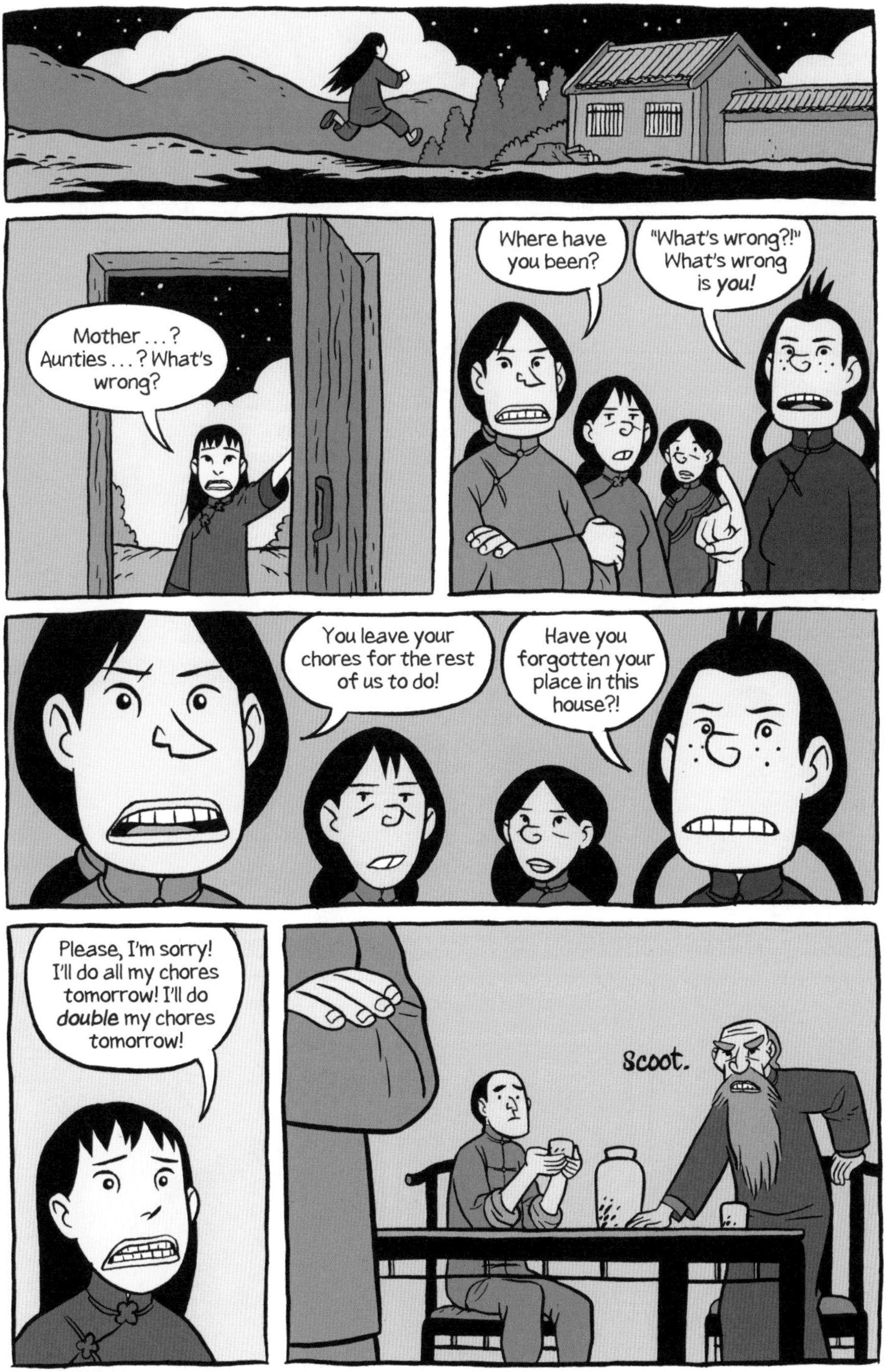
Mother . . . ? Aunties . . . ? What's wrong?
Where have you been?
"What's wrong?!" What's wrong is *you!*
You leave your chores for the rest of us to do!
Have you forgotten your place in this house?!
Please, I'm sorry! I'll do all my chores tomorrow! I'll do *double* my chores tomorrow!
Scoot.

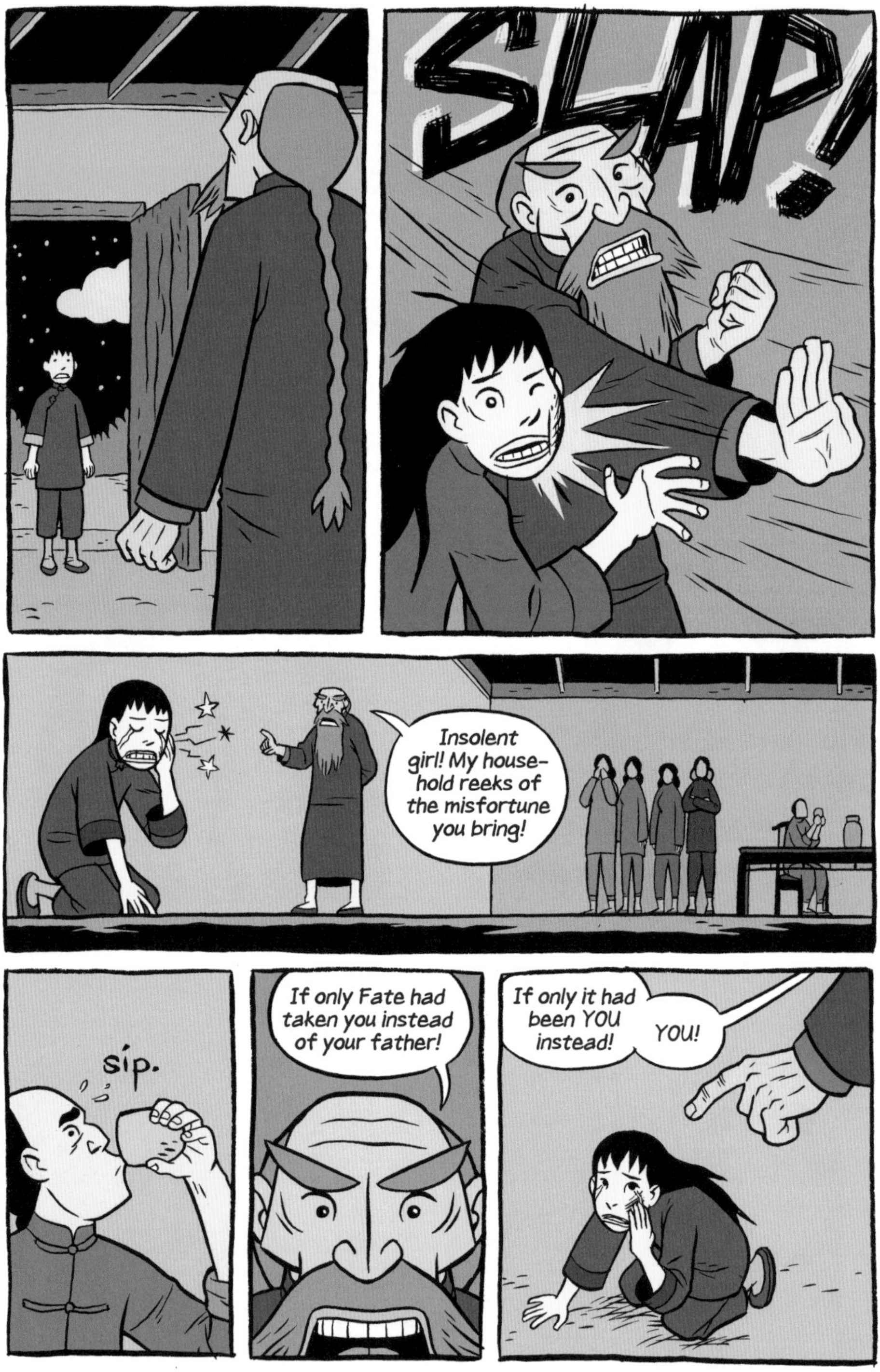
SLAP!
Insolent girl! My household reeks of the misfortune you bring!
sip.
If only Fate had taken you instead of your father!
If only it had been YOU instead!
YOU!

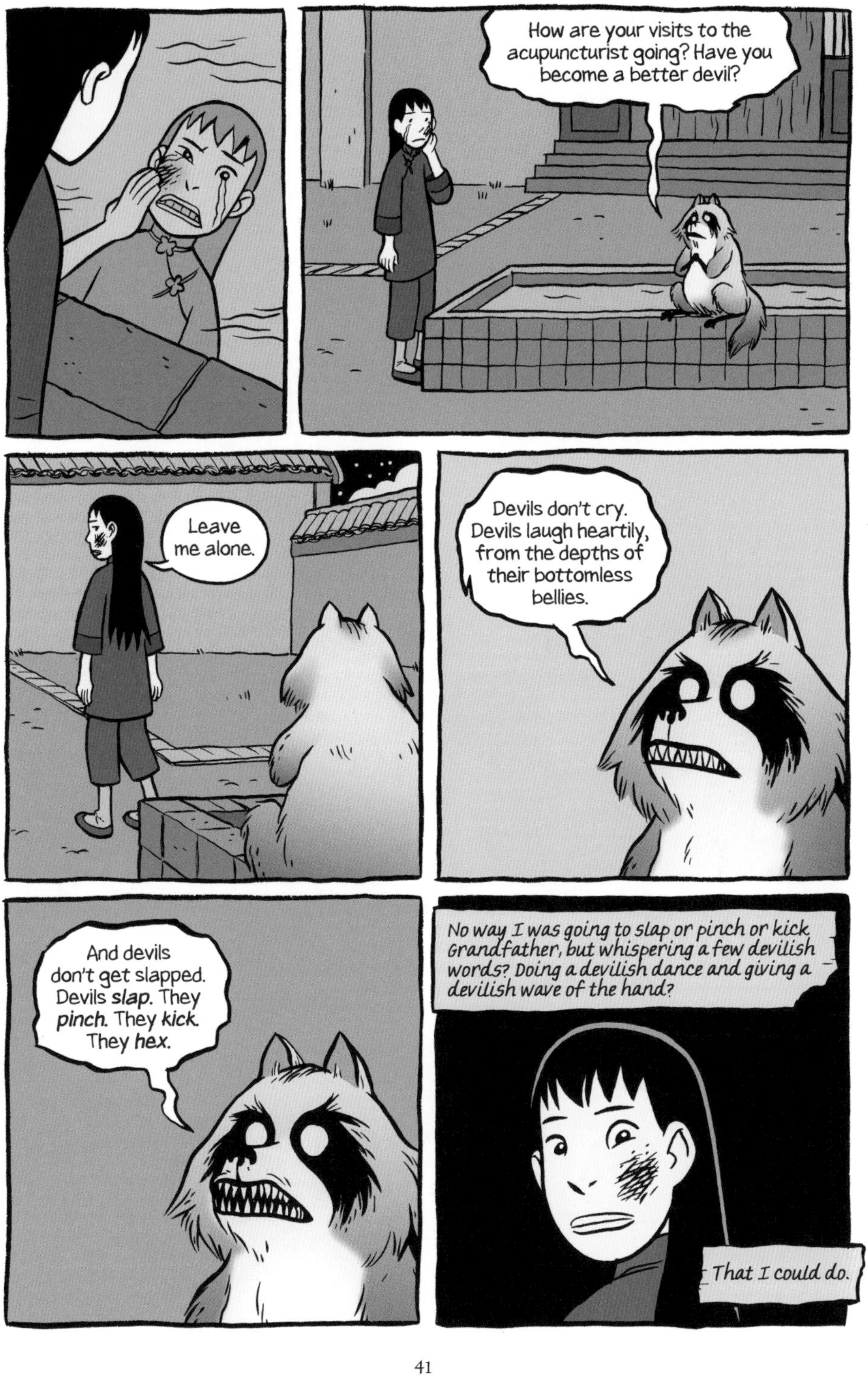
How are your visits to the acupuncturist going? Have you become a better devil?
Leave me alone.
Devils don't cry. Devils laugh heartily, from the depths of their bottomless bellies.
And devils don't get slapped. Devils *slap*. They *pinch*. They *kick*. They *hex*.
No way I was going to slap or pinch or kick Grandfather, but whispering a few devilish words? Doing a devilish dance and giving a devilish wave of the hand?
That I could do.

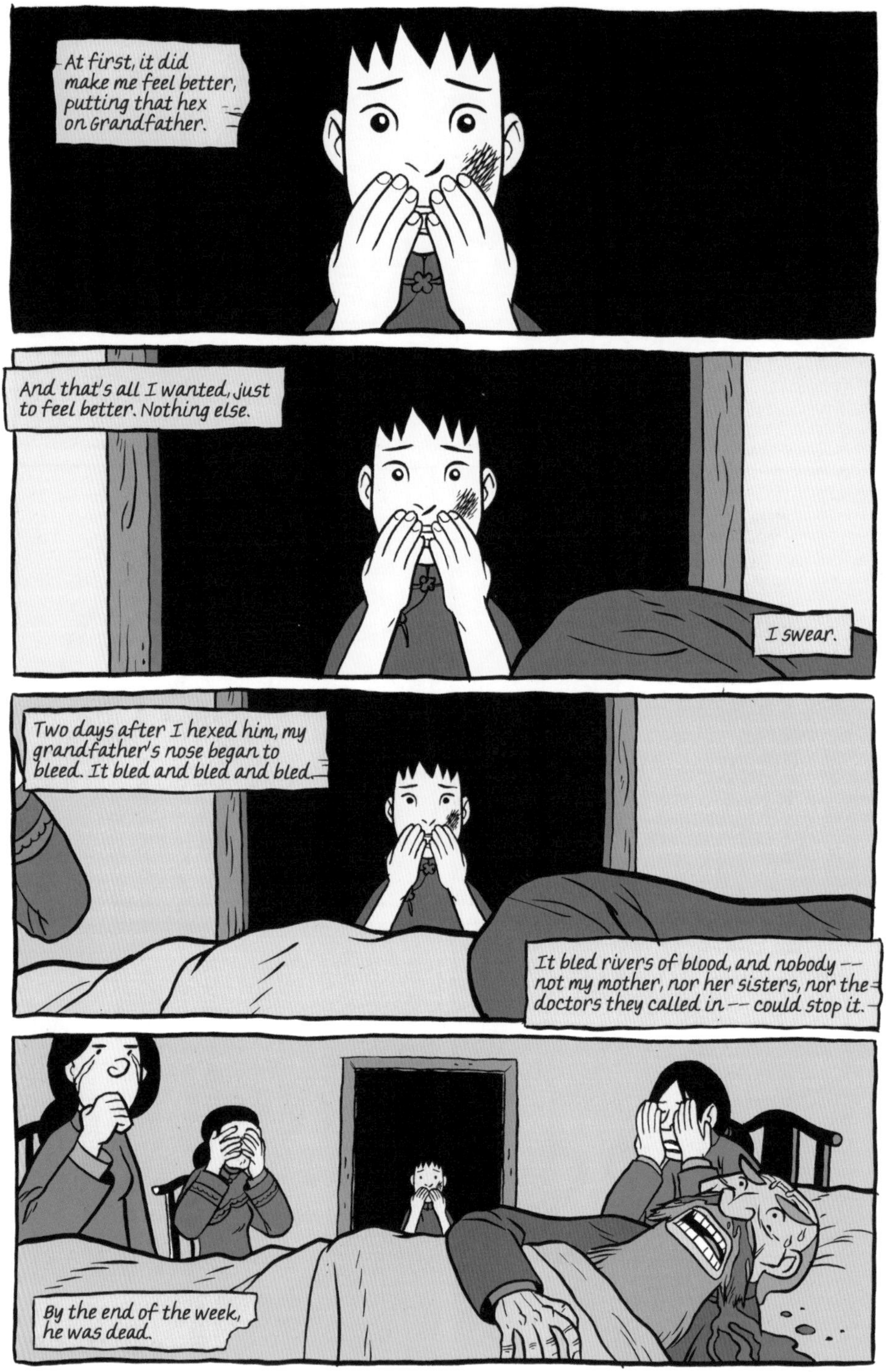
At first, it did make me feel better, putting that hex on Grandfather.
And that's all I wanted, just to feel better. Nothing else.
I swear.
Two days after I hexed him, my grandfather's nose began to bleed. It bled and bled and bled.
It bled rivers of blood, and nobody -- not my mother, nor her sisters, nor the doctors they called in -- could stop it.
By the end of the week, he was dead.

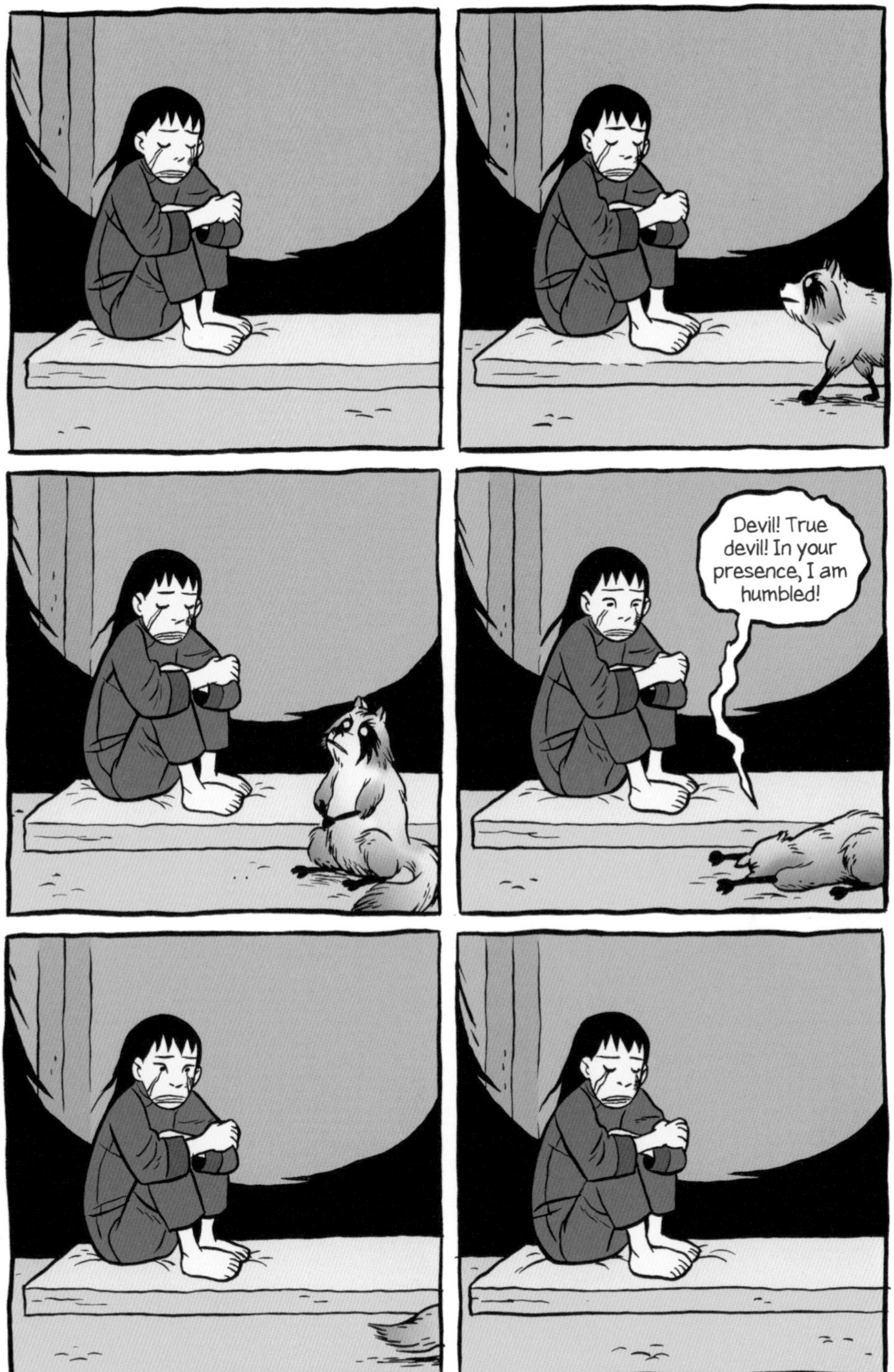
Devil! True devil! In your presence, I am humbled!

第三章

Age 9

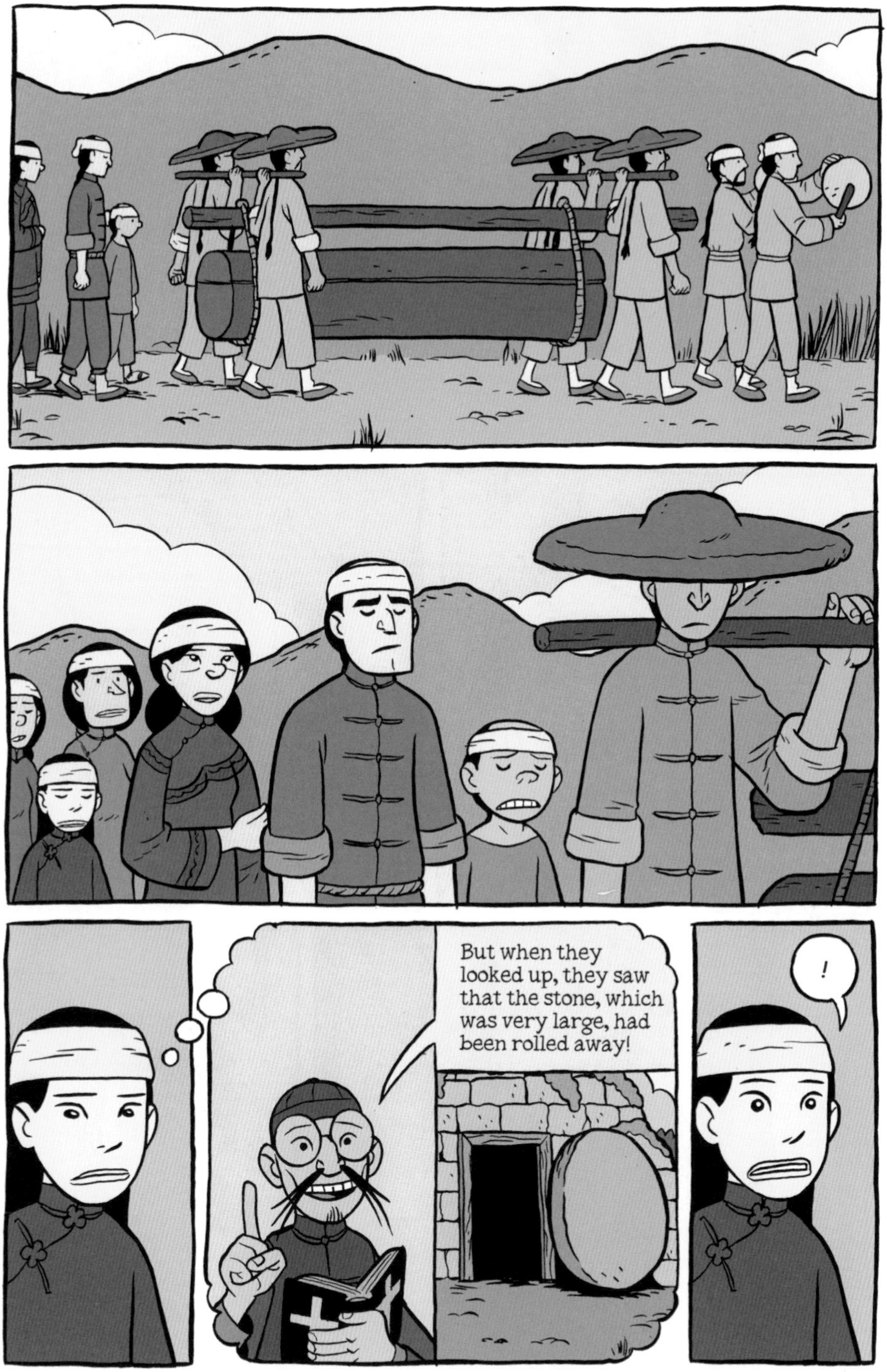
But when they looked up, they saw that the stone, which was very large, had been rolled away!
!

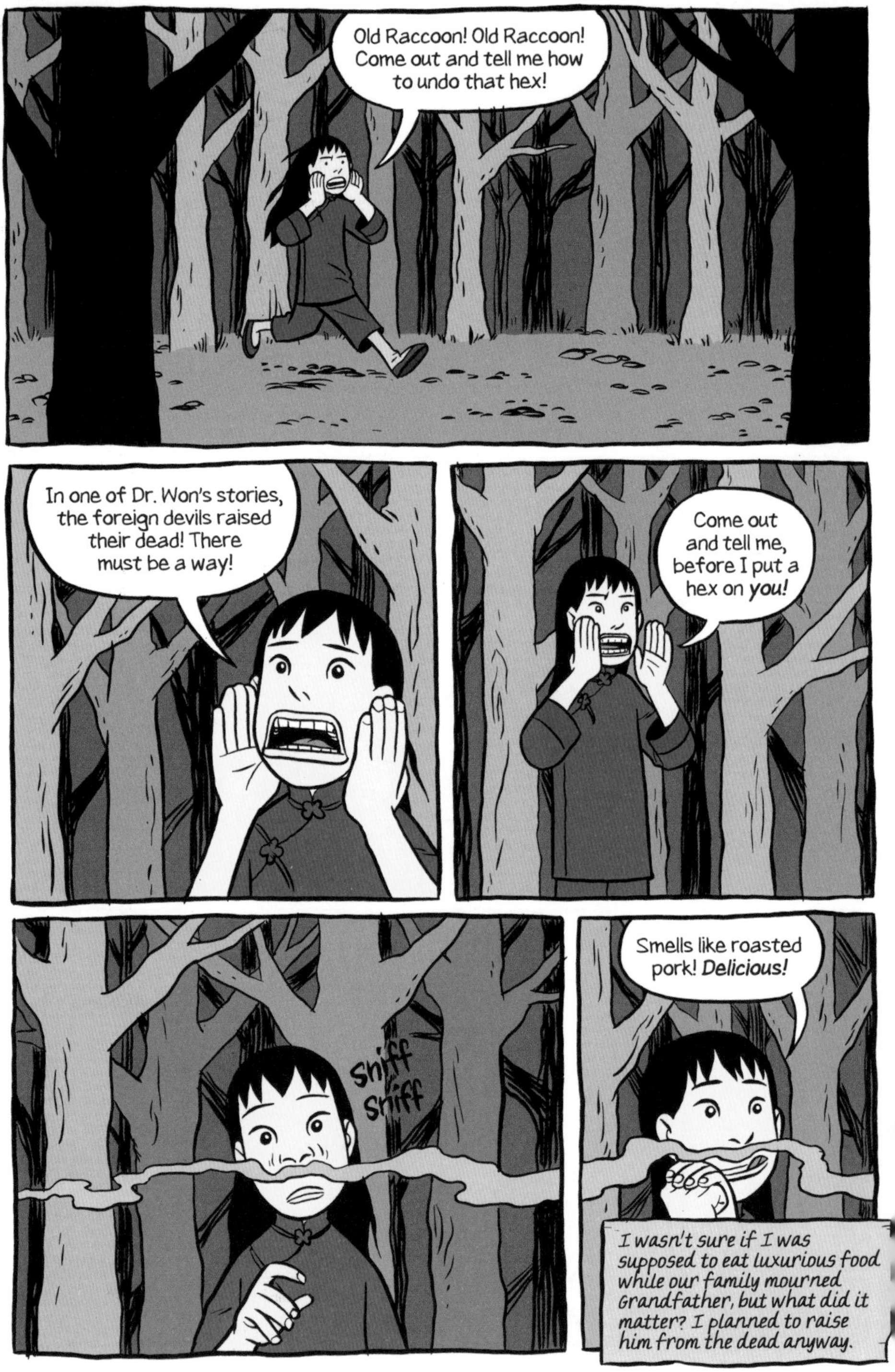

Old Raccoon! Old Raccoon! Come out and tell me how to undo that hex!
In one of Dr. Won's stories, the foreign devils raised their dead! There must be a way!
Come out and tell me, before I put a hex on *you!*
Sniff Sniff
Smells like roasted pork! *Delicious!*
I wasn't sure if I was supposed to eat luxurious food while our family mourned Grandfather, but what did it matter? I planned to raise him from the dead anyway.

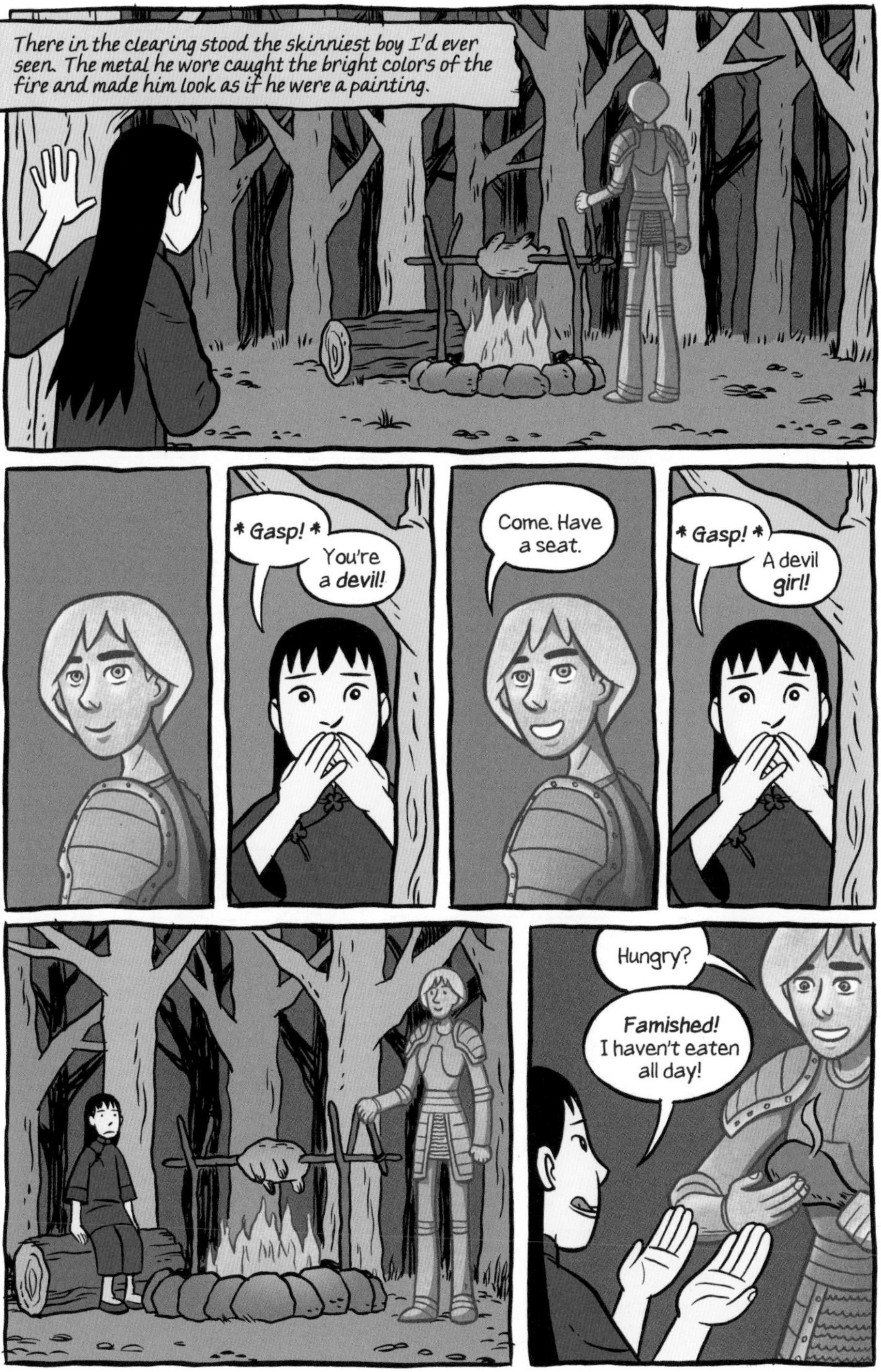
There in the clearing stood the skinniest boy I'd ever seen. The metal he wore caught the bright colors of the fire and made him look as if he were a painting.
* Gasp! *
You're a devil!
Come. Have a seat.
* Gasp! *
A devil girl!
Hungry?
Famished! I haven't eaten all day!

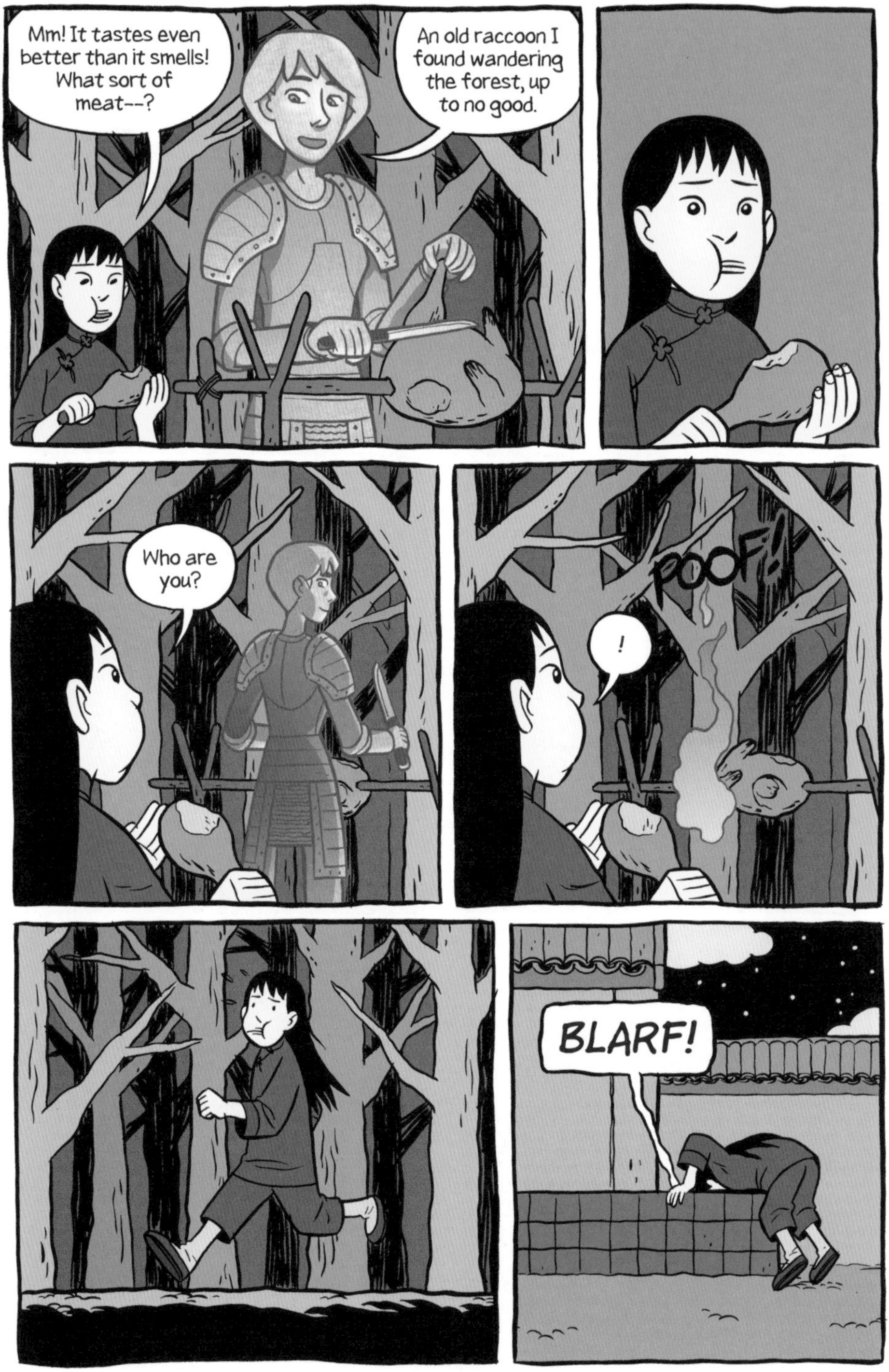
Mm! It tastes even better than it smells! What sort of meat--?
An old raccoon I found wandering the forest, up to no good.
Who are you?
POOF!
!
BLARF!

KNOCK!
KNOCK!

Four-Girl! Ha ha! Again, I thought you'd gone for good! And again, the power of the Gospel has compelled you to return!

Um... yeah.

Doctor, I've been visited by a *devil!* Not the *foreign* kind, but the *real* kind! The kind that disappears in a puff of smoke--

--and leaves you with a heaviness in your *heart*.

That heaviness was probably guilt from killing Grandfather, but Dr. Won didn't need to know that.

I described to him my encounter with the devil boy-girl.

Hm. I... I'm not sure what to say.

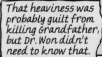

scratch scratch

What is there to say?! She raves like a *lunatic!* Take her to see the priest!

munch munch

51

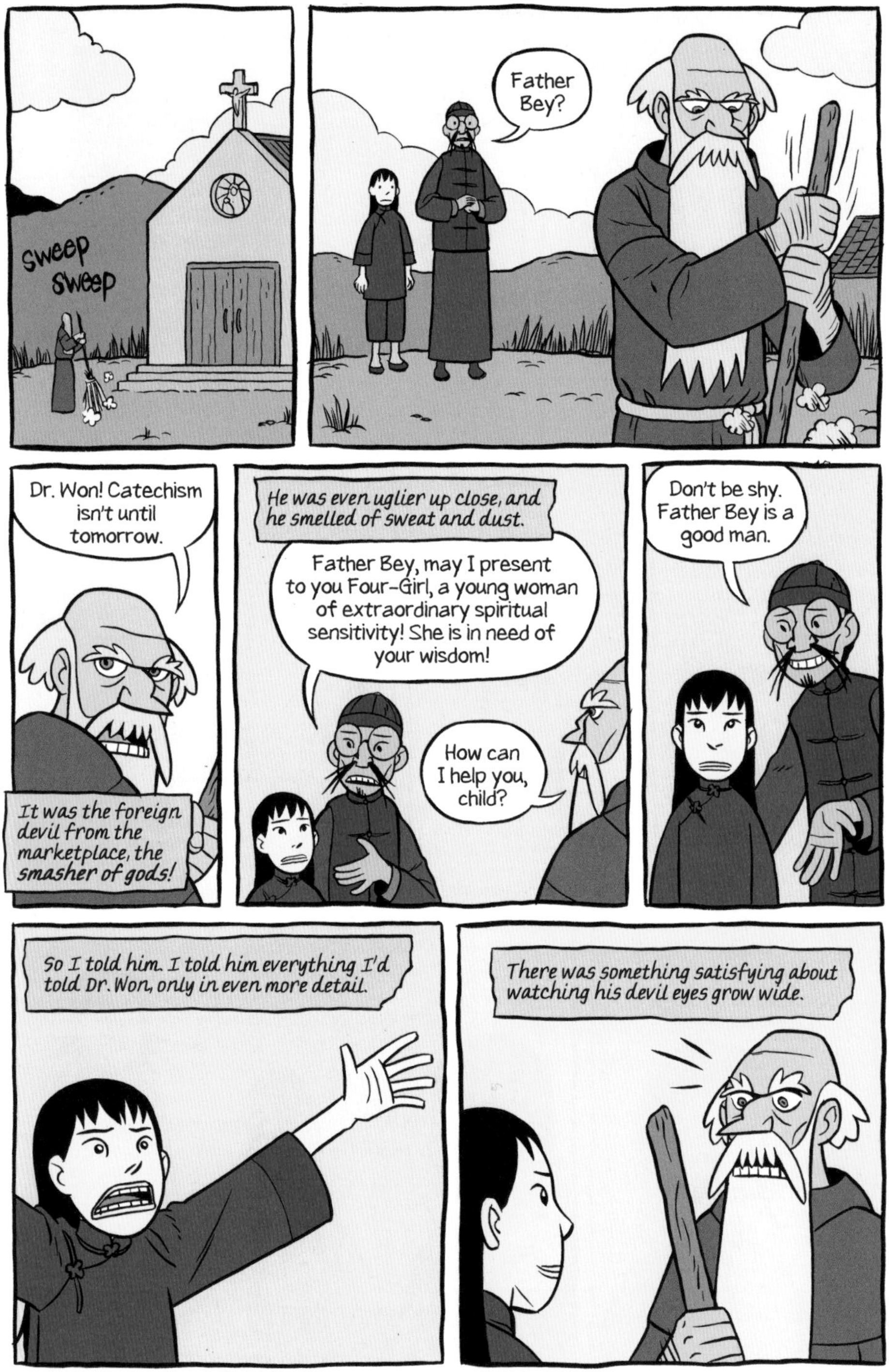
SWEEP
SWEEP
Father Bey?
Dr. Won! Catechism isn't until tomorrow.
It was the foreign devil from the marketplace, the smasher of gods!
He was even uglier up close, and he smelled of sweat and dust.
Father Bey, may I present to you Four-Girl, a young woman of extraordinary spiritual sensitivity! She is in need of your wisdom!
How can I help you, child?
Don't be shy. Father Bey is a good man.
So I told him. I told him everything I'd told Dr. Won, only in even more detail.
There was something satisfying about watching his devil eyes grow wide.

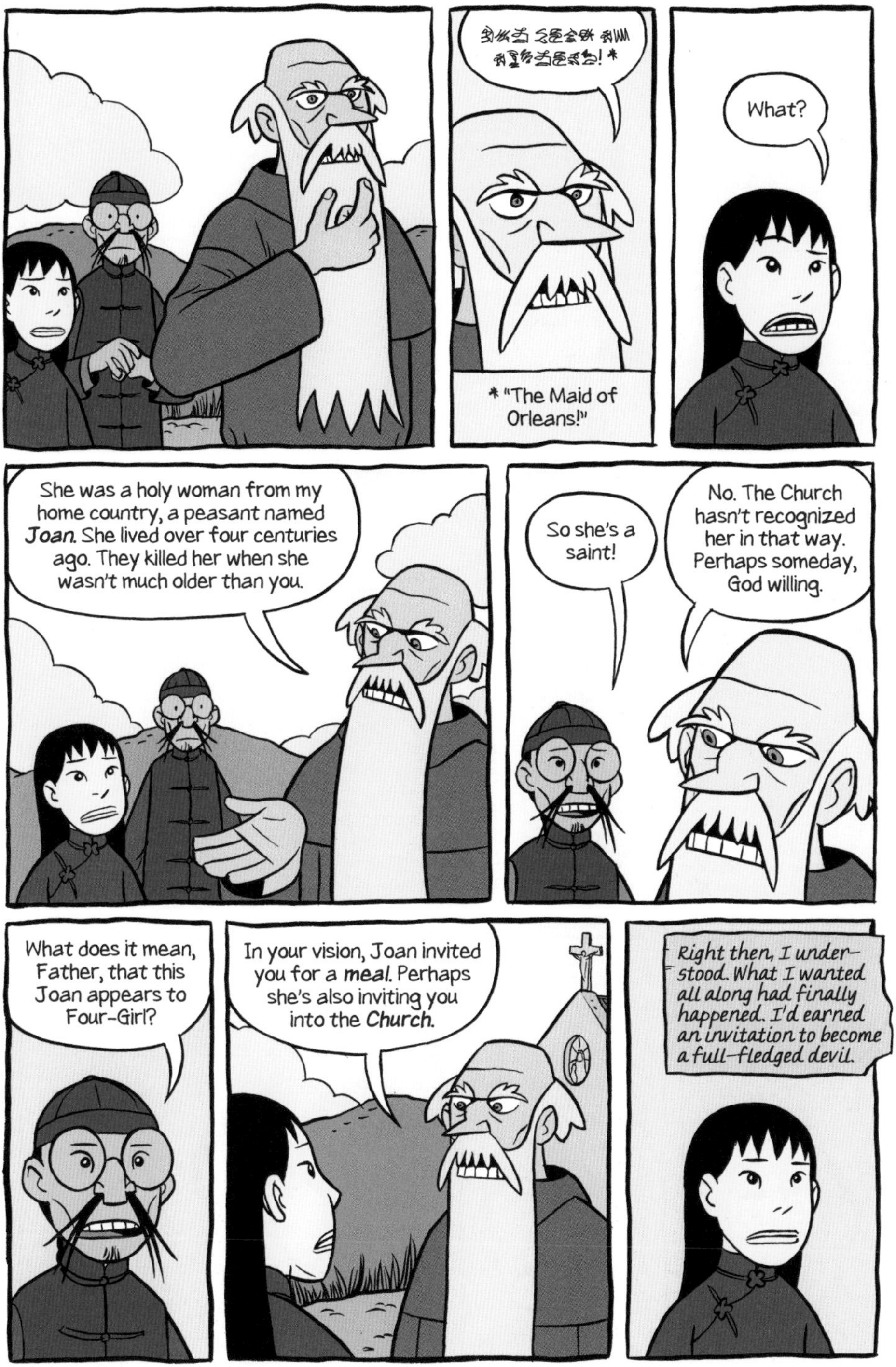
* "The Maid of Orleans!"
What?
She was a holy woman from my home country, a peasant named Joan. She lived over four centuries ago. They killed her when she wasn't much older than you.
So she's a saint!
No. The Church hasn't recognized her in that way. Perhaps someday, God willing.
What does it mean, Father, that this Joan appears to Four-Girl?
In your vision, Joan invited you for a meal. Perhaps she's also inviting you into the Church.
Right then, I understood. What I wanted all along had finally happened. I'd earned an invitation to become a full-fledged devil.

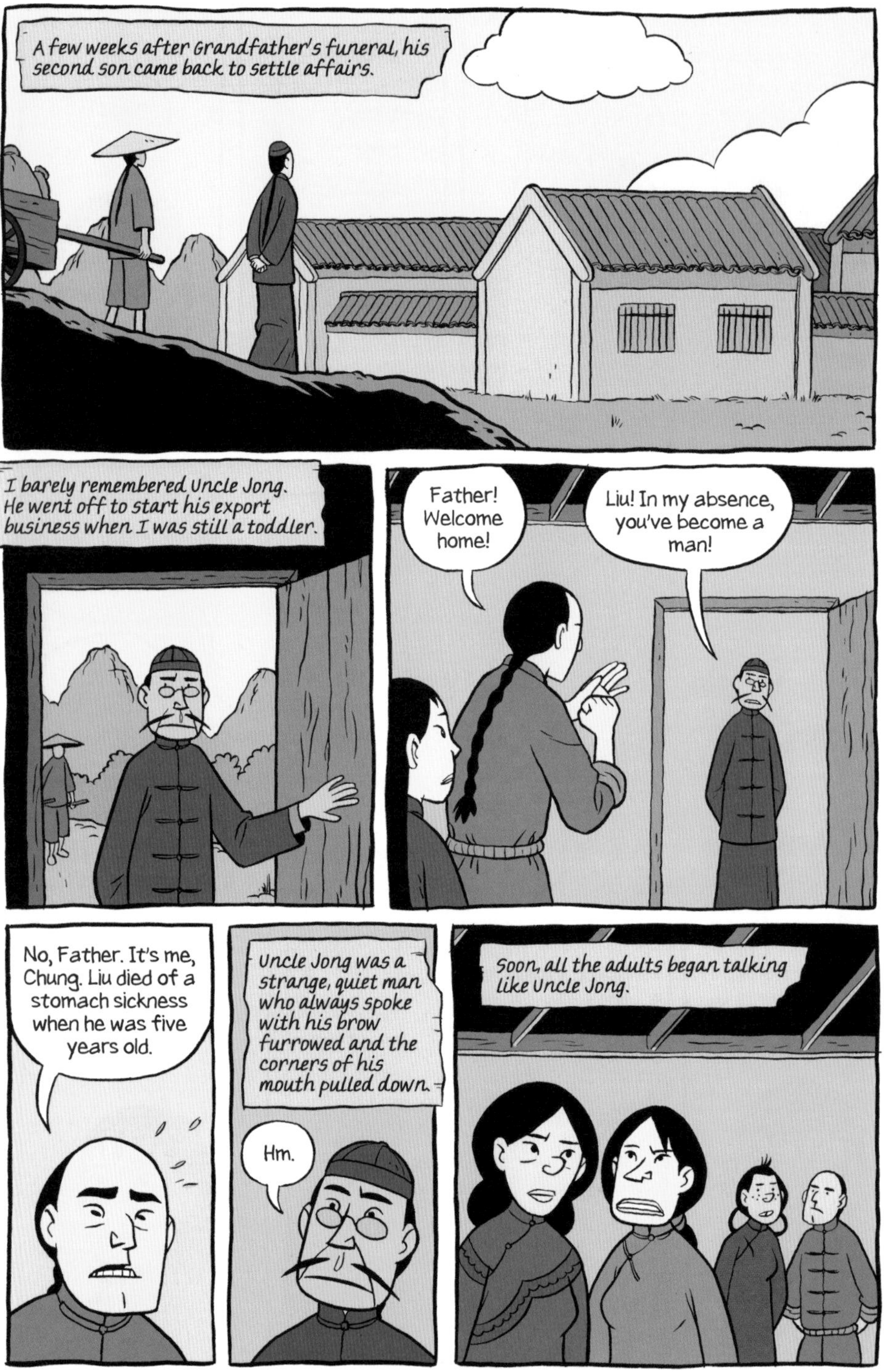
A few weeks after Grandfather's funeral, his second son came back to settle affairs.
I barely remembered Uncle Jong. He went off to start his export business when I was still a toddler.
Father! Welcome home!
Liu! In my absence, you've become a man!
No, Father. It's me, Chung. Liu died of a stomach sickness when he was five years old.
Uncle Jong was a strange, quiet man who always spoke with his brow furrowed and the corners of his mouth pulled down.
Hm.
Soon, all the adults began talking like Uncle Jong.

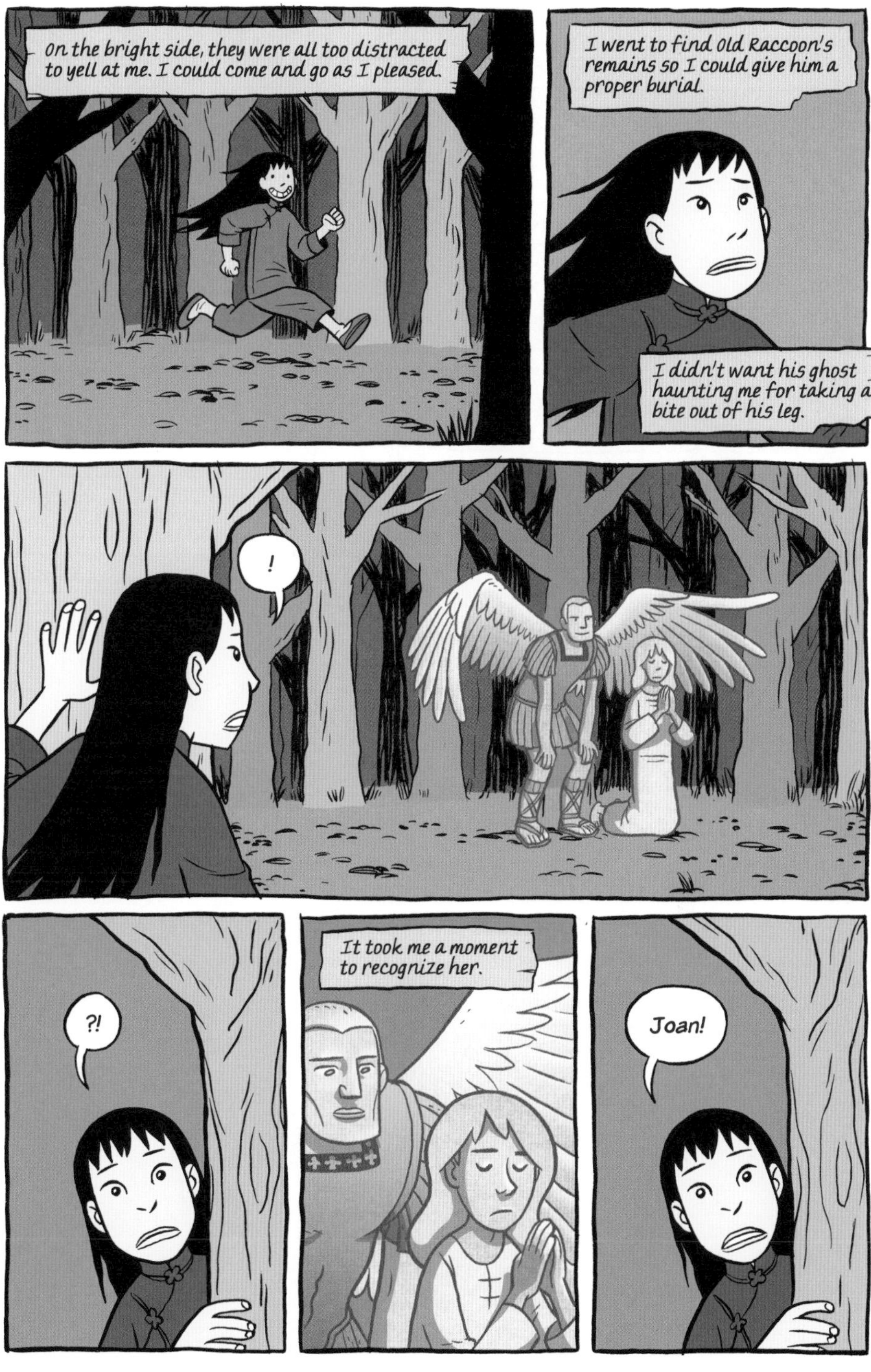
On the bright side, they were all too distracted to yell at me. I could come and go as I pleased.
I went to find Old Raccoon's remains so I could give him a proper burial.
I didn't want his ghost haunting me for taking a bite out of his leg.
!
?!
It took me a moment to recognize her.
Joan!

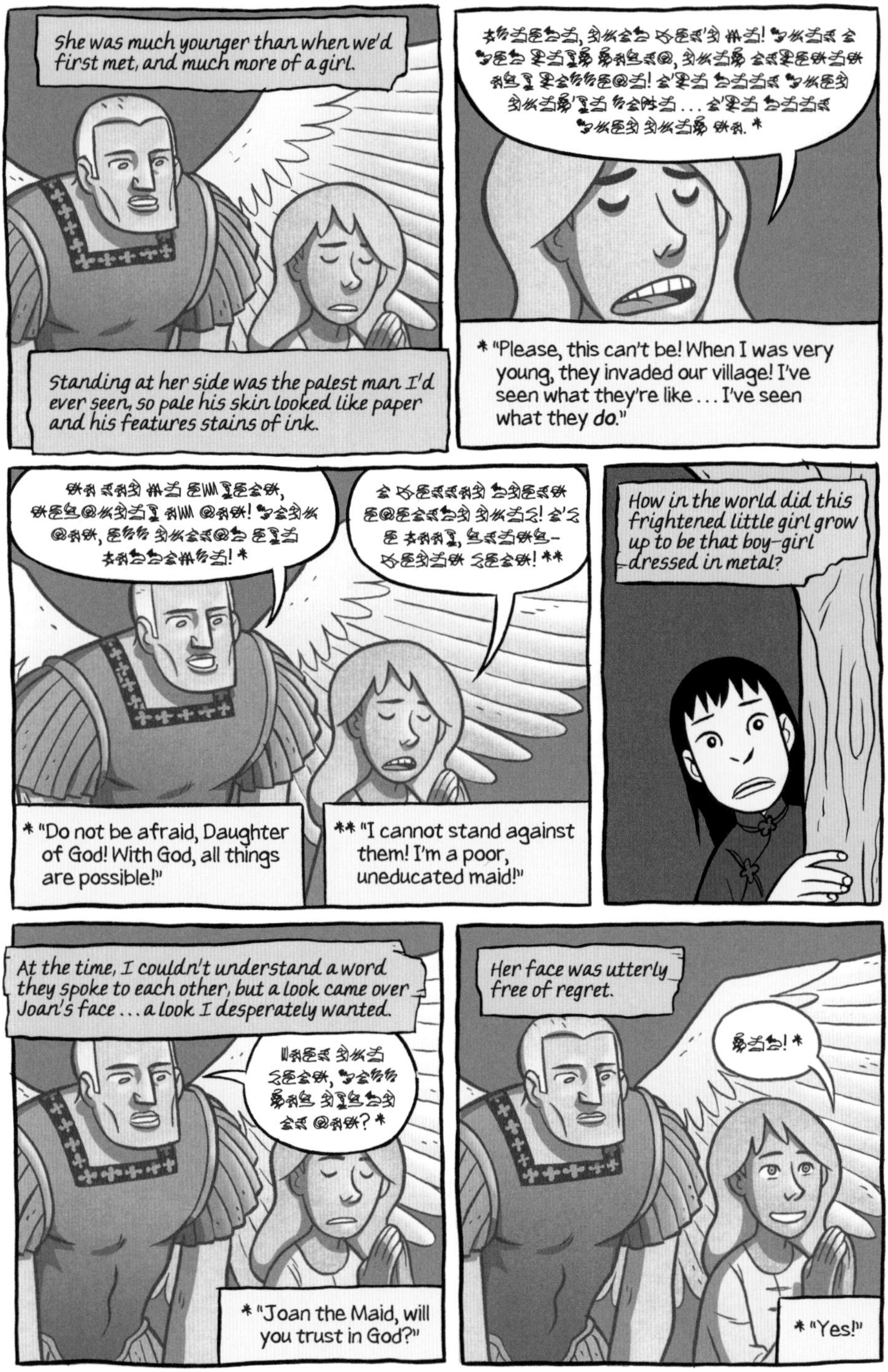
She was much younger than when we'd first met, and much more of a girl.
Standing at her side was the palest man I'd ever seen, so pale his skin looked like paper and his features stains of ink.
* "Please, this can't be! When I was very young, they invaded our village! I've seen what they're like . . . I've seen what they *do*."
* "Do not be afraid, Daughter of God! With God, all things are possible!"
** "I cannot stand against them! I'm a poor, uneducated maid!"
How in the world did this frightened little girl grow up to be that boy-girl dressed in metal?
At the time, I couldn't understand a word they spoke to each other, but a look came over Joan's face . . . a look I desperately wanted.
* "Joan the Maid, will you trust in God?"
Her face was utterly free of regret.
* "Yes!"

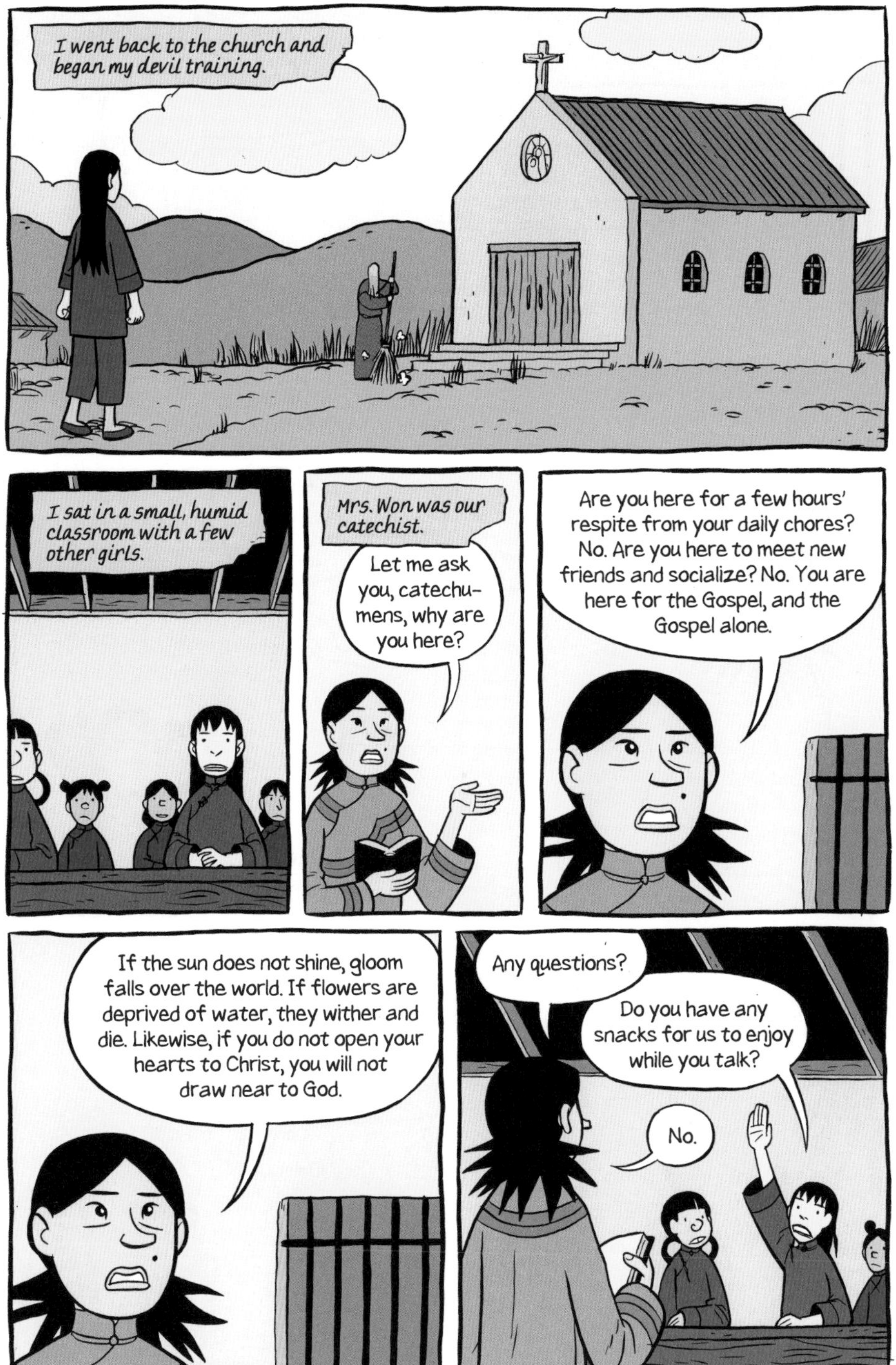
I went back to the church and began my devil training.
I sat in a small, humid classroom with a few other girls.
Mrs. Won was our catechist.
Let me ask you, catechumens, why are you here?
Are you here for a few hours' respite from your daily chores? No. Are you here to meet new friends and socialize? No. You are here for the Gospel, and the Gospel alone.
If the sun does not shine, gloom falls over the world. If flowers are deprived of water, they wither and die. Likewise, if you do not open your hearts to Christ, you will not draw near to God.
Any questions?
Do you have any snacks for us to enjoy while you talk?
No.

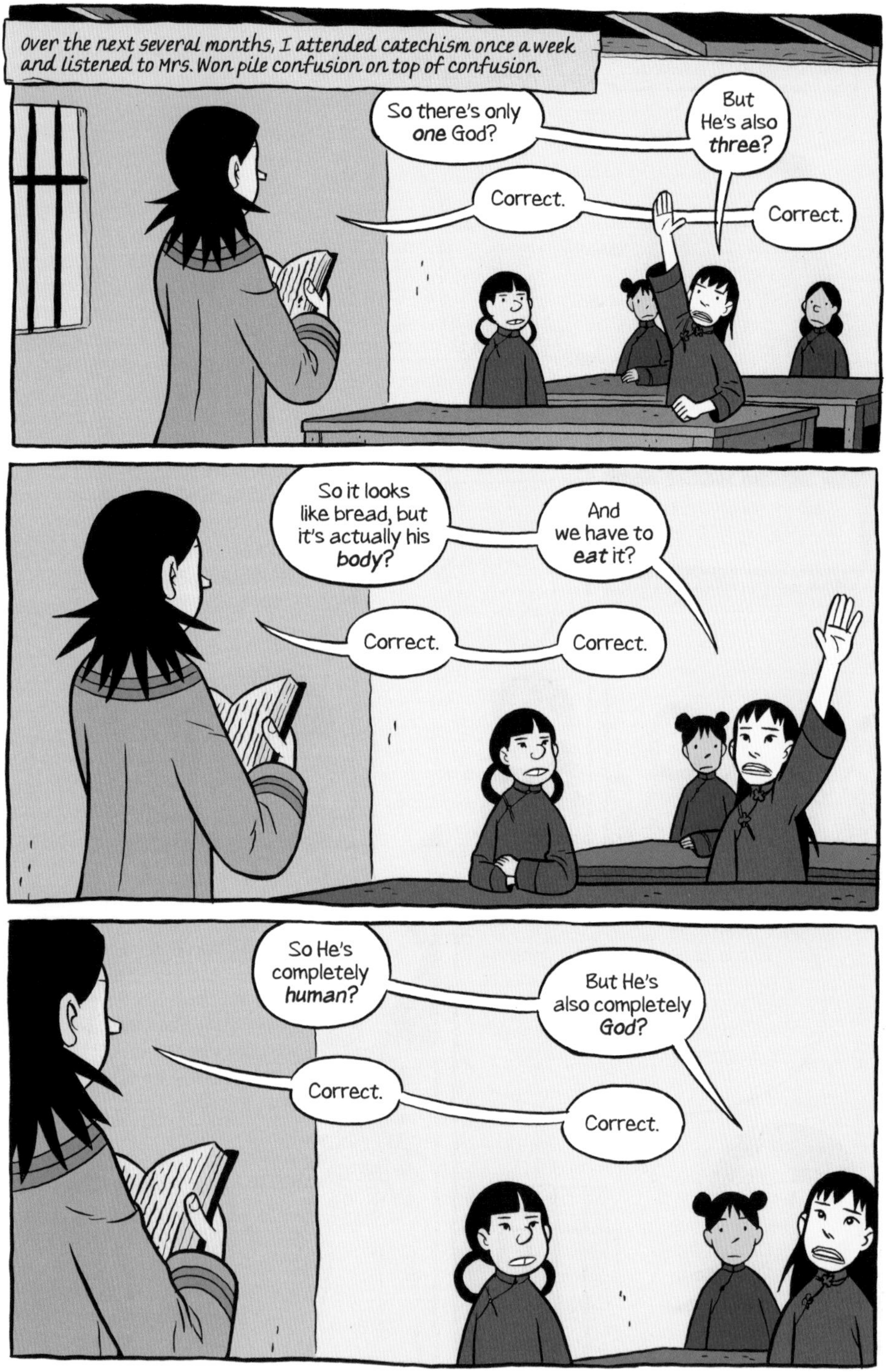
Over the next several months, I attended catechism once a week and listened to Mrs. Won pile confusion on top of confusion.
So there's only *one* God?
But He's also *three*?
Correct.
Correct.
So it looks like bread, but it's actually his *body*?
And we have to *eat* it?
Correct.
Correct.
So He's completely *human*?
But He's also completely *God*?
Correct.
Correct.

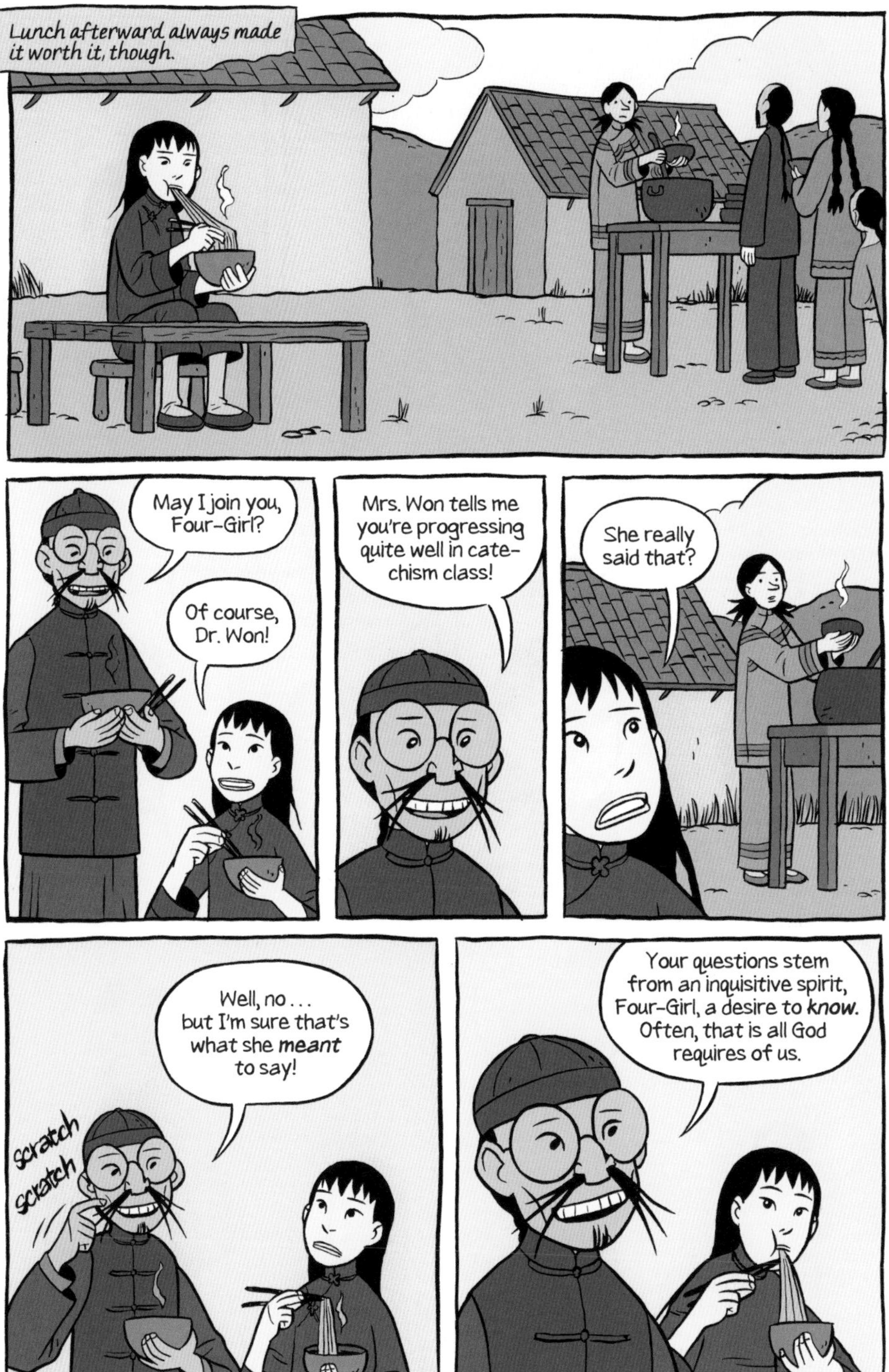
Lunch afterward always made it worth it, though.
May I join you, Four-Girl?
Of course, Dr. Won!
Mrs. Won tells me you're progressing quite well in catechism class!
She really said that?
Well, no . . . but I'm sure that's what she *meant* to say!
scratch scratch
Your questions stem from an inquisitive spirit, Four-Girl, a desire to *know*. Often, that is all God requires of us.

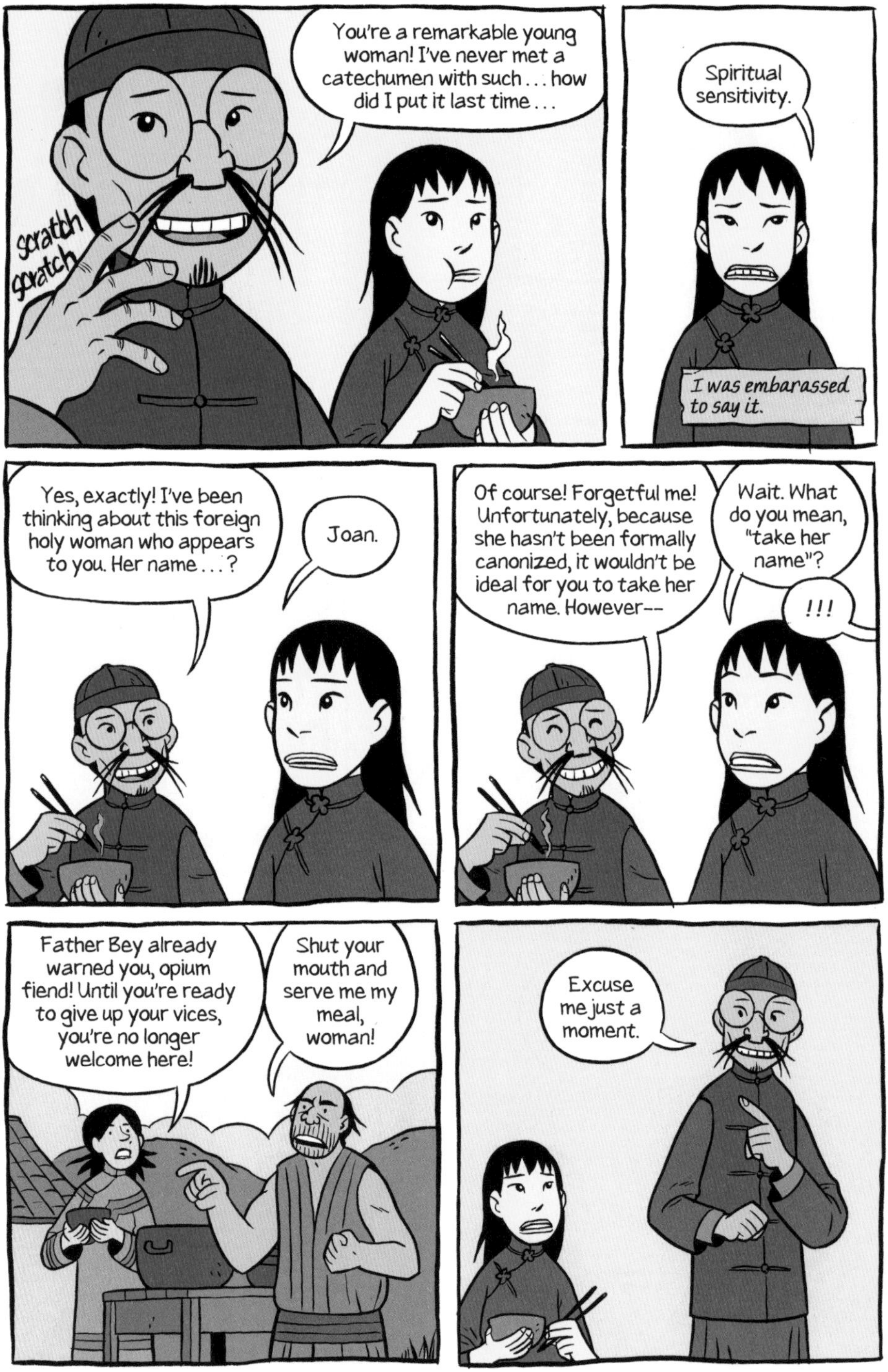
You're a remarkable young woman! I've never met a catechumen with such . . . how did I put it last time . . .
scratch scratch
Spiritual sensitivity.
I was embarassed to say it.
Yes, exactly! I've been thinking about this foreign holy woman who appears to you. Her name . . . ?
Joan.
Of course! Forgetful me! Unfortunately, because she hasn't been formally canonized, it wouldn't be ideal for you to take her name. However--
Wait. What do you mean, "take her name"?
!!!
Father Bey already warned you, opium fiend! Until you're ready to give up your vices, you're no longer welcome here!
Shut your mouth and serve me my meal, woman!
Excuse me just a moment.

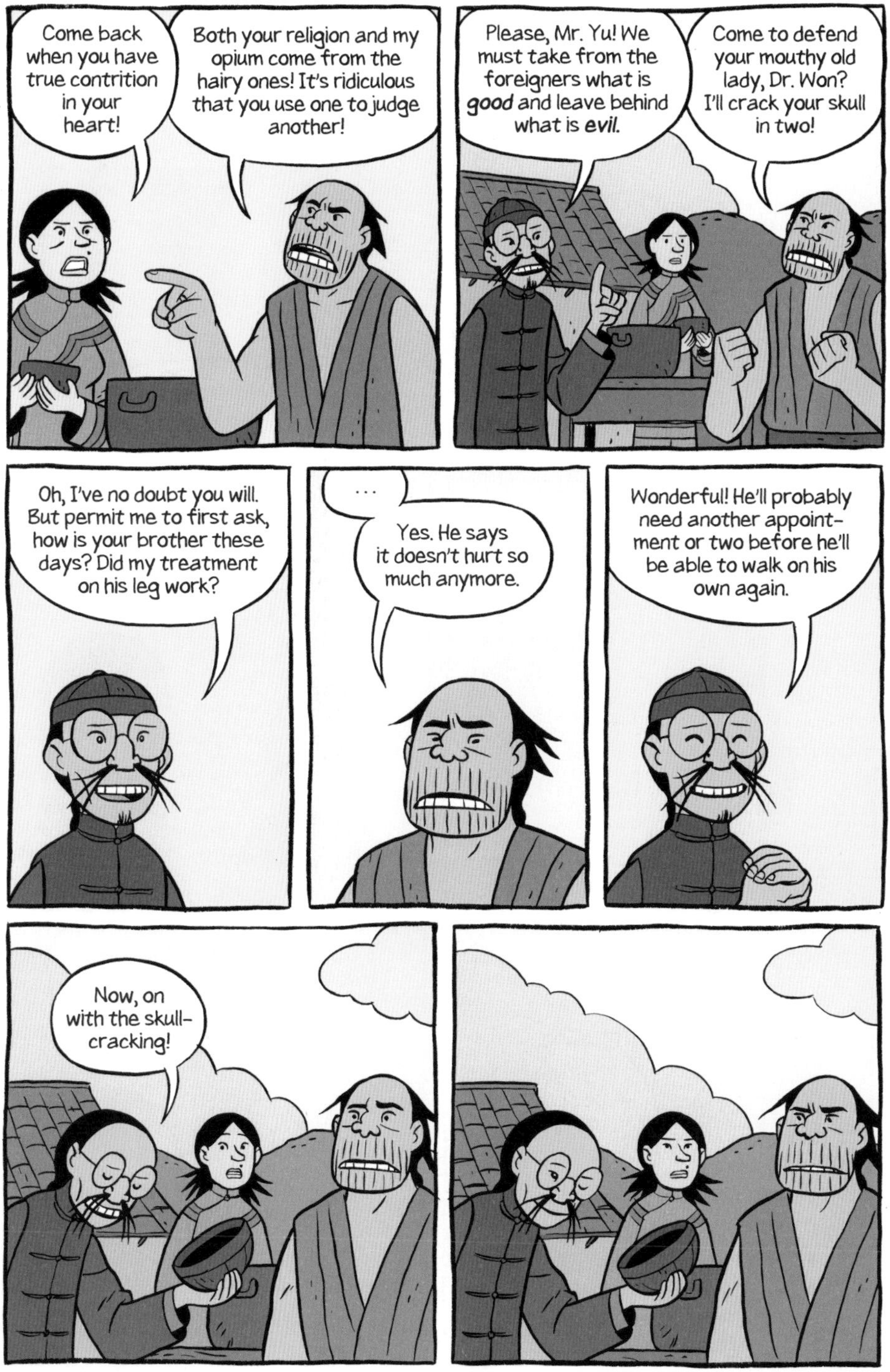
Come back when you have true contrition in your heart!
Both your religion and my opium come from the hairy ones! It's ridiculous that you use one to judge another!
Please, Mr. Yu! We must take from the foreigners what is *good* and leave behind what is *evil.*
Come to defend your mouthy old lady, Dr. Won? I'll crack your skull in two!
Oh, I've no doubt you will. But permit me to first ask, how is your brother these days? Did my treatment on his leg work?
...
Yes. He says it doesn't hurt so much anymore.
Wonderful! He'll probably need another appoint-ment or two before he'll be able to walk on his own again.
Now, on with the skull-cracking!

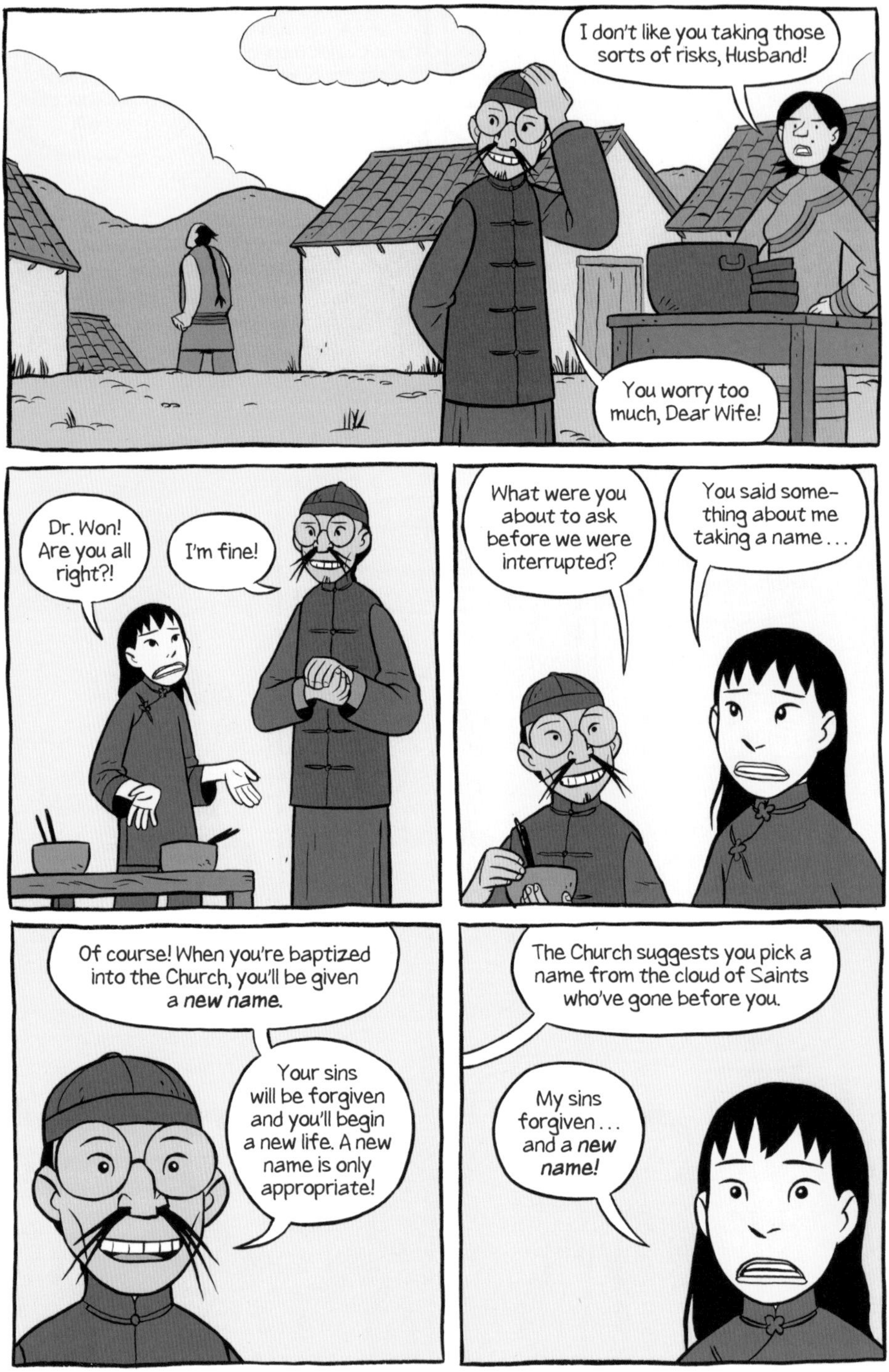
I don't like you taking those sorts of risks, Husband!
You worry too much, Dear Wife!
Dr. Won! Are you all right?!
I'm fine!
What were you about to ask before we were interrupted?
You said some-thing about me taking a name . . .
Of course! When you're baptized into the Church, you'll be given a *new name.*
Your sins will be forgiven and you'll begin a new life. A new name is only appropriate!
The Church suggests you pick a name from the cloud of Saints who've gone before you.
My sins forgiven . . . and a *new name!*

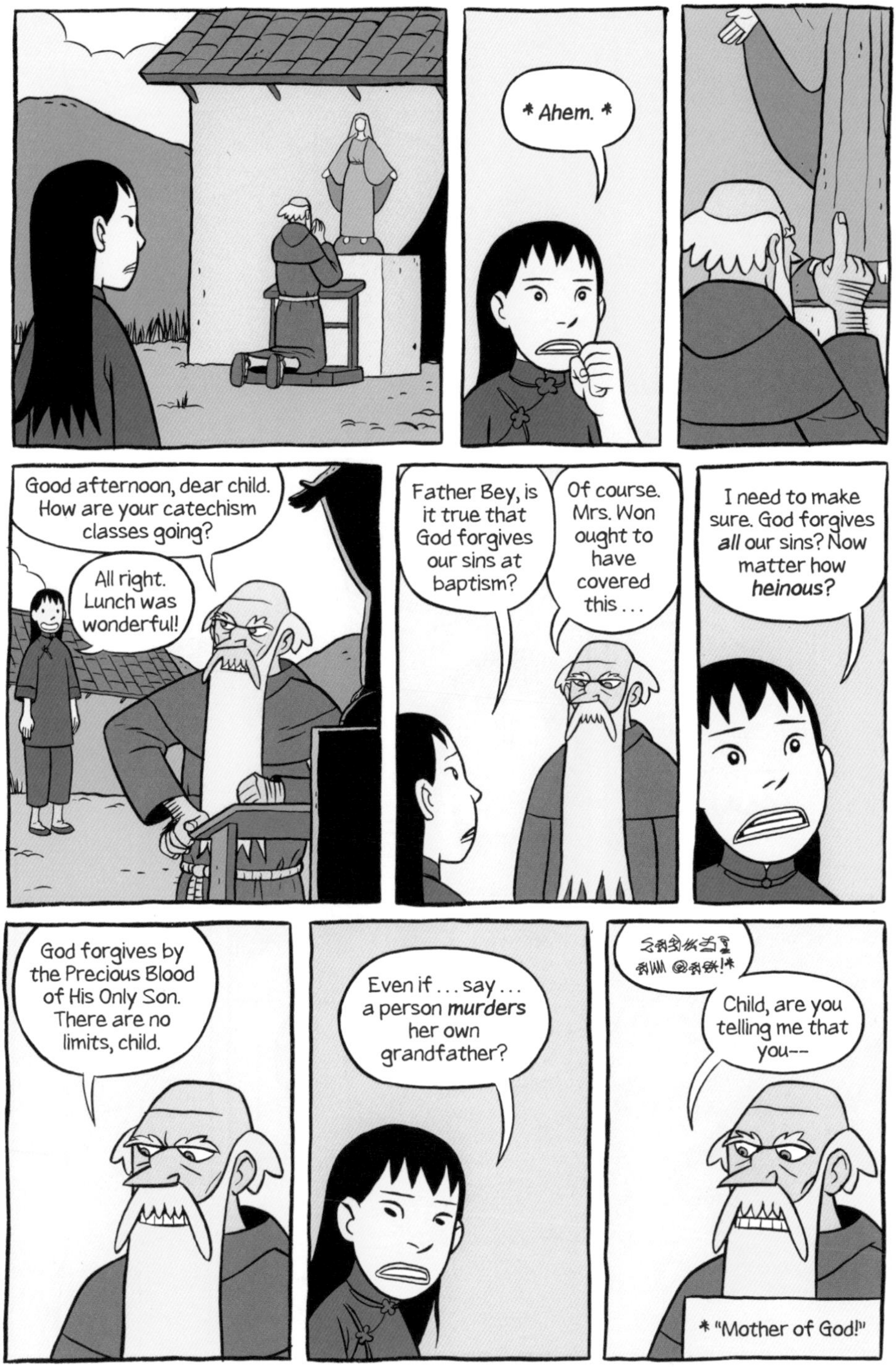
* Ahem. *
Good afternoon, dear child. How are your catechism classes going?
All right. Lunch was wonderful!
Father Bey, is it true that God forgives our sins at baptism?
Of course. Mrs. Won ought to have covered this . . .
I need to make sure. God forgives *all* our sins? No matter how ***heinous***?
God forgives by the Precious Blood of His Only Son. There are no limits, child.
Even if . . . say . . . a person ***murders*** her own grandfather?
Child, are you telling me that you--
* "Mother of God!"

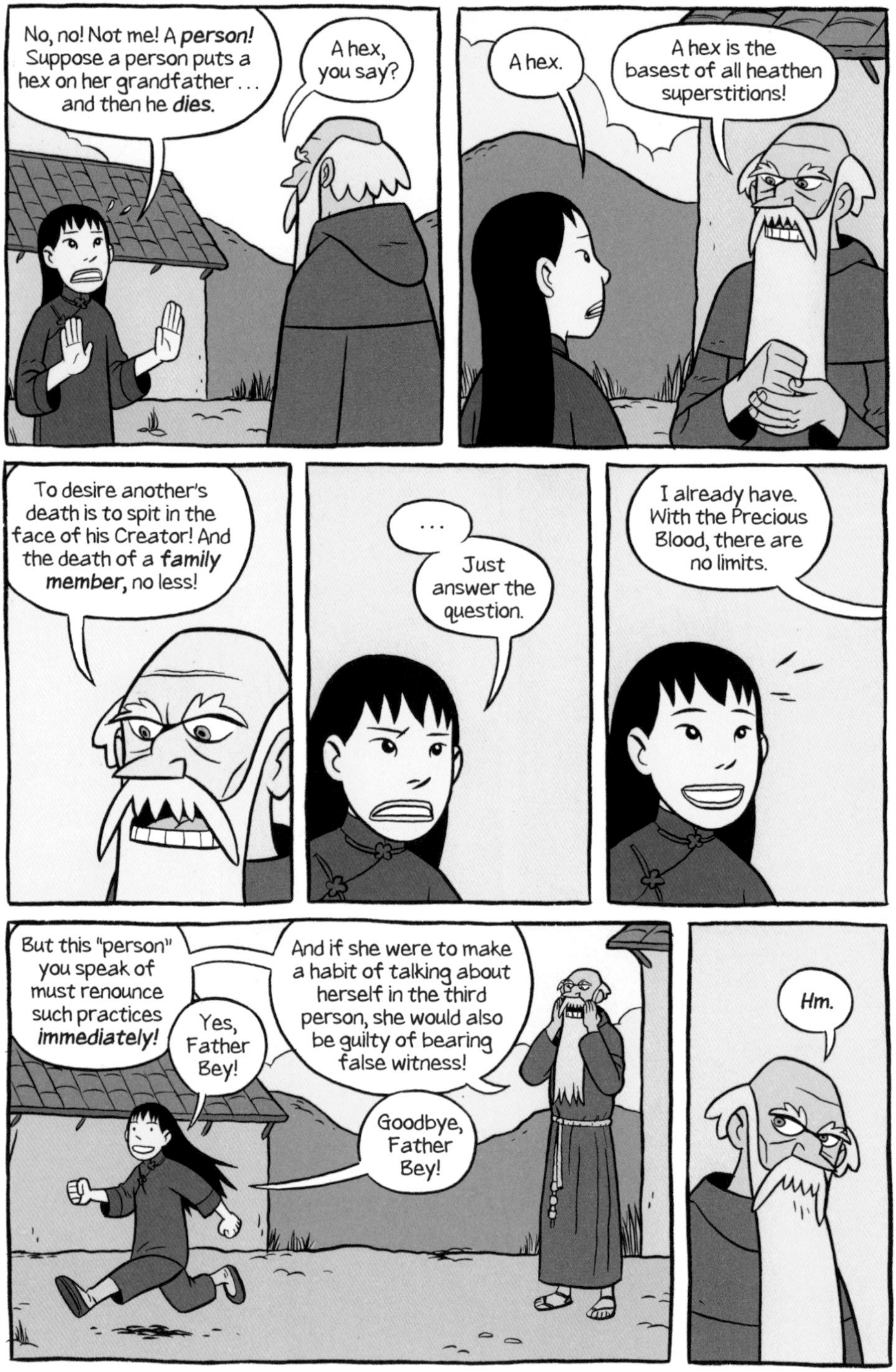
No, no! Not me! A person! Suppose a person puts a hex on her grandfather . . . and then he dies.
A hex, you say?
A hex.
A hex is the basest of all heathen superstitions!
To desire another's death is to spit in the face of his Creator! And the death of a family member, no less!
. . .
Just answer the question.
I already have. With the Precious Blood, there are no limits.
But this "person" you speak of must renounce such practices immediately!
Yes, Father Bey!
And if she were to make a habit of talking about herself in the third person, she would also be guilty of bearing false witness!
Goodbye, Father Bey!
Hm.

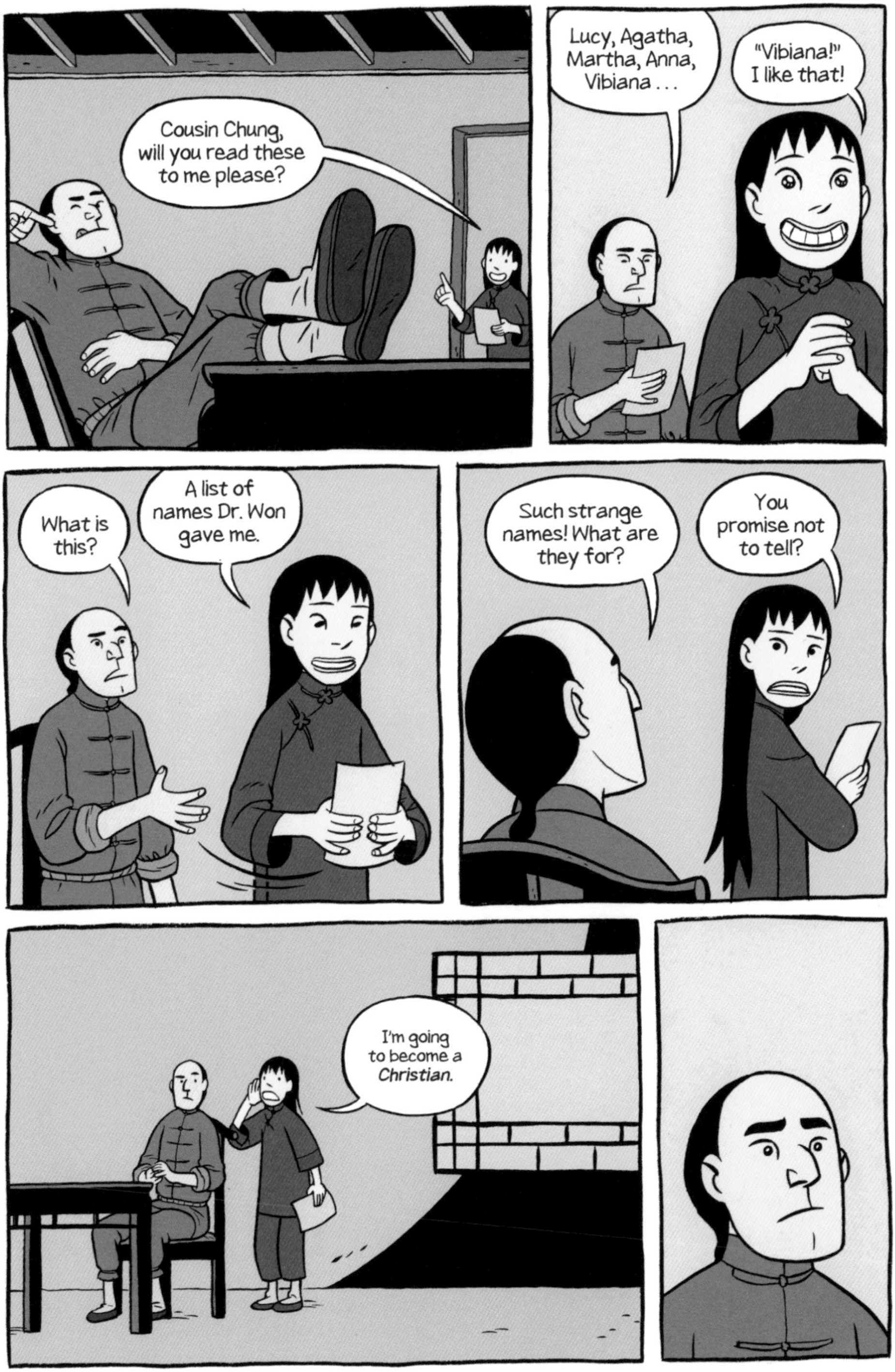

Cousin Chung, will you read these to me please?
Lucy, Agatha, Martha, Anna, Vibiana . . .
"Vibiana!" I like that!
What is this?
A list of names Dr. Won gave me.
Such strange names! What are they for?
You promise not to tell?
I'm going to become a *Christian.*

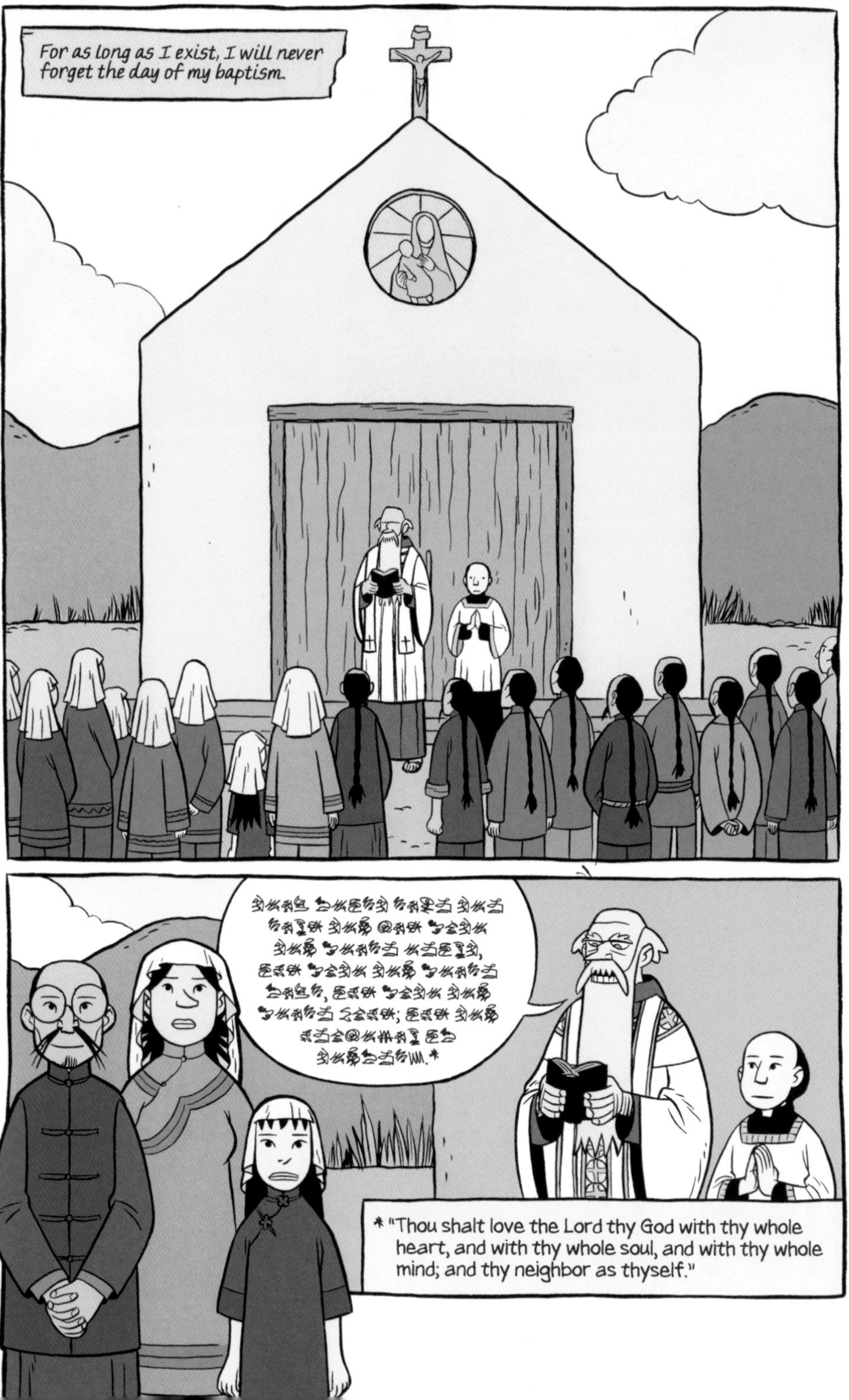
For as long as I exist, I will never forget the day of my baptism.
* "Thou shalt love the Lord thy God with thy whole heart, and with thy whole soul, and with thy whole mind; and thy neighbor as thyself."

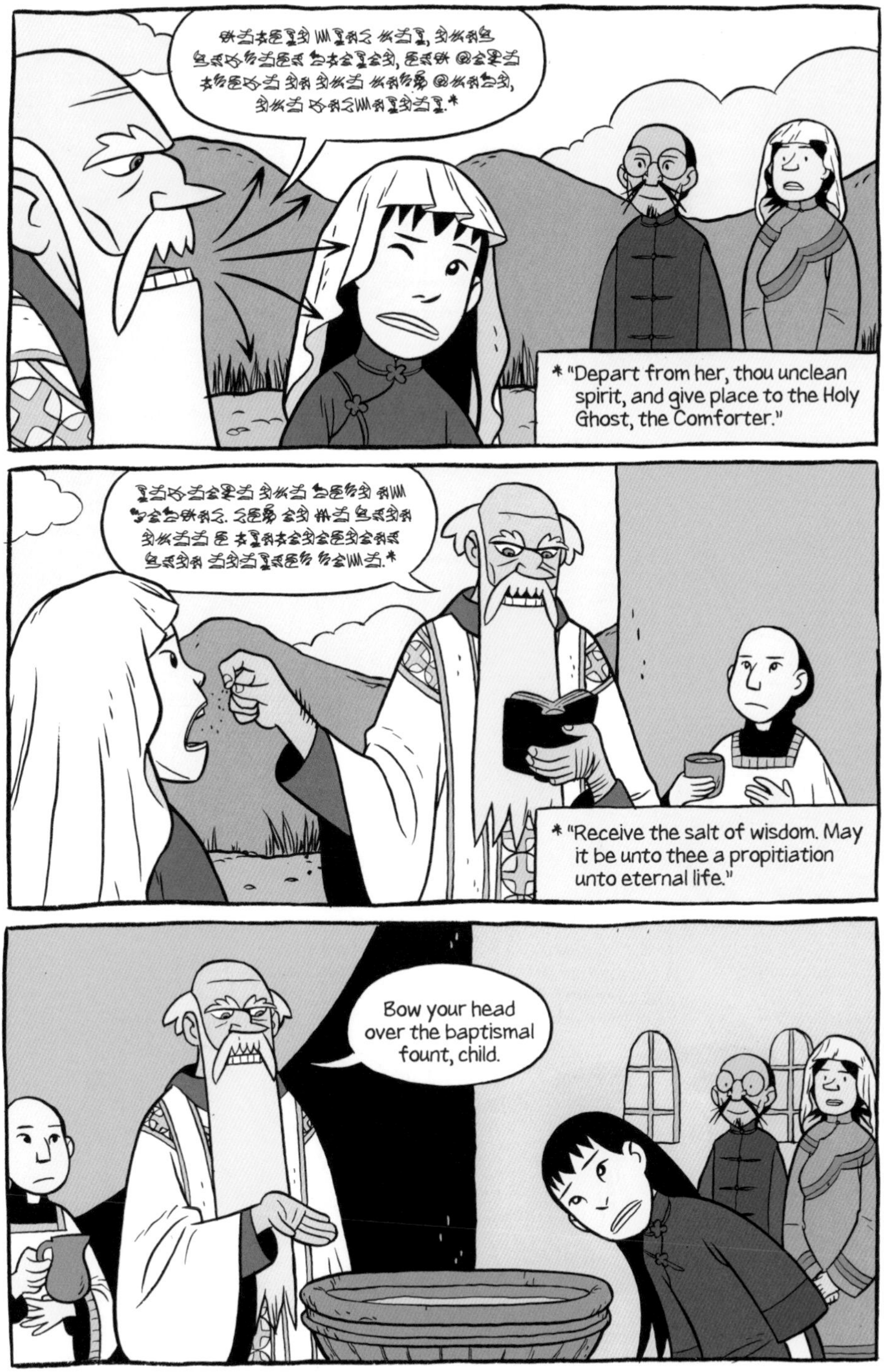
* "Depart from her, thou unclean spirit, and give place to the Holy Ghost, the Comforter."
* "Receive the salt of wisdom. May it be unto thee a propitiation unto eternal life."
Bow your head over the baptismal fount, child.

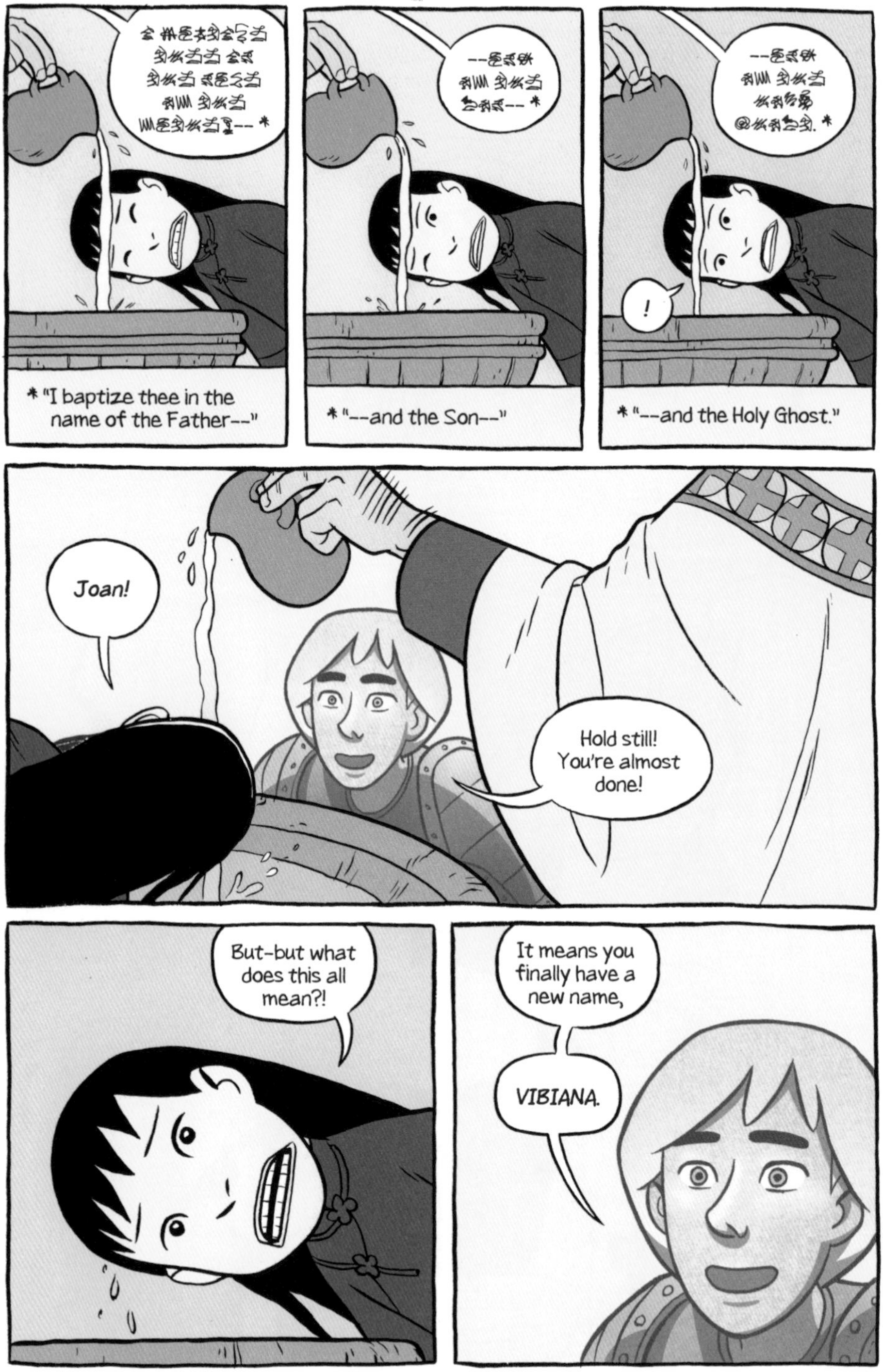
* "I baptize thee in the name of the Father--"
* "--and the Son--"
!
* "--and the Holy Ghost."
Joan!
Hold still! You're almost done!
But-but what does this all mean?!
It means you finally have a new name,
VIBIANA.

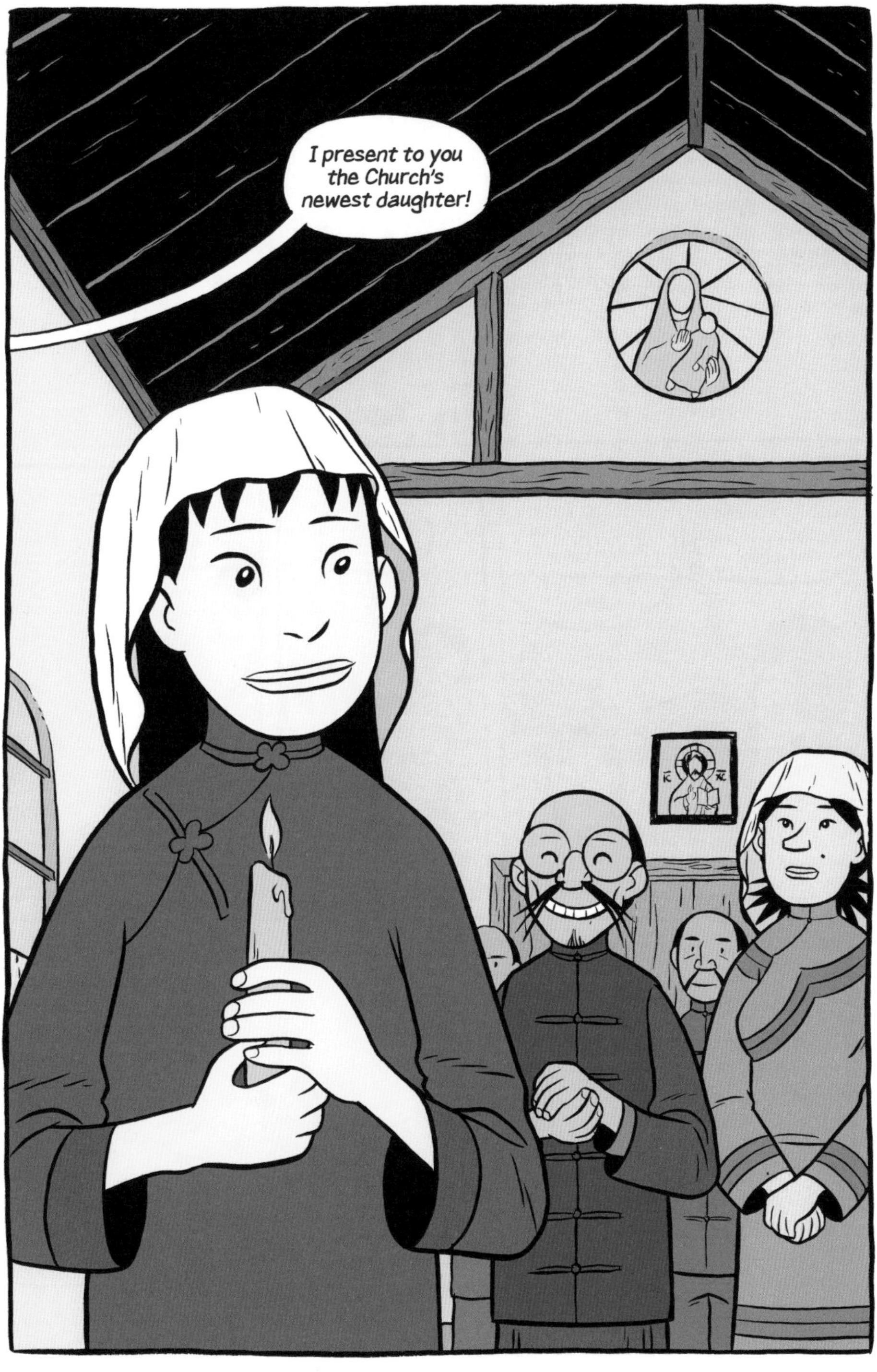
I present to you the Church's newest daughter!

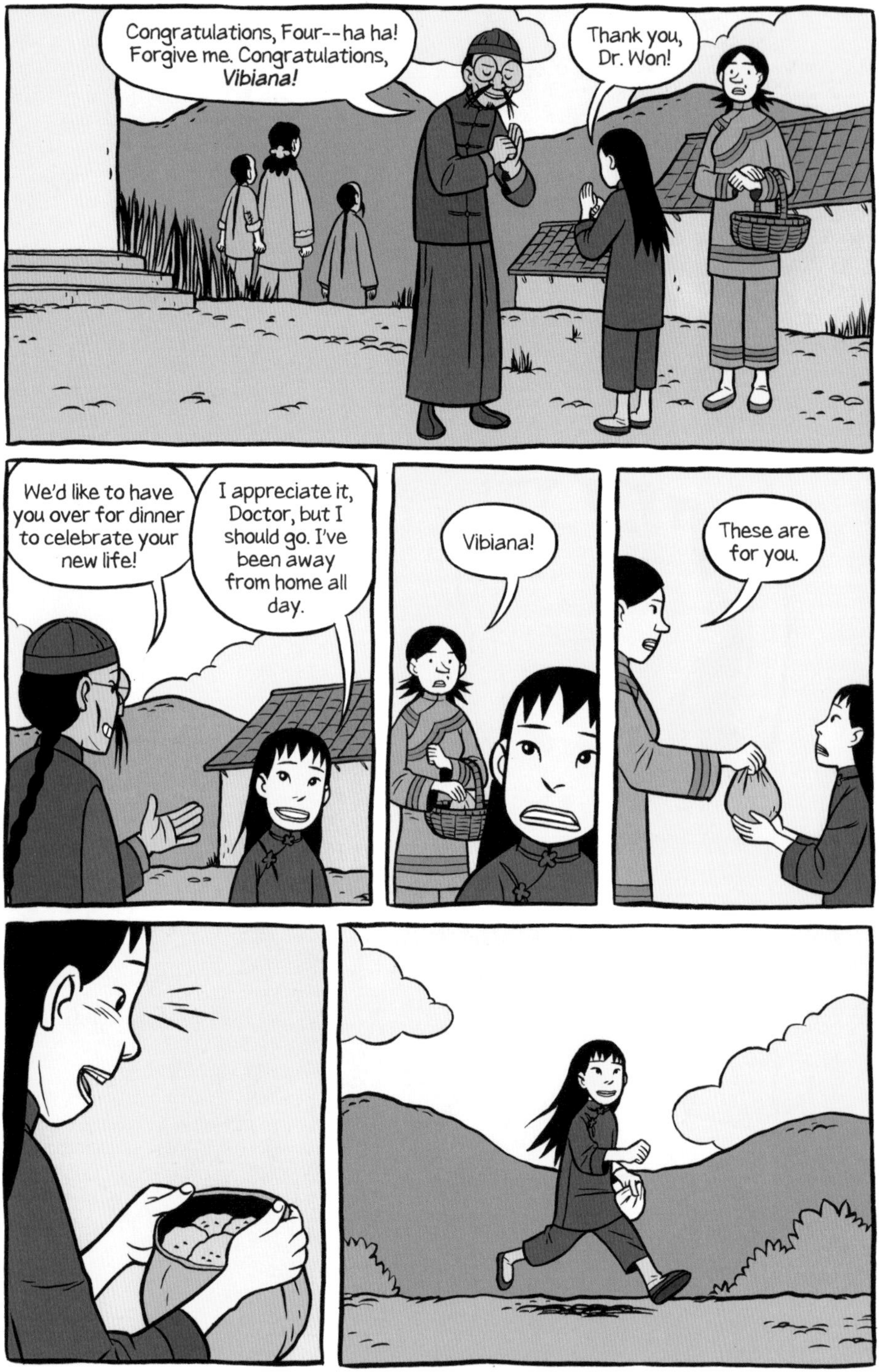
Congratulations, Four--ha ha! Forgive me. Congratulations, *Vibiana!*
Thank you, Dr. Won!
We'd like to have you over for dinner to celebrate your new life!
I appreciate it, Doctor, but I should go. I've been away from home all day.
Vibiana!
These are for you.

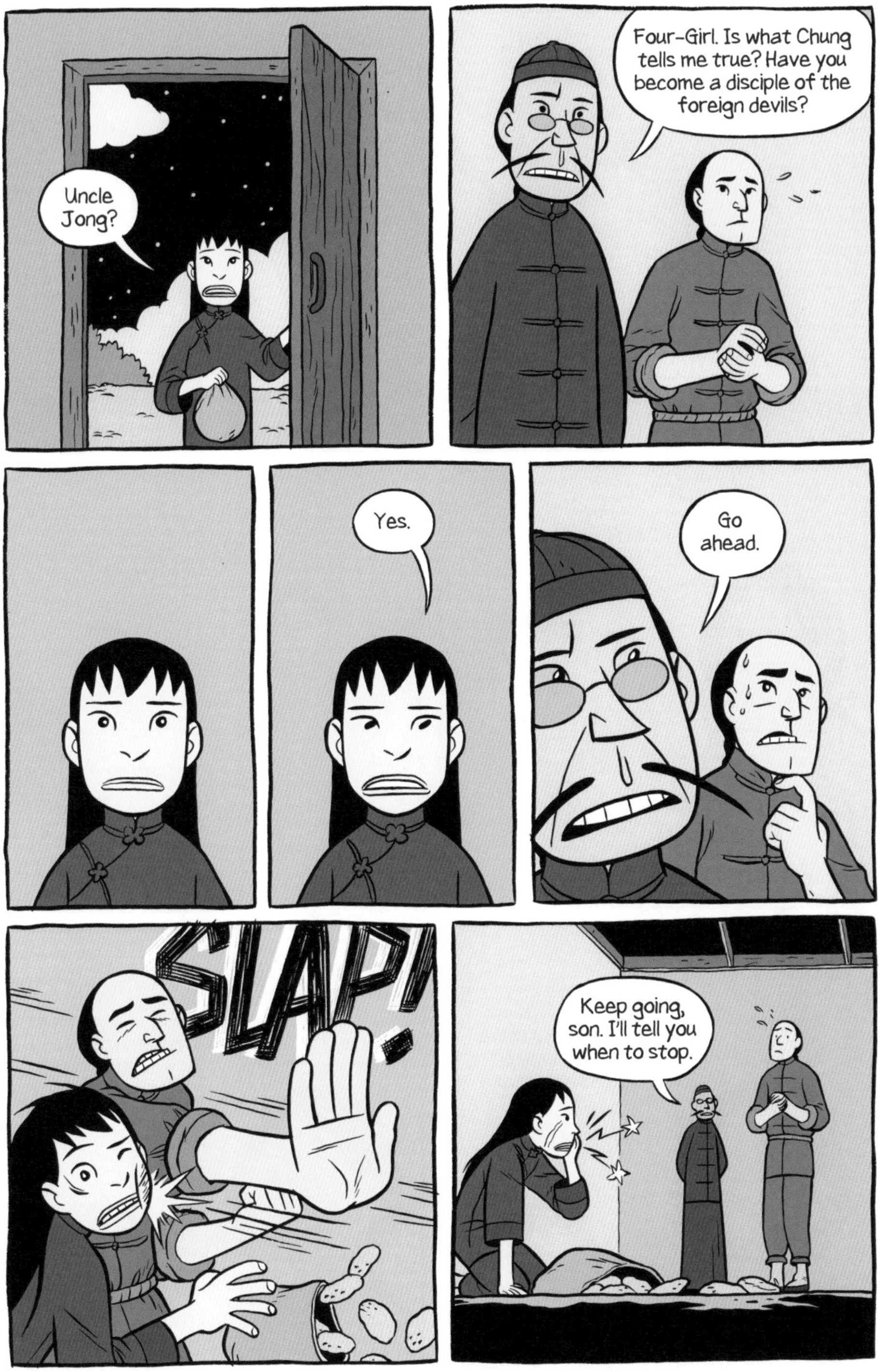
Uncle Jong?
Four-Girl. Is what Chung tells me true? Have you become a disciple of the foreign devils?
Yes.
Go ahead.
SLAP!
Keep going, son. I'll tell you when to stop.

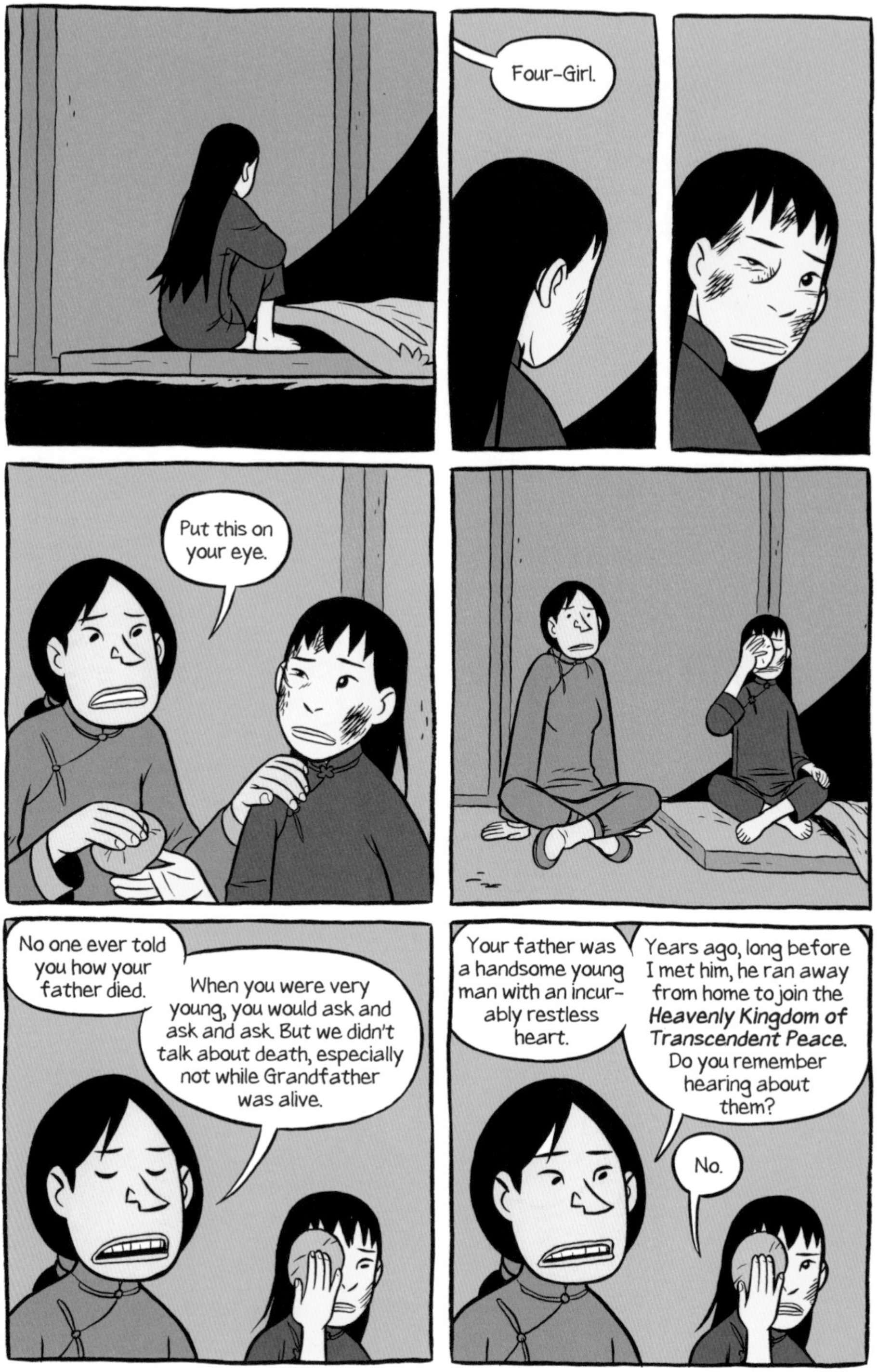
Four-Girl.
Put this on your eye.
No one ever told you how your father died.
When you were very young, you would ask and ask and ask. But we didn't talk about death, especially not while Grandfather was alive.
Your father was a handsome young man with an incurably restless heart.
Years ago, long before I met him, he ran away from home to join the *Heavenly Kingdom of Transcendent Peace*. Do you remember hearing about them?
No.

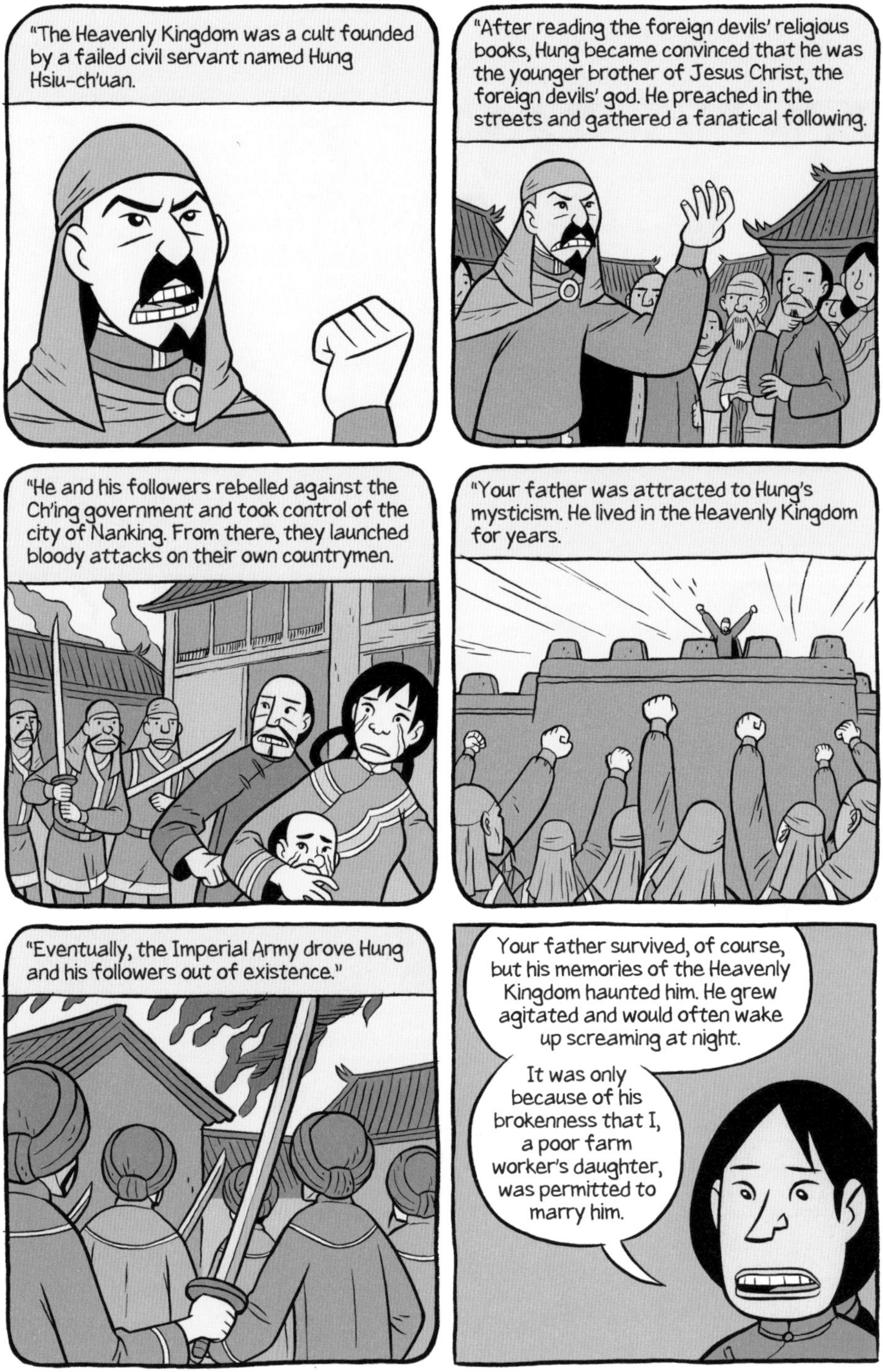
"The Heavenly Kingdom was a cult founded by a failed civil servant named Hung Hsiu-ch'uan.
"After reading the foreign devils' religious books, Hung became convinced that he was the younger brother of Jesus Christ, the foreign devils' god. He preached in the streets and gathered a fanatical following.
"He and his followers rebelled against the Ch'ing government and took control of the city of Nanking. From there, they launched bloody attacks on their own countrymen.
"Your father was attracted to Hung's mysticism. He lived in the Heavenly Kingdom for years.
"Eventually, the Imperial Army drove Hung and his followers out of existence."
Your father survived, of course, but his memories of the Heavenly Kingdom haunted him. He grew agitated and would often wake up screaming at night.
It was only because of his brokenness that I, a poor farm worker's daughter, was permitted to marry him.

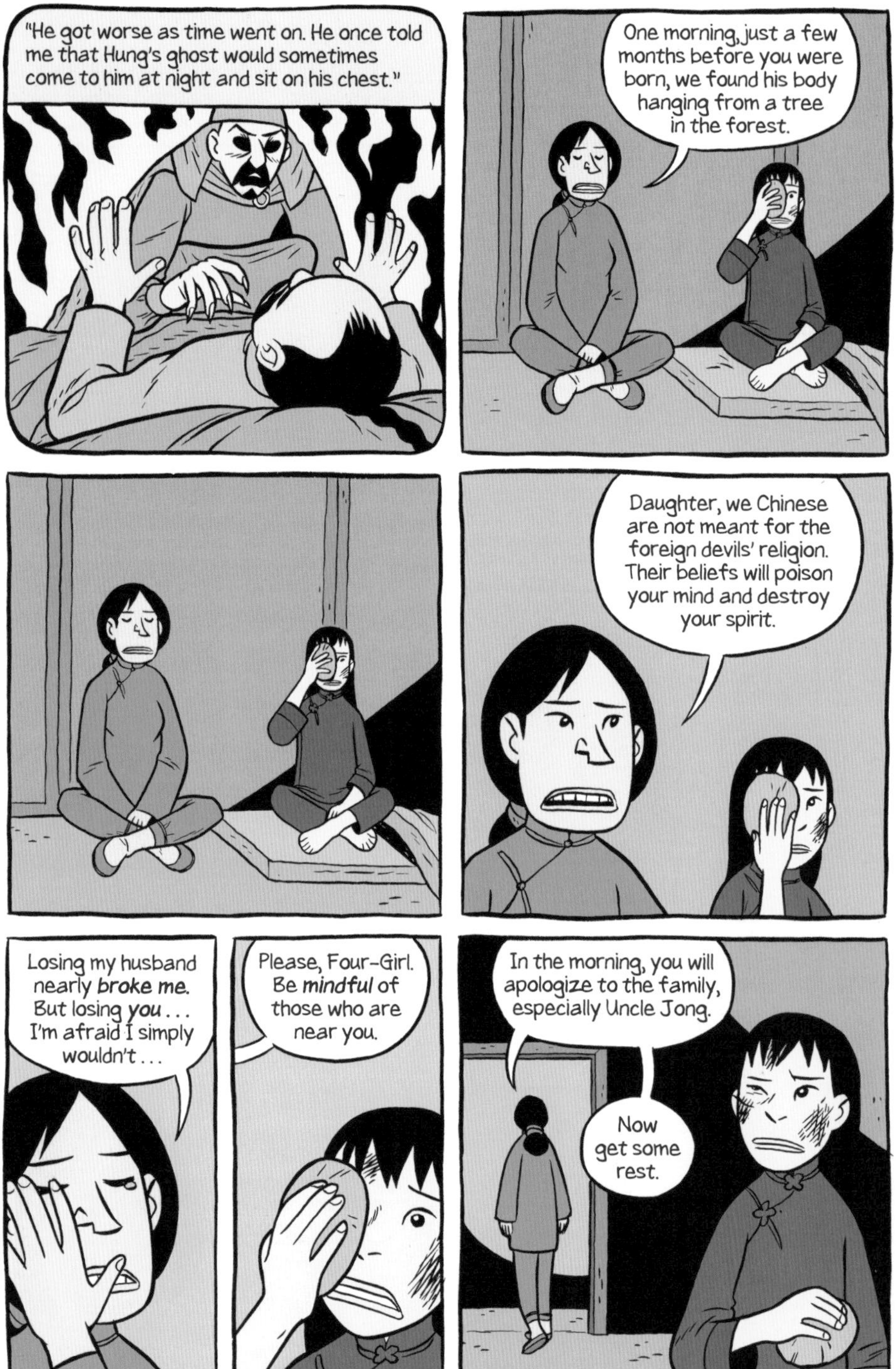
"He got worse as time went on. He once told me that Hung's ghost would sometimes come to him at night and sit on his chest."
One morning, just a few months before you were born, we found his body hanging from a tree in the forest.
Daughter, we Chinese are not meant for the foreign devils' religion. Their beliefs will poison your mind and destroy your spirit.
Losing my husband nearly **broke me.** But losing *you*... I'm afraid I simply wouldn't...
Please, Four-Girl. Be *mindful* of those who are near you.
In the morning, you will apologize to the family, especially Uncle Jong.
Now get some rest.

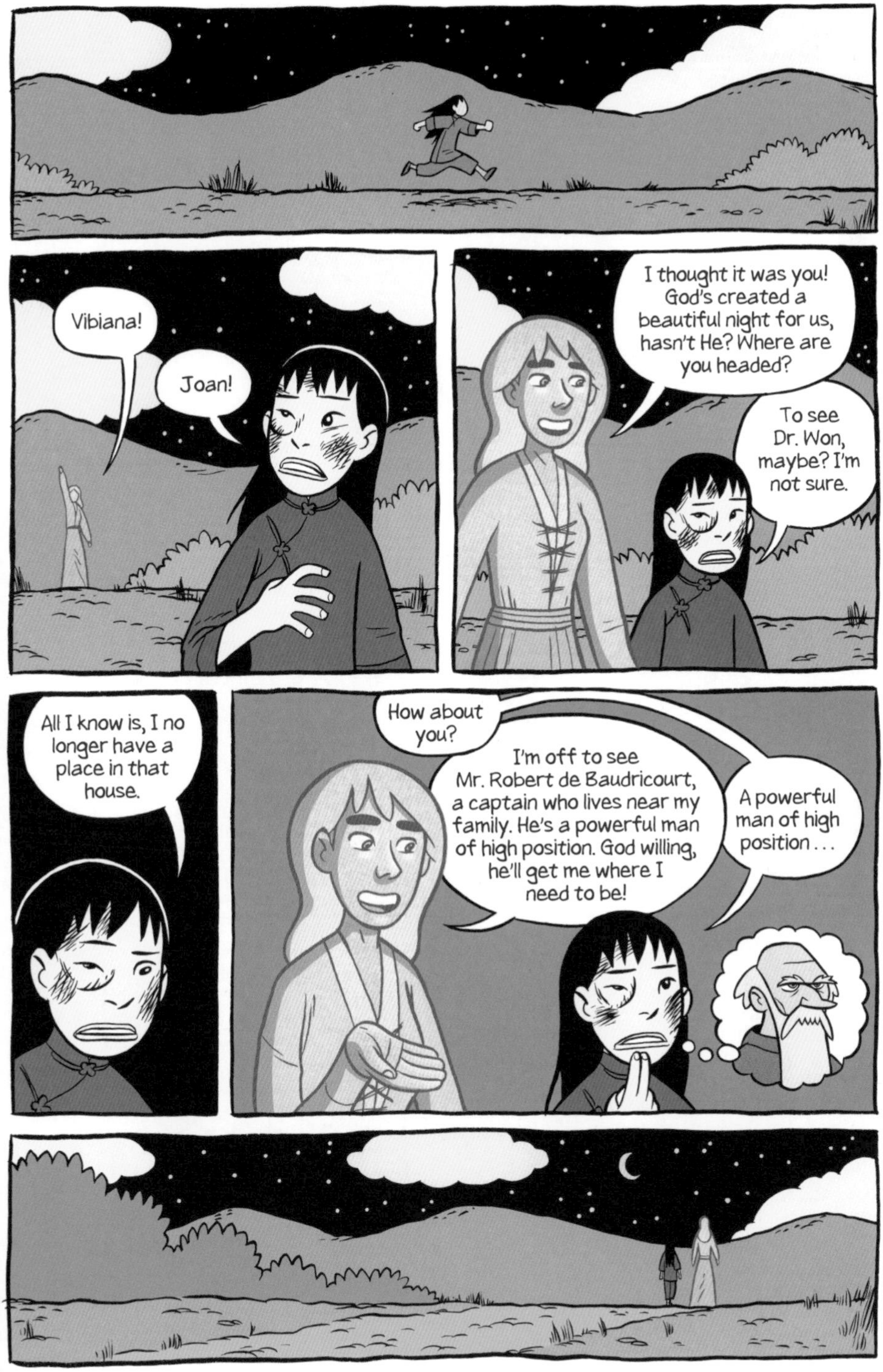
Vibiana!
Joan!
I thought it was you! God's created a beautiful night for us, hasn't He? Where are you headed?
To see Dr. Won, maybe? I'm not sure.
All I know is, I no longer have a place in that house.
How about you?
I'm off to see Mr. Robert de Baudricourt, a captain who lives near my family. He's a powerful man of high position. God willing, he'll get me where I need to be!
A powerful man of high position . . .

I enjoyed sharing that stretch of road, but I'm headed this way now.

Will we meet each other again?

Of course, Vibiana! Of course!

God be with you!

桃兆我正長我妹!
桃兆我正長我妹 桃妹
匆光会我匆合兆片兆妹
妹我么妹么! *

Father Bey?

* "Betrayed! Betrayed by whitewashed tombs!"

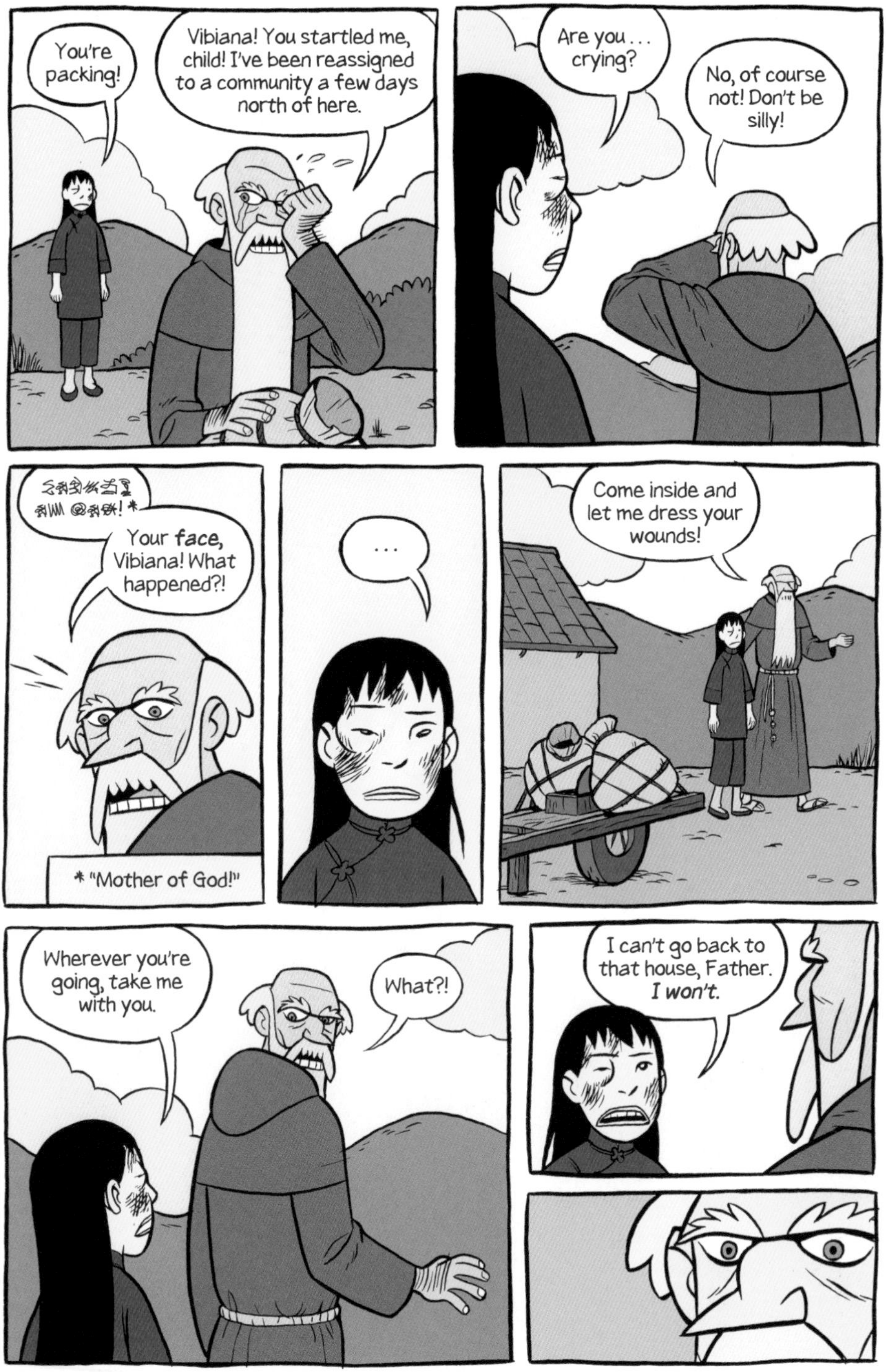
You're packing!
Vibiana! You startled me, child! I've been reassigned to a community a few days north of here.
Are you . . . crying?
No, of course not! Don't be silly!
Your **face,** Vibiana! What happened?!
* "Mother of God!"
. . .
Come inside and let me dress your wounds!
Wherever you're going, take me with you.
What?!
I can't go back to that house, Father. *I won't.*

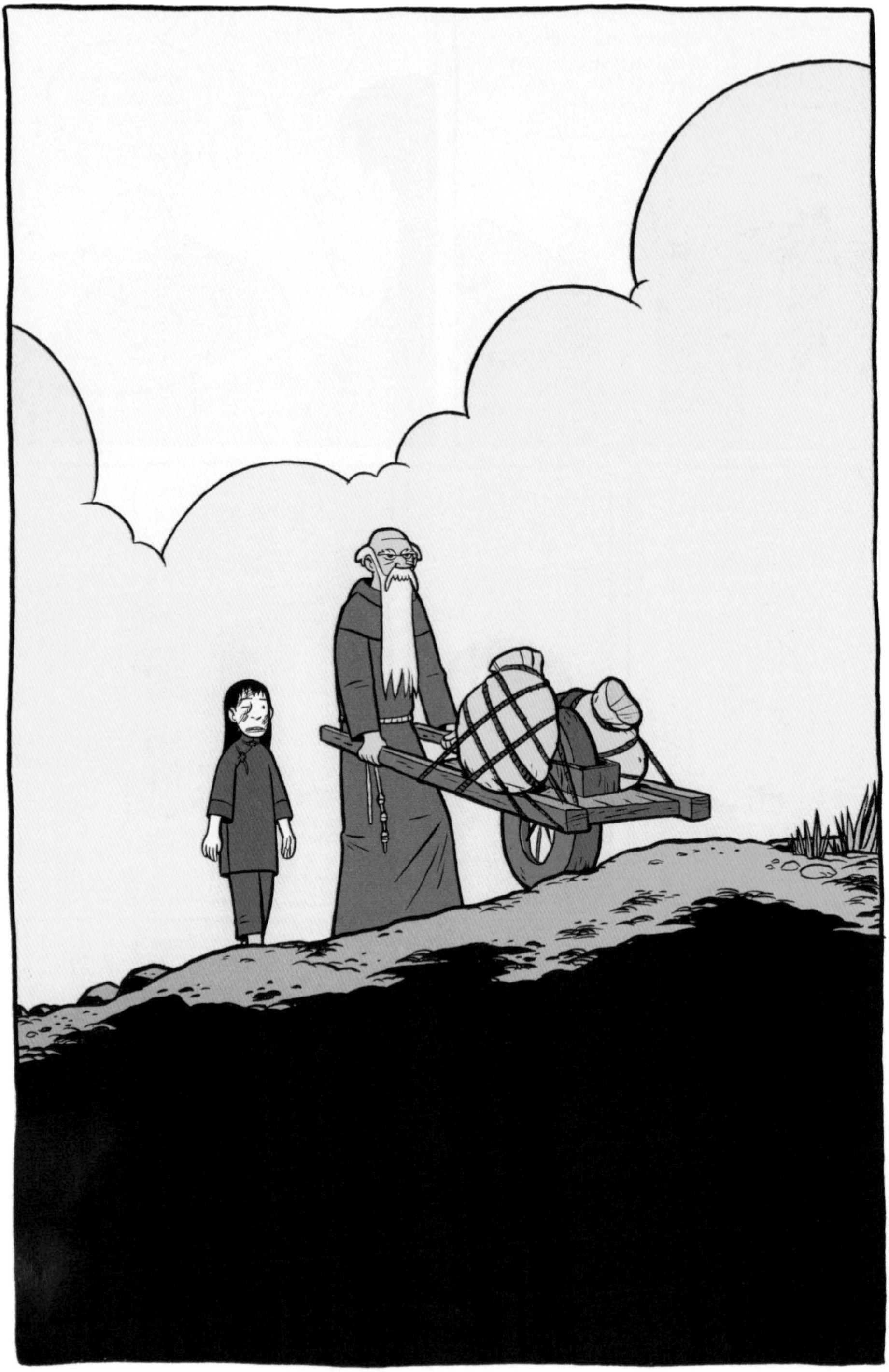

第四章

Age 14

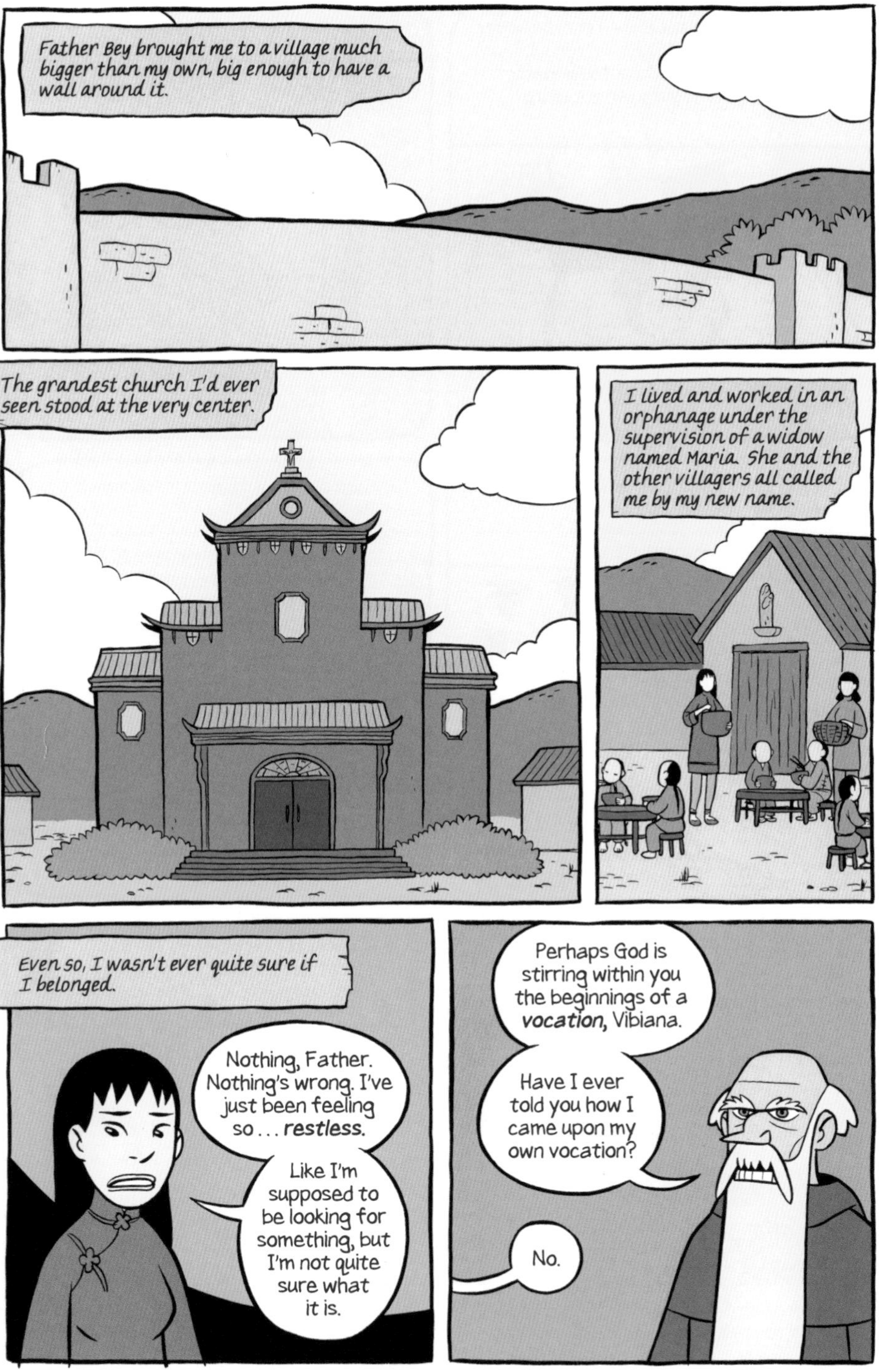
Father Bey brought me to a village much bigger than my own, big enough to have a wall around it.
The grandest church I'd ever seen stood at the very center.
I lived and worked in an orphanage under the supervision of a widow named Maria. She and the other villagers all called me by my new name.
Even so, I wasn't ever quite sure if I belonged.
Nothing, Father. Nothing's wrong. I've just been feeling so . . . restless.
Like I'm supposed to be looking for something, but I'm not quite sure what it is.
Perhaps God is stirring within you the beginnings of a vocation, Vibiana.
Have I ever told you how I came upon my own vocation?
No.

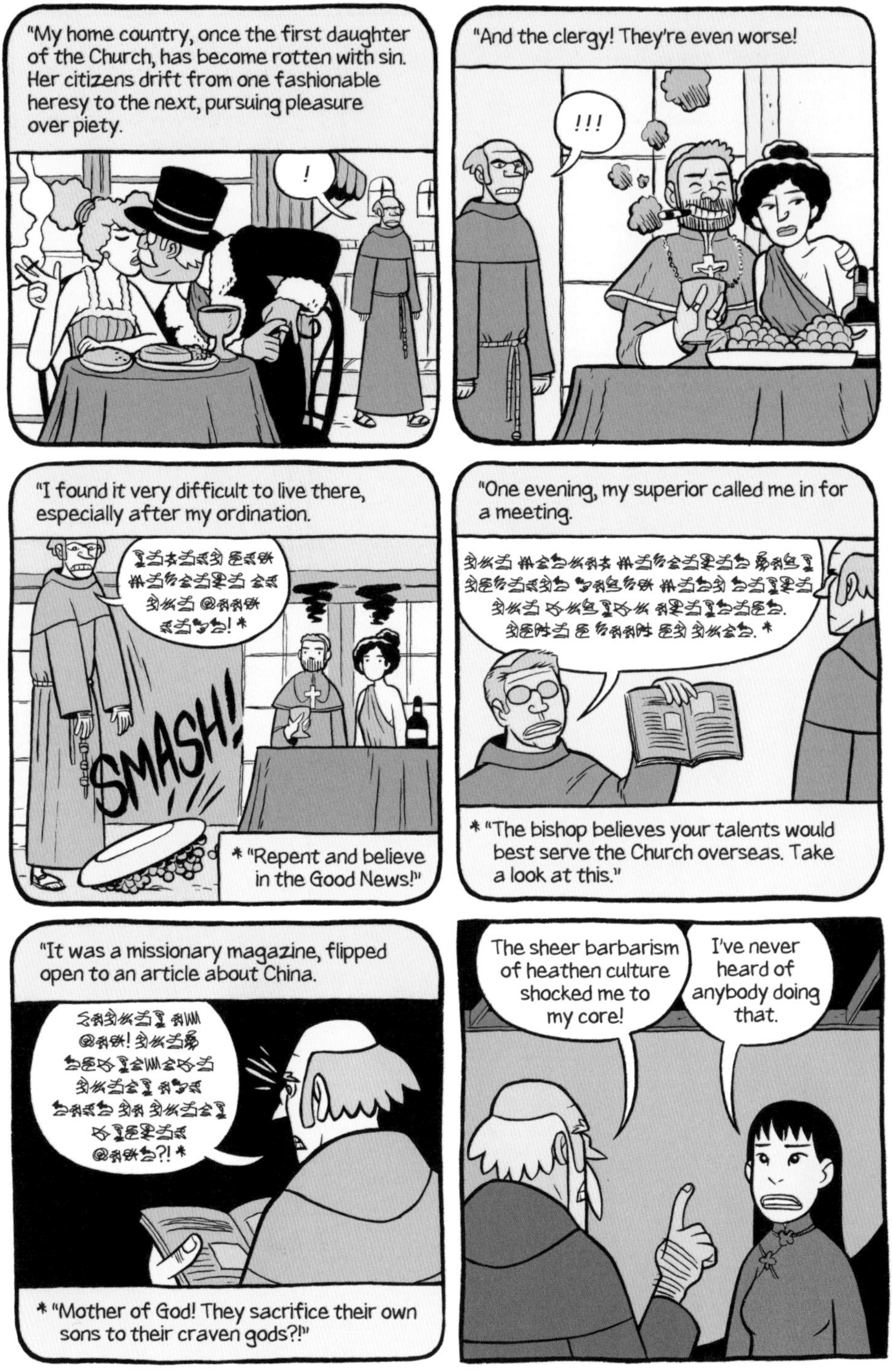
"My home country, once the first daughter of the Church, has become rotten with sin. Her citizens drift from one fashionable heresy to the next, pursuing pleasure over piety.
!
"And the clergy! They're even worse!
!!!
"I found it very difficult to live there, especially after my ordination.
SMASH!
* "Repent and believe in the Good News!"
"One evening, my superior called me in for a meeting.
* "The bishop believes your talents would best serve the Church overseas. Take a look at this."
"It was a missionary magazine, flipped open to an article about China.
* "Mother of God! They sacrifice their own sons to their craven gods?!"
The sheer barbarism of heathen culture shocked me to my core!
I've never heard of anybody doing that.

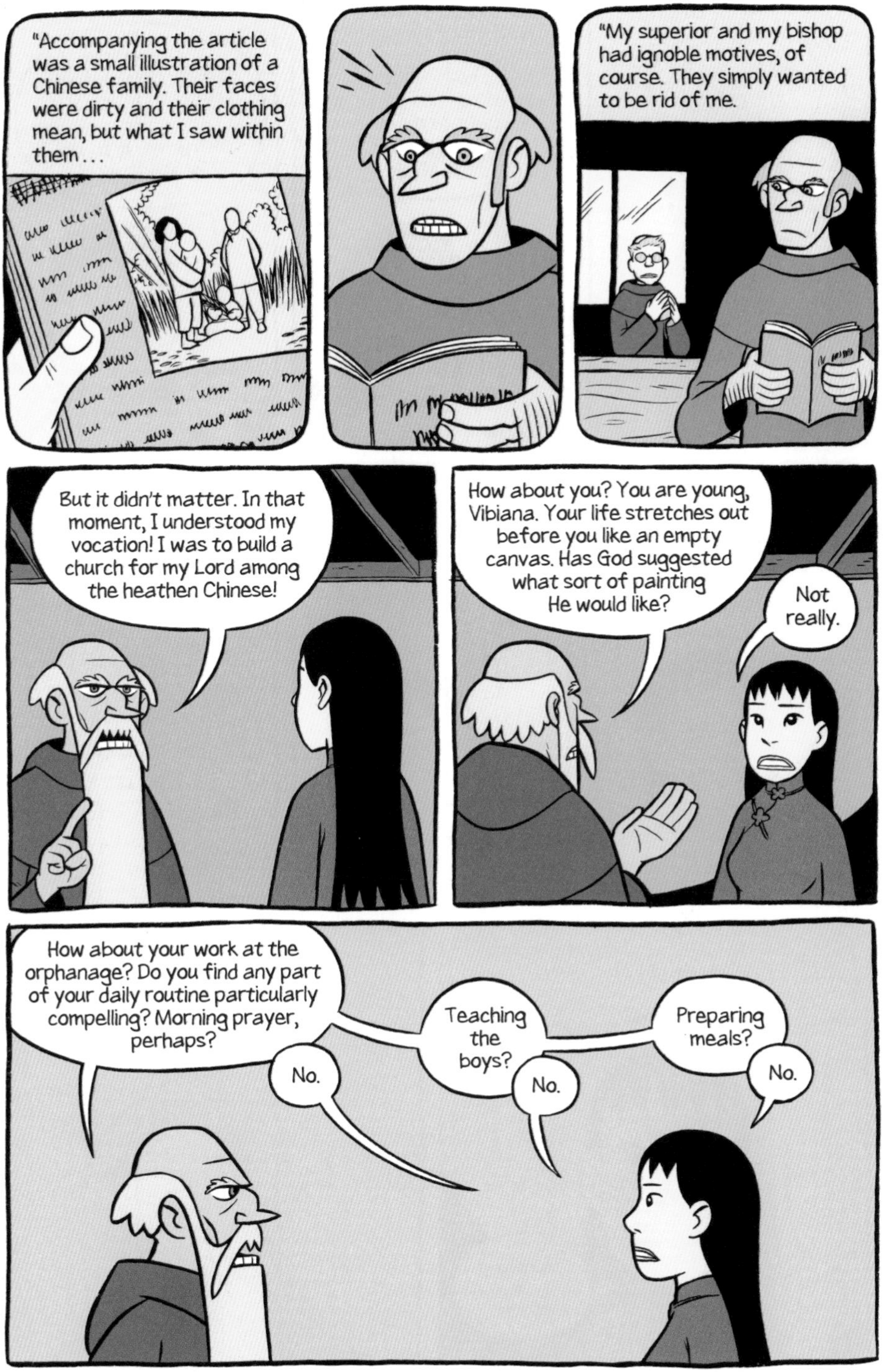
"Accompanying the article was a small illustration of a Chinese family. Their faces were dirty and their clothing mean, but what I saw within them...
"My superior and my bishop had ignoble motives, of course. They simply wanted to be rid of me.
But it didn't matter. In that moment, I understood my vocation! I was to build a church for my Lord among the heathen Chinese!
How about you? You are young, Vibiana. Your life stretches out before you like an empty canvas. Has God suggested what sort of painting He would like?
Not really.
How about your work at the orphanage? Do you find any part of your daily routine particularly compelling? Morning prayer, perhaps?
No.
Teaching the boys?
No.
Preparing meals?
No.

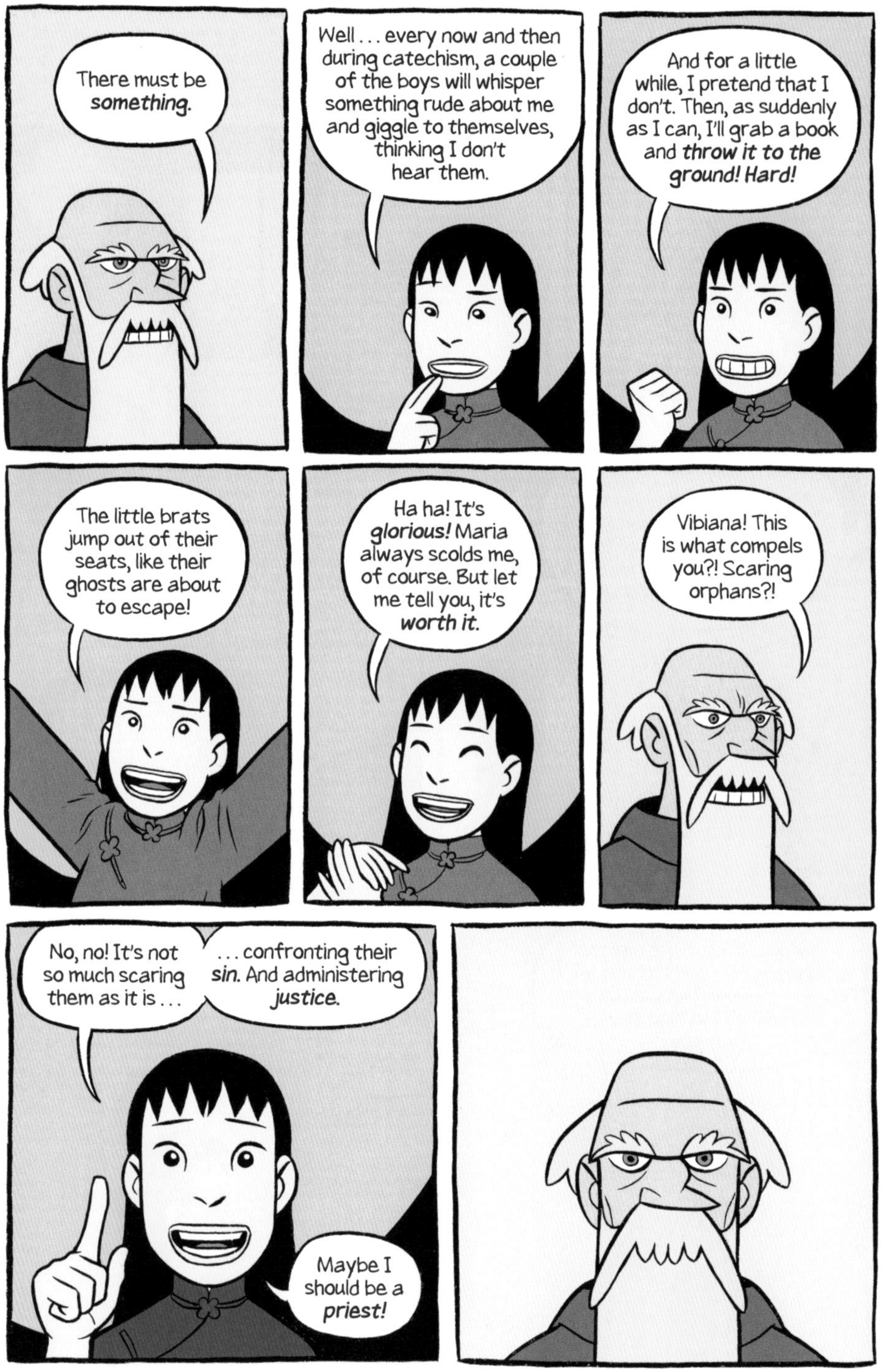

There must be *something*.
Well . . . every now and then during catechism, a couple of the boys will whisper something rude about me and giggle to themselves, thinking I don't hear them.
And for a little while, I pretend that I don't. Then, as suddenly as I can, I'll grab a book and ***throw it to the ground! Hard!***
The little brats jump out of their seats, like their ghosts are about to escape!
Ha ha! It's ***glorious!*** Maria always scolds me, of course. But let me tell you, it's ***worth it***.
Vibiana! This is what compels you?! Scaring orphans?!
No, no! It's not so much scaring them as it is . . .
. . . confronting their *sin*. And administering ***justice***.
Maybe I should be a ***priest!***

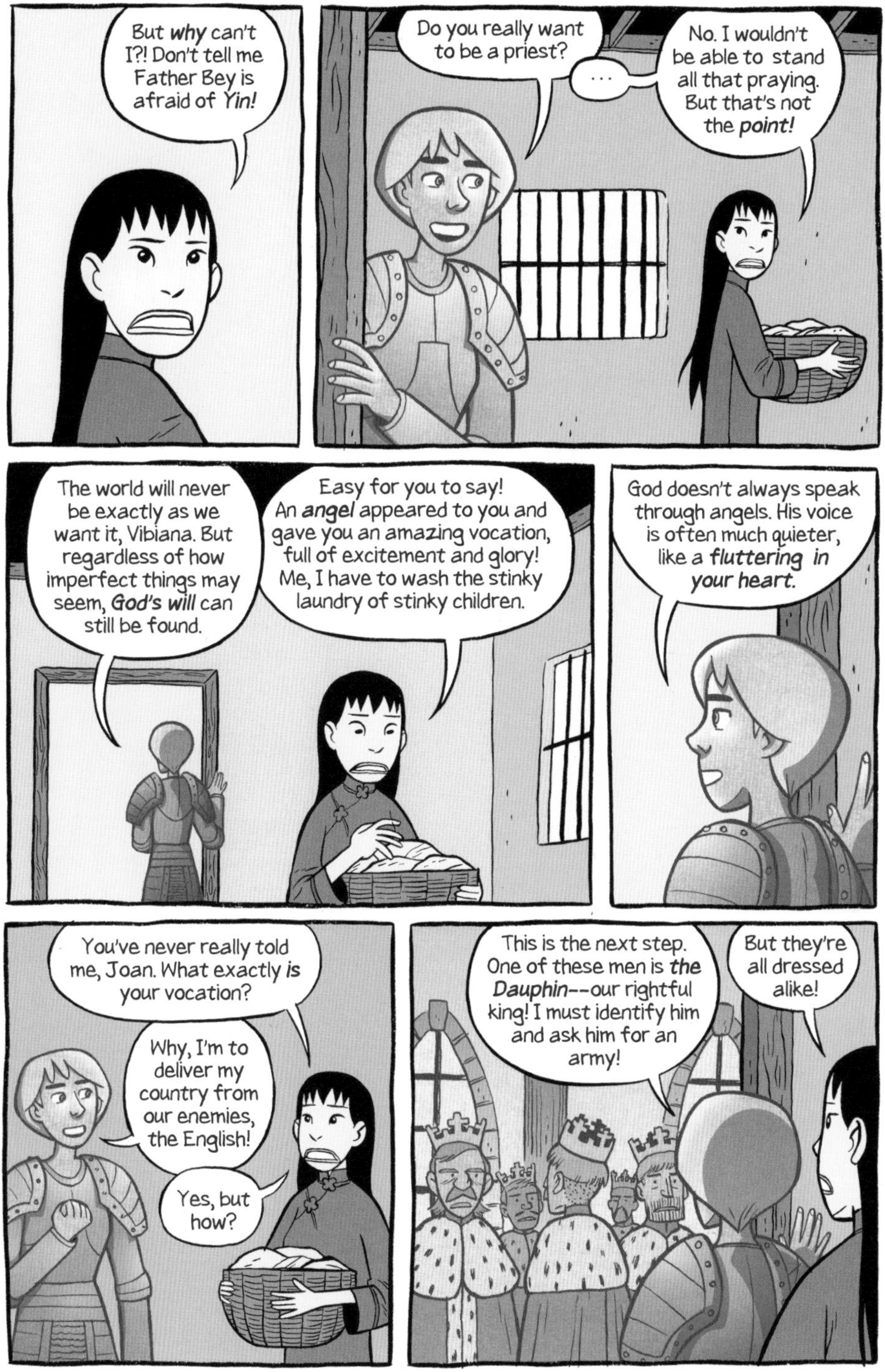
But why can't I?! Don't tell me Father Bey is afraid of Yin!
Do you really want to be a priest?
...
No. I wouldn't be able to stand all that praying. But that's not the point!
The world will never be exactly as we want it, Vibiana. But regardless of how imperfect things may seem, God's will can still be found.
Easy for you to say! An angel appeared to you and gave you an amazing vocation, full of excitement and glory! Me, I have to wash the stinky laundry of stinky children.
God doesn't always speak through angels. His voice is often much quieter, like a fluttering in your heart.
You've never really told me, Joan. What exactly is your vocation?
Why, I'm to deliver my country from our enemies, the English!
Yes, but how?
This is the next step. One of these men is the Dauphin--our rightful king! I must identify him and ask him for an army!
But they're all dressed alike!

It's a test. The Dauphin wants to confirm the nature of my calling.

It's him!

How do you know?

I know.

That man is to be your king?! He's the ugliest man I've ever seen! I mean, that nose, even for a foreigner--!

Seek and you will find, Vibiana!

!

ⵗⵗ ⵗⵗⵗ'ⵗ ⵗⵗⵗⵗ, ⵗⵗⵗ ⵗⵗⵗⵗⵗ ⵗⵗ ⵗⵗⵗ ⵗⵗⵗⵗ@ⵗⵗⵗ ⵗⵗⵗ ⵗⵗⵗⵗ!*

* Sigh. *

* "In God's name, you shall be the king and none other!"

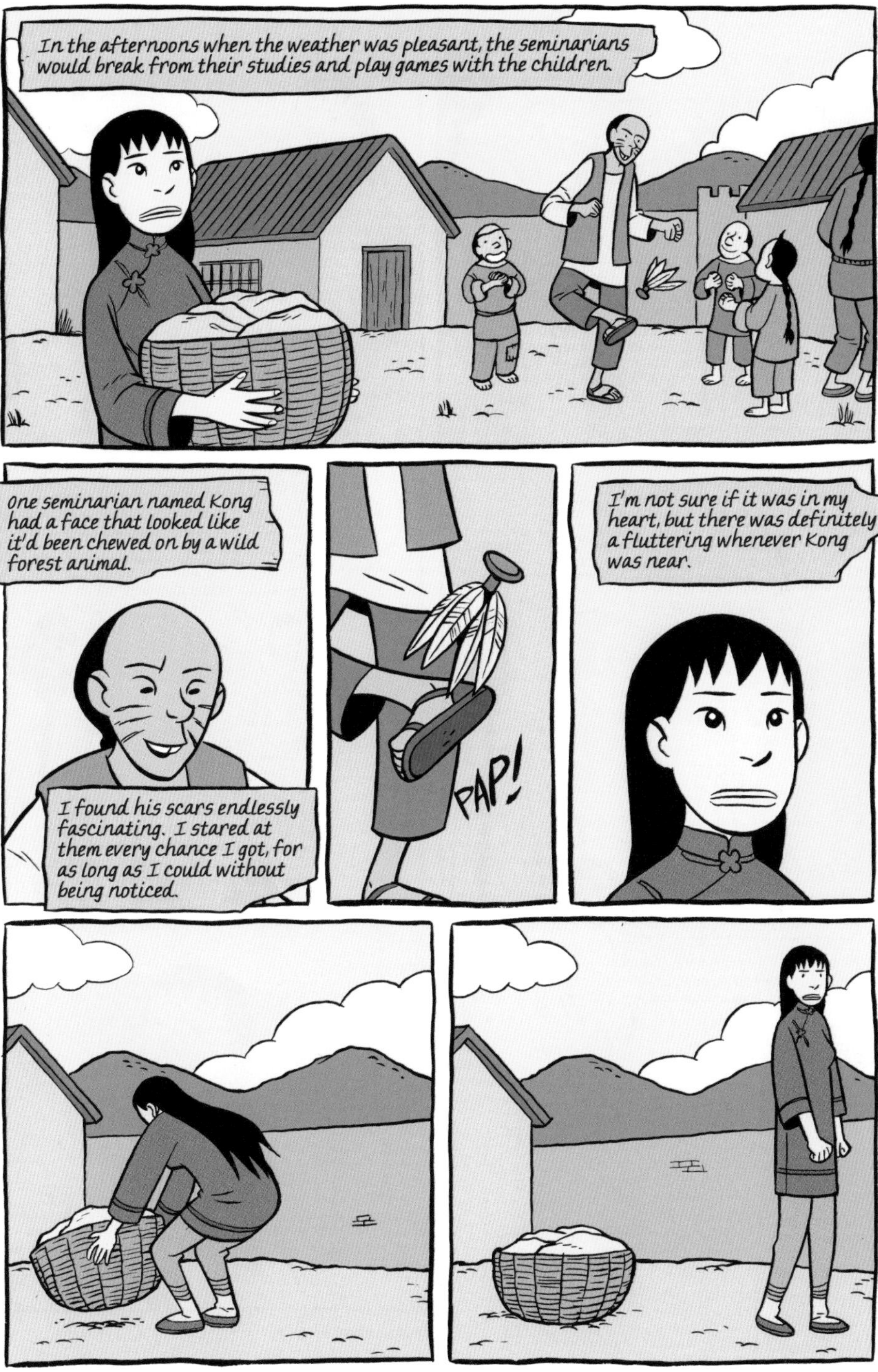
In the afternoons when the weather was pleasant, the seminarians would break from their studies and play games with the children.
One seminarian named Kong had a face that looked like it'd been chewed on by a wild forest animal.
I found his scars endlessly fascinating. I stared at them every chance I got, for as long as I could without being noticed.
PAP!
I'm not sure if it was in my heart, but there was definitely a fluttering whenever Kong was near.

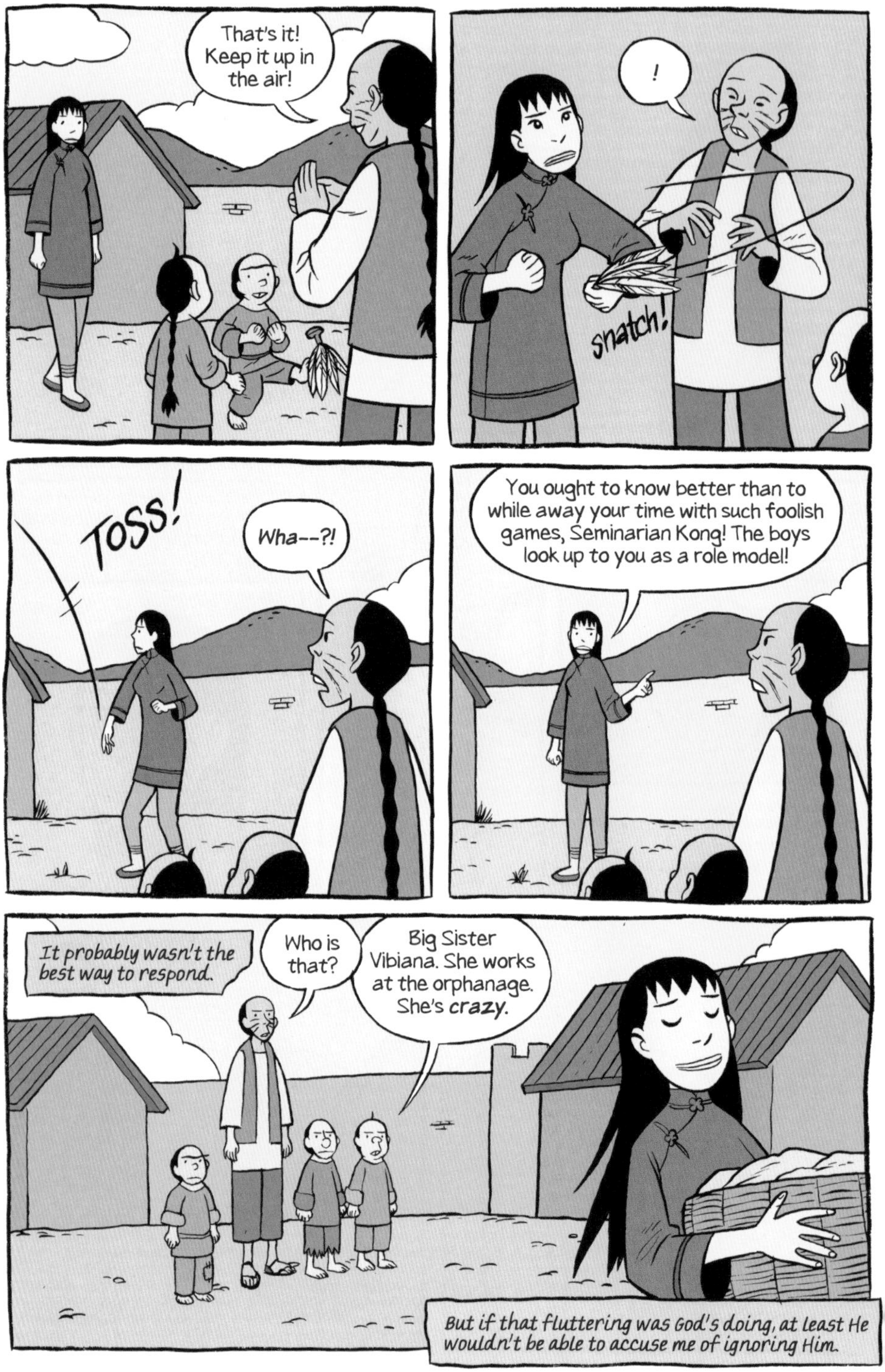
That's it! Keep it up in the air!
!
snatch!
TOSS!
Wha--?!
You ought to know better than to while away your time with such foolish games, Seminarian Kong! The boys look up to you as a role model!
It probably wasn't the best way to respond.
Who is that?
Big Sister Vibiana. She works at the orphanage. She's crazy.
But if that fluttering was God's doing, at least He wouldn't be able to accuse me of ignoring Him.

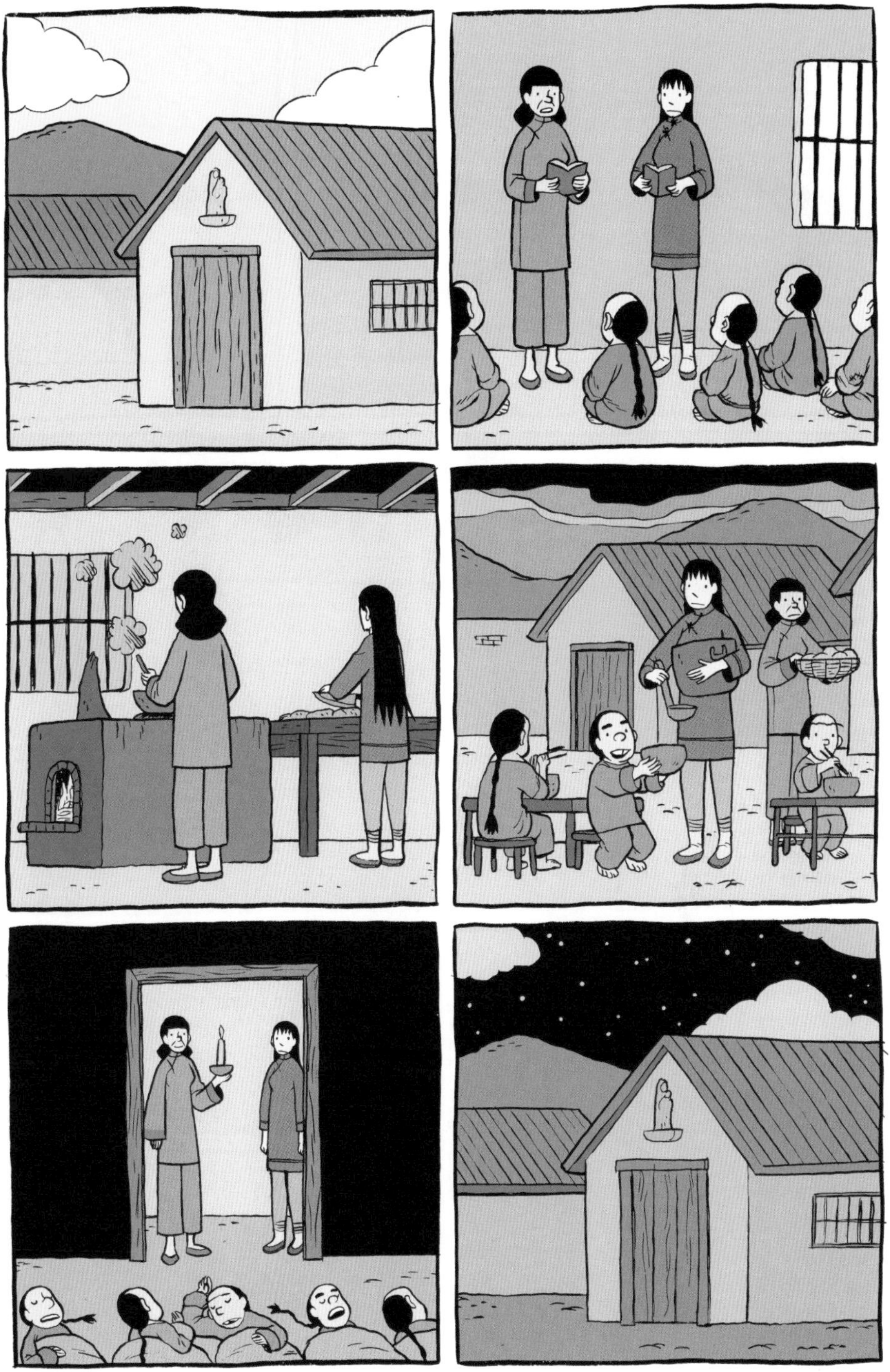

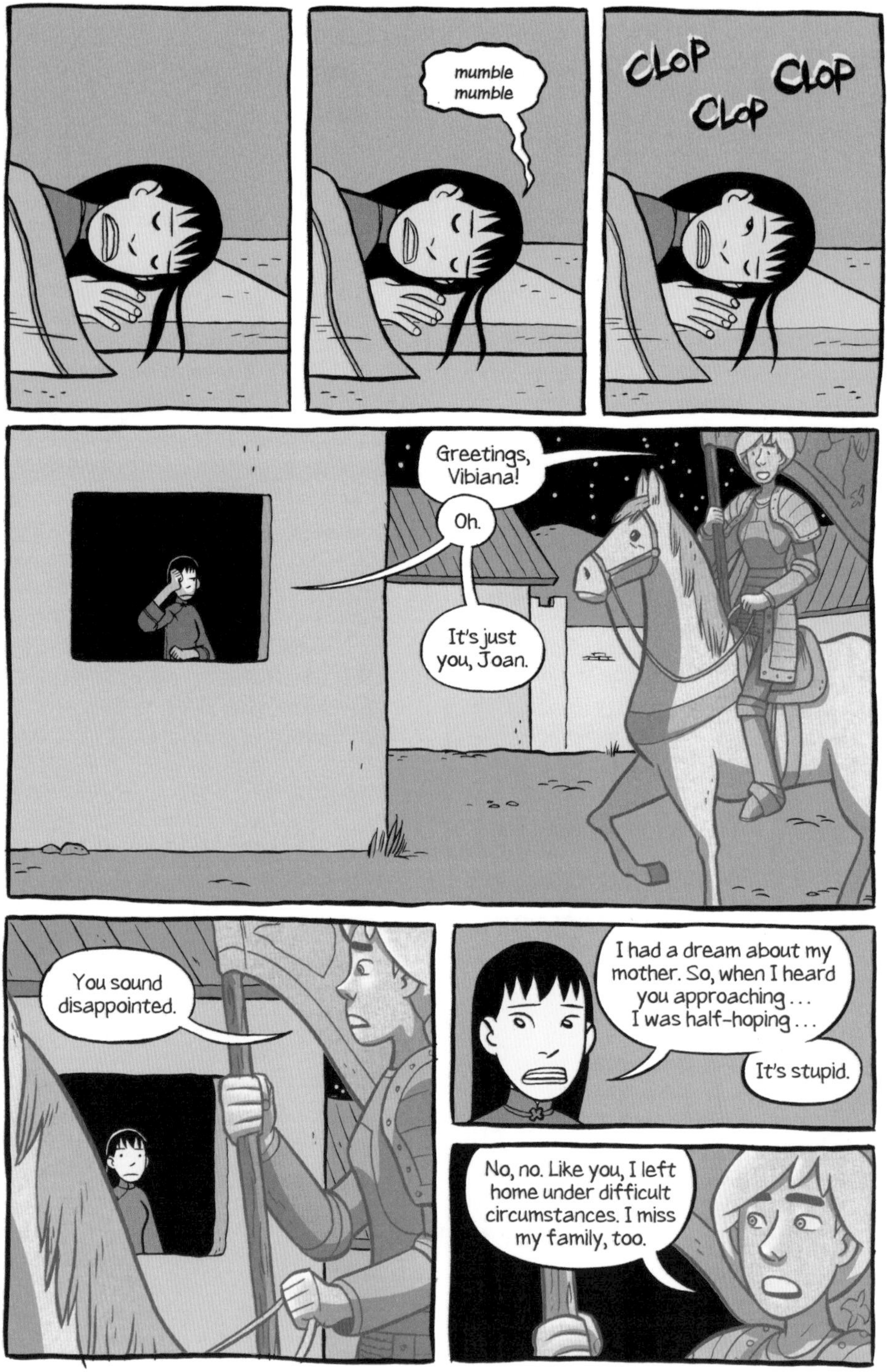
mumble
mumble
CLOP
CLOP
CLOP
Greetings, Vibiana!
Oh.
It's just you, Joan.
You sound disappointed.
I had a dream about my mother. So, when I heard you approaching . . . I was half-hoping . . .
It's stupid.
No, no. Like you, I left home under difficult circumstances. I miss my family, too.

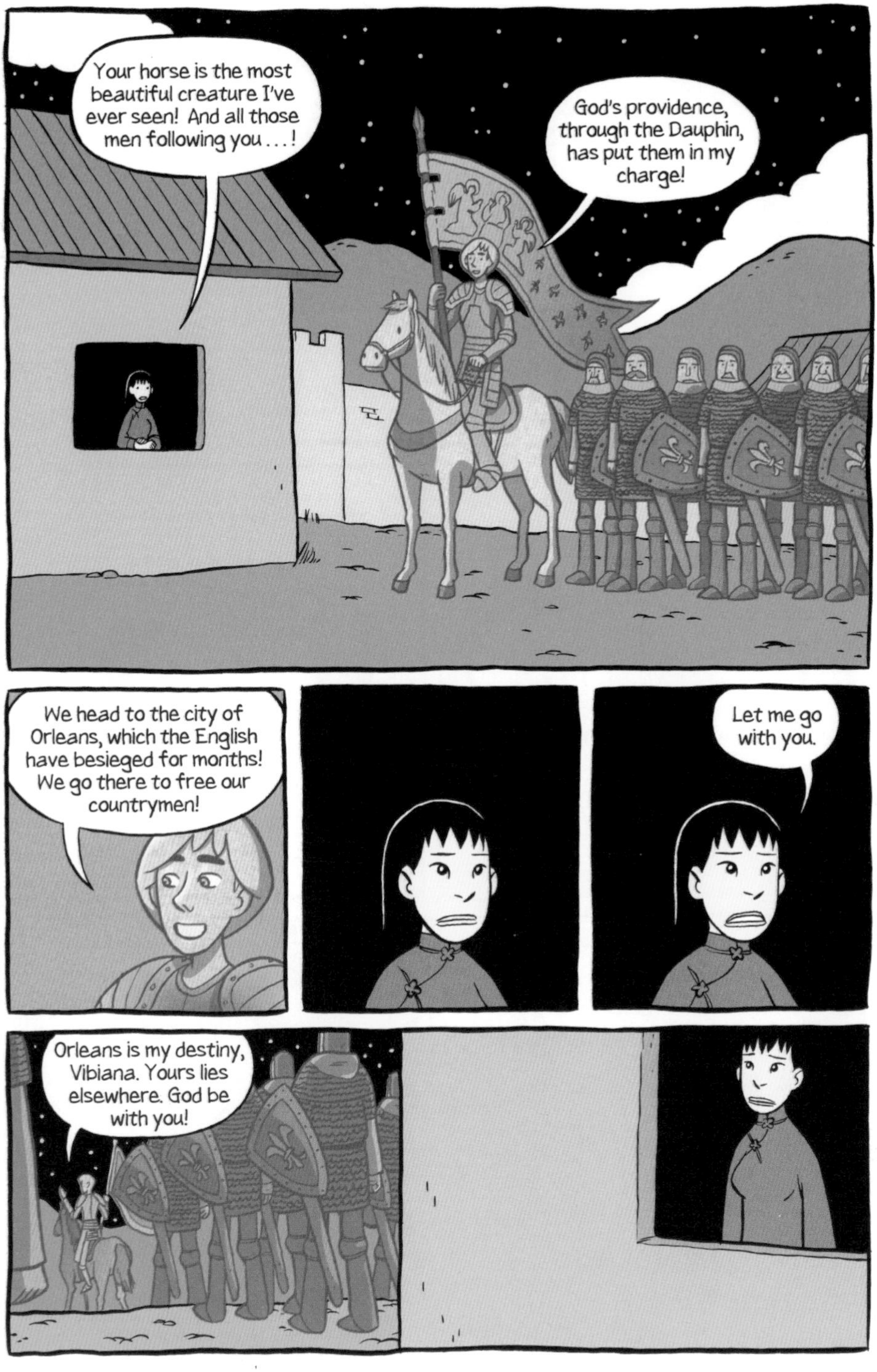
Your horse is the most beautiful creature I've ever seen! And all those men following you . . . !
God's providence, through the Dauphin, has put them in my charge!
We head to the city of Orleans, which the English have besieged for months! We go there to free our countrymen!
Let me go with you.
Orleans is my destiny, Vibiana. Yours lies elsewhere. God be with you!

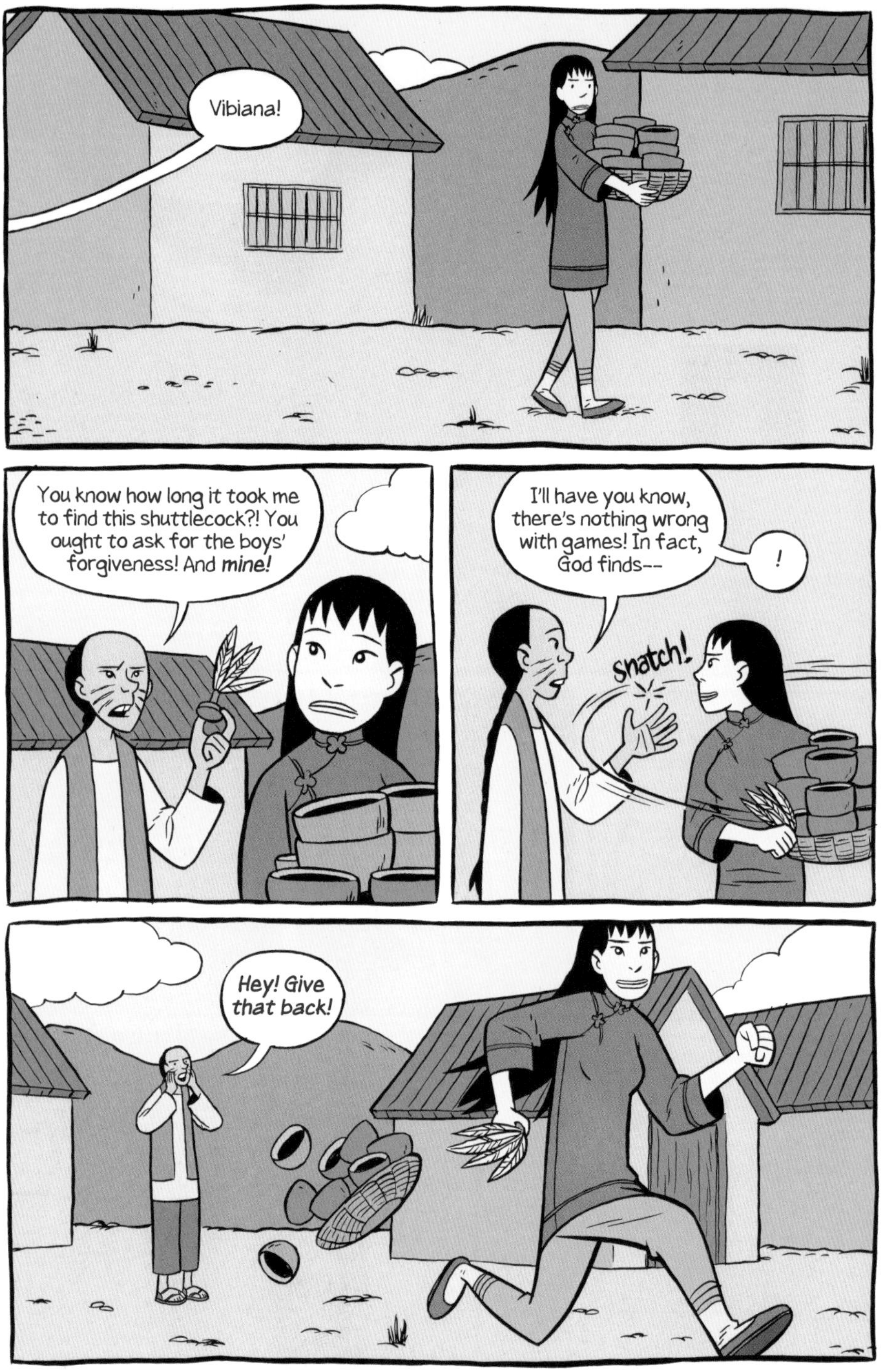
Vibiana!
You know how long it took me to find this shuttlecock?! You ought to ask for the boys' forgiveness! And *mine!*
I'll have you know, there's nothing wrong with games! In fact, God finds--
!
Snatch!
Hey! Give that back!

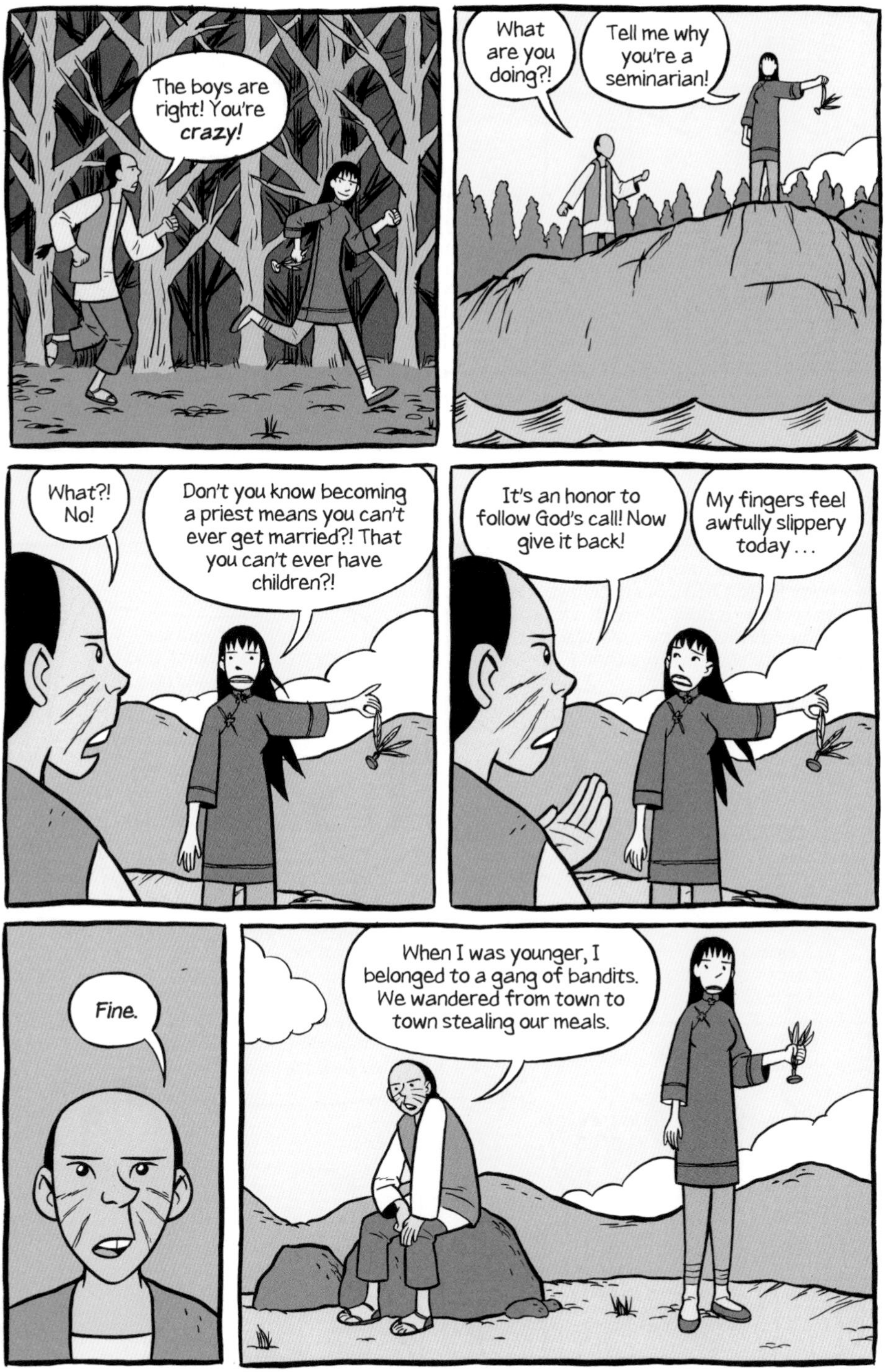
The boys are right! You're *crazy!*
What are you doing?!
Tell me why you're a seminarian!
What?! No!
Don't you know becoming a priest means you can't ever get married?! That you can't ever have children?!
It's an honor to follow God's call! Now give it back!
My fingers feel awfully slippery today . . .
Fine.
When I was younger, I belonged to a gang of bandits. We wandered from town to town stealing our meals.

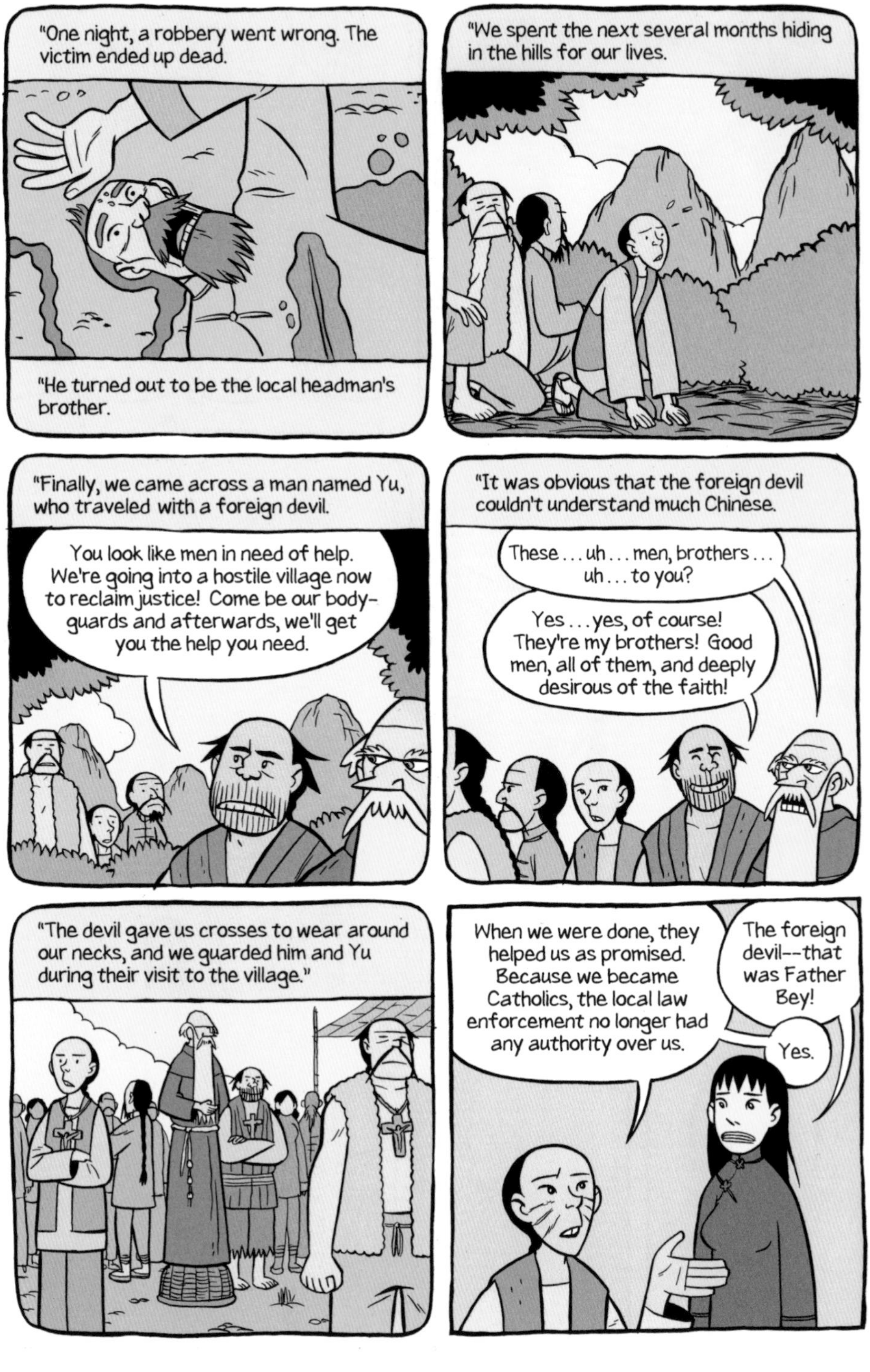
"One night, a robbery went wrong. The victim ended up dead.
"He turned out to be the local headman's brother.
"We spent the next several months hiding in the hills for our lives.
"Finally, we came across a man named Yu, who traveled with a foreign devil.
You look like men in need of help. We're going into a hostile village now to reclaim justice! Come be our body-guards and afterwards, we'll get you the help you need.
"It was obvious that the foreign devil couldn't understand much Chinese.
These . . . uh . . . men, brothers . . . uh . . . to you?
Yes . . . yes, of course! They're my brothers! Good men, all of them, and deeply desirous of the faith!
"The devil gave us crosses to wear around our necks, and we guarded him and Yu during their visit to the village."
When we were done, they helped us as promised. Because we became Catholics, the local law enforcement no longer had any authority over us.
The foreign devil--that was Father Bey!
Yes.

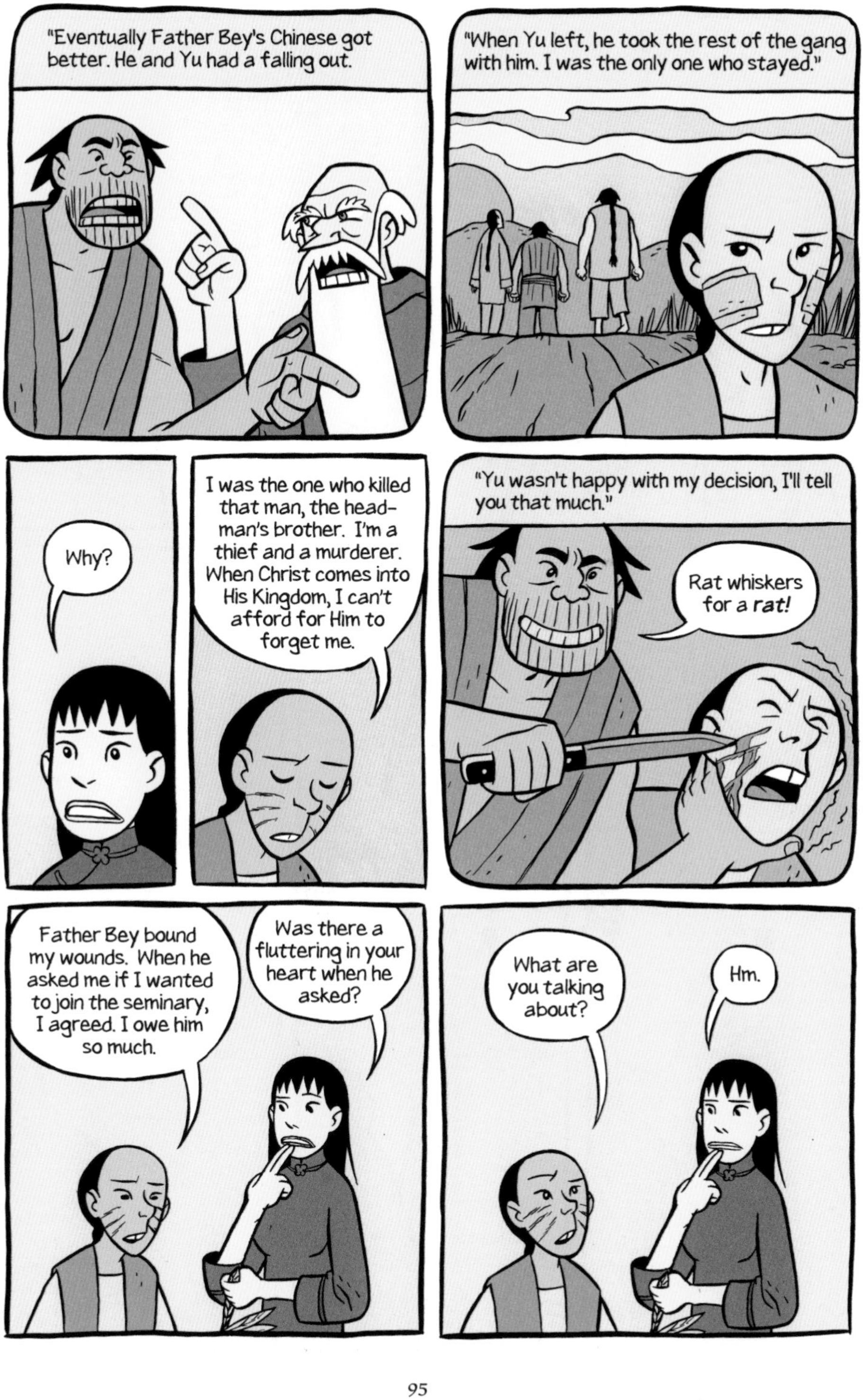
"Eventually Father Bey's Chinese got better. He and Yu had a falling out.
"When Yu left, he took the rest of the gang with him. I was the only one who stayed."
Why?
I was the one who killed that man, the head-man's brother. I'm a thief and a murderer. When Christ comes into His Kingdom, I can't afford for Him to forget me.
"Yu wasn't happy with my decision, I'll tell you that much."
Rat whiskers for a *rat!*
Father Bey bound my wounds. When he asked me if I wanted to join the seminary, I agreed. I owe him so much.
Was there a fluttering in your heart when he asked?
What are you talking about?
Hm.

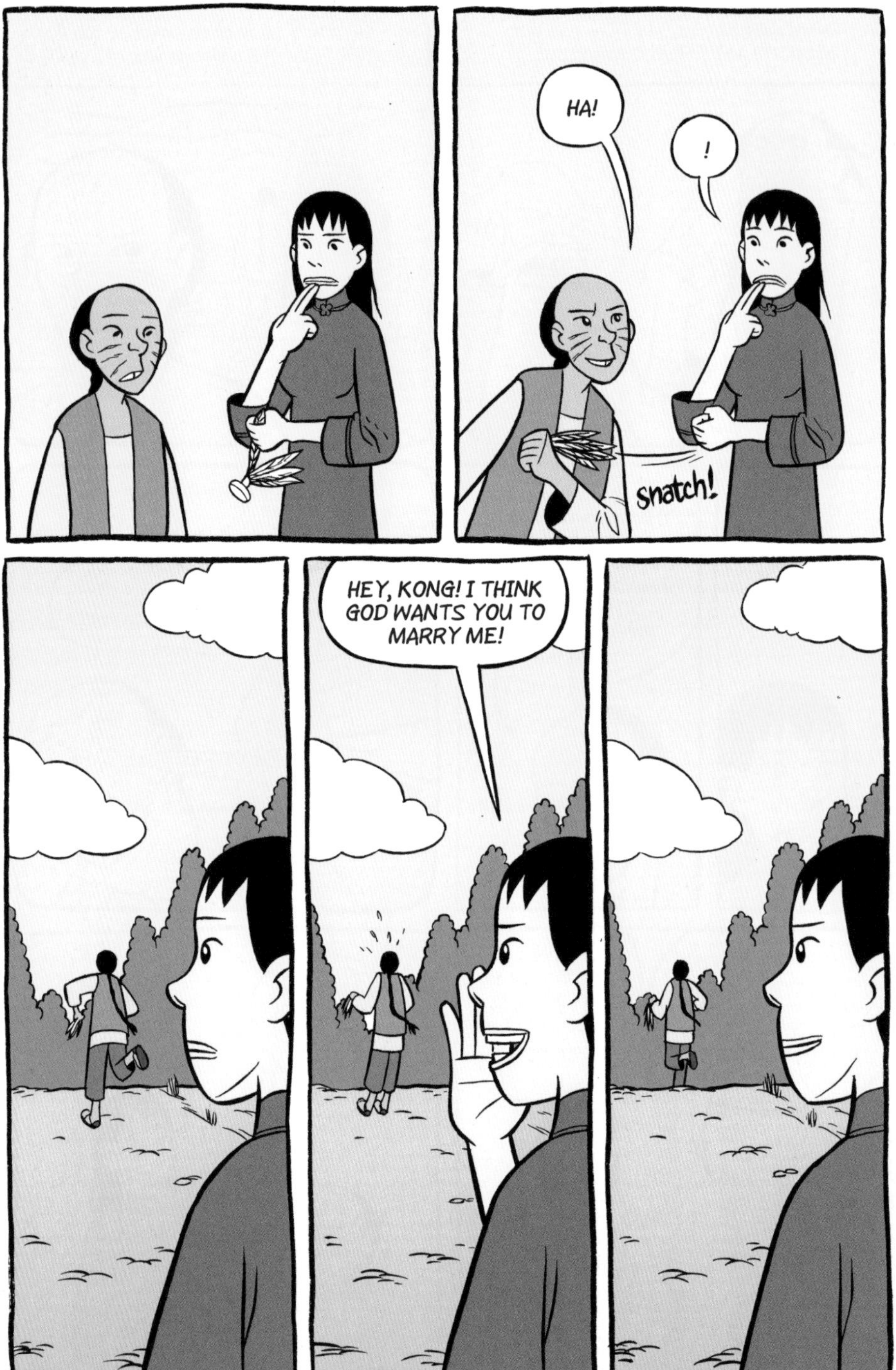
HA!
!
Snatch!
HEY, KONG! I THINK GOD WANTS YOU TO MARRY ME!

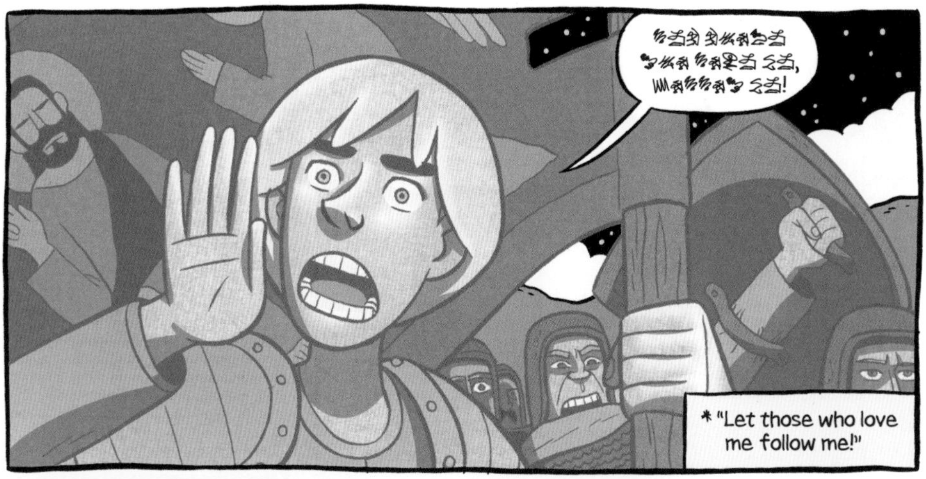
* "Let those who love me follow me!"

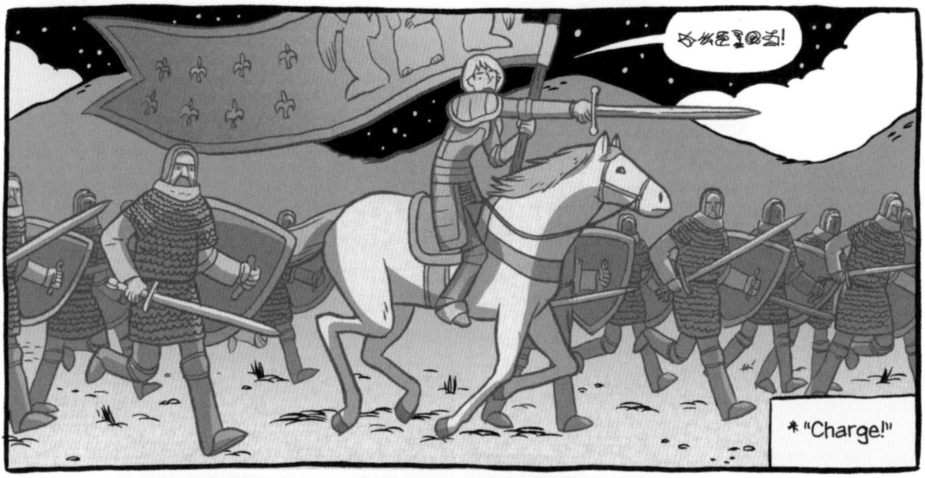
* "Charge!"

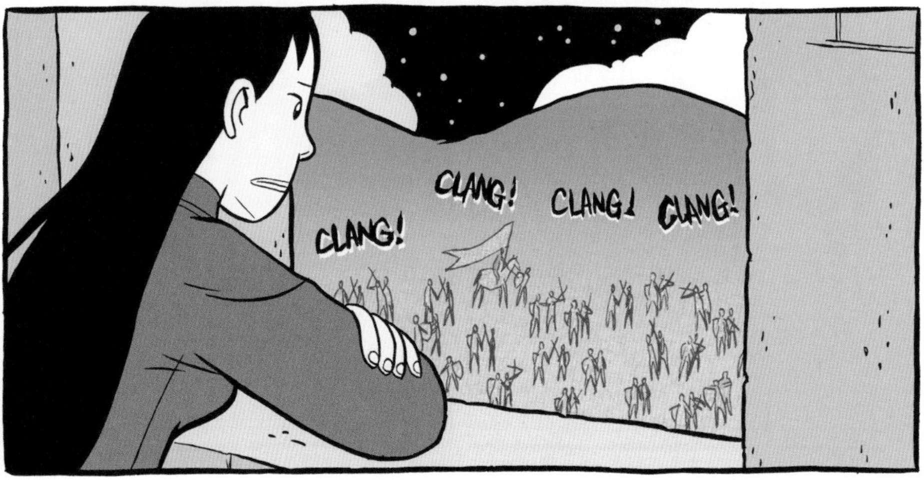
CLANG!
CLANG!
CLANG!
CLANG!

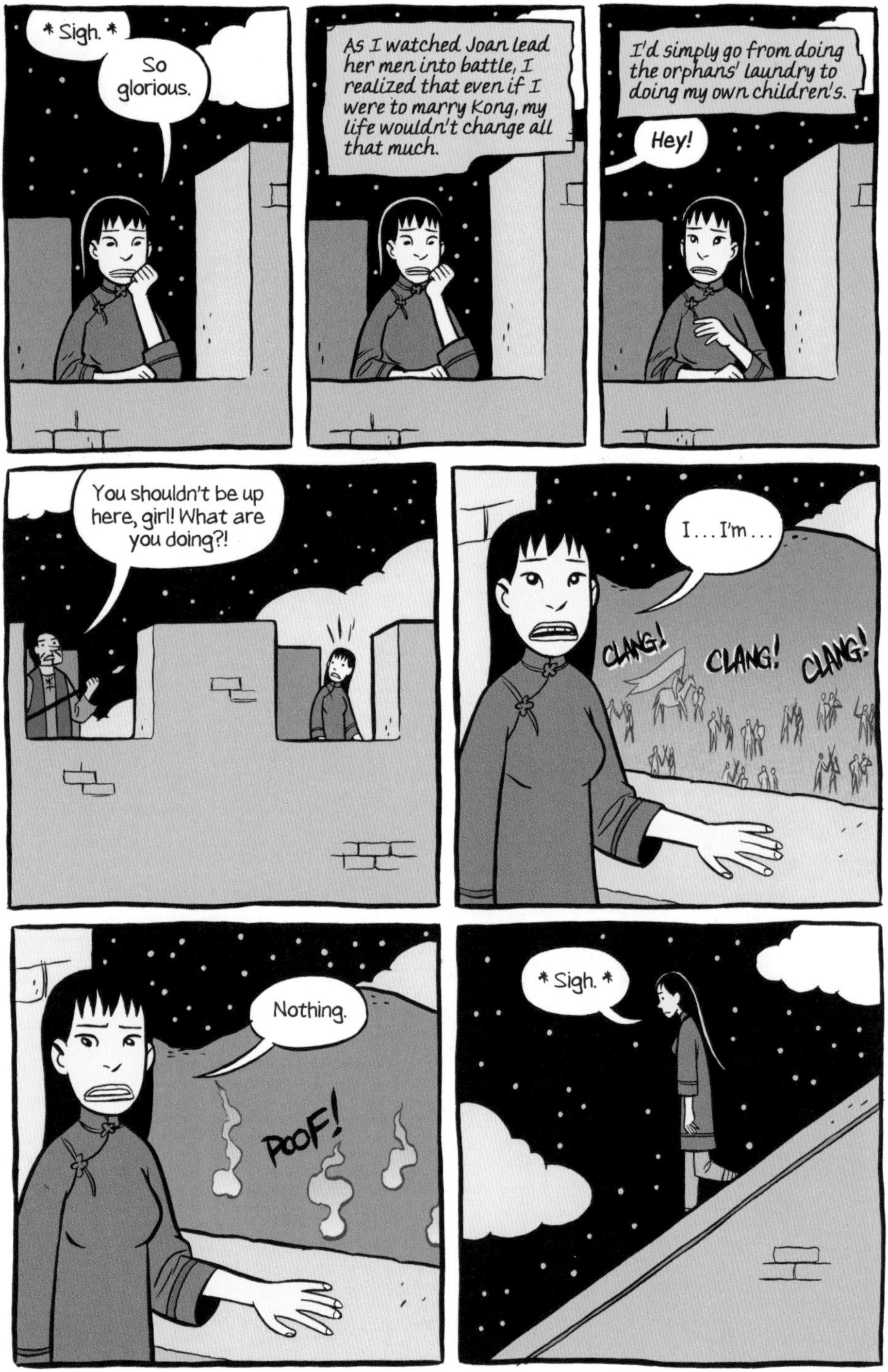

* Sigh. *
So glorious.
As I watched Joan lead her men into battle, I realized that even if I were to marry Kong, my life wouldn't change all that much.
I'd simply go from doing the orphans' laundry to doing my own children's.
Hey!
You shouldn't be up here, girl! What are you doing?!
I... I'm...
CLANG!
CLANG!
CLANG!
Nothing.
POOF!
* Sigh. *

Big Sister! Big Sister! Stop!

What? If you're asking to go to the bathroom again--!

Who are those women talking to Father Bey?

ᓭᔑᑊᔭᔑ ᑦᔭᔑ #ᔭᵚᑊᔭᔑ, ᵚᔭᔑᑧᔭᔑ ᔭᵎᔑᔐ ᔭᔭᗰᵷᔭᔐᔭᗰᔭᔐᔭᗰᔭᔐᔭᔑᔐ ᔭᔐᗰᔐᔭᔐᔑᔑᔐ.*

* "We've met before, Father. I'm a Congregationalist missionary."

99

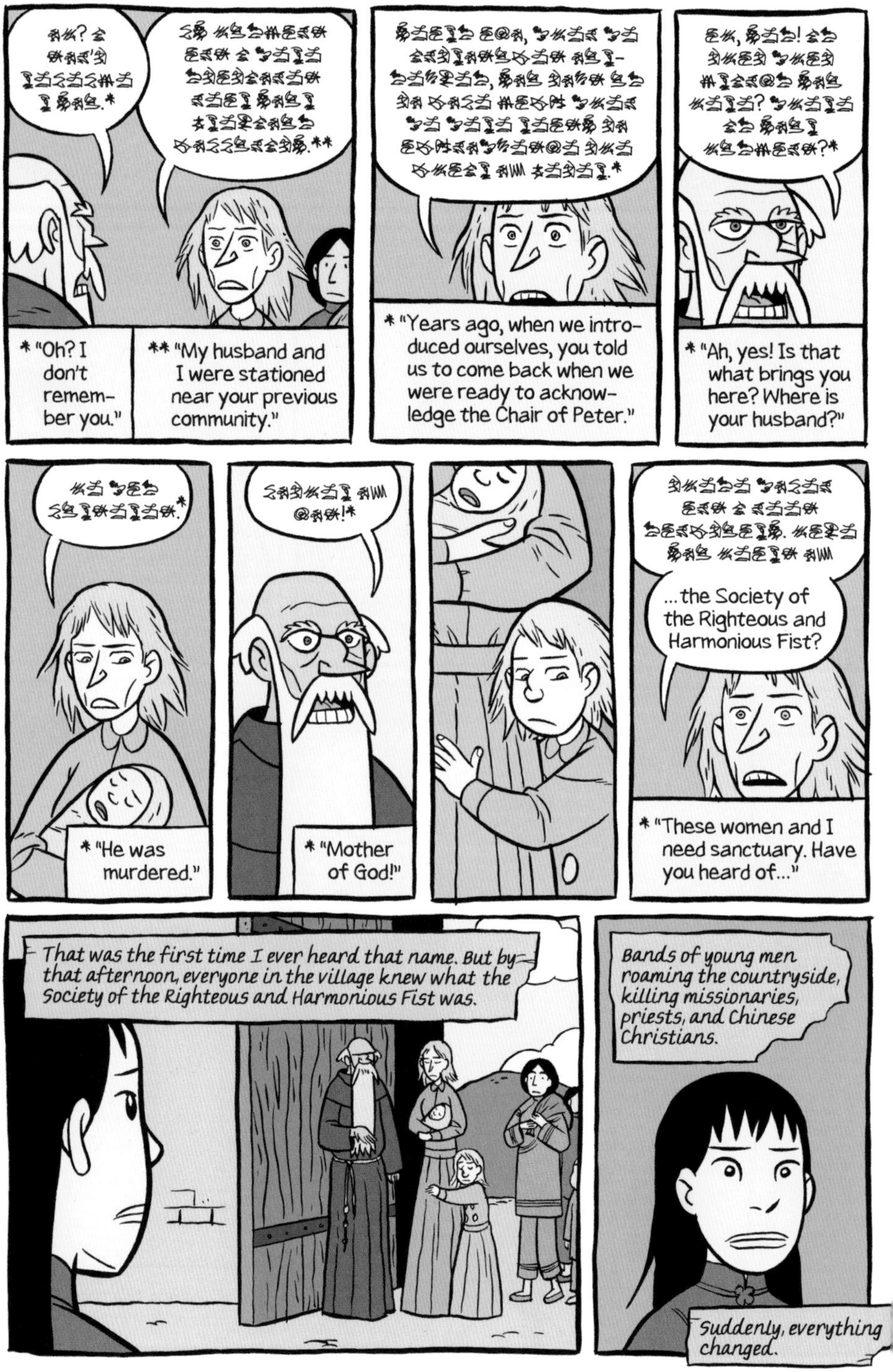
* "Oh? I don't remember you."
** "My husband and I were stationed near your previous community."
* "Years ago, when we introduced ourselves, you told us to come back when we were ready to acknowledge the Chair of Peter."
* "Ah, yes! Is that what brings you here? Where is your husband?"
* "He was murdered."
* "Mother of God!"
* "These women and I need sanctuary. Have you heard of..."
...the Society of the Righteous and Harmonious Fist?
That was the first time I ever heard that name. But by that afternoon, everyone in the village knew what the Society of the Righteous and Harmonious Fist was.
Bands of young men roaming the countryside, killing missionaries, priests, and Chinese Christians.
Suddenly, everything changed.

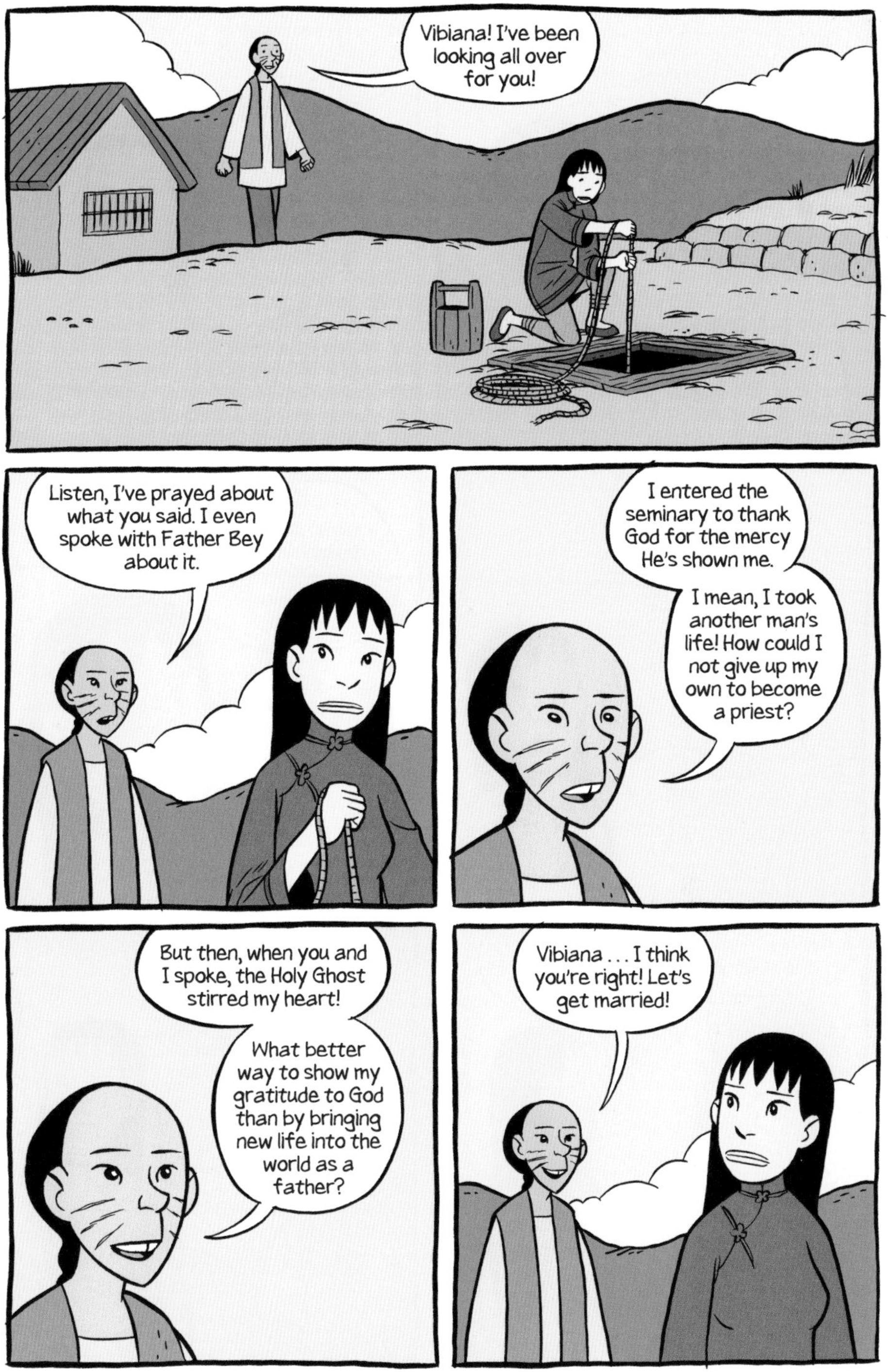
Vibiana! I've been looking all over for you!
Listen, I've prayed about what you said. I even spoke with Father Bey about it.
I entered the seminary to thank God for the mercy He's shown me.
I mean, I took another man's life! How could I not give up my own to become a priest?
But then, when you and I spoke, the Holy Ghost stirred my heart!
What better way to show my gratitude to God than by bringing new life into the world as a father?
Vibiana . . . I think you're right! Let's get married!

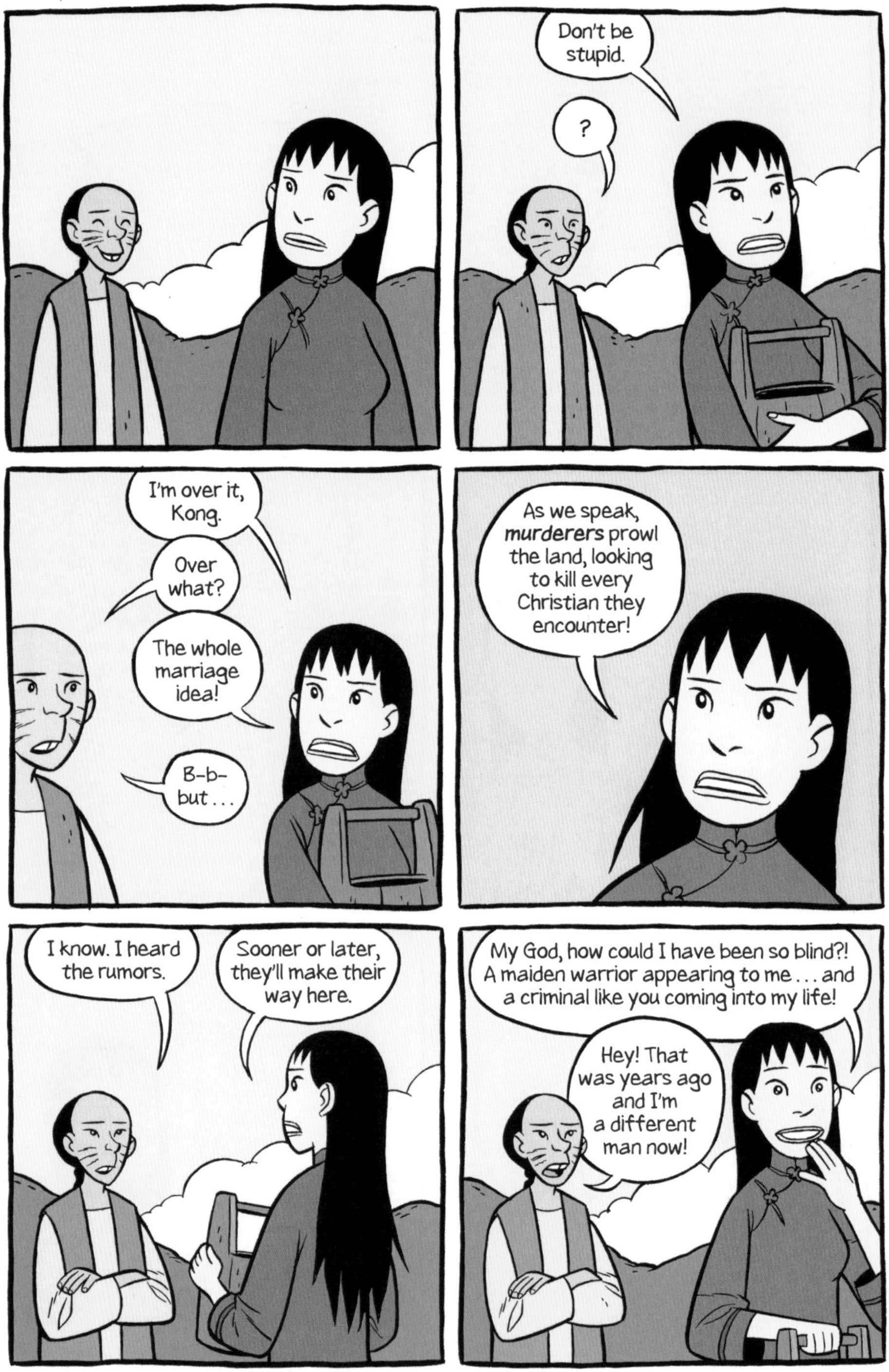
Don't be stupid.
?
I'm over it, Kong.
Over what?
The whole marriage idea!
B-b-but . . .
As we speak, **murderers** prowl the land, looking to kill every Christian they encounter!
I know. I heard the rumors.
Sooner or later, they'll make their way here.
My God, how could I have been so blind?! A maiden warrior appearing to me . . . and a criminal like you coming into my life!
Hey! That was years ago and I'm a different man now!

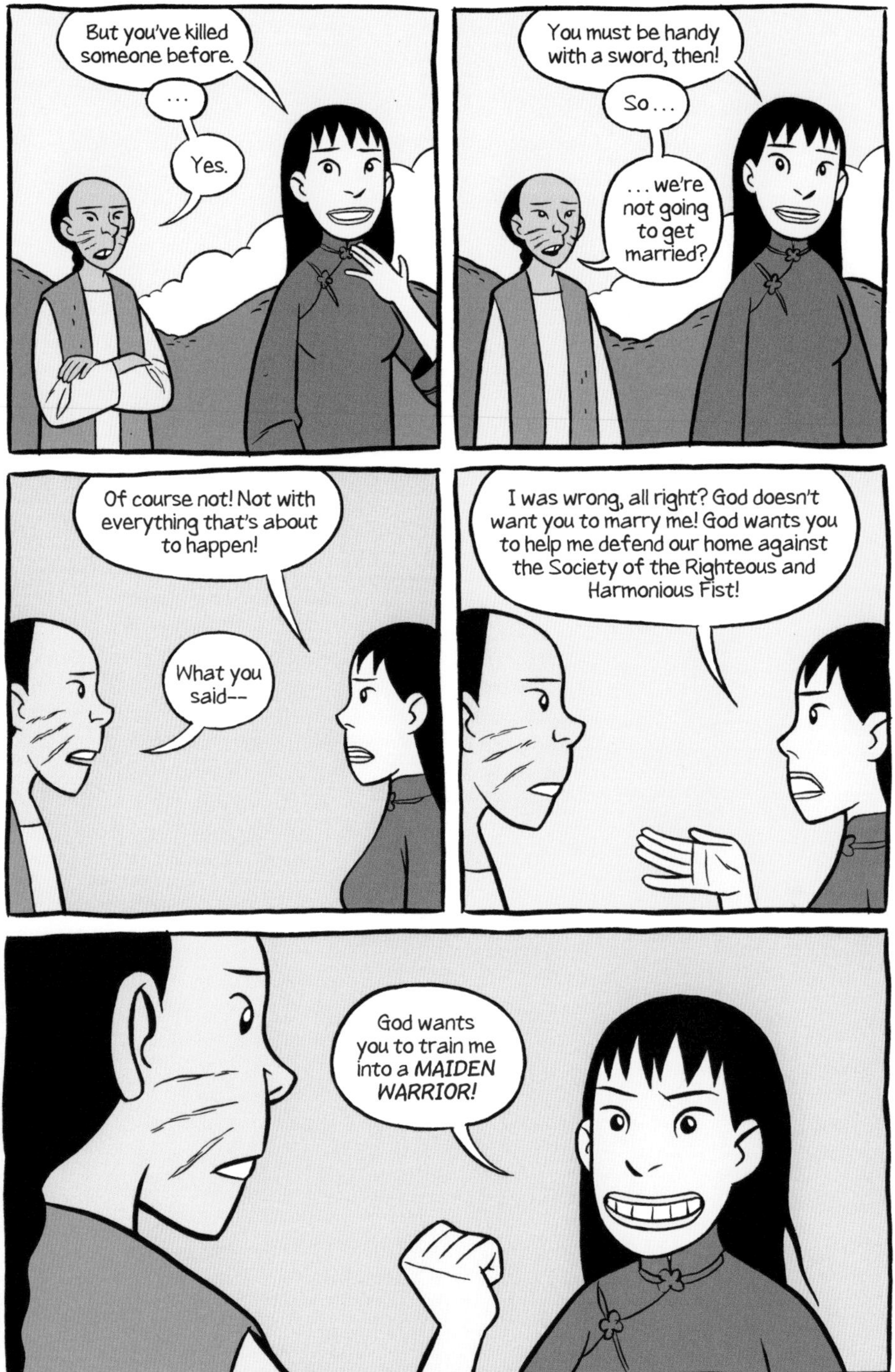
But you've killed someone before.
. . .
Yes.
You must be handy with a sword, then!
So . . .
. . . we're not going to get married?
Of course not! Not with everything that's about to happen!
What you said--
I was wrong, all right? God doesn't want you to marry me! God wants you to help me defend our home against the Society of the Righteous and Harmonious Fist!
God wants you to train me into a *MAIDEN WARRIOR!*

第五章

Age 15

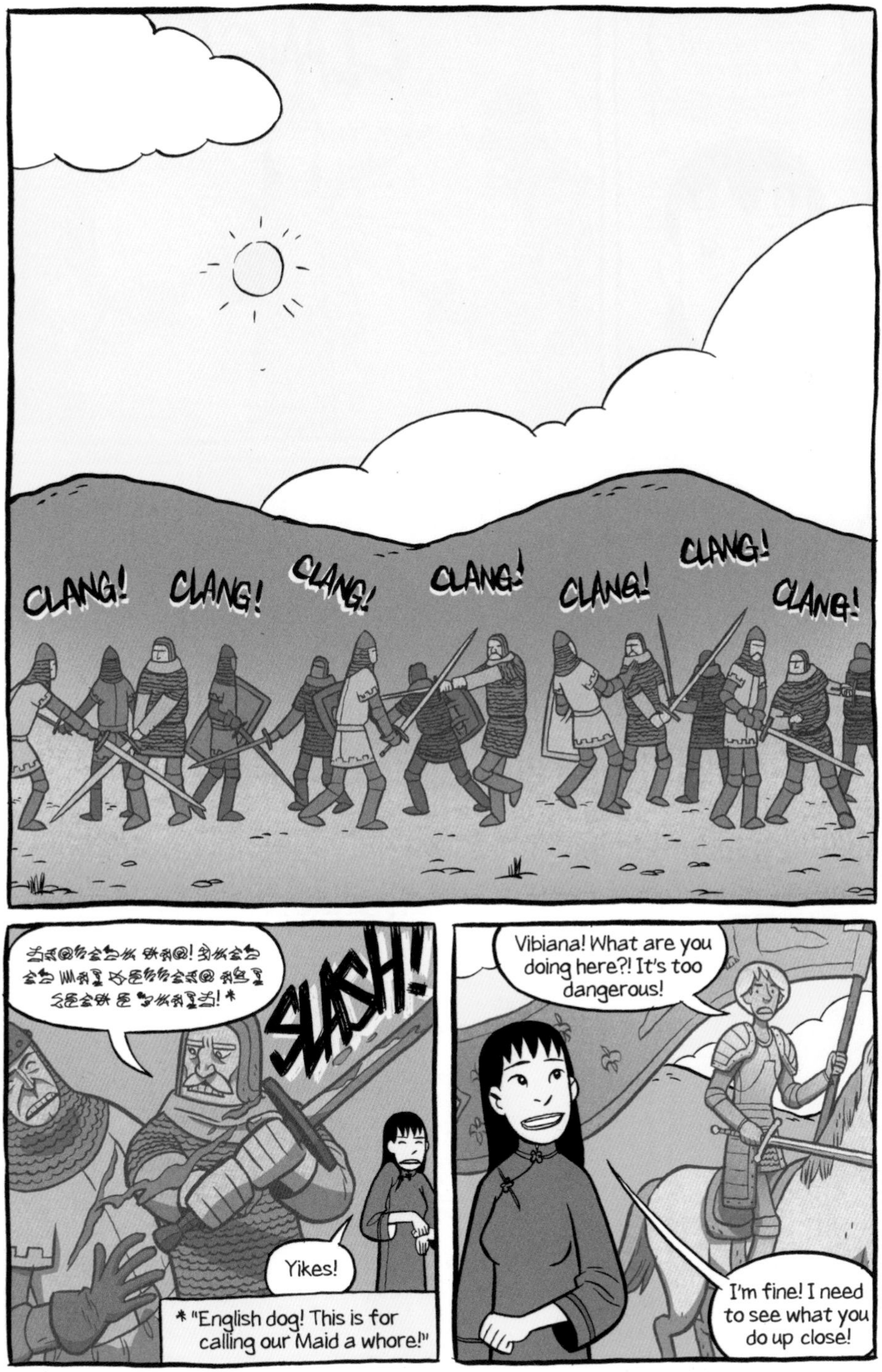
CLANG!
CLANG!
CLANG!
CLANG!
CLANG!
CLANG!
CLANG!
SLASH!
Yikes!
* "English dog! This is for calling our Maid a whore!"
Vibiana! What are you doing here?! It's too dangerous!
I'm fine! I need to see what you do up close!

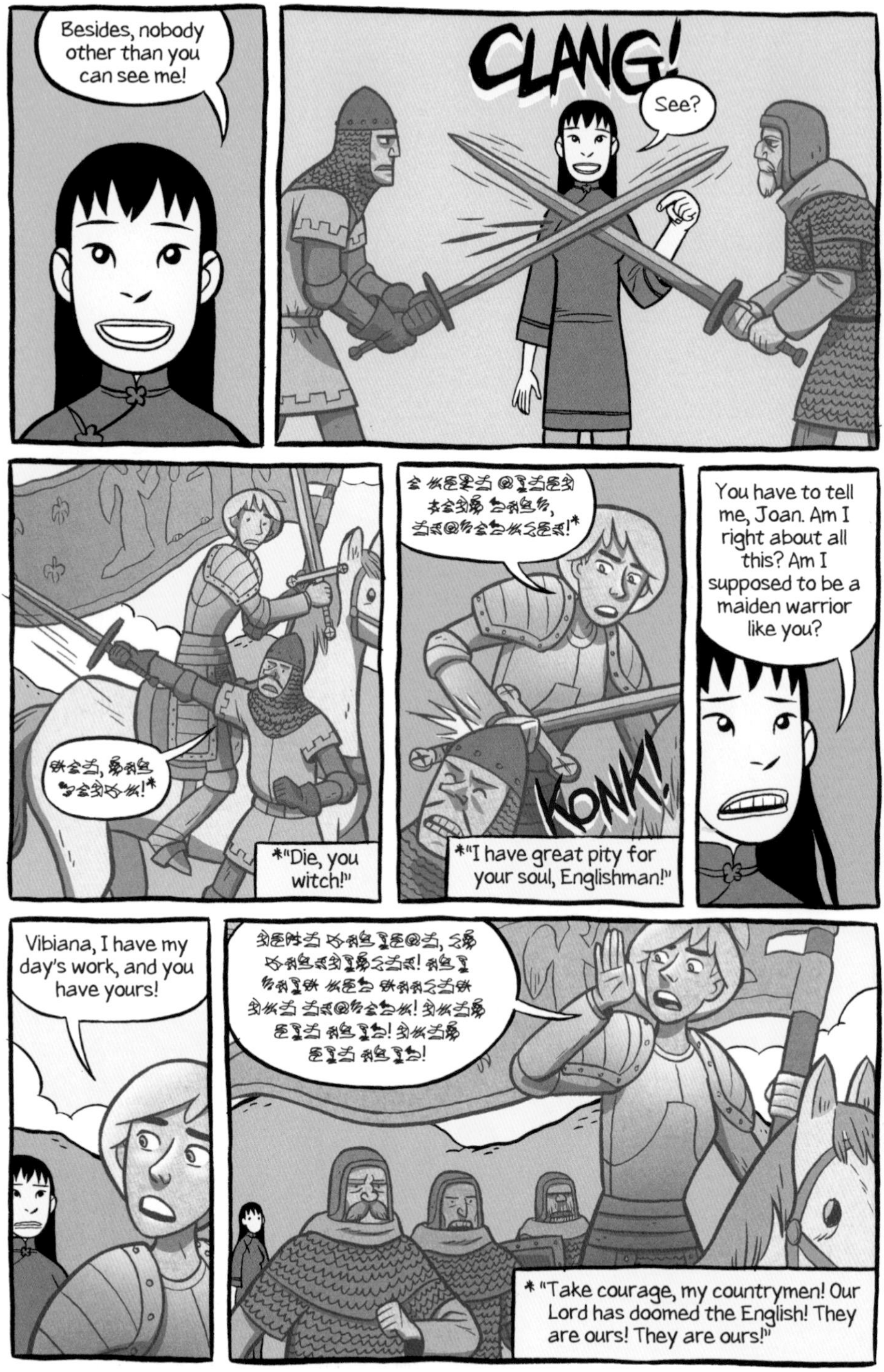
Besides, nobody other than you can see me!
CLANG!
See?
*"Die, you witch!"
*"I have great pity for your soul, Englishman!"
KONK!
You have to tell me, Joan. Am I right about all this? Am I supposed to be a maiden warrior like you?
Vibiana, I have my day's work, and you have yours!
*"Take courage, my countrymen! Our Lord has doomed the English! They are ours! They are ours!"

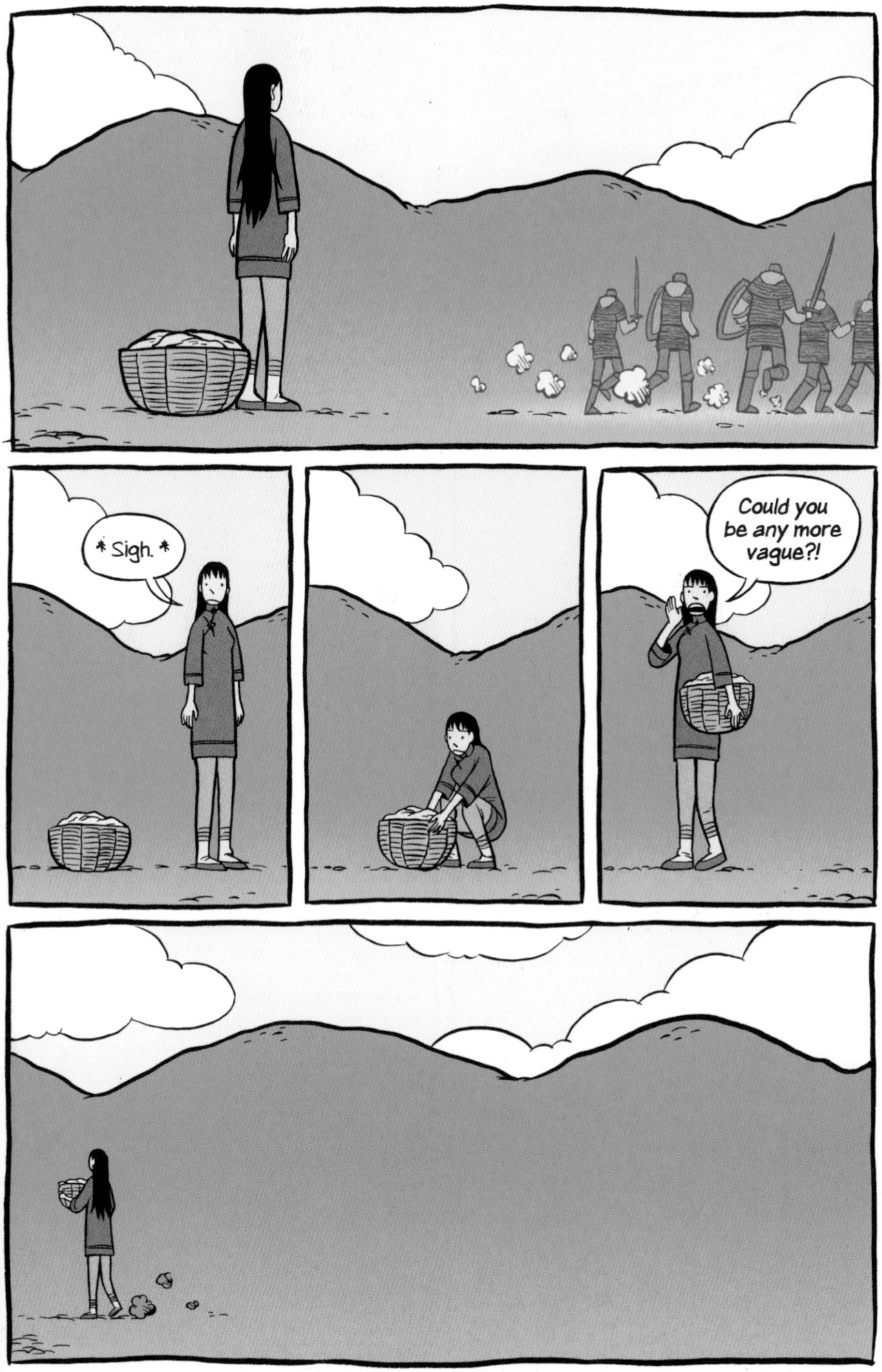
* Sigh. *
Could you be any more vague?!

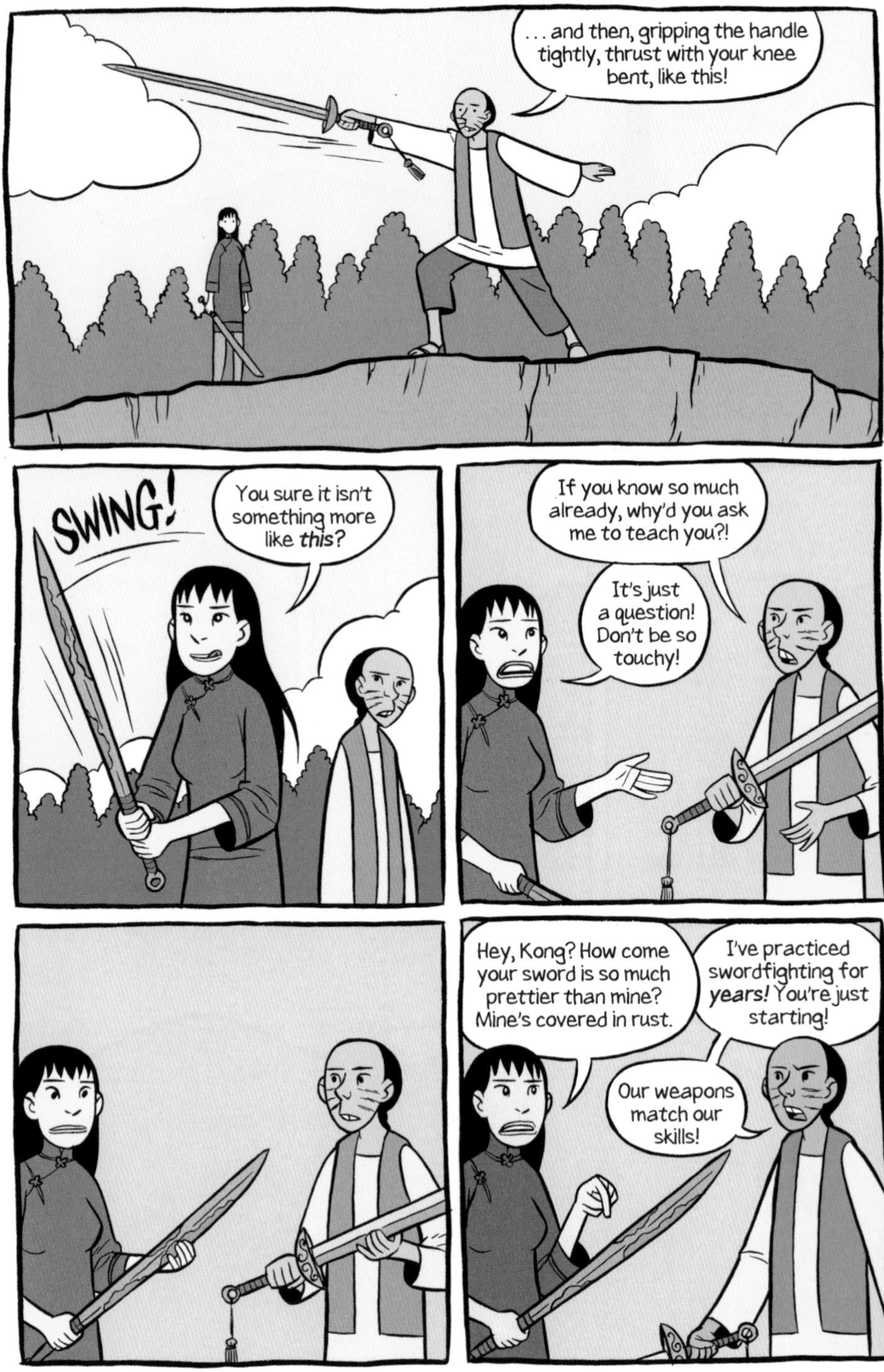
. . . and then, gripping the handle tightly, thrust with your knee bent, like this!
SWING!
You sure it isn't something more like *this*?
If you know so much already, why'd you ask me to teach you?!
It's just a question! Don't be so touchy!
Hey, Kong? How come your sword is so much prettier than mine? Mine's covered in rust.
I've practiced swordfighting for *years!* You're just starting!
Our weapons match our skills!

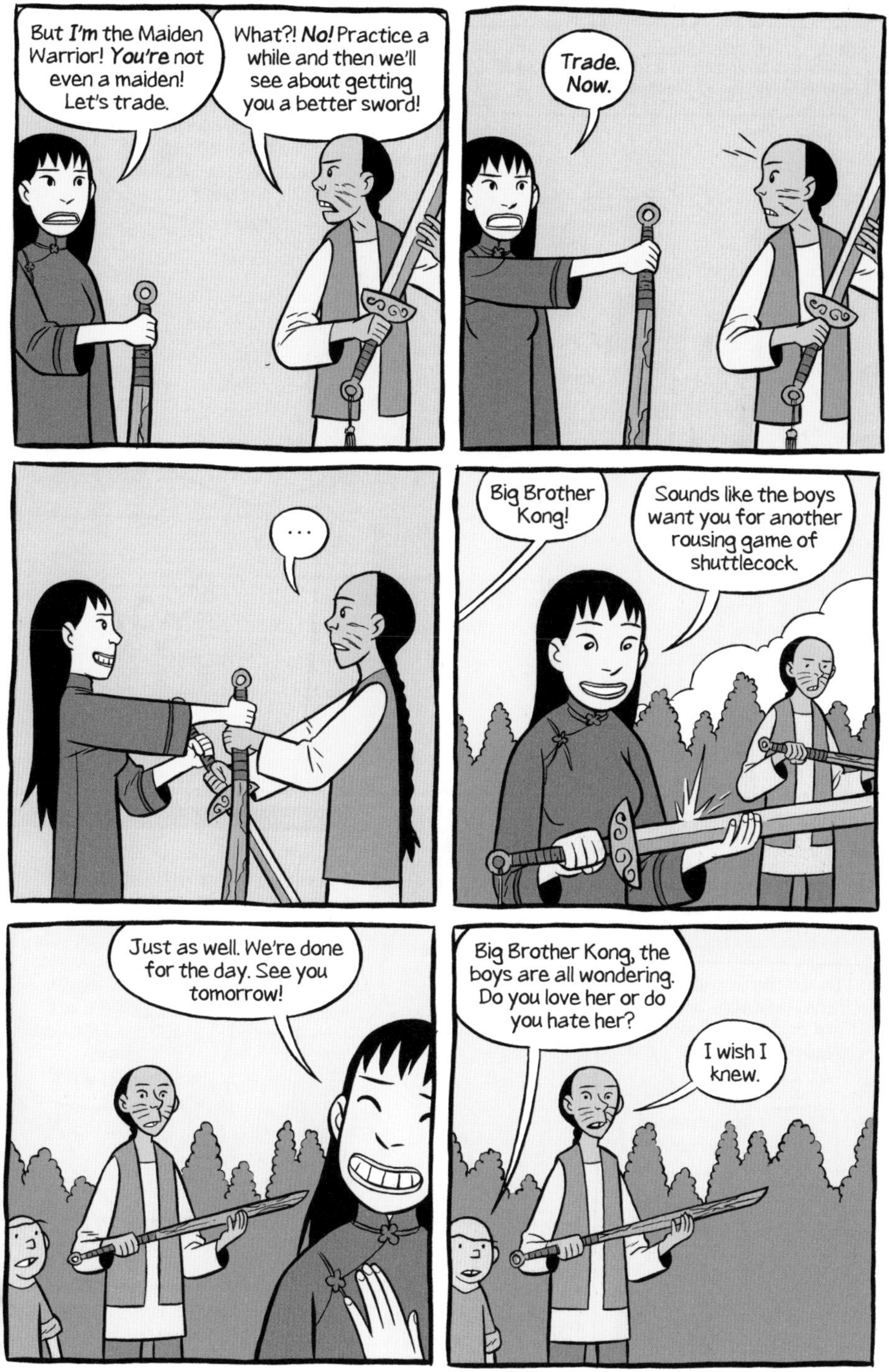
But I'm the Maiden Warrior! You're not even a maiden! Let's trade.
What?! No! Practice a while and then we'll see about getting you a better sword!
Trade. Now.
. . .
Big Brother Kong!
Sounds like the boys want you for another rousing game of shuttlecock.
Just as well. We're done for the day. See you tomorrow!
Big Brother Kong, the boys are all wondering. Do you love her or do you hate her?
I wish I knew.

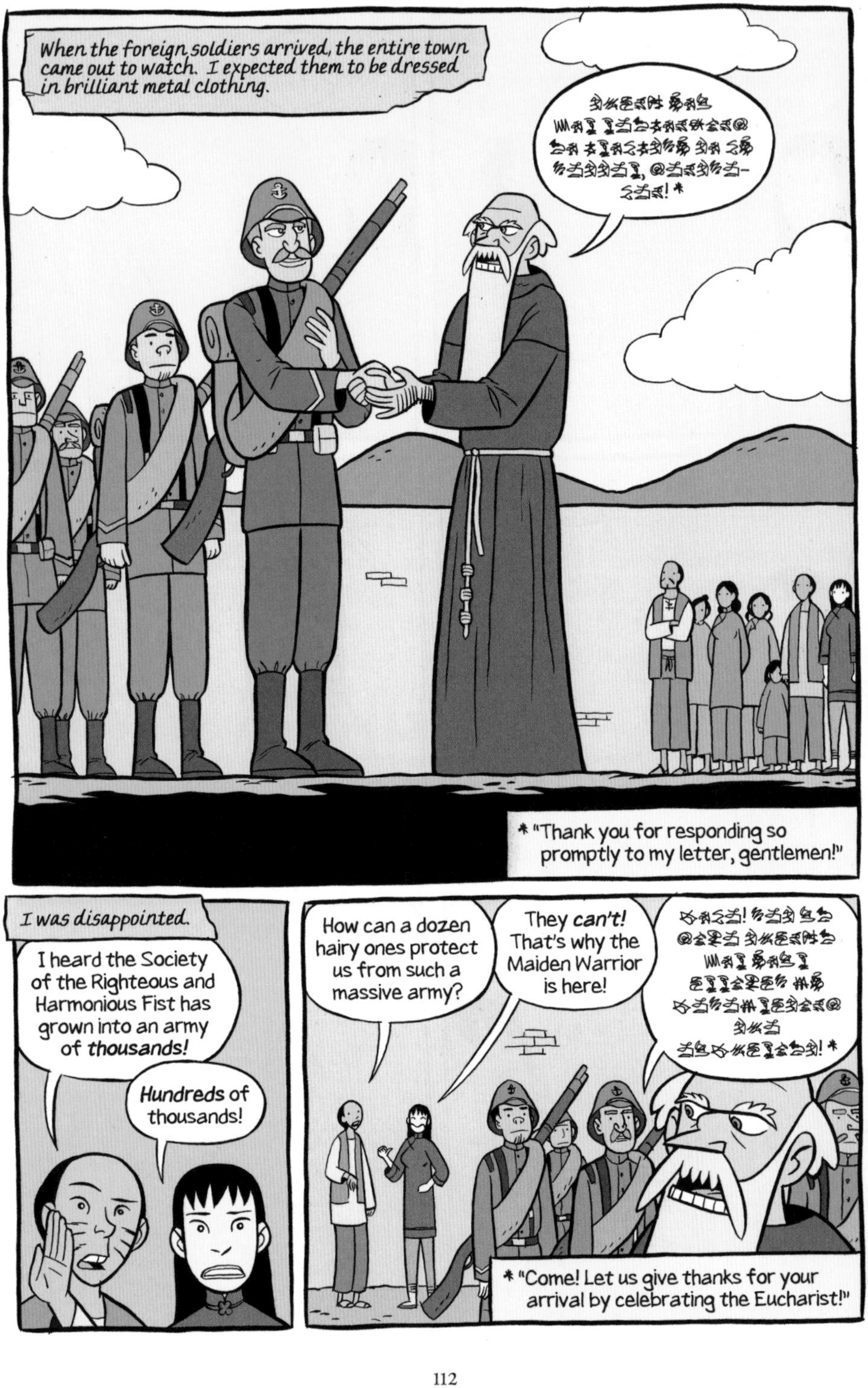
When the foreign soldiers arrived, the entire town came out to watch. I expected them to be dressed in brilliant metal clothing.
* "Thank you for responding so promptly to my letter, gentlemen!"
I was disappointed.
I heard the Society of the Righteous and Harmonious Fist has grown into an army of *thousands!*
Hundreds of thousands!
How can a dozen hairy ones protect us from such a massive army?
They *can't!* That's why the Maiden Warrior is here!
* "Come! Let us give thanks for your arrival by celebrating the Eucharist!"

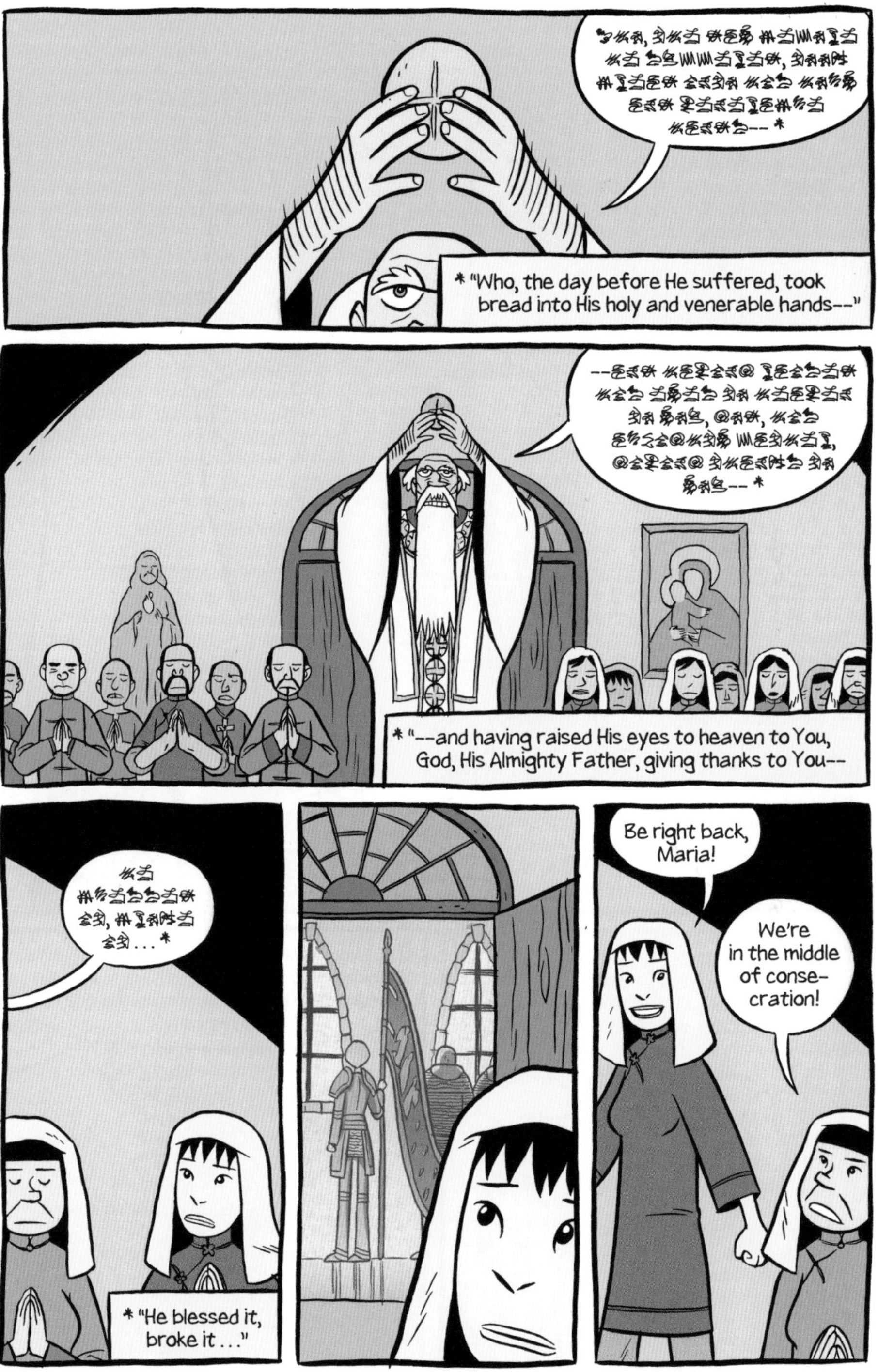
* "Who, the day before He suffered, took bread into His holy and venerable hands--"
* "--and having raised His eyes to heaven to You, God, His Almighty Father, giving thanks to You--
* "He blessed it, broke it . . ."
Be right back, Maria!
We're in the middle of conse-cration!

Joan...?

Shhh! My king receives his crown!

Ah. So the ugly man gets a fancy new hat.

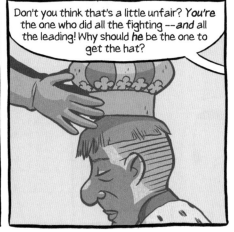

Don't you think that's a little unfair? *You're* the one who did all the fighting --*and* all the leading! Why should *he* be the one to get the hat?

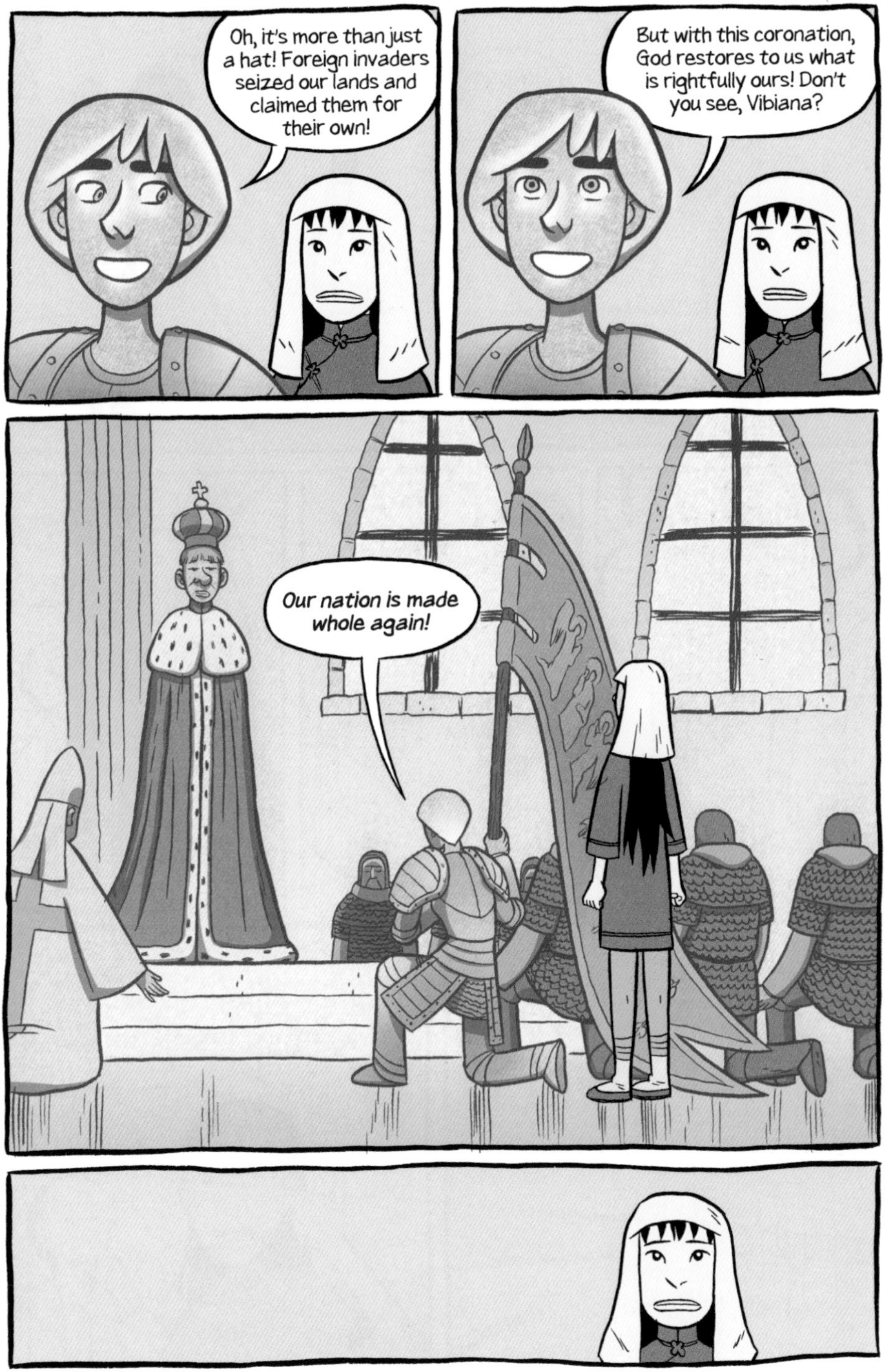
Oh, it's more than just a hat! Foreign invaders seized our lands and claimed them for their own!
But with this coronation, God restores to us what is rightfully ours! Don't you see, Vibiana?
Our nation is made whole again!

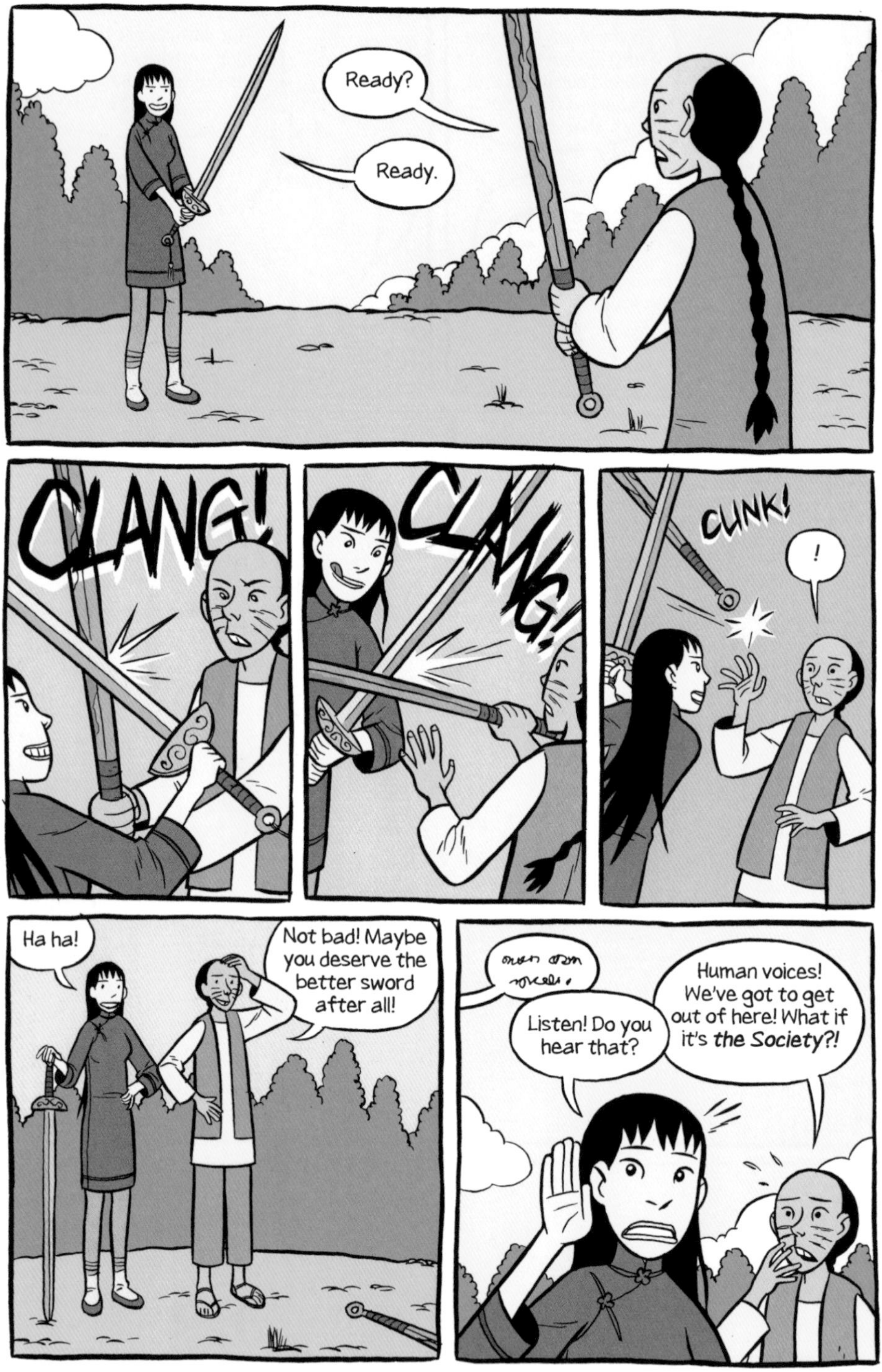
Ready?
Ready.
CLANG!
CLANG!
CLUNK!
!
Ha ha!
Not bad! Maybe you deserve the better sword after all!
Listen! Do you hear that?
Human voices! We've got to get out of here! What if it's *the Society*?!

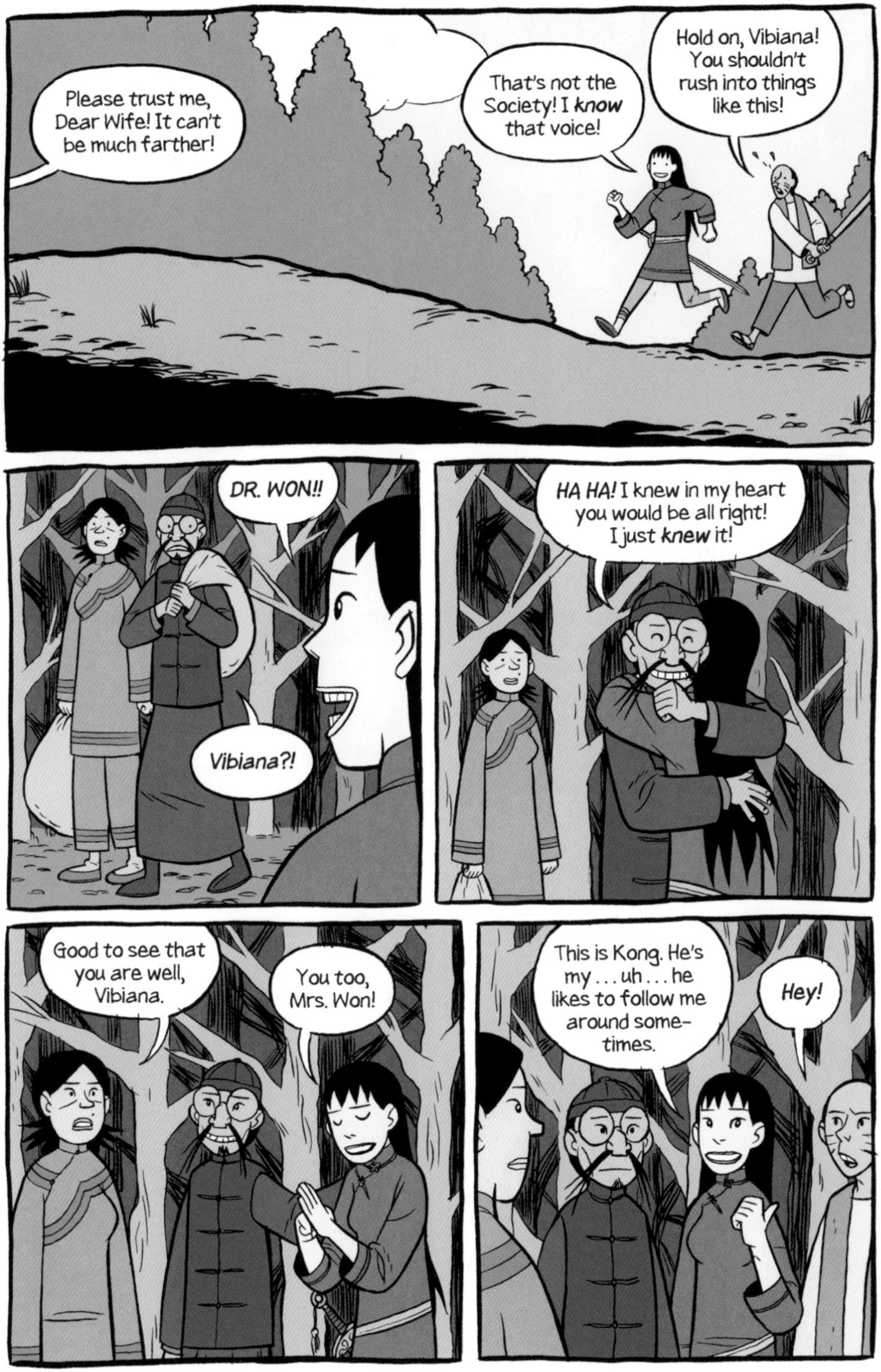
Please trust me, Dear Wife! It can't be much farther!
That's not the Society! I *know* that voice!
Hold on, Vibiana! You shouldn't rush into things like this!
DR. WON!!
Vibiana?!
HA HA! I knew in my heart you would be all right! I just *knew* it!
Good to see that you are well, Vibiana.
You too, Mrs. Won!
This is Kong. He's my . . . uh . . . he likes to follow me around some-times.
Hey!

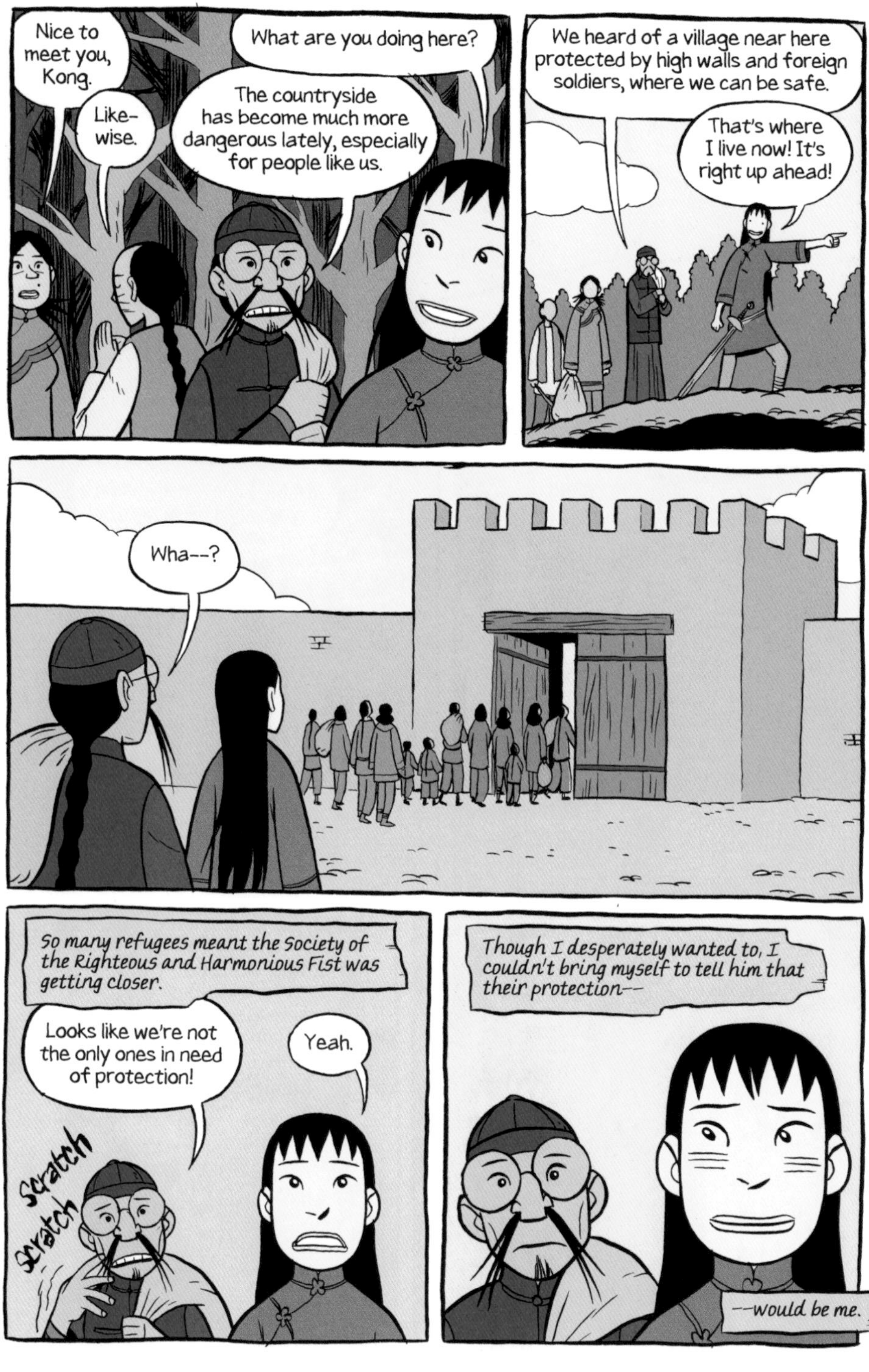

Nice to meet you, Kong.
Like-wise.
What are you doing here?
The countryside has become much more dangerous lately, especially for people like us.
We heard of a village near here protected by high walls and foreign soldiers, where we can be safe.
That's where I live now! It's right up ahead!
Wha--?
So many refugees meant the Society of the Righteous and Harmonious Fist was getting closer.
Looks like we're not the only ones in need of protection!
Yeah.
Scratch scratch
Though I desperately wanted to, I couldn't bring myself to tell him that their protection--
--would be me.

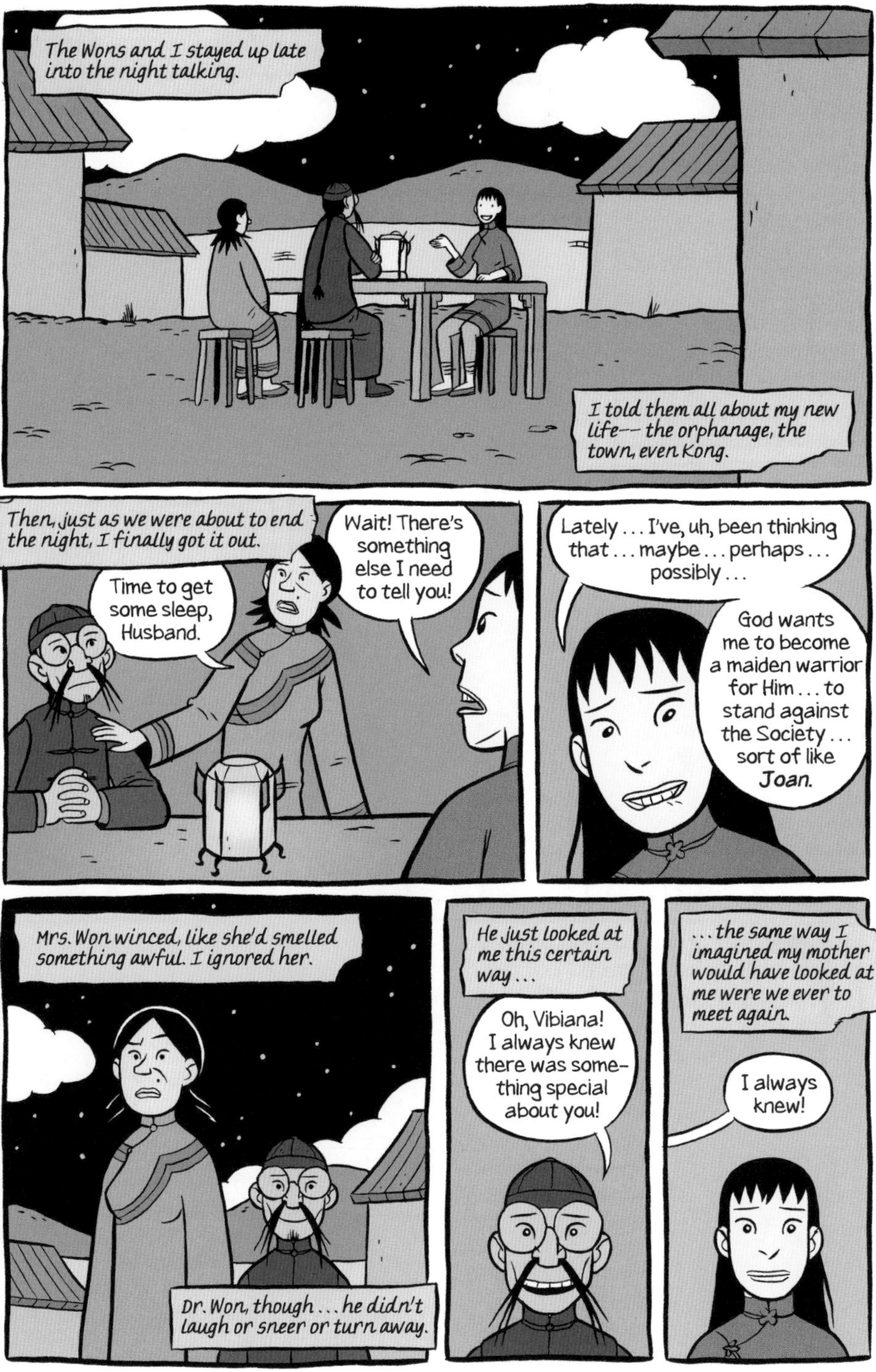
The Wons and I stayed up late into the night talking.
I told them all about my new life-- the orphanage, the town, even Kong.
Then, just as we were about to end the night, I finally got it out.
Time to get some sleep, Husband.
Wait! There's something else I need to tell you!
Lately . . . I've, uh, been thinking that . . . maybe . . . perhaps . . . possibly . . .
God wants me to become a maiden warrior for Him . . . to stand against the Society . . . sort of like Joan.
Mrs. Won winced, like she'd smelled something awful. I ignored her.
Dr. Won, though . . . he didn't laugh or sneer or turn away.
He just looked at me this certain way . . .
Oh, Vibiana! I always knew there was some-thing special about you!
. . . the same way I imagined my mother would have looked at me were we ever to meet again.
I always knew!

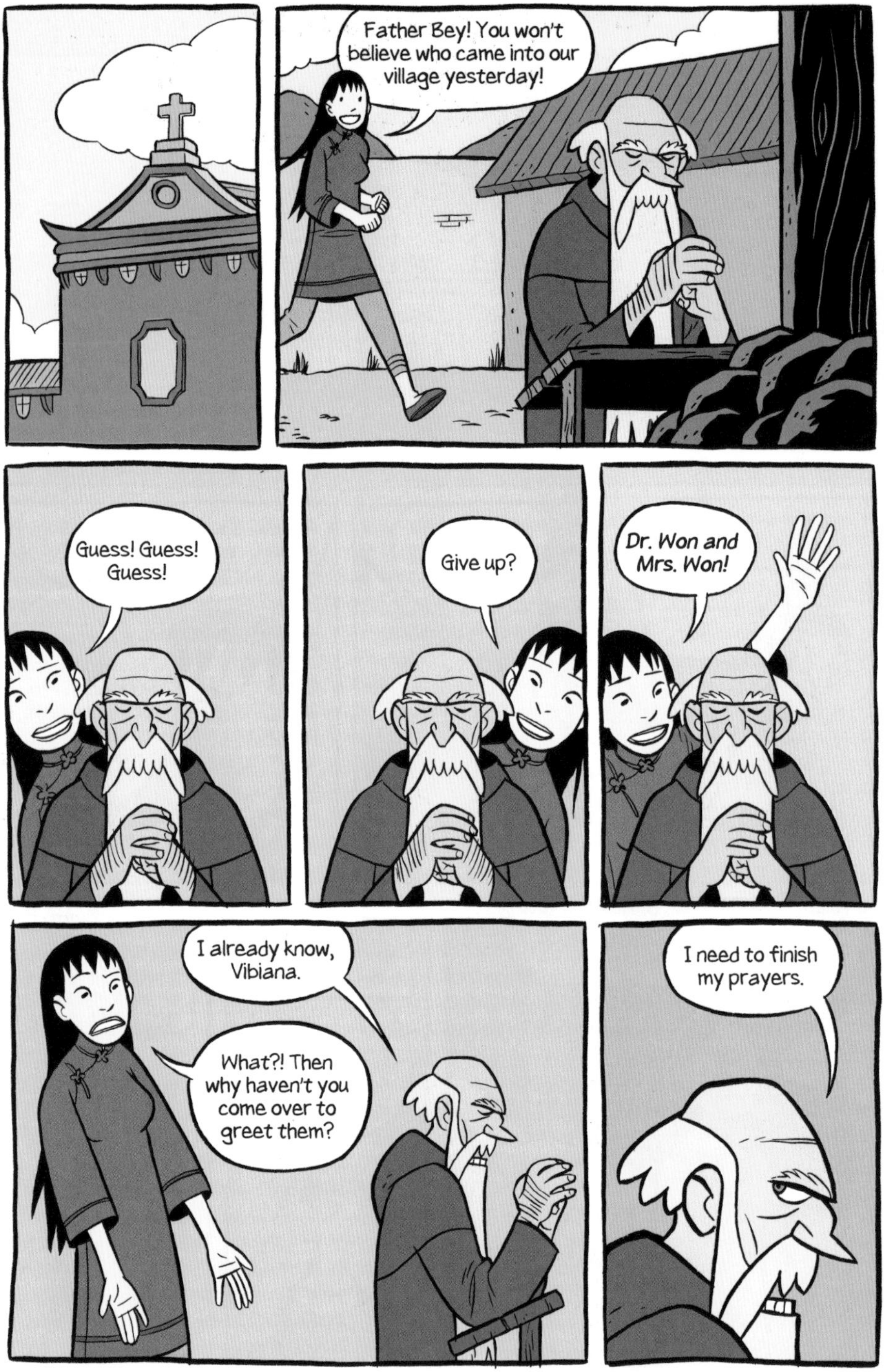
Father Bey! You won't believe who came into our village yesterday!
Guess! Guess! Guess!
Give up?
Dr. Won and Mrs. Won!
I already know, Vibiana.
What?! Then why haven't you come over to greet them?
I need to finish my prayers.

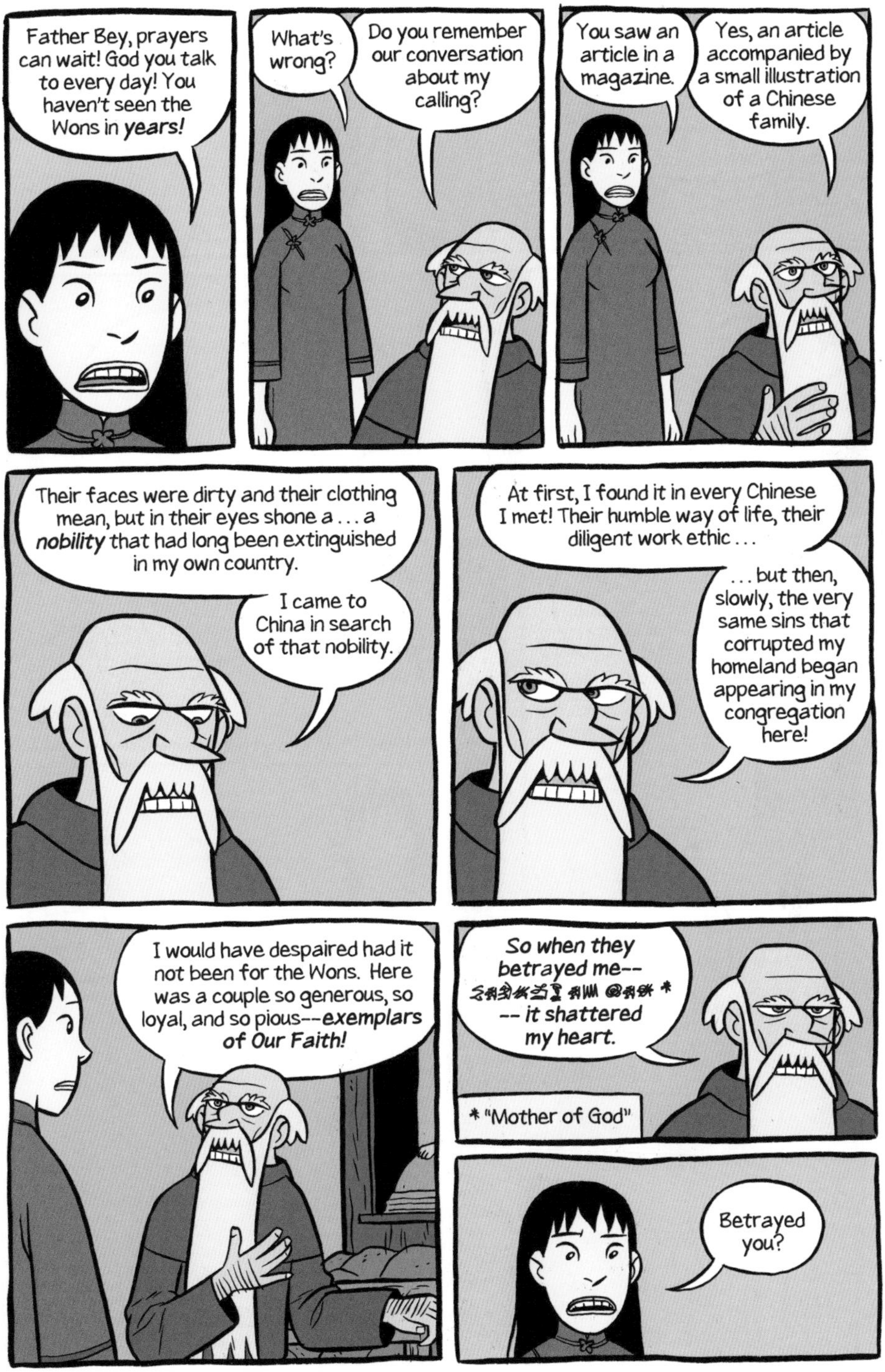
Father Bey, prayers can wait! God you talk to every day! You haven't seen the Wons in *years!*
What's wrong?
Do you remember our conversation about my calling?
You saw an article in a magazine.
Yes, an article accompanied by a small illustration of a Chinese family.
Their faces were dirty and their clothing mean, but in their eyes shone a . . . a *nobility* that had long been extinguished in my own country.
I came to China in search of that nobility.
At first, I found it in every Chinese I met! Their humble way of life, their diligent work ethic . . .
. . . but then, slowly, the very same sins that corrupted my homeland began appearing in my congregation here!
I would have despaired had it not been for the Wons. Here was a couple so generous, so loyal, and so pious--*exemplars of Our Faith!*
So when they betrayed me--
-- it shattered my heart.
* "Mother of God"
Betrayed you?

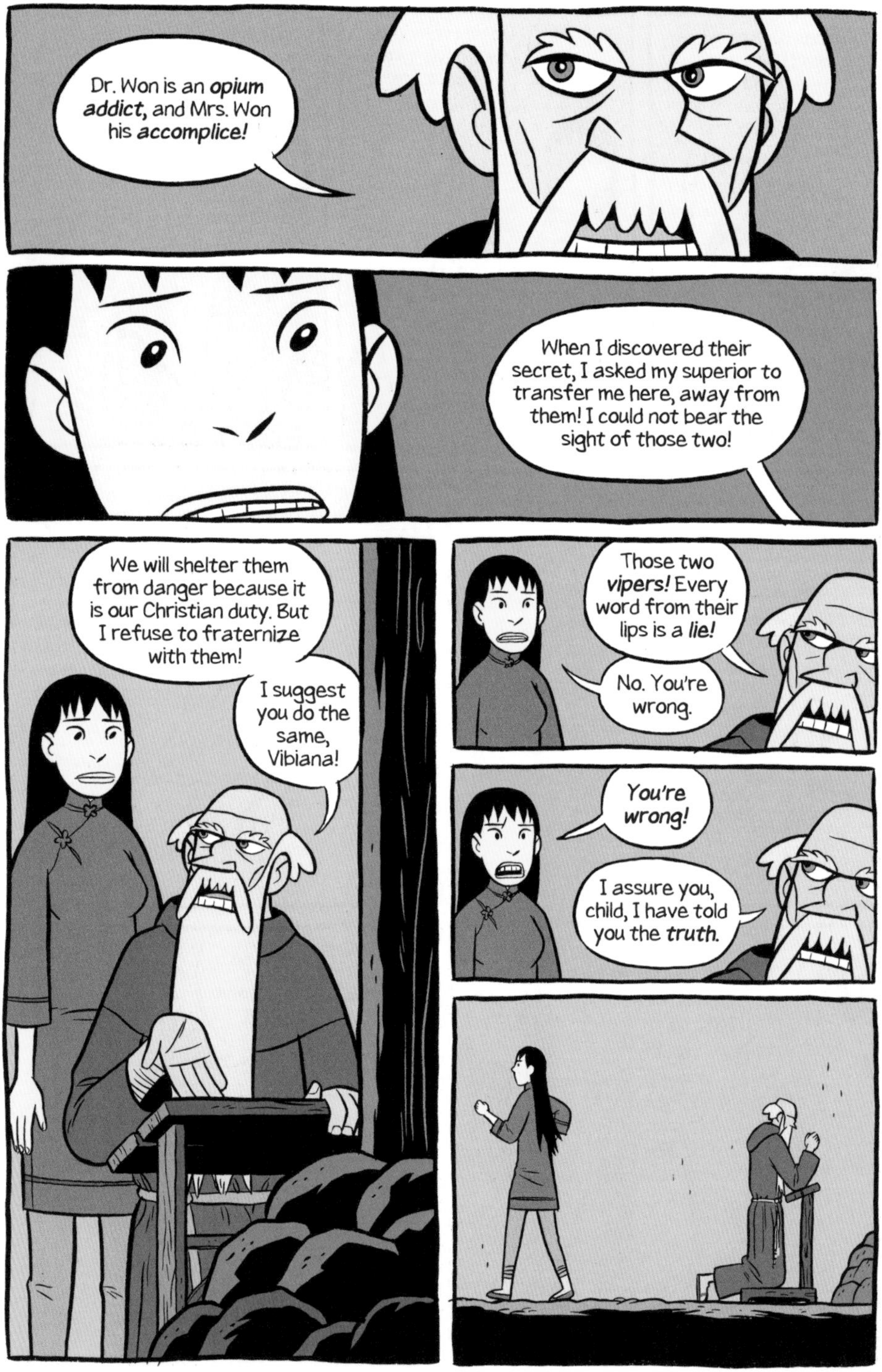
Dr. Won is an *opium addict,* and Mrs. Won his *accomplice!*
When I discovered their secret, I asked my superior to transfer me here, away from them! I could not bear the sight of those two!
We will shelter them from danger because it is our Christian duty. But I refuse to fraternize with them!
I suggest you do the same, Vibiana!
Those two *vipers!* Every word from their lips is a *lie!*
No. You're wrong.
You're wrong!
I assure you, child, I have told you the *truth.*

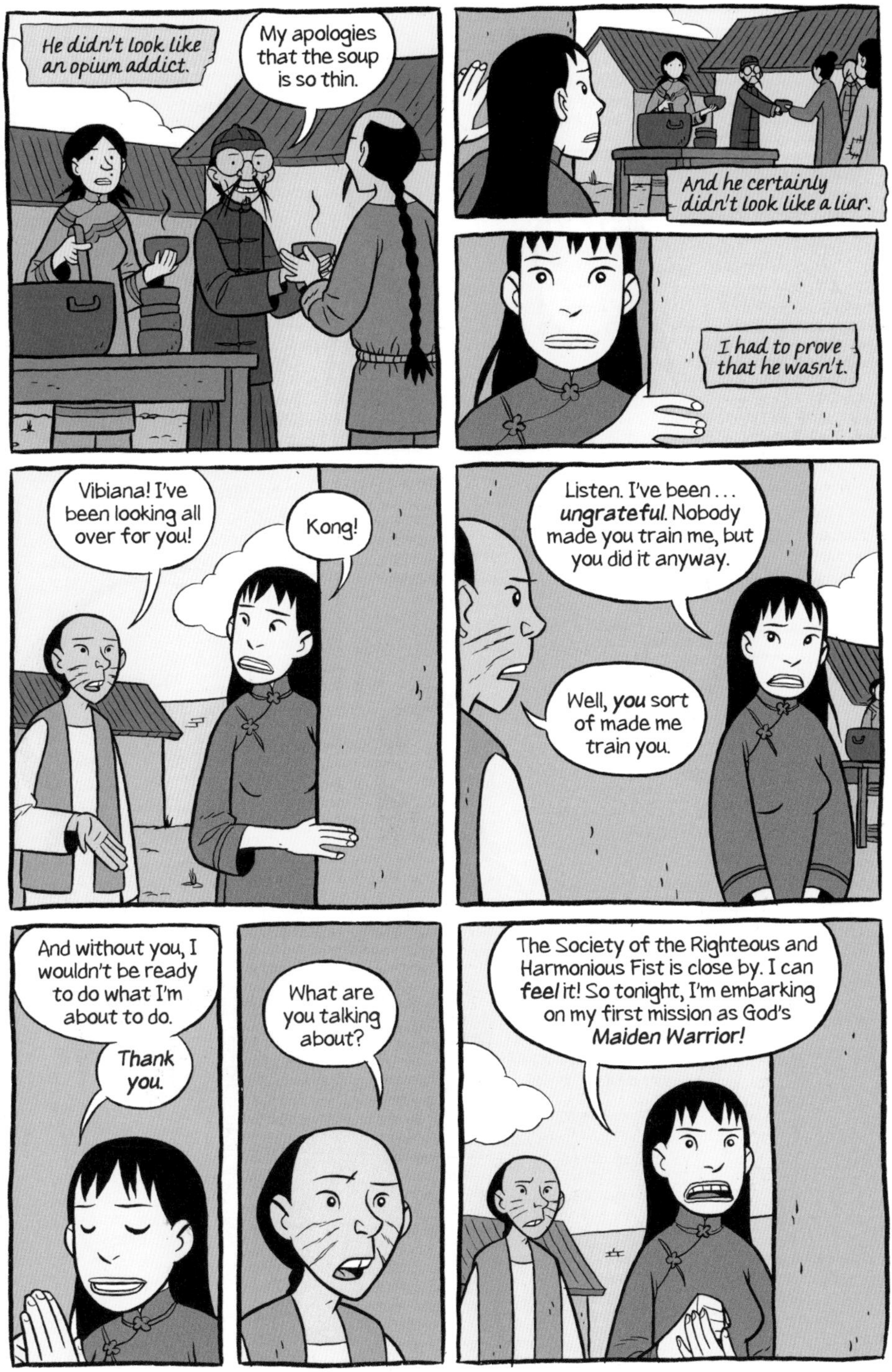
He didn't look like an opium addict.
My apologies that the soup is so thin.
And he certainly didn't look like a liar.
I had to prove that he wasn't.
Vibiana! I've been looking all over for you!
Kong!
Listen. I've been . . . *ungrateful*. Nobody made you train me, but you did it anyway.
Well, *you* sort of made me train you.
And without you, I wouldn't be ready to do what I'm about to do.
Thank you.
What are you talking about?
The Society of the Righteous and Harmonious Fist is close by. I can *feel* it! So tonight, I'm embarking on my first mission as God's *Maiden Warrior!*

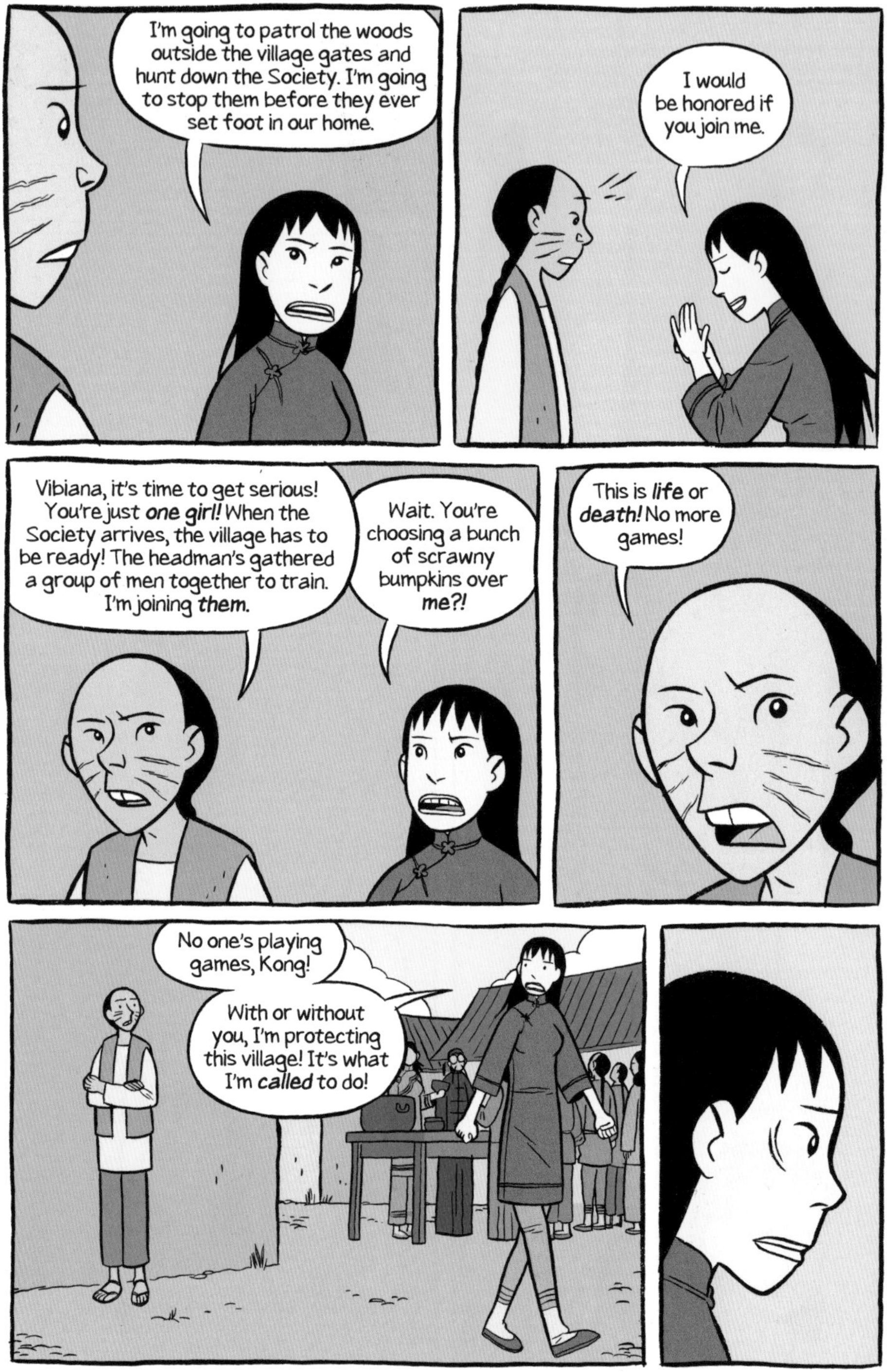

I'm going to patrol the woods outside the village gates and hunt down the Society. I'm going to stop them before they ever set foot in our home.
I would be honored if you join me.
Vibiana, it's time to get serious! You're just *one girl!* When the Society arrives, the village has to be ready! The headman's gathered a group of men together to train. I'm joining *them.*
Wait. You're choosing a bunch of scrawny bumpkins over *me?!*
This is *life* or *death!* No more games!
No one's playing games, Kong!
With or without you, I'm protecting this village! It's what I'm *called* to do!

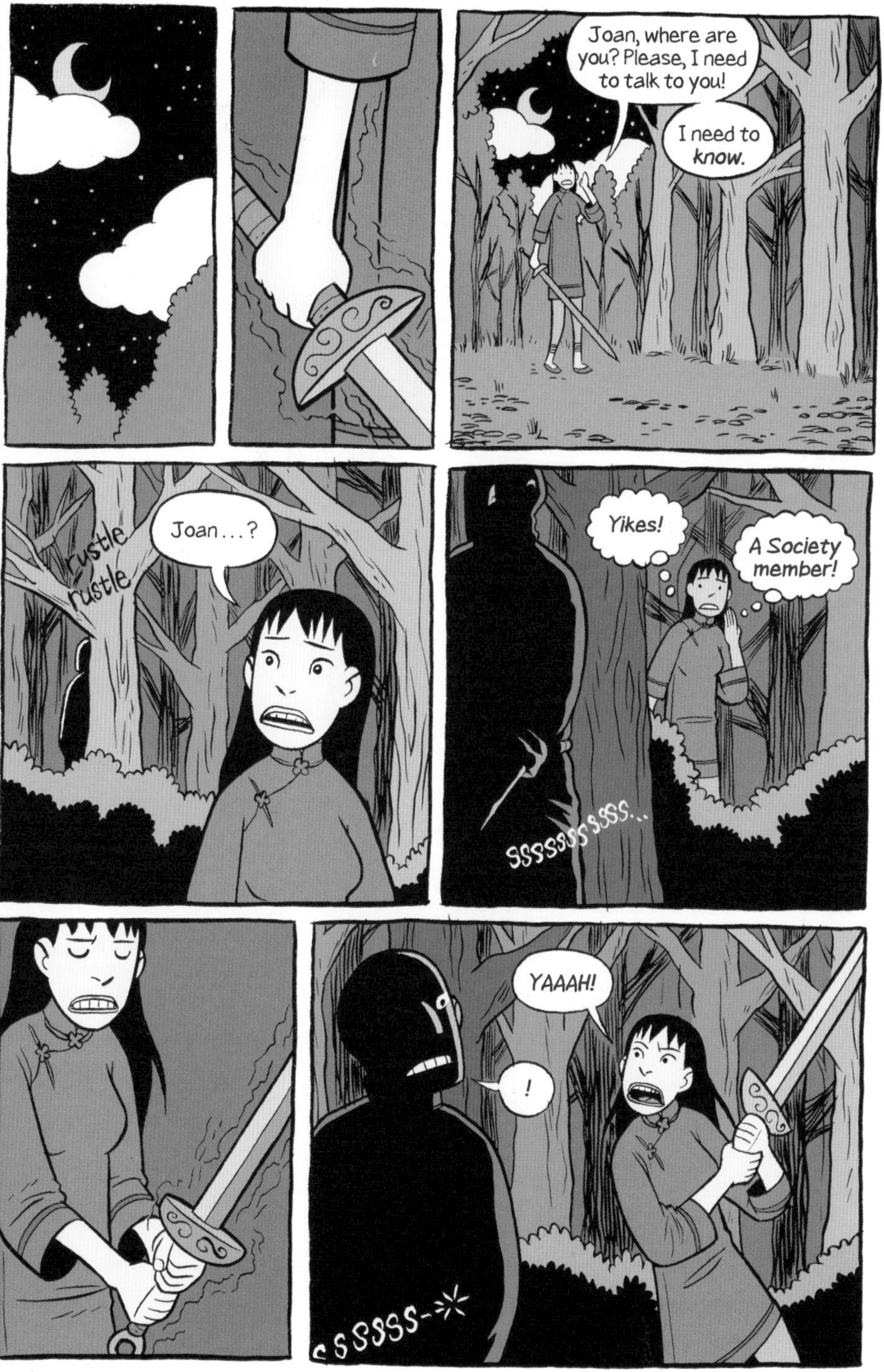

Joan, where are you? Please, I need to talk to you!
I need to know.
rustle
rustle
Joan...?
Yikes!
A Society member!
SSSSSSSSSSS...
YAAAH!
!
SSSSS-

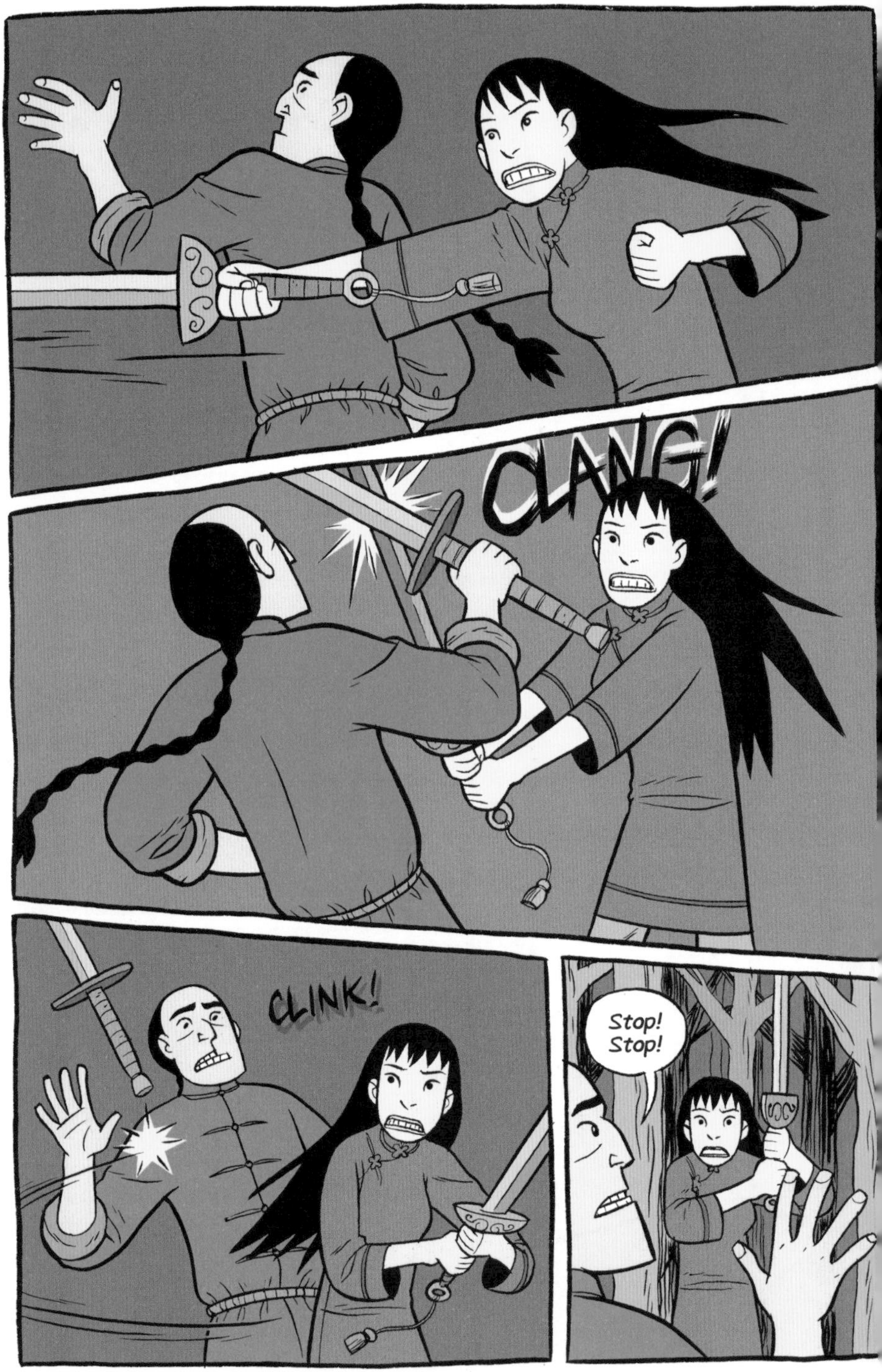
CLANG!
CLINK!
Stop! Stop!

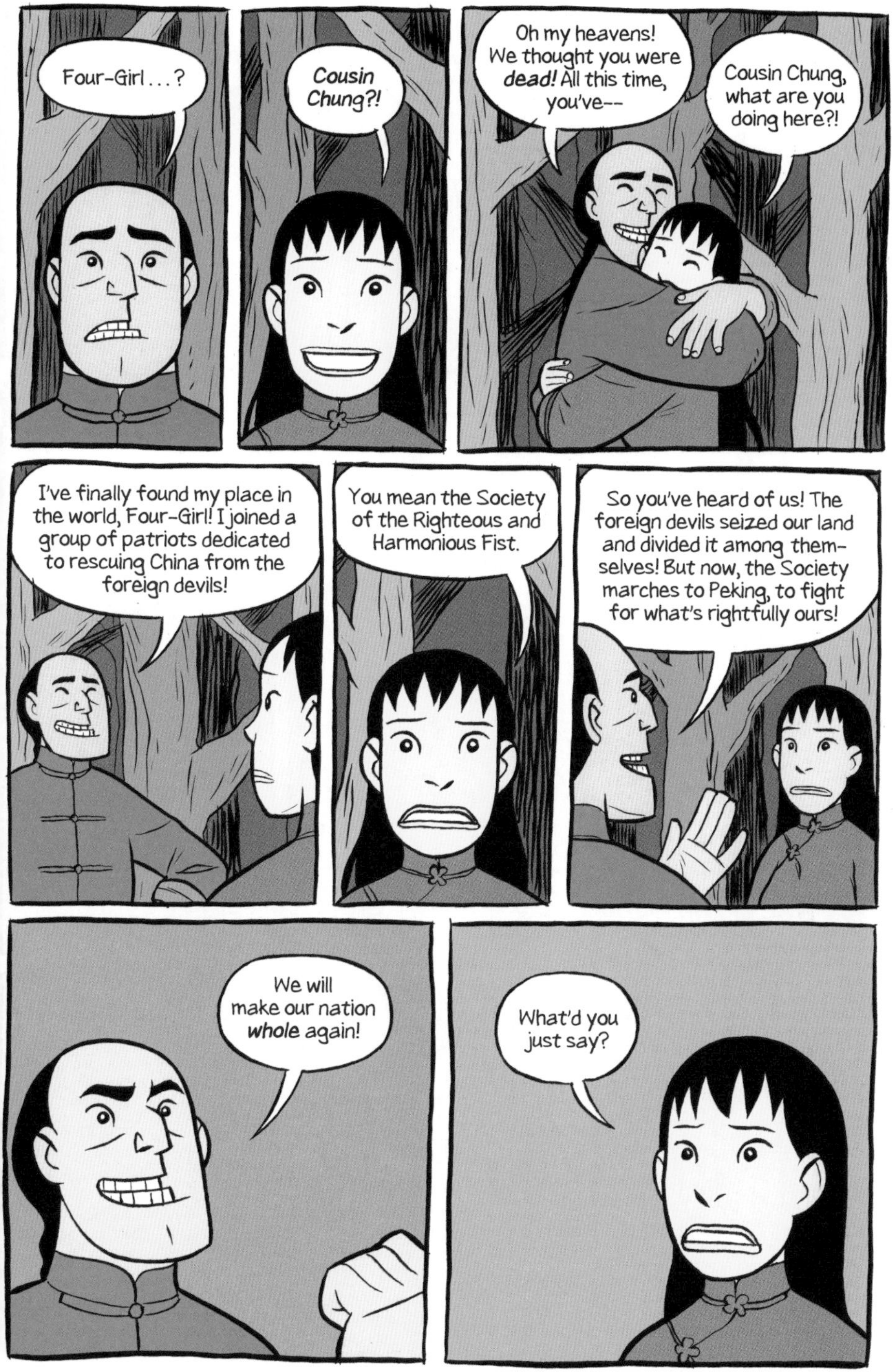

Four-Girl...?
Cousin Chung?!
Oh my heavens! We thought you were dead! All this time, you've--
Cousin Chung, what are you doing here?!
I've finally found my place in the world, Four-Girl! I joined a group of patriots dedicated to rescuing China from the foreign devils!
You mean the Society of the Righteous and Harmonious Fist.
So you've heard of us! The foreign devils seized our land and divided it among them-selves! But now, the Society marches to Peking, to fight for what's rightfully ours!
We will make our nation whole again!
What'd you just say?

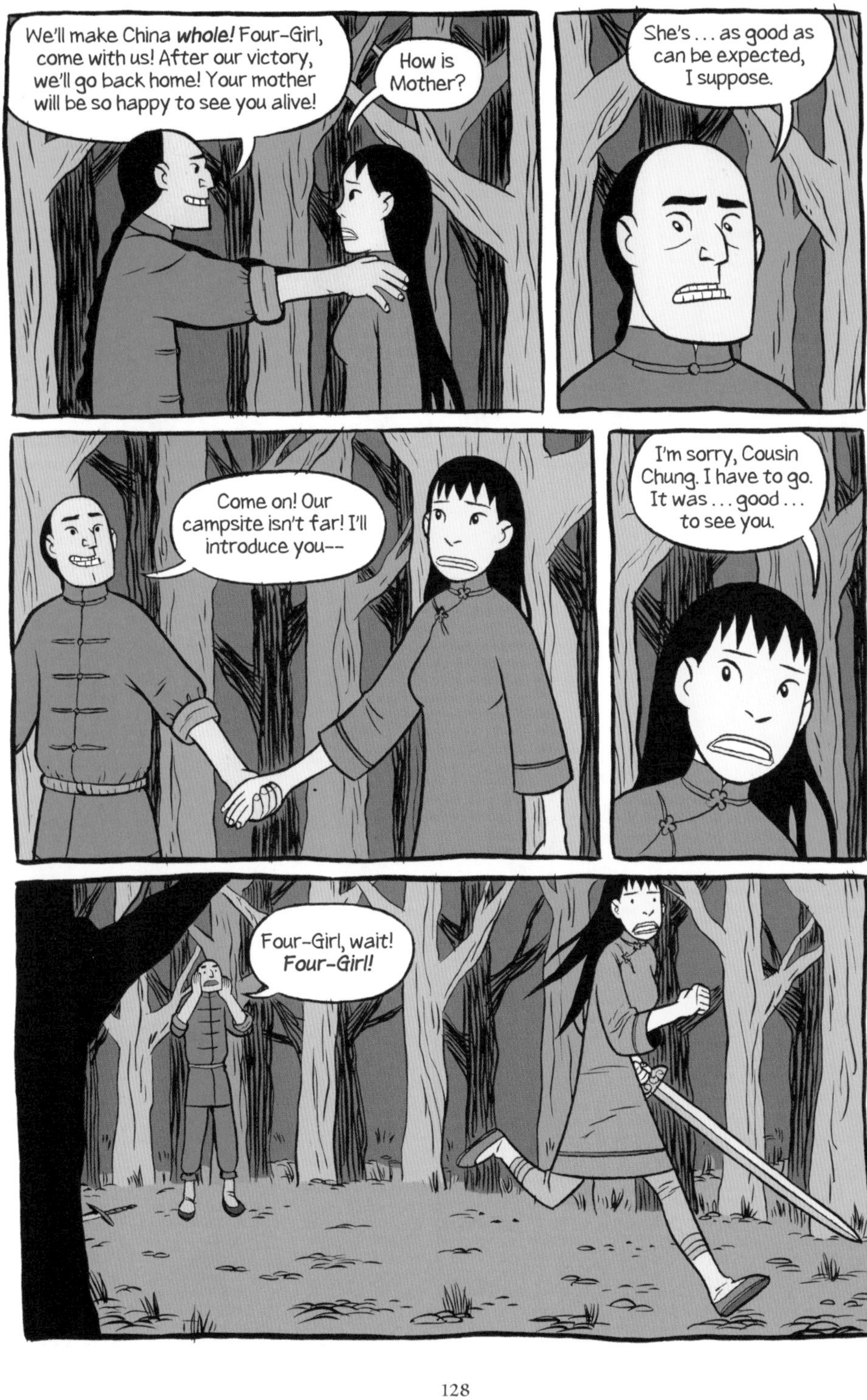
We'll make China ***whole!*** Four-Girl, come with us! After our victory, we'll go back home! Your mother will be so happy to see you alive!
How is Mother?
She's . . . as good as can be expected, I suppose.
Come on! Our campsite isn't far! I'll introduce you--
I'm sorry, Cousin Chung. I have to go. It was . . . good . . . to see you.
Four-Girl, wait! **Four-Girl!**

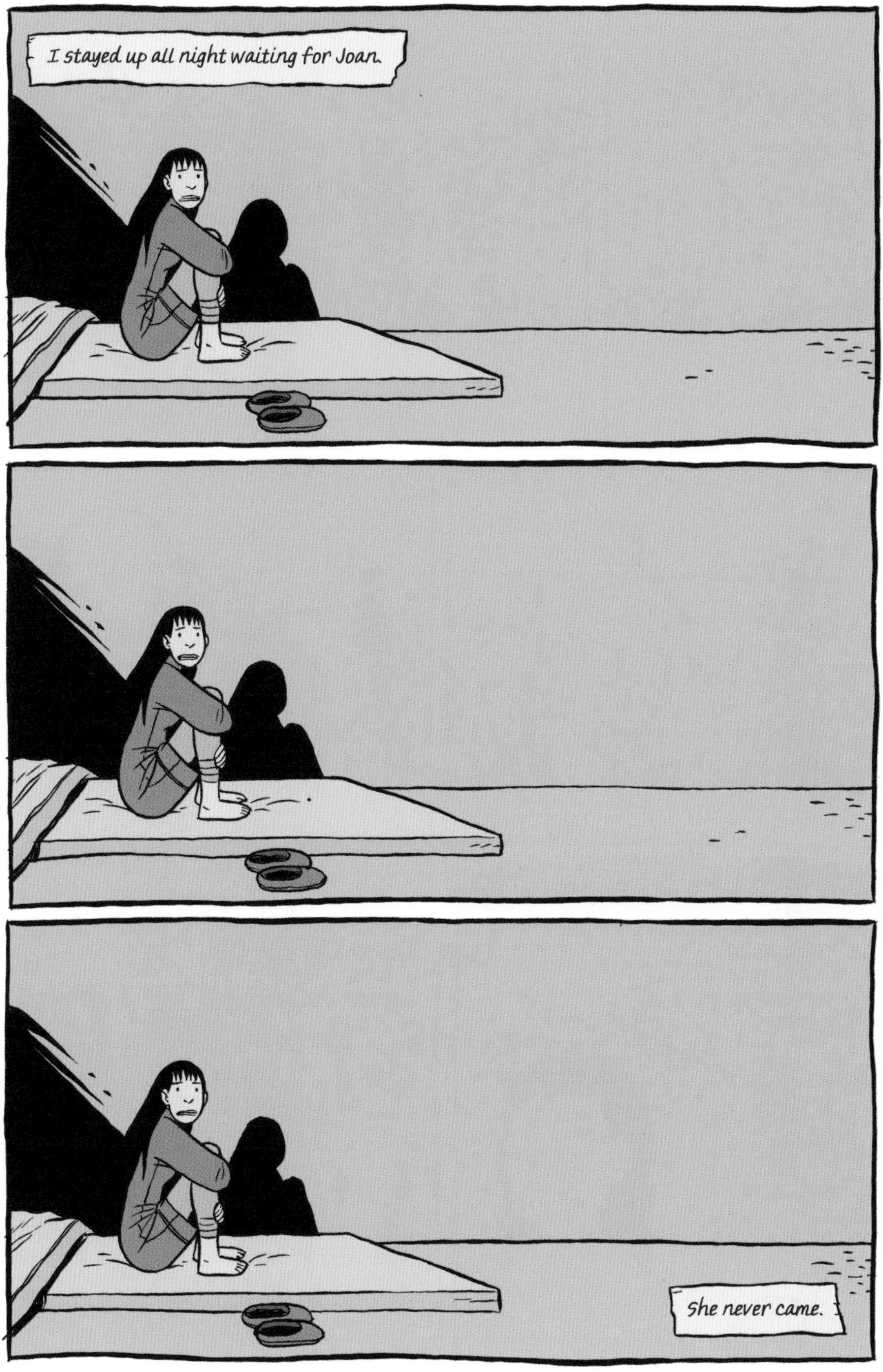
I stayed up all night waiting for Joan.
She never came.

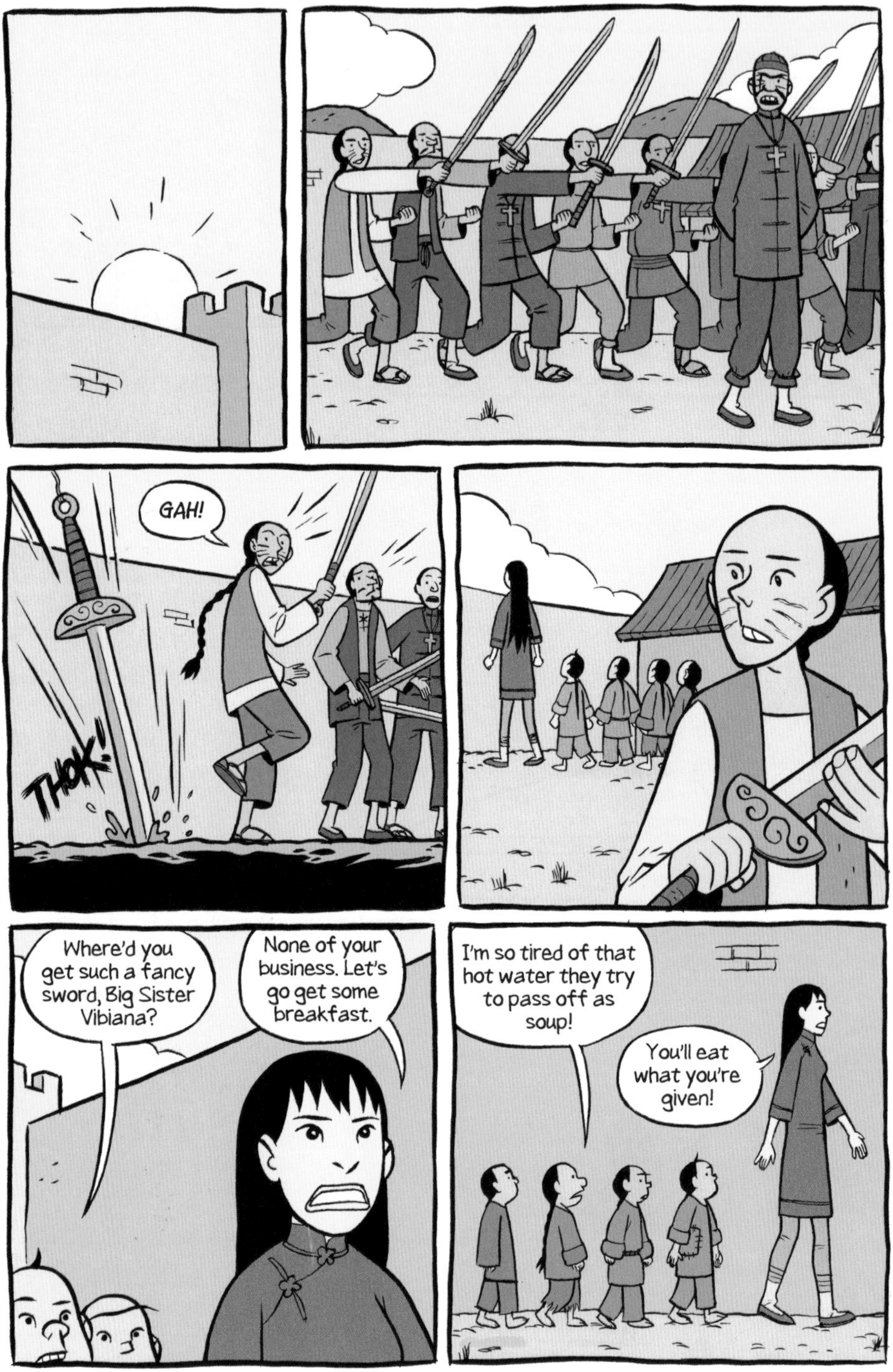
GAH!
THOK!
Where'd you get such a fancy sword, Big Sister Vibiana?
None of your business. Let's go get some breakfast.
I'm so tired of that hot water they try to pass off as soup!
You'll eat what you're given!

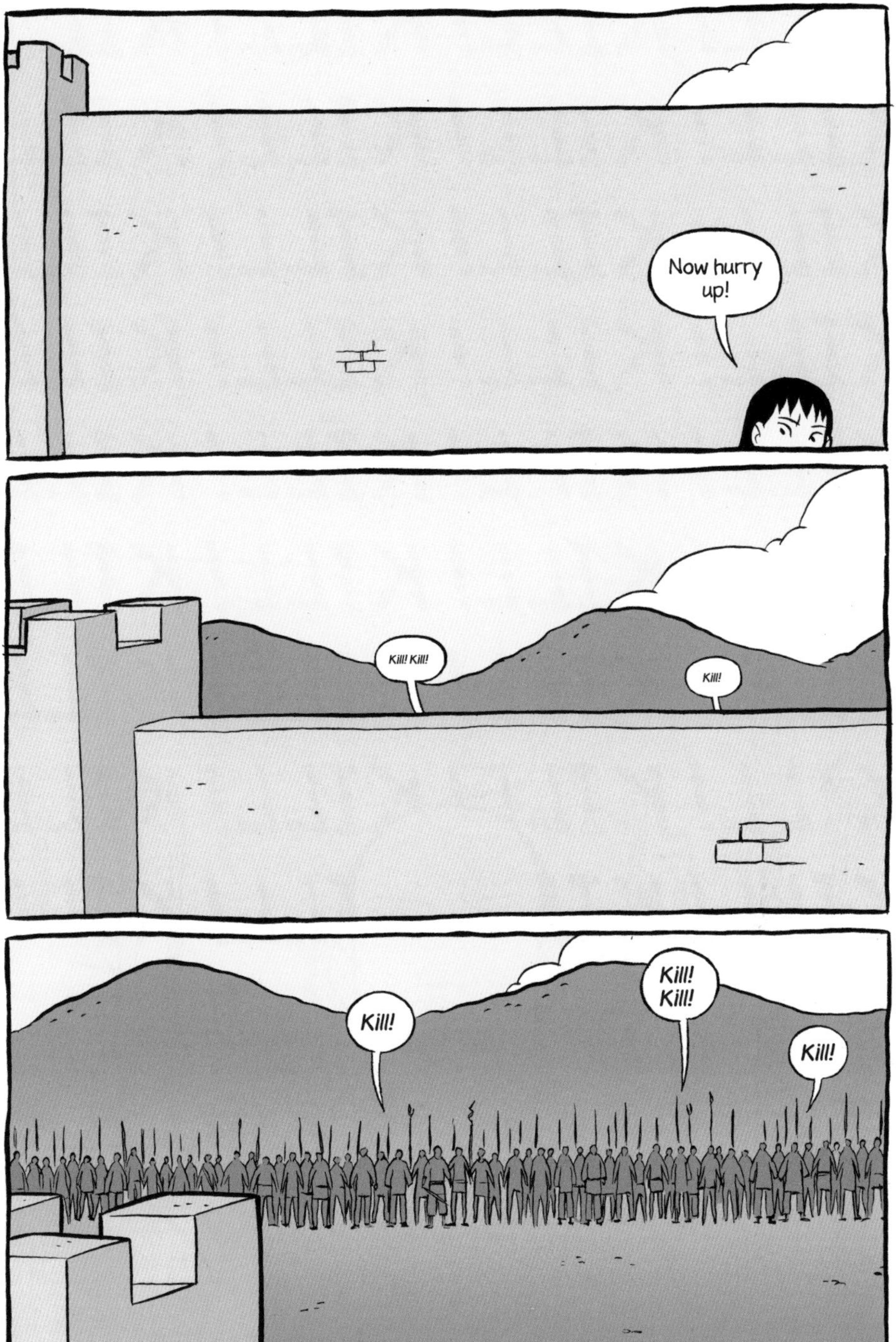
Now hurry up!
Kill! Kill!
Kill!
Kill!
Kill! Kill!
Kill!

第六章

Age 15

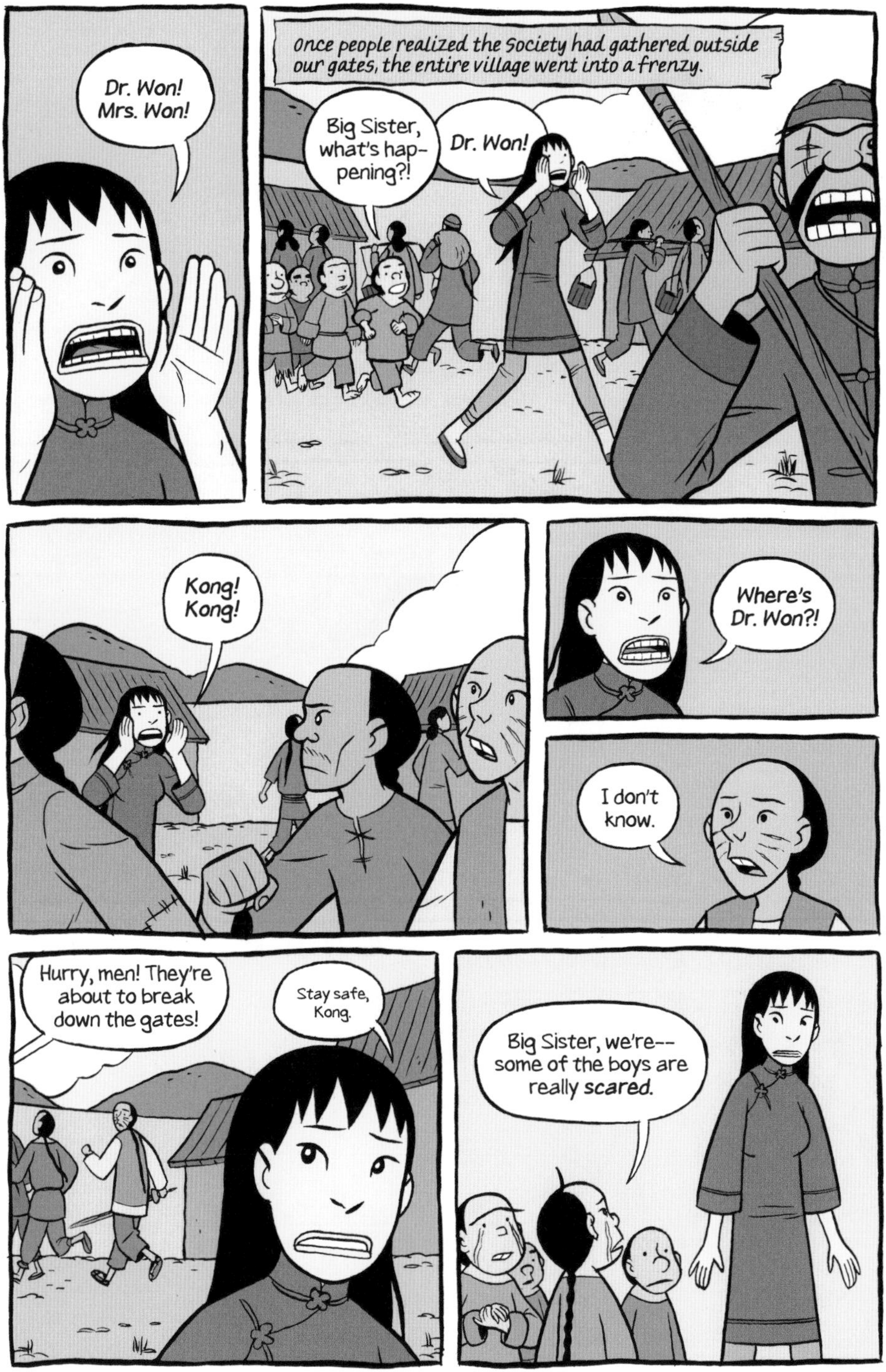
Dr. Won! Mrs. Won!
Once people realized the Society had gathered outside our gates, the entire village went into a frenzy.
Big Sister, what's hap-pening?!
Dr. Won!
Kong! Kong!
Where's Dr. Won?!
I don't know.
Hurry, men! They're about to break down the gates!
Stay safe, Kong.
Big Sister, we're-- some of the boys are really scared.

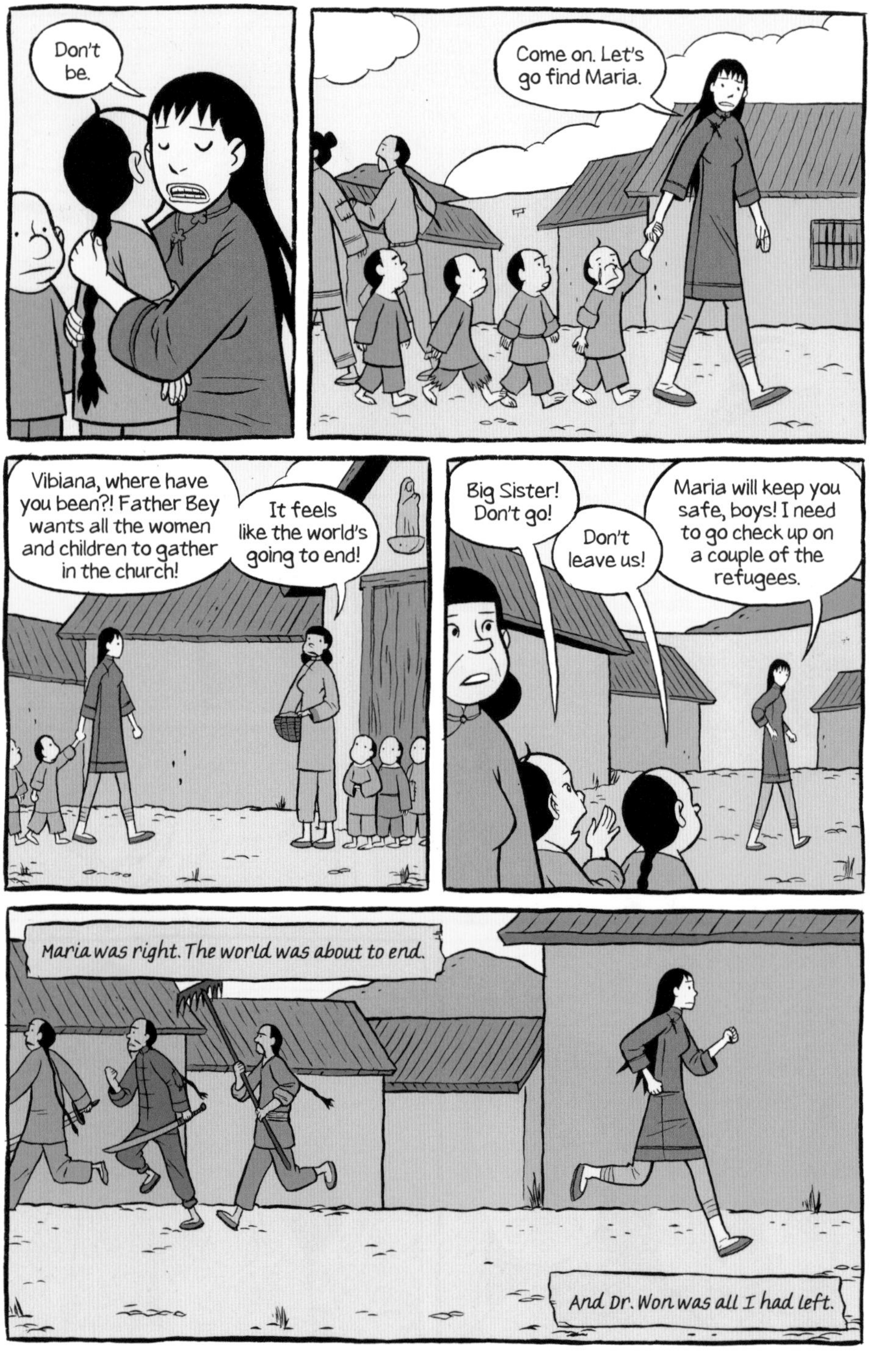
Don't be.
Come on. Let's go find Maria.
Vibiana, where have you been?! Father Bey wants all the women and children to gather in the church!
It feels like the world's going to end!
Big Sister! Don't go!
Don't leave us!
Maria will keep you safe, boys! I need to go check up on a couple of the refugees.
Maria was right. The world was about to end.
And Dr. Won was all I had left.

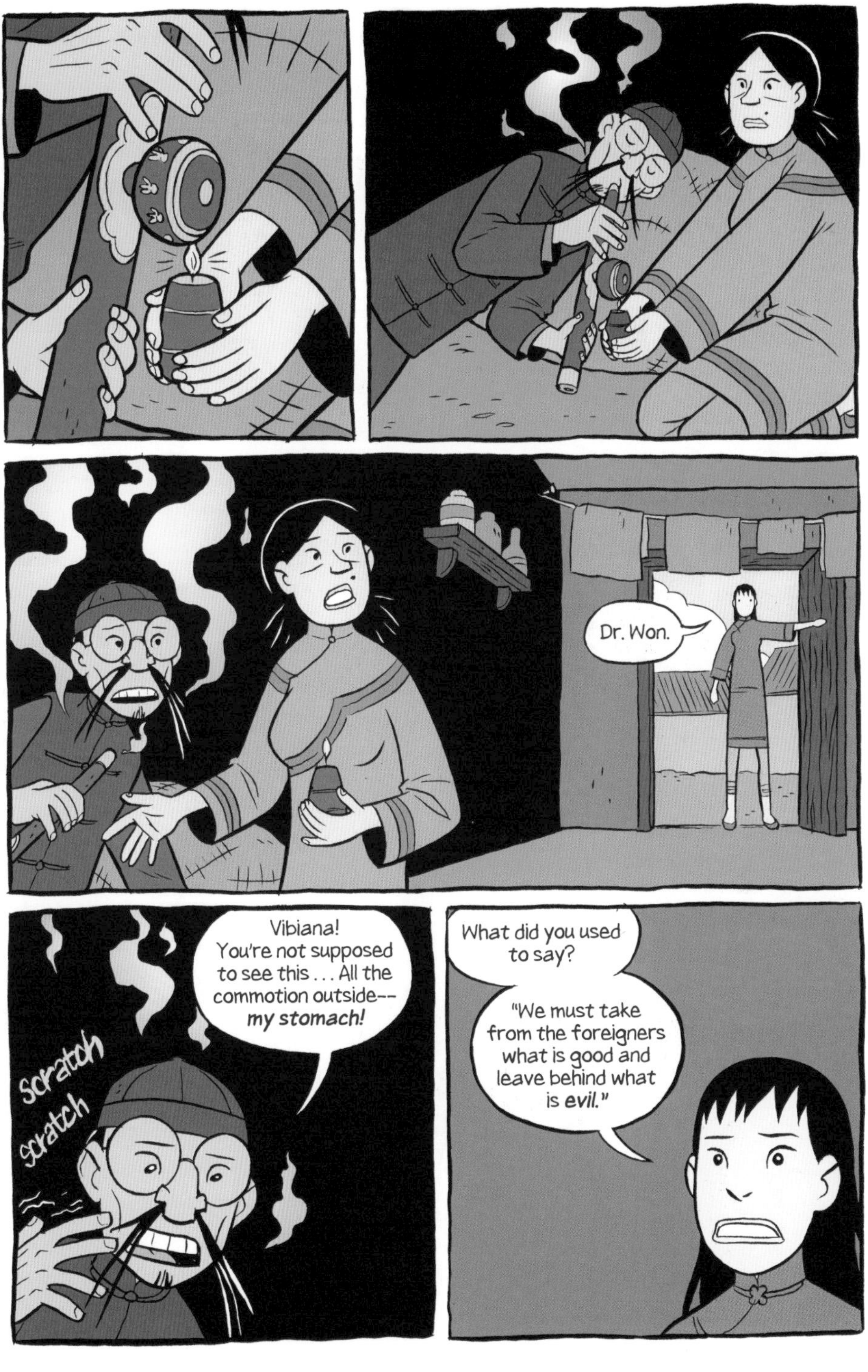
Dr. Won.
Vibiana! You're not supposed to see this . . . All the commotion outside-- my stomach!
scratch scratch
What did you used to say?
"We must take from the foreigners what is good and leave behind what is evil."

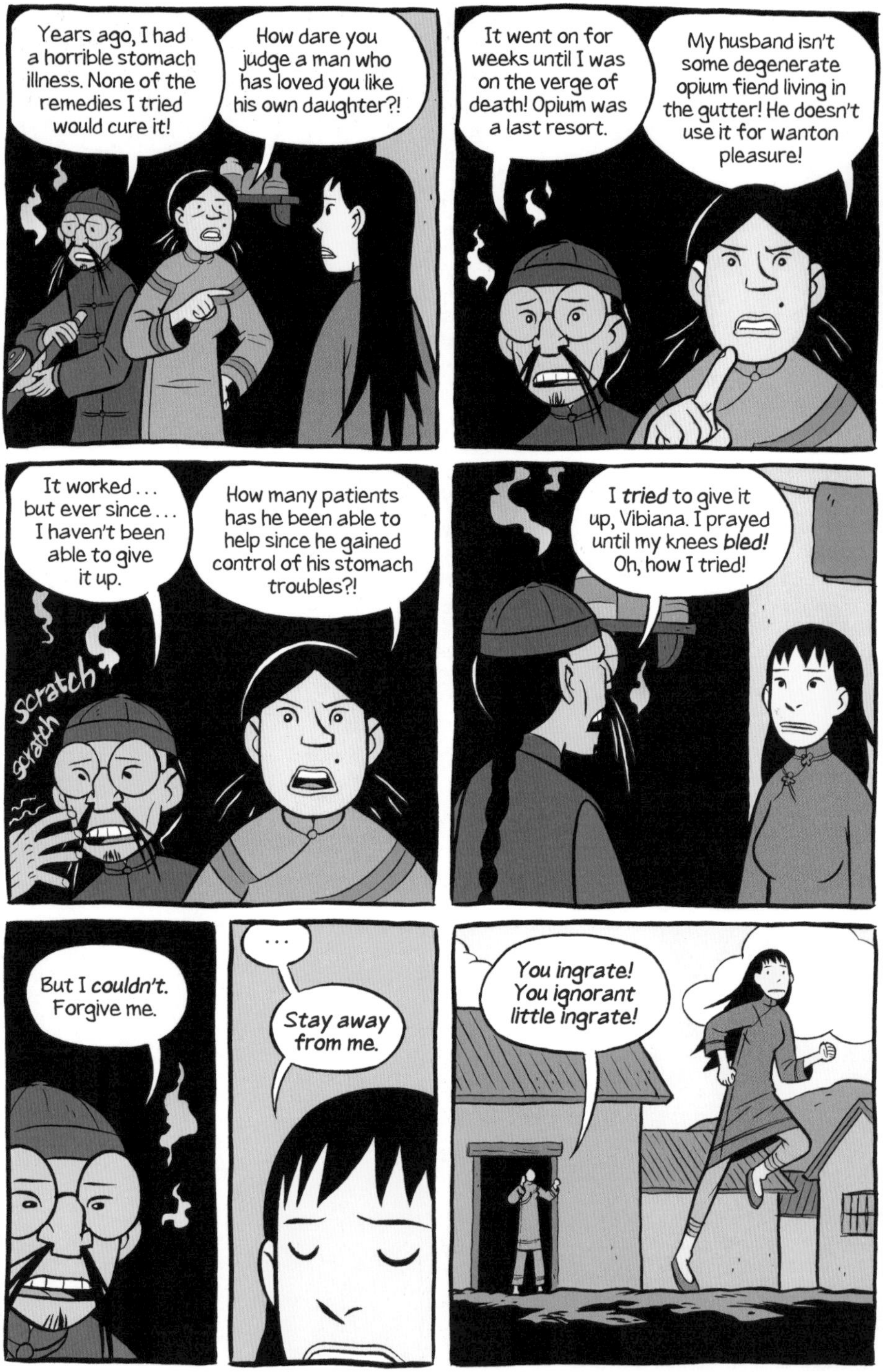
Years ago, I had a horrible stomach illness. None of the remedies I tried would cure it!
How dare you judge a man who has loved you like his own daughter?!
It went on for weeks until I was on the verge of death! Opium was a last resort.
My husband isn't some degenerate opium fiend living in the gutter! He doesn't use it for wanton pleasure!
It worked... but ever since... I haven't been able to give it up.
How many patients has he been able to help since he gained control of his stomach troubles?!
scratch
scratch
I *tried* to give it up, Vibiana. I prayed until my knees *bled!* Oh, how I tried!
But I *couldn't.* Forgive me.
...
Stay away from me.
You ingrate! You ignorant little ingrate!

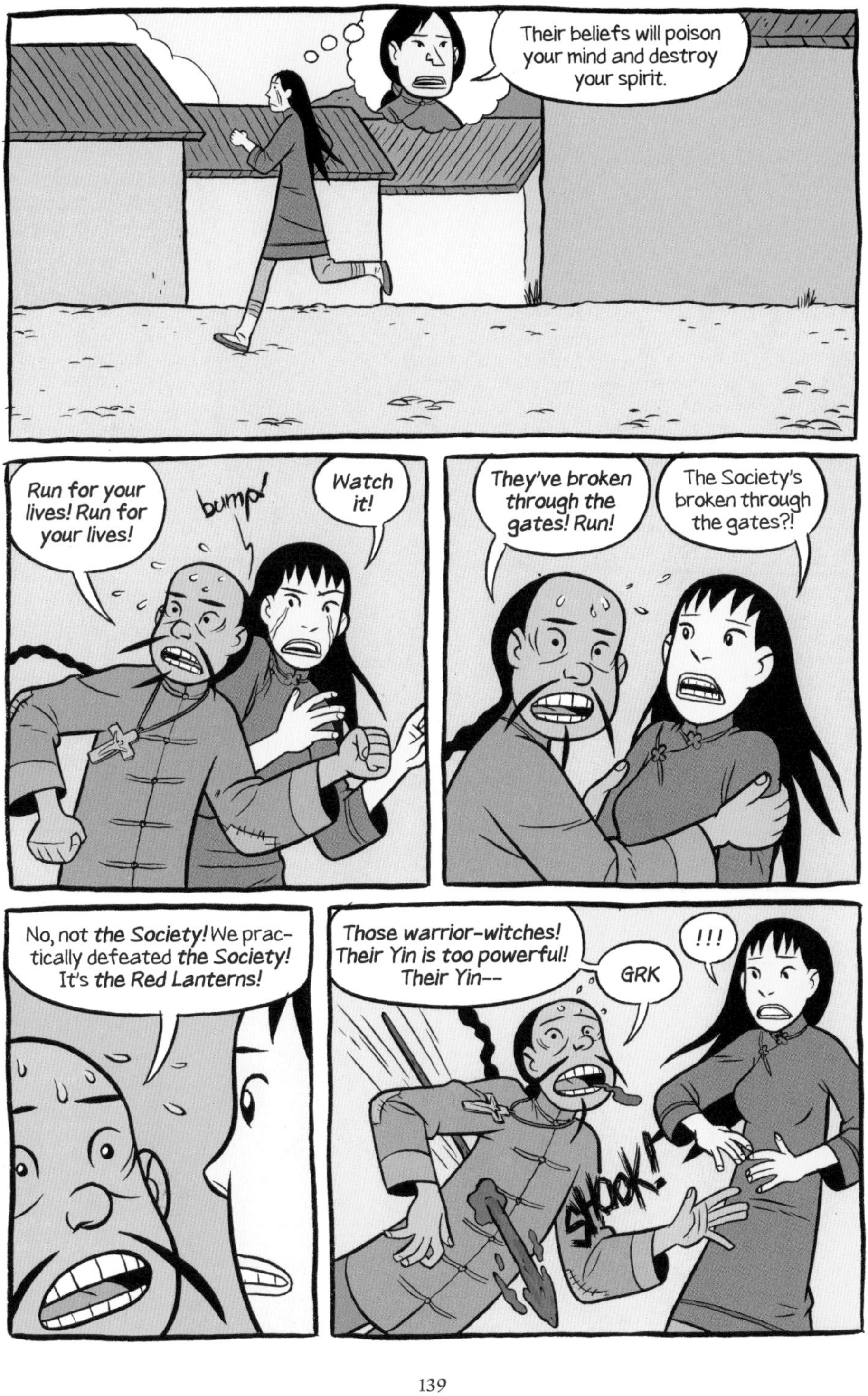
Their beliefs will poison your mind and destroy your spirit.
Run for your lives! Run for your lives!
bump!
Watch it!
They've broken through the gates! Run!
The Society's broken through the gates?!
No, not *the Society!* We practically defeated *the Society!* It's *the Red Lanterns!*
Those warrior-witches! Their Yin is too powerful! Their Yin--
GRK
!!!
SHOOK!

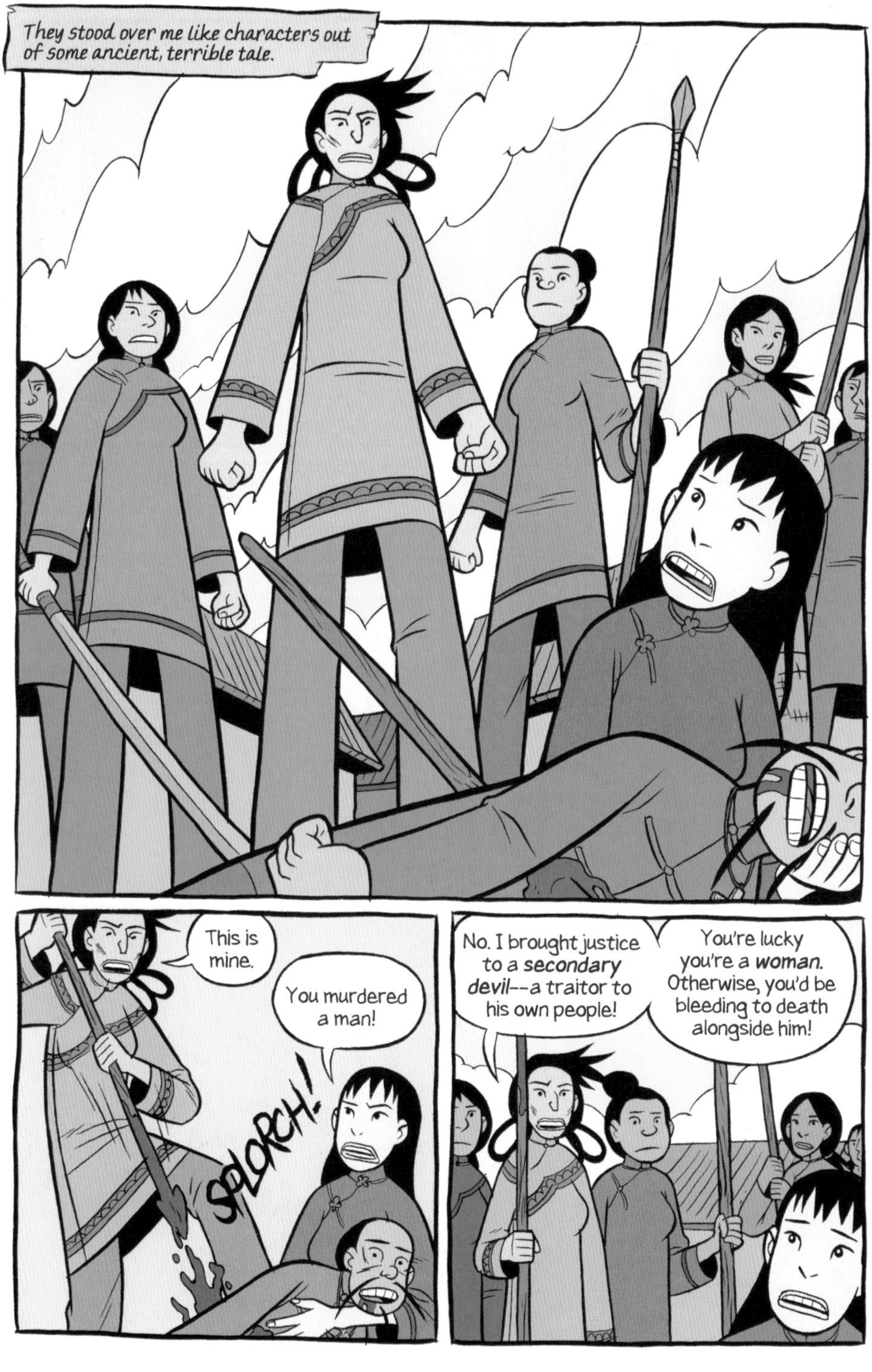
They stood over me like characters out of some ancient, terrible tale.
This is mine.
You murdered a man!
SPLORCH!
No. I brought justice to a *secondary devil*--a traitor to his own people!
You're lucky you're a *woman*. Otherwise, you'd be bleeding to death alongside him!

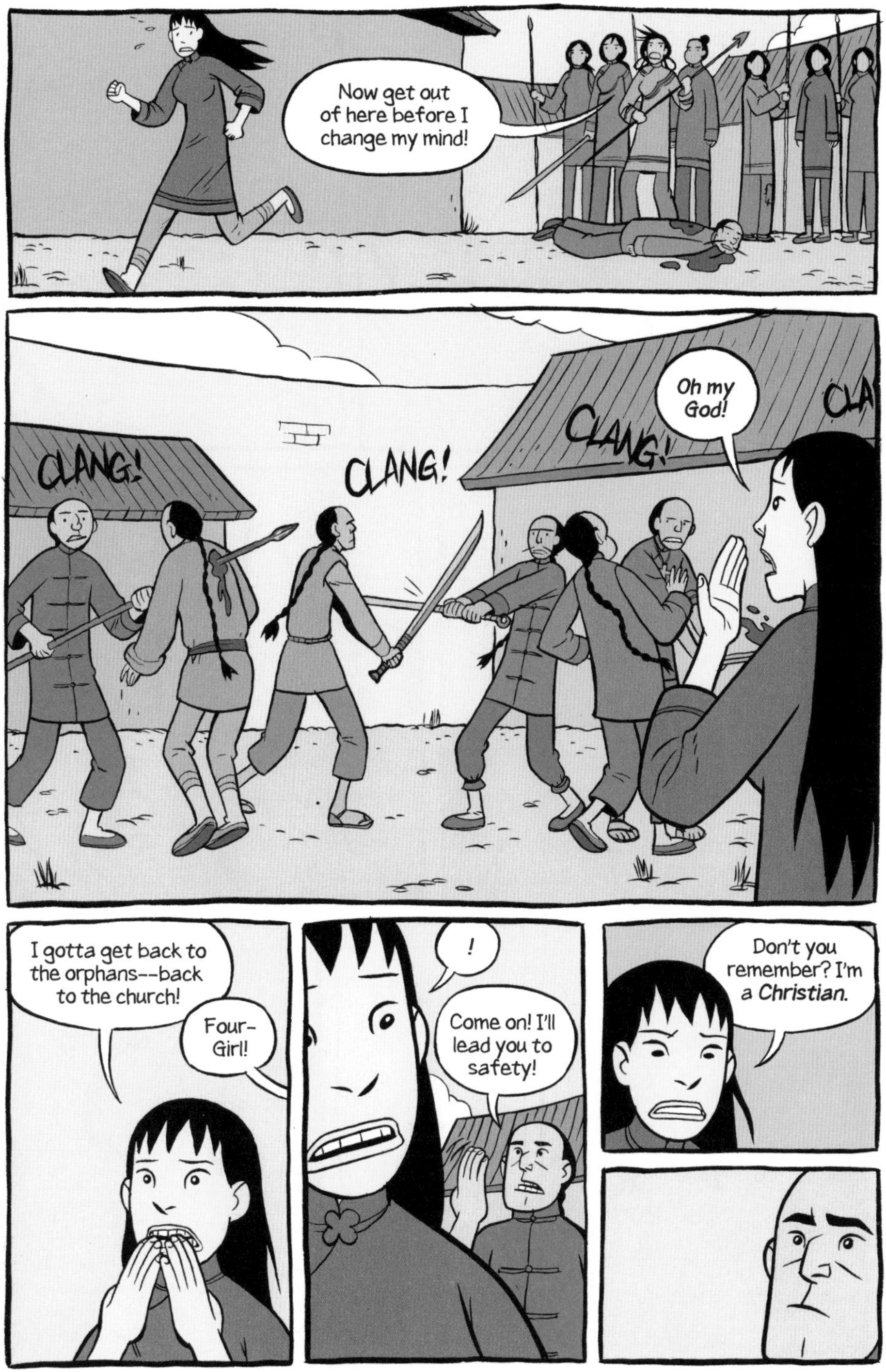
Now get out of here before I change my mind!
CLANG!
CLANG!
CLANG!
CLA
Oh my God!
I gotta get back to the orphans--back to the church!
Four-Girl!
!
Come on! I'll lead you to safety!
Don't you remember? I'm a *Christian*.

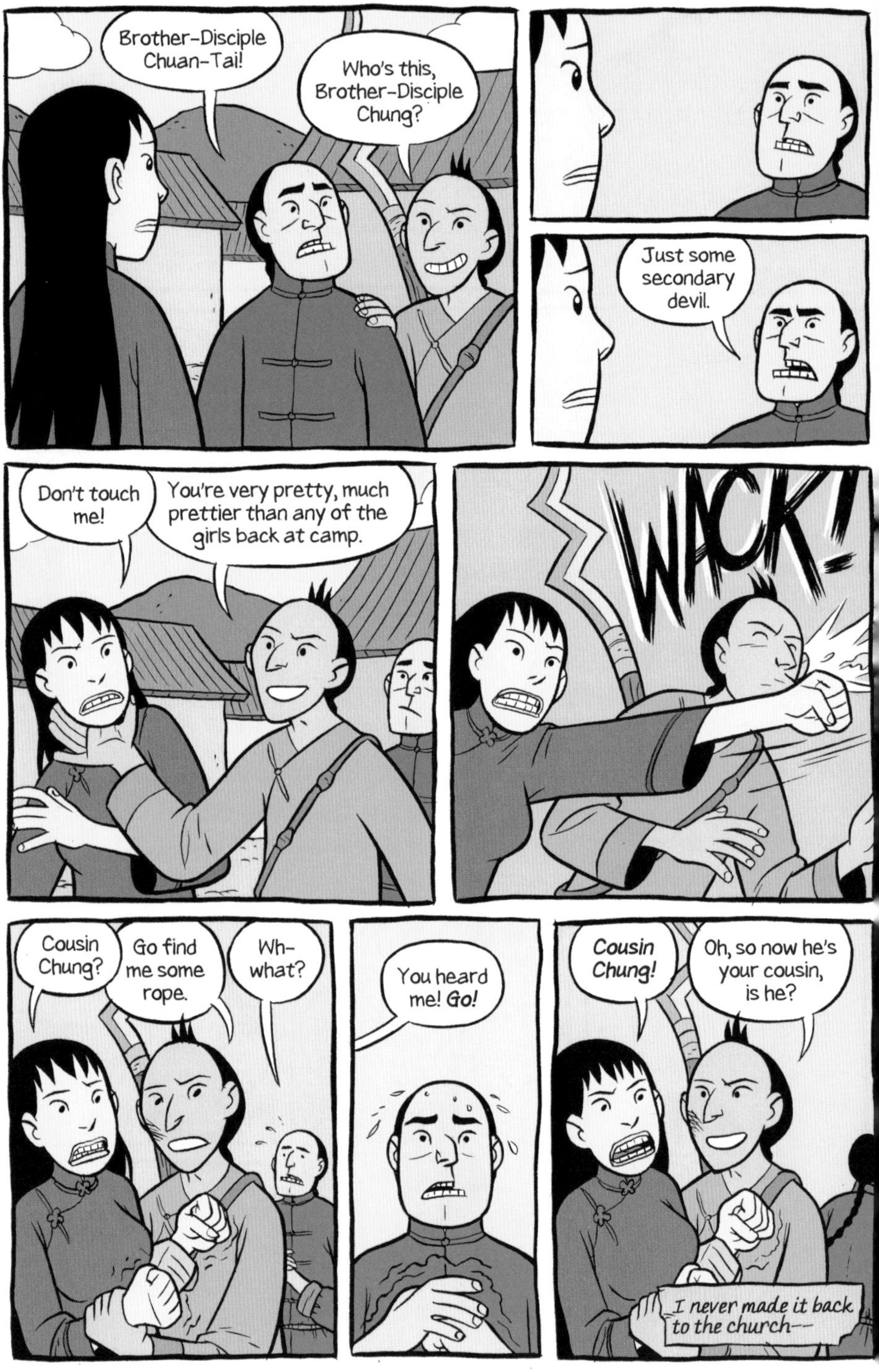
Brother-Disciple Chuan-Tai!
Who's this, Brother-Disciple Chung?
Just some secondary devil.
Don't touch me!
You're very pretty, much prettier than any of the girls back at camp.
WACK!
Cousin Chung?
Go find me some rope.
Wh-what?
You heard me! **Go!**
Cousin Chung!
Oh, so now he's your cousin, is he?
I never made it back to the church--

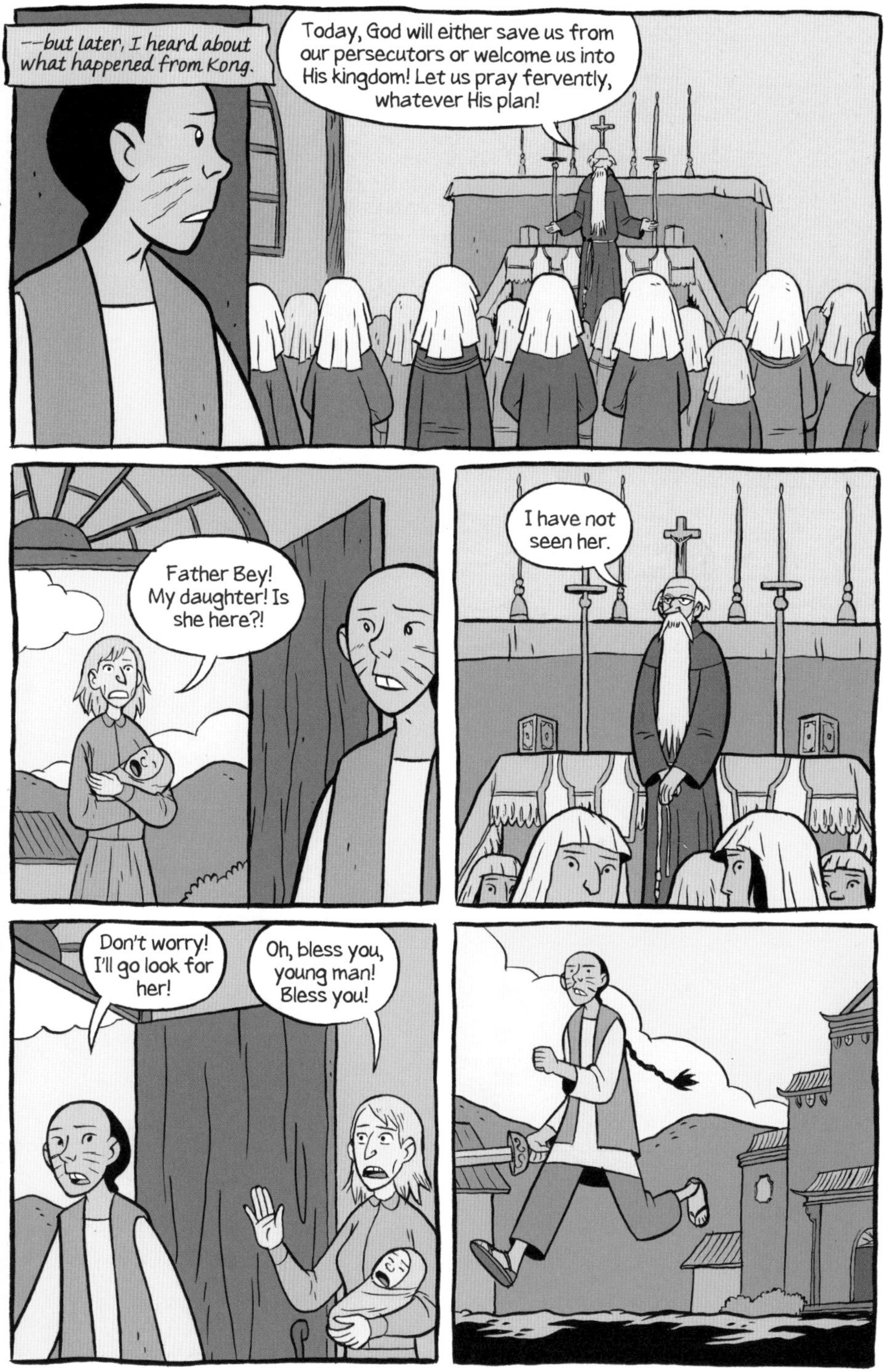
--but later, I heard about what happened from Kong.
Today, God will either save us from our persecutors or welcome us into His kingdom! Let us pray fervently, whatever His plan!
Father Bey! My daughter! Is she here?!
I have not seen her.
Don't worry! I'll go look for her!
Oh, bless you, young man! Bless you!

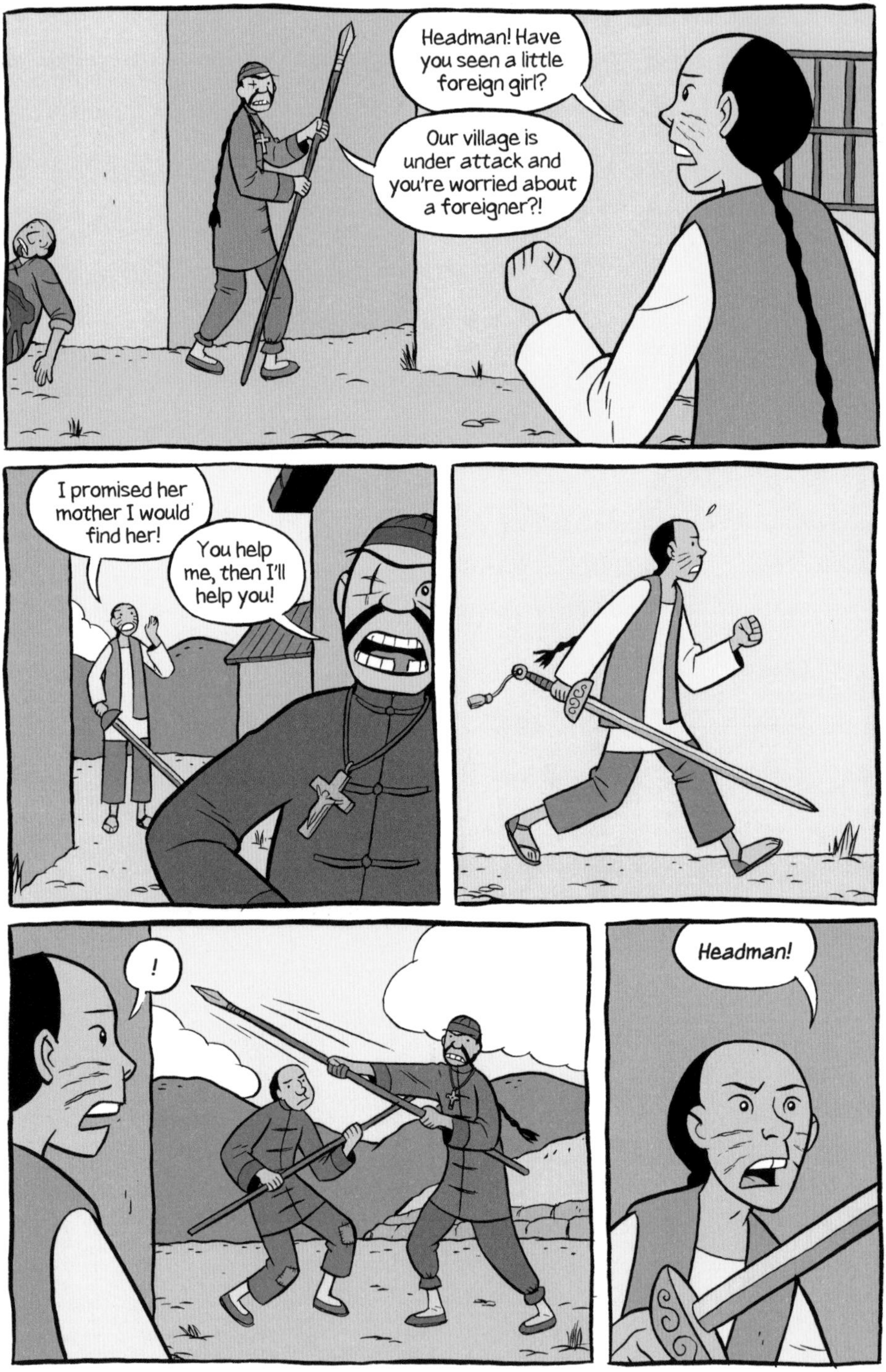
Headman! Have you seen a little foreign girl?
Our village is under attack and you're worried about a foreigner?!
I promised her mother I would find her!
You help me, then I'll help you!
!
Headman!

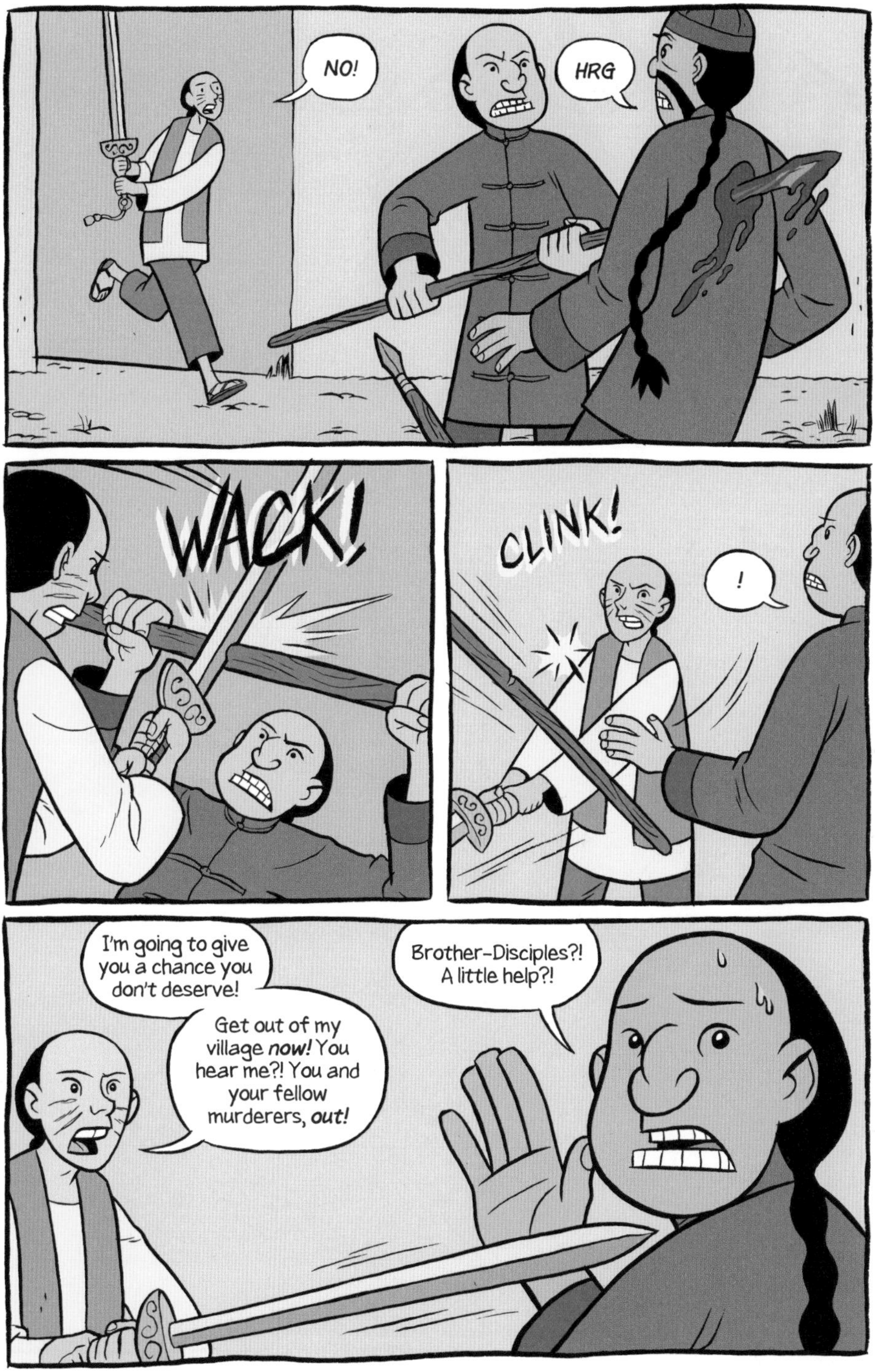
NO!
HRG
WACK!
CLINK!
!
I'm going to give you a chance you don't deserve!
Get out of my village *now!* You hear me?! You and your fellow murderers, *out!*
Brother-Disciples?! A little help?!

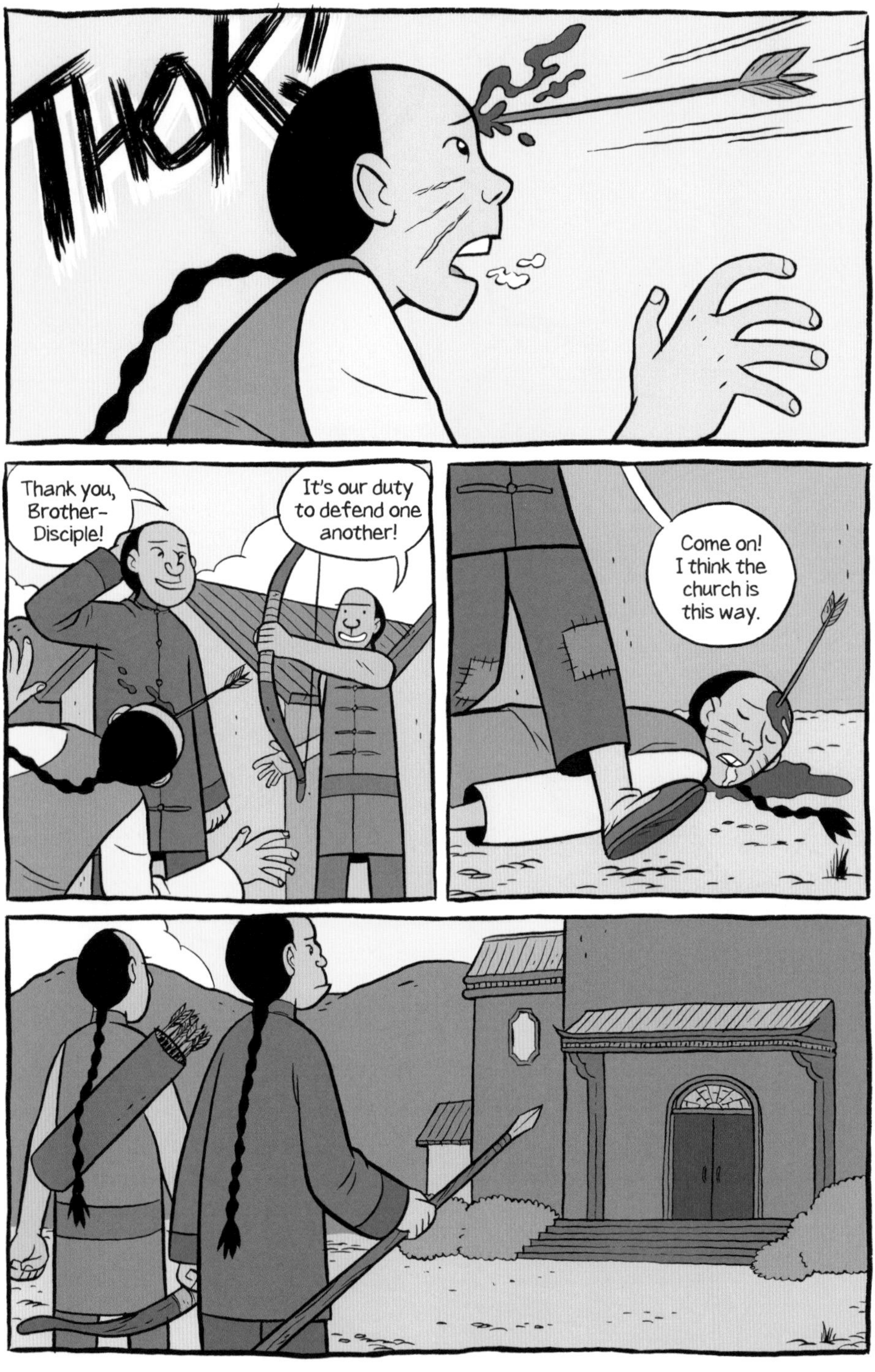
THOK!
Thank you, Brother-Disciple!
It's our duty to defend one another!
Come on! I think the church is this way.

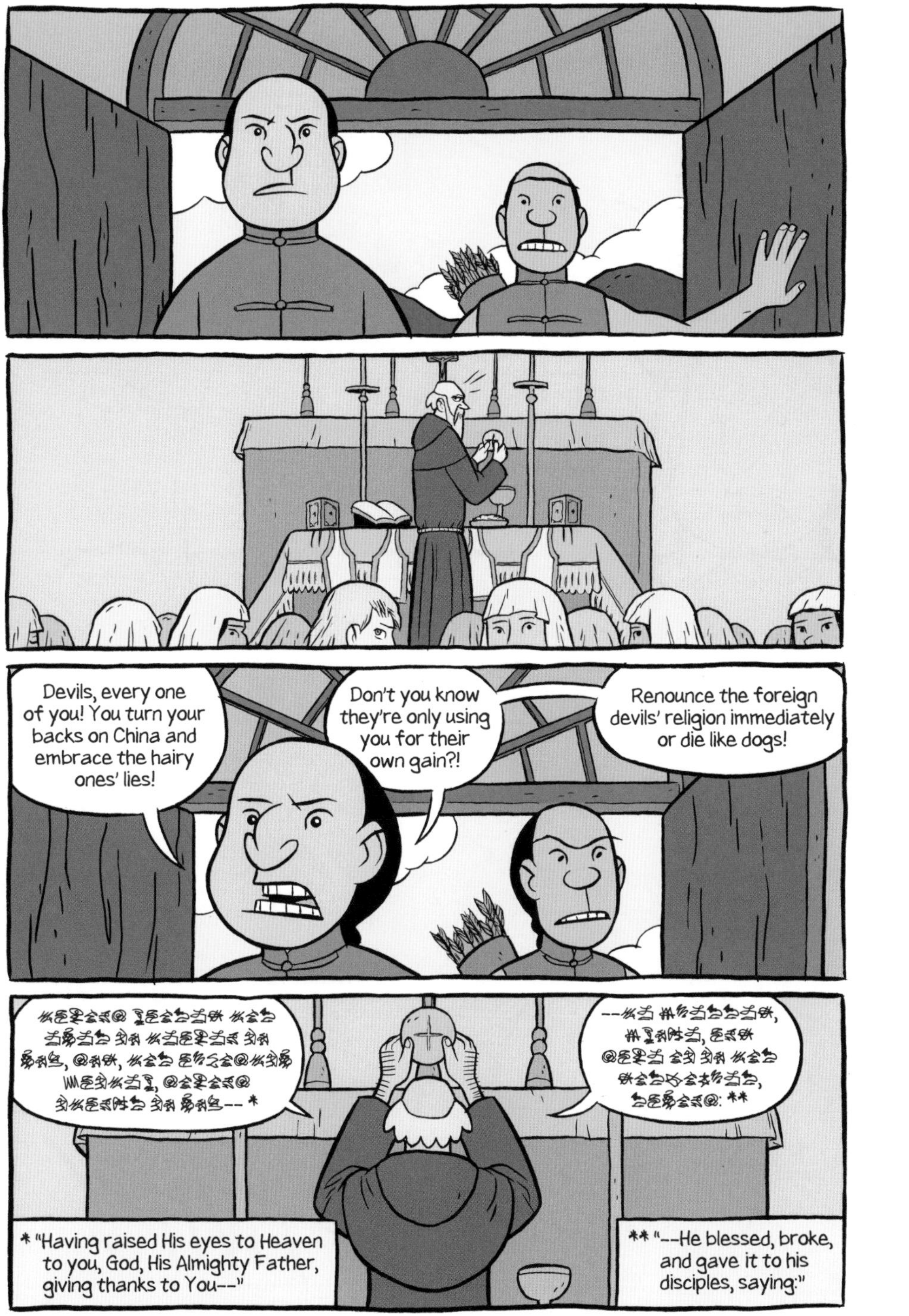
Devils, every one of you! You turn your backs on China and embrace the hairy ones' lies!
Don't you know they're only using you for their own gain?!
Renounce the foreign devils' religion immediately or die like dogs!
* "Having raised His eyes to Heaven to you, God, His Almighty Father, giving thanks to You--"
** "--He blessed, broke, and gave it to his disciples, saying:"

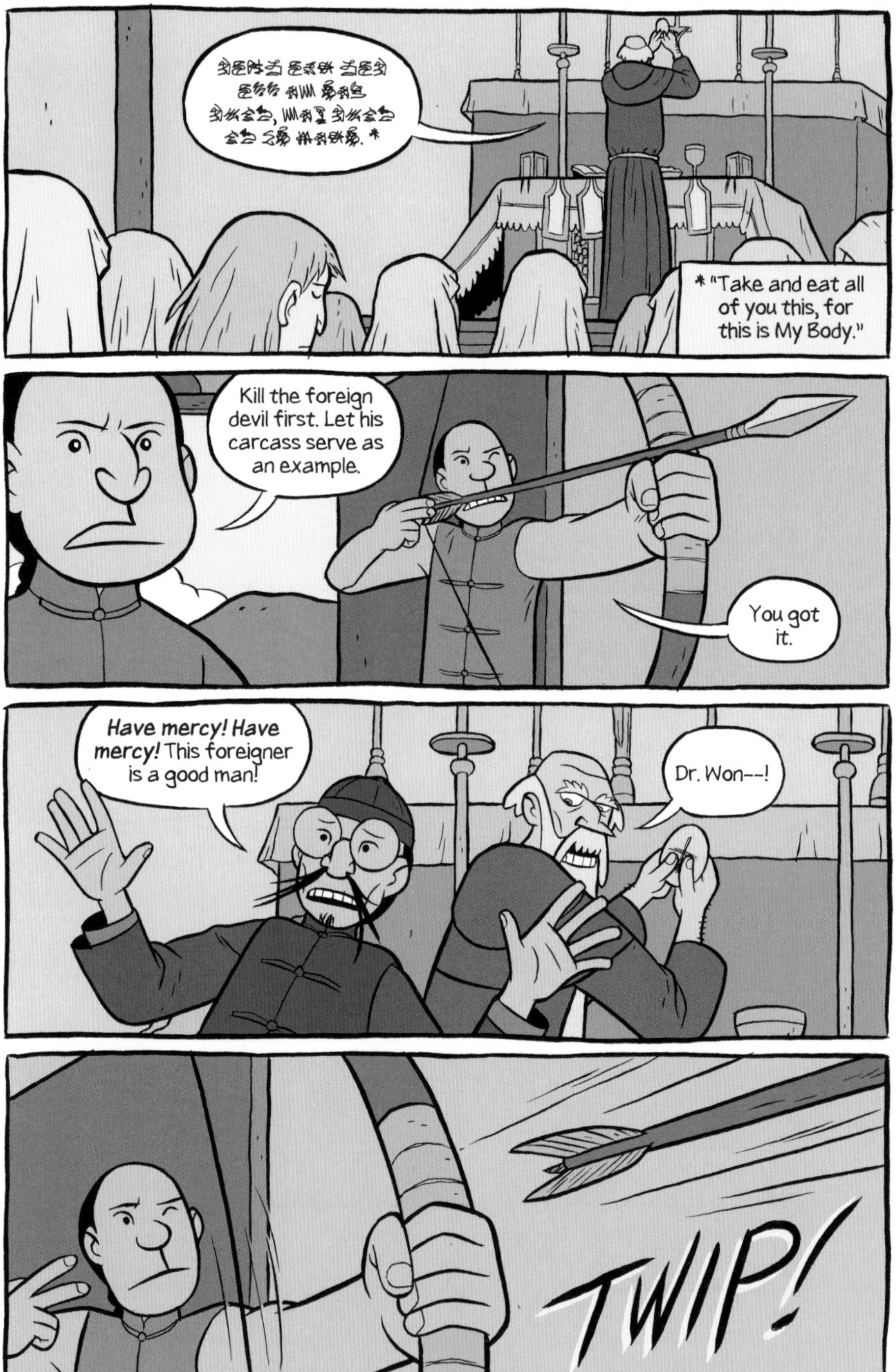

* "Take and eat all of you this, for this is My Body."
Kill the foreign devil first. Let his carcass serve as an example.
You got it.
Have mercy! Have mercy! This foreigner is a good man!
Dr. Won--!
TWIP!

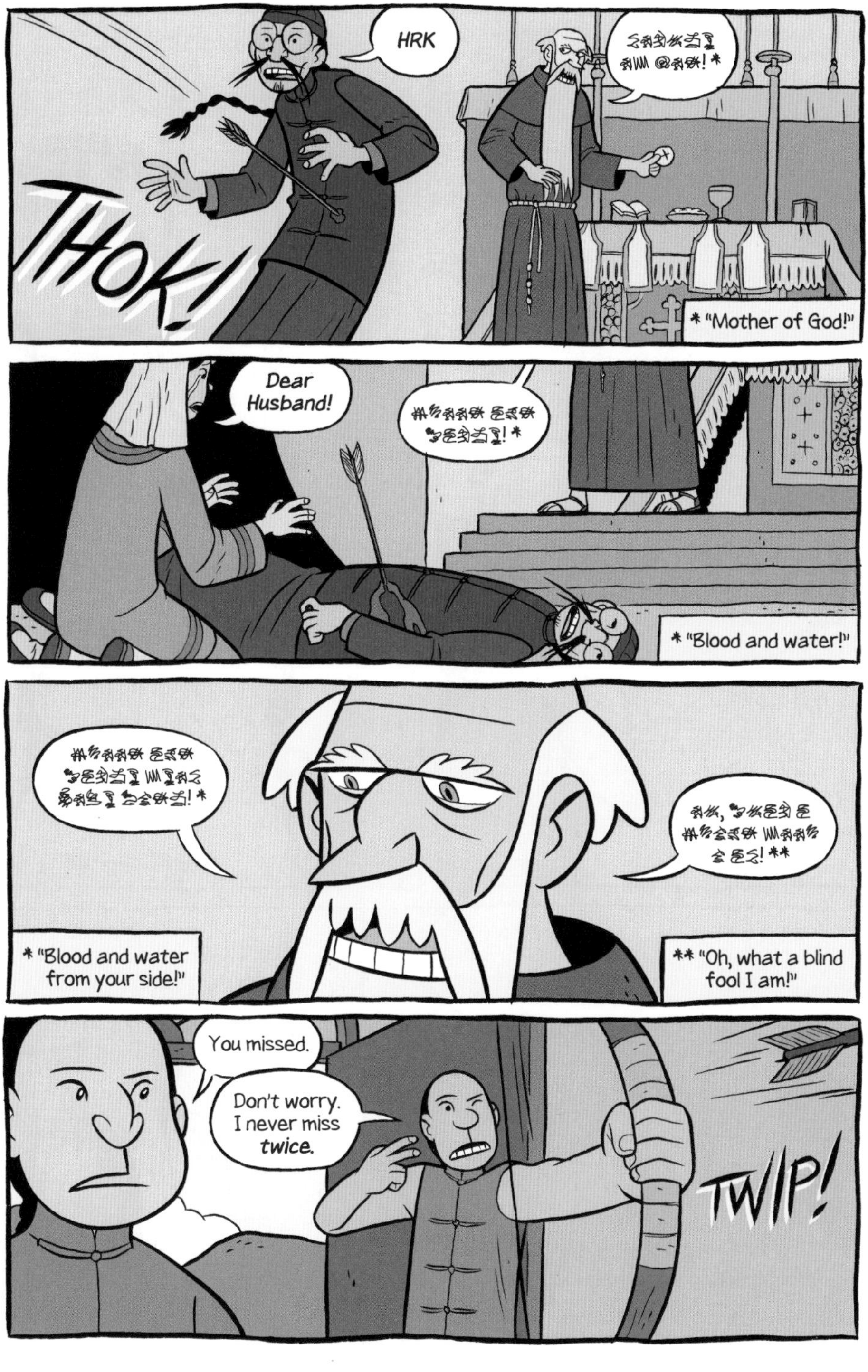
THOK!
HRK
* "Mother of God!"
Dear Husband!
* "Blood and water!"
* "Blood and water from your side!"
** "Oh, what a blind fool I am!"
You missed.
Don't worry. I never miss *twice*.
TWIP!

I thought I wanted... something from you, but not like this... This isn't what I want at all.

Then let me go!

Shut your mouth for a minute! Let me think!

Second Brother?! What are you doing?!

Bao! This is one of the secondary devils!

What do you think he's doing?!

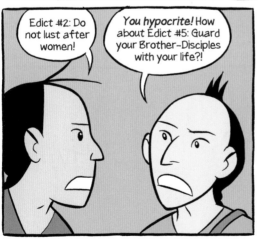

Edict #2: Do not lust after women!

You hypocrite! How about Edict #5: Guard your Brother-Disciples with your life?!

How is it that Big Brother is dead, but you're still alive?

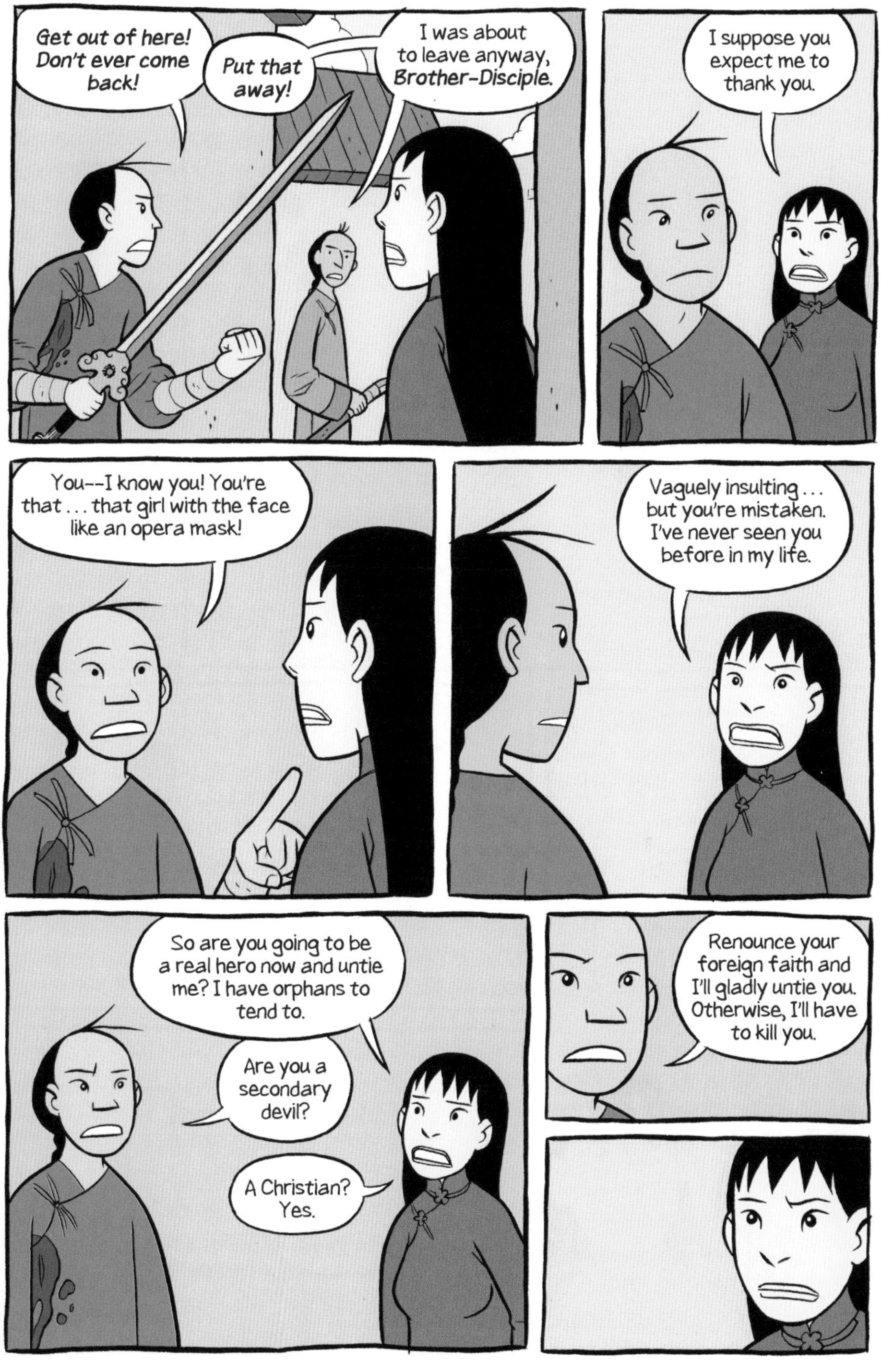

Get out of here! Don't ever come back!
Put that away!
I was about to leave anyway, Brother-Disciple.
I suppose you expect me to thank you.
You--I know you! You're that . . . that girl with the face like an opera mask!
Vaguely insulting . . . but you're mistaken. I've never seen you before in my life.
So are you going to be a real hero now and untie me? I have orphans to tend to.
Are you a secondary devil?
A Christian? Yes.
Renounce your foreign faith and I'll gladly untie you. Otherwise, I'll have to kill you.

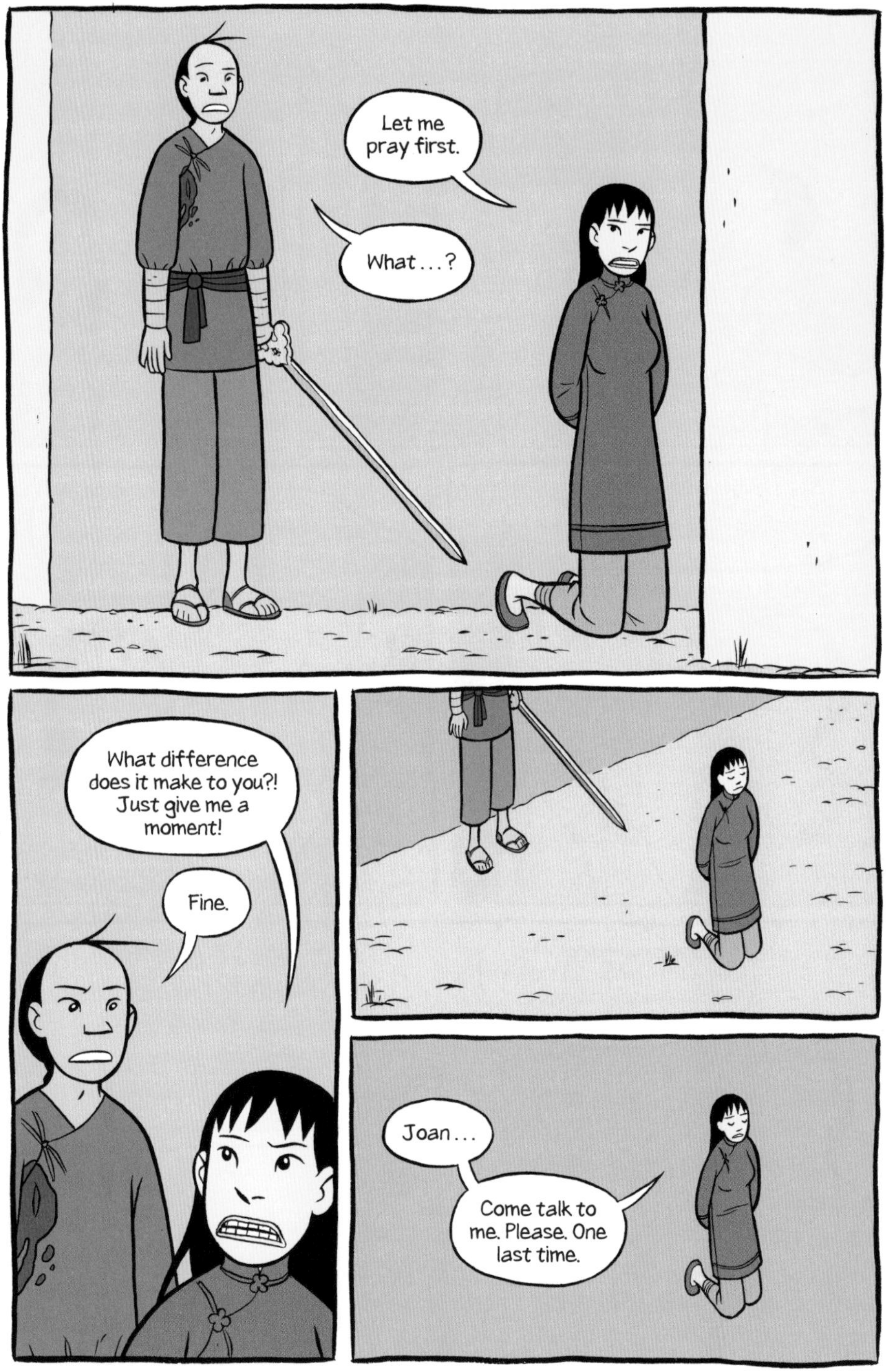
Let me pray first.
What...?
What difference does it make to you?! Just give me a moment!
Fine.
Joan...
Come talk to me. Please. One last time.

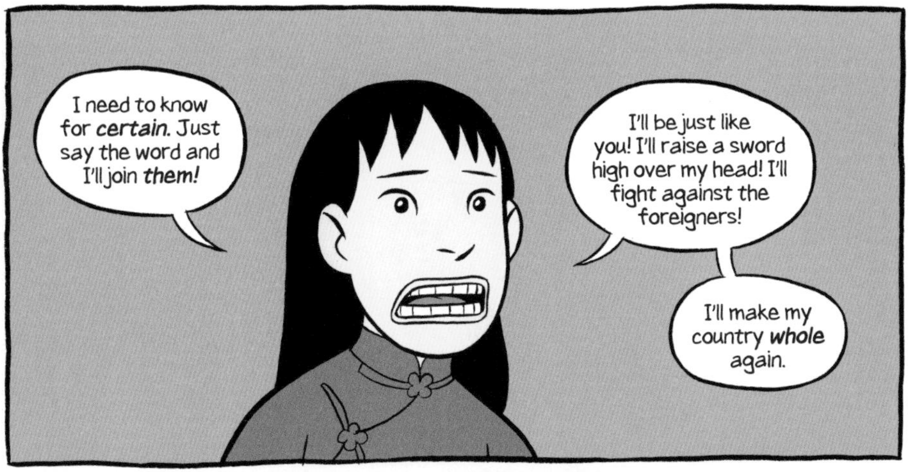
I need to know for *certain*. Just say the word and I'll join *them!*
I'll be just like you! I'll raise a sword high over my head! I'll fight against the foreigners!
I'll make my country **whole** again.

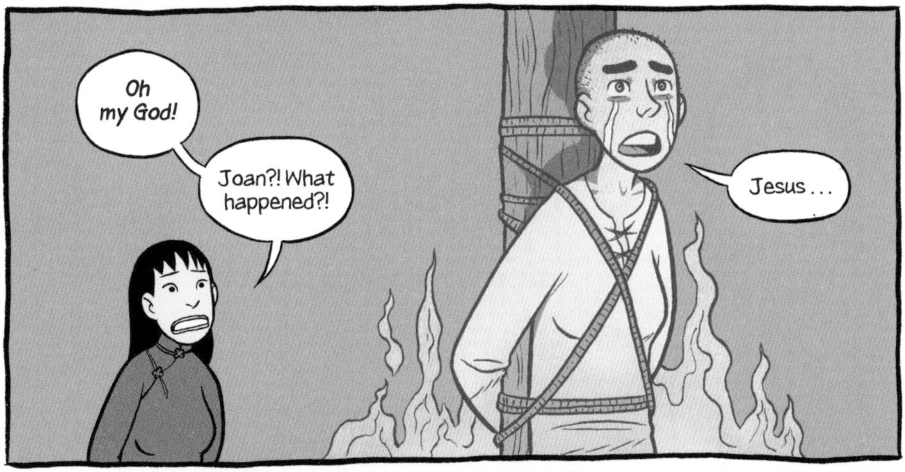
Oh my God!
Joan?! What happened?!
Jesus . . .

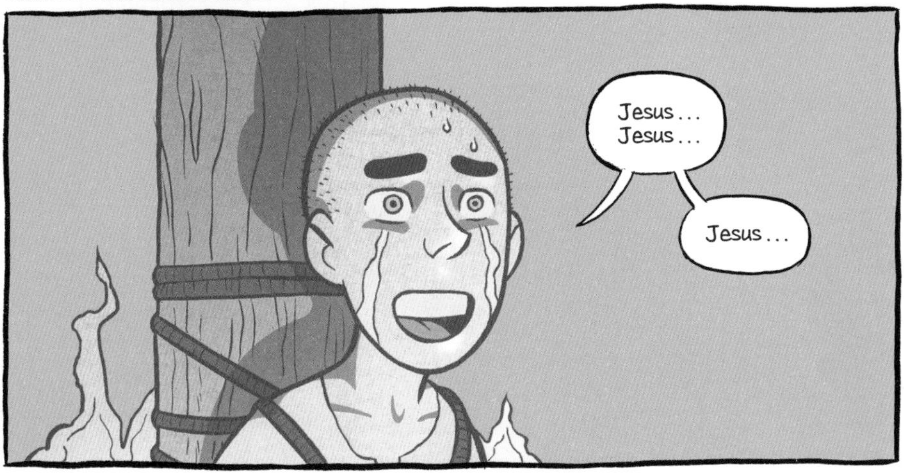
Jesus . . .
Jesus . . .
Jesus . . .

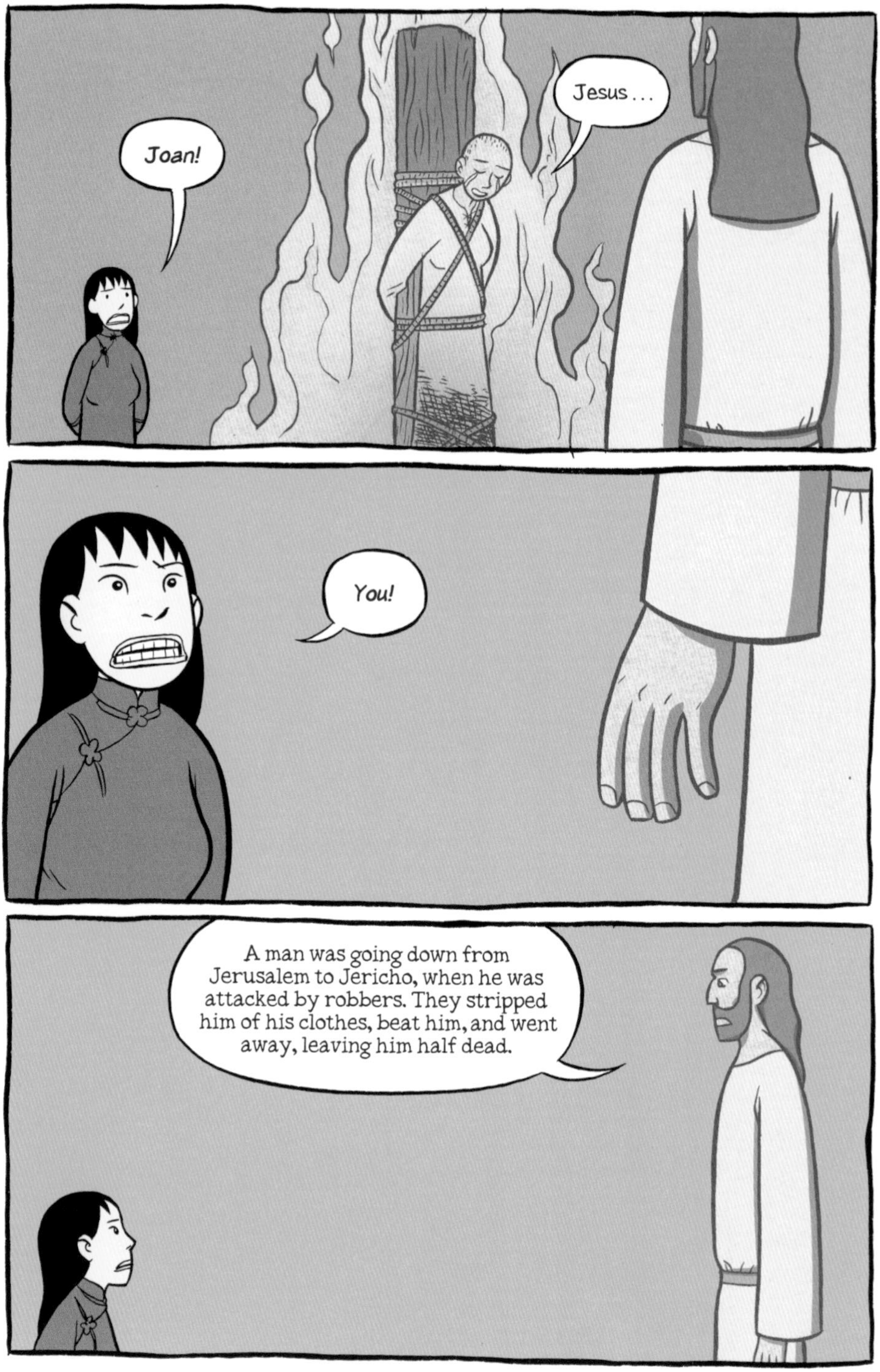
Joan!
Jesus...
You!
A man was going down from Jerusalem to Jericho, when he was attacked by robbers. They stripped him of his clothes, beat him, and went away, leaving him half dead.

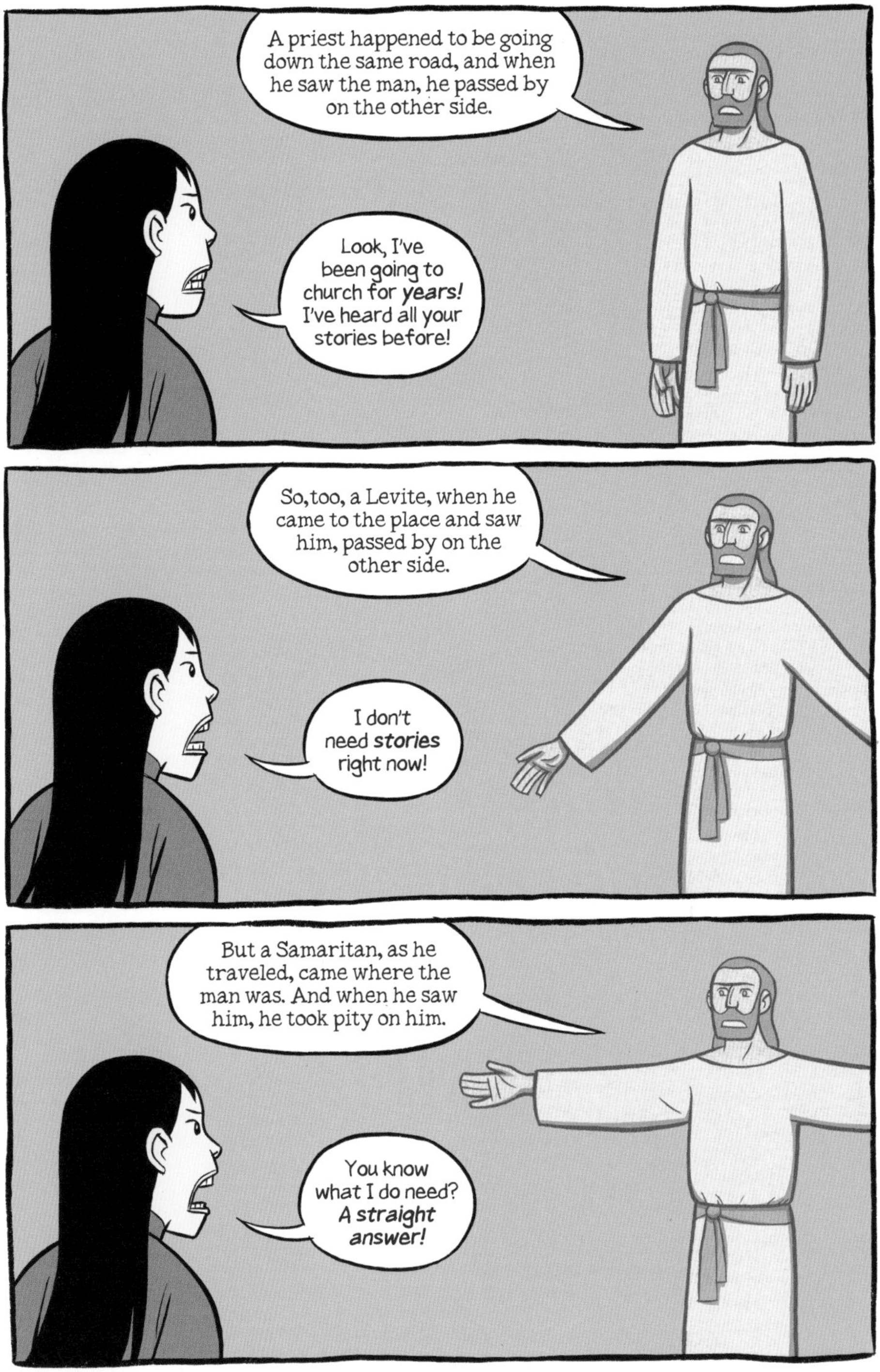
A priest happened to be going down the same road, and when he saw the man, he passed by on the other side.
Look, I've been going to church for *years!* I've heard all your stories before!
So, too, a Levite, when he came to the place and saw him, passed by on the other side.
I don't need *stories* right now!
But a Samaritan, as he traveled, came where the man was. And when he saw him, he took pity on him.
You know what I do need? *A straight answer!*

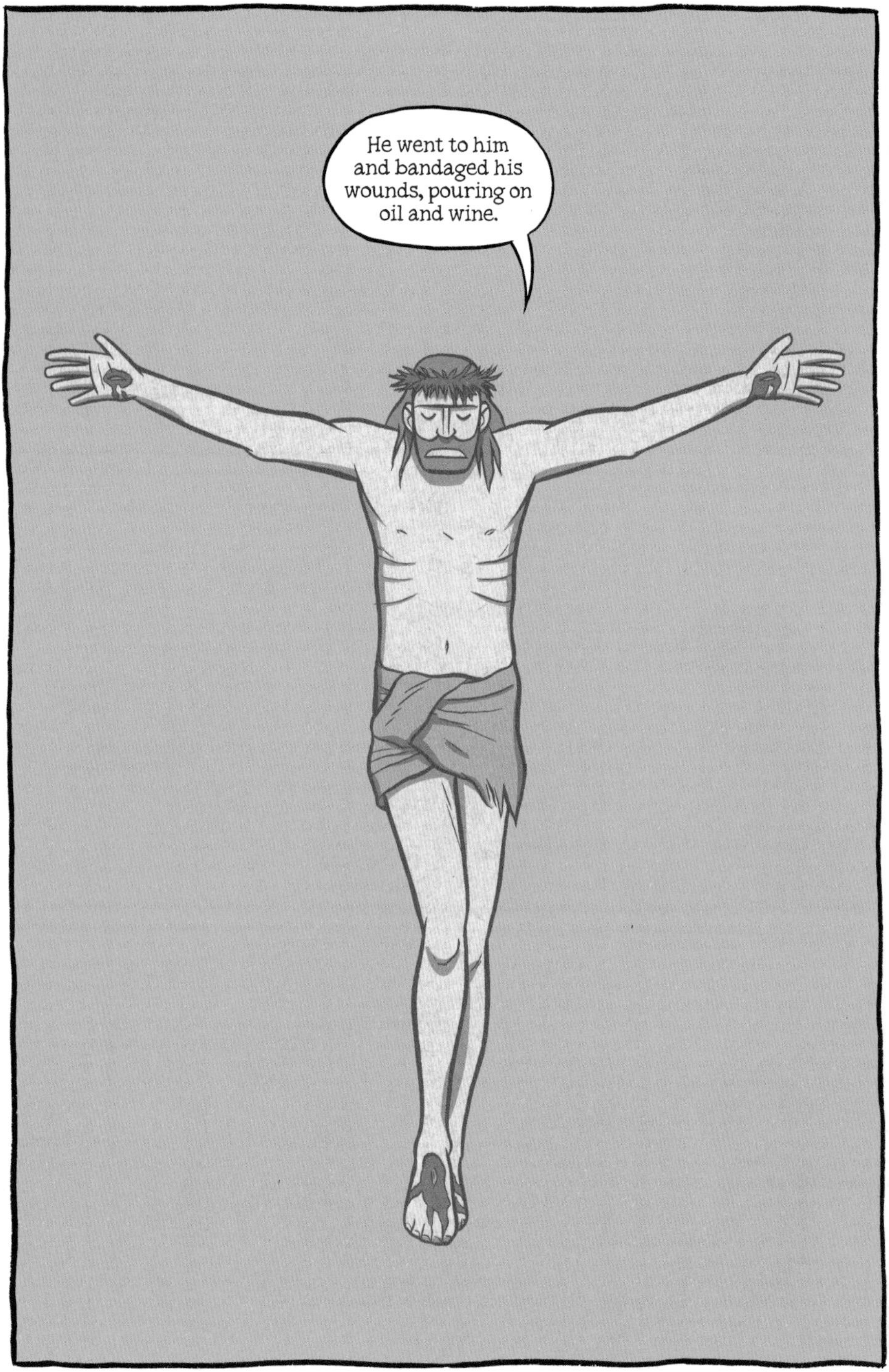
He went to him and bandaged his wounds, pouring on oil and wine.

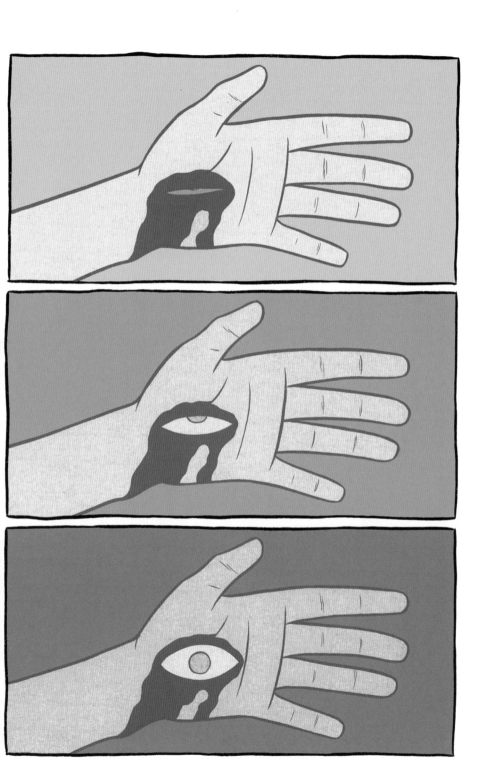

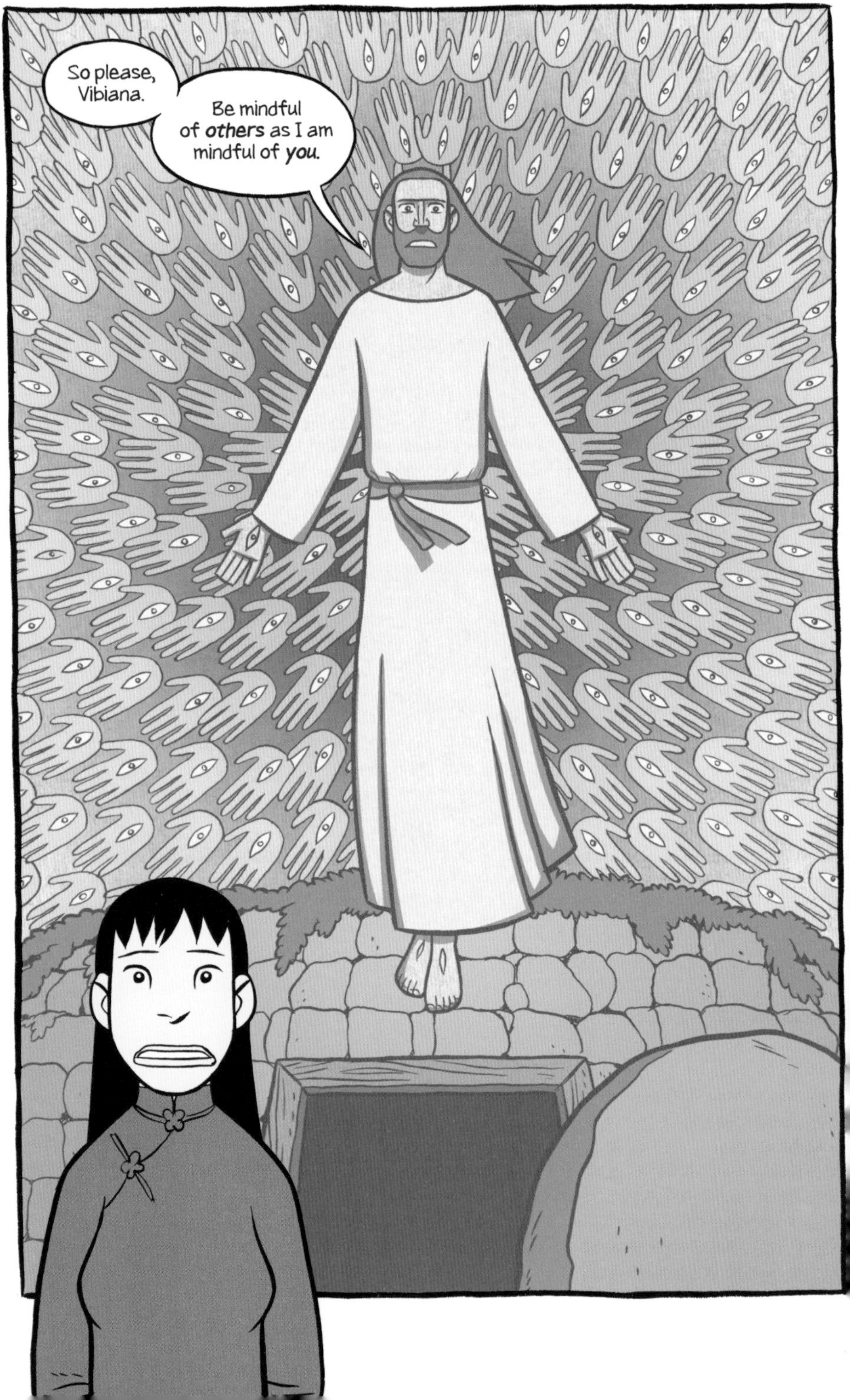
So please, Vibiana.
Be mindful of *others* as I am mindful of *you.*

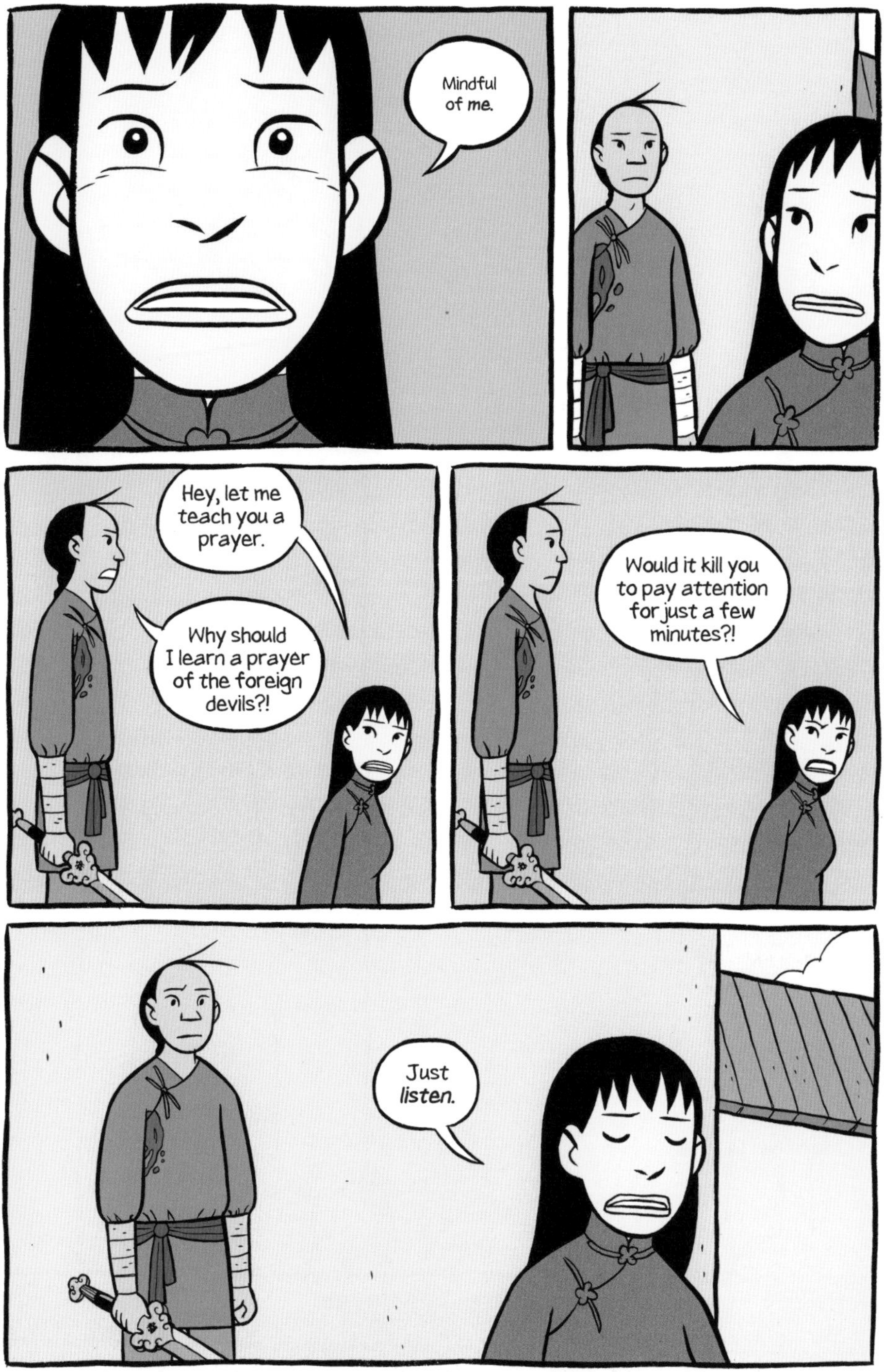
Mindful of me.
Hey, let me teach you a prayer.
Why should I learn a prayer of the foreign devils?!
Would it kill you to pay attention for just a few minutes?!
Just *listen.*

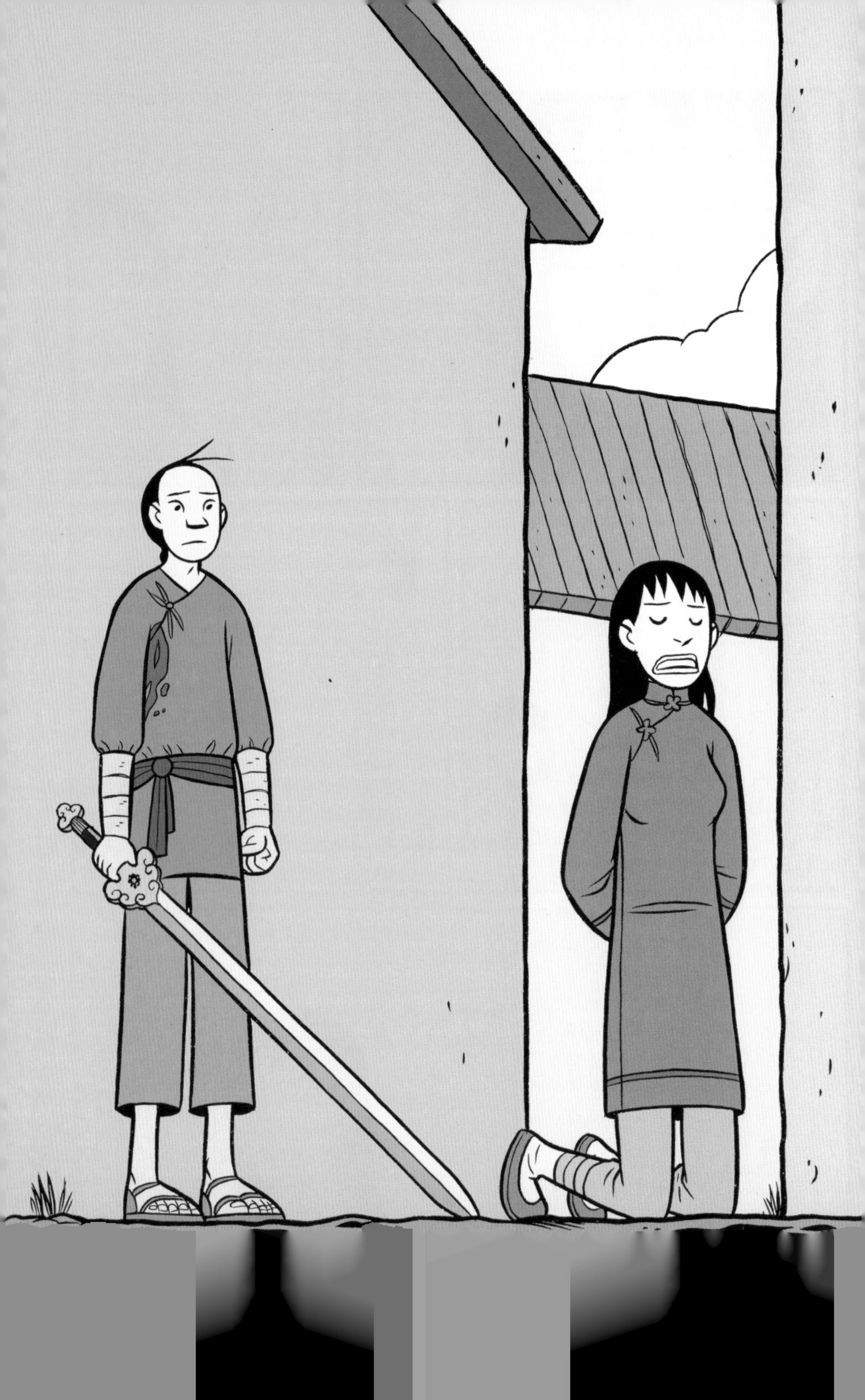

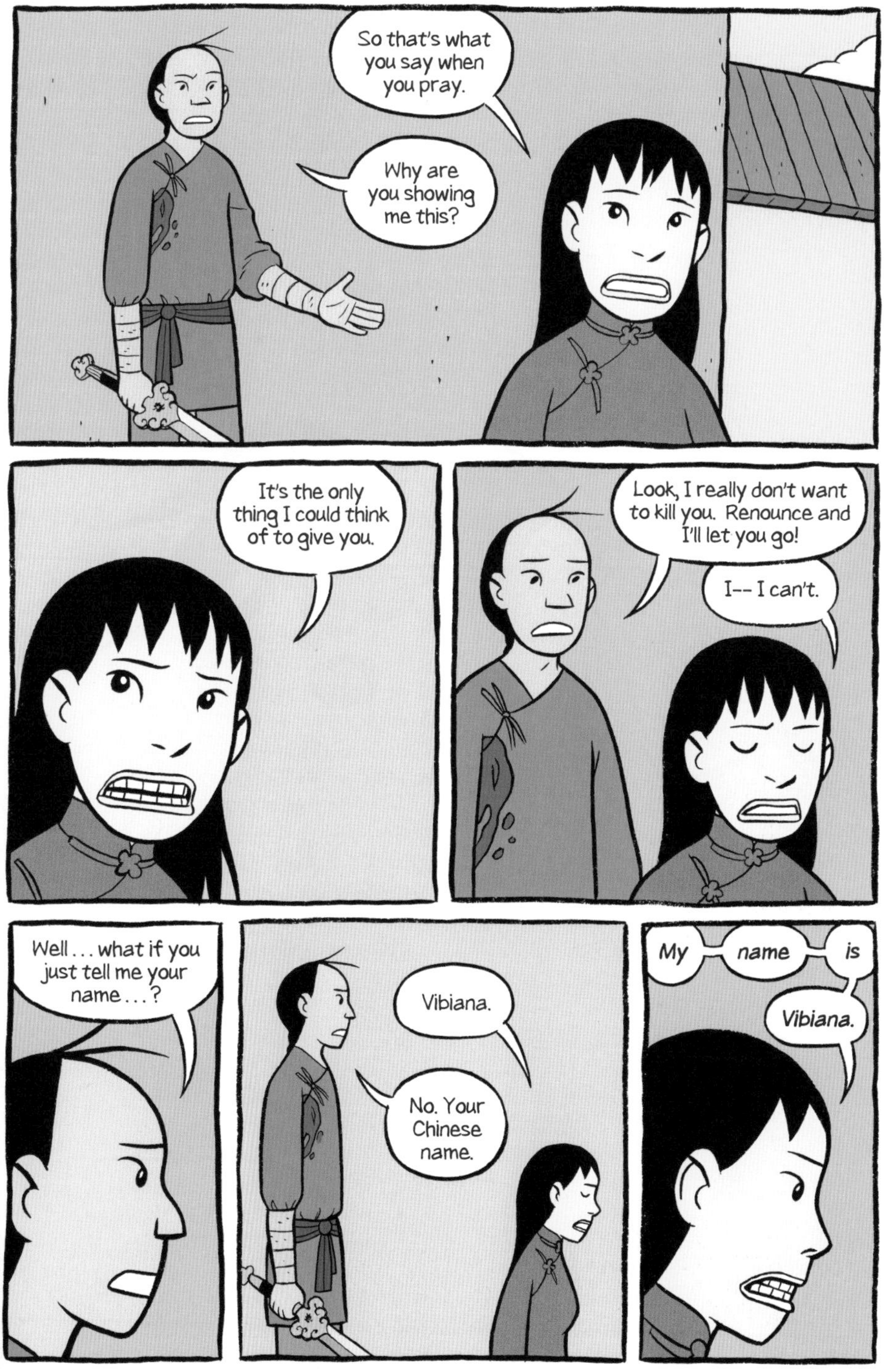
So that's what you say when you pray.
Why are you showing me this?
It's the only thing I could think of to give you.
Look, I really don't want to kill you. Renounce and I'll let you go!
I-- I can't.
Well . . . what if you just tell me your name . . . ?
Vibiana.
No. Your Chinese name.
My
name
is
Vibiana.

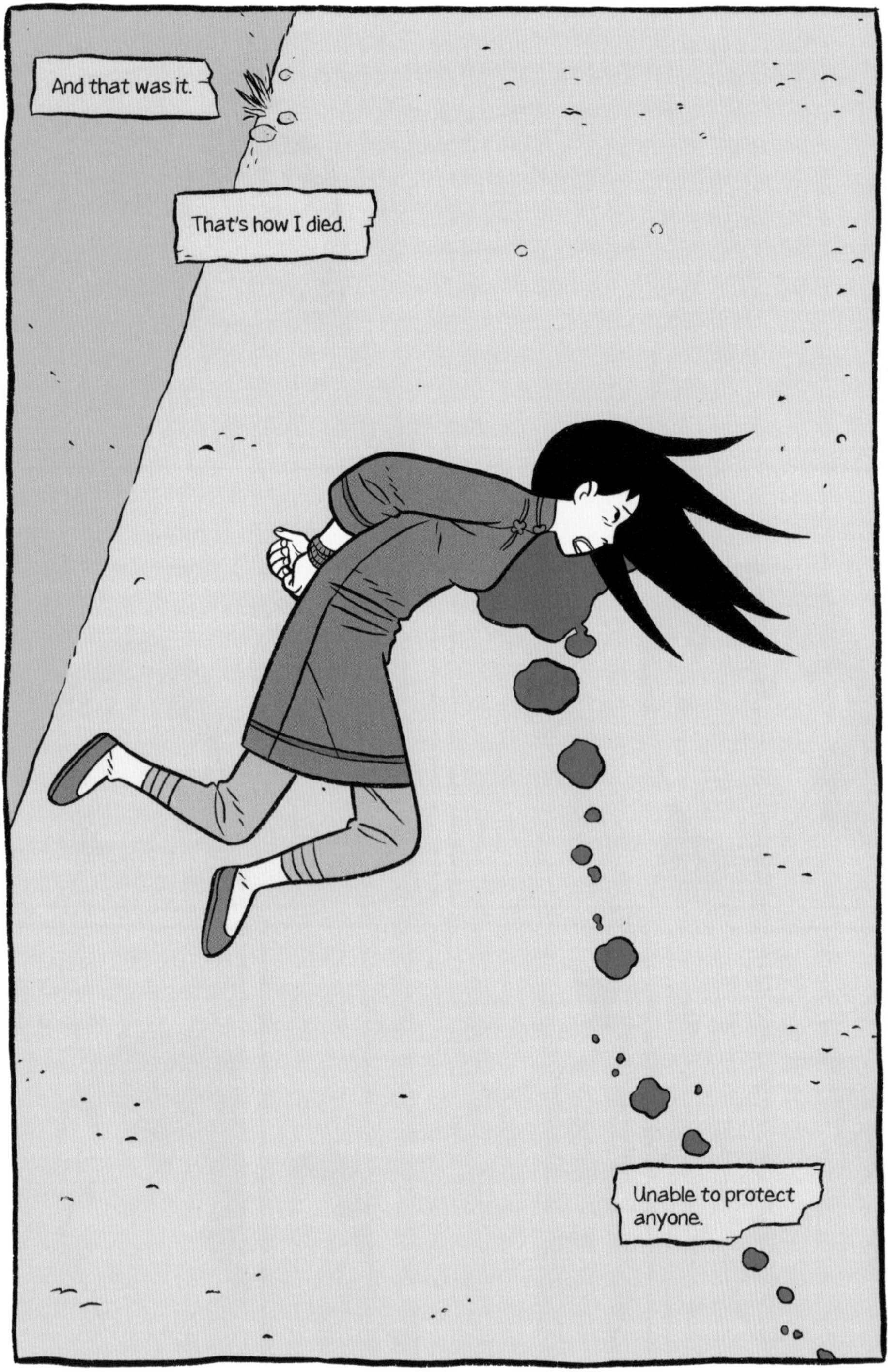
And that was it.
That's how I died.
Unable to protect anyone.

结语

Epilogue

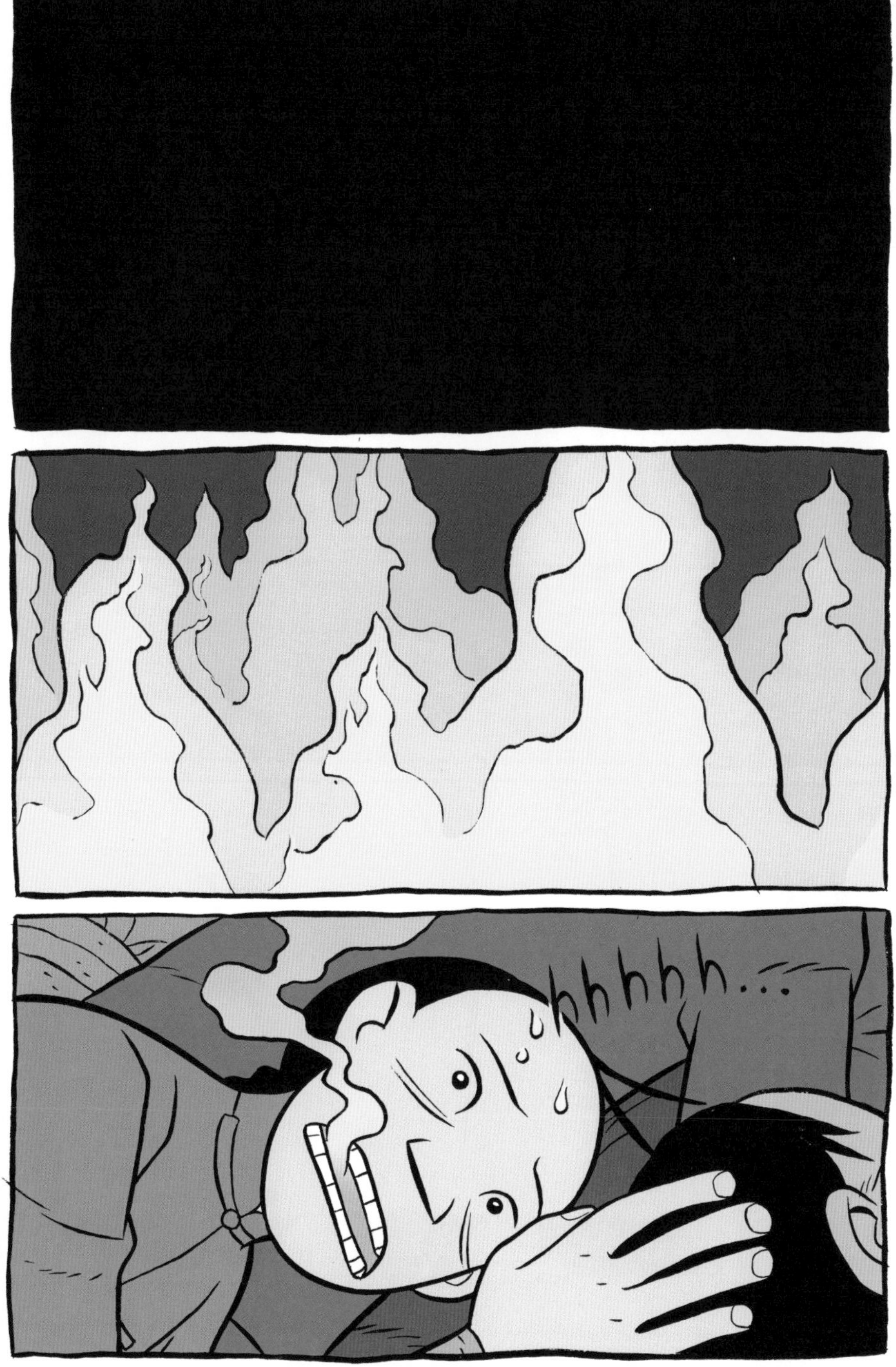
hhhhh...

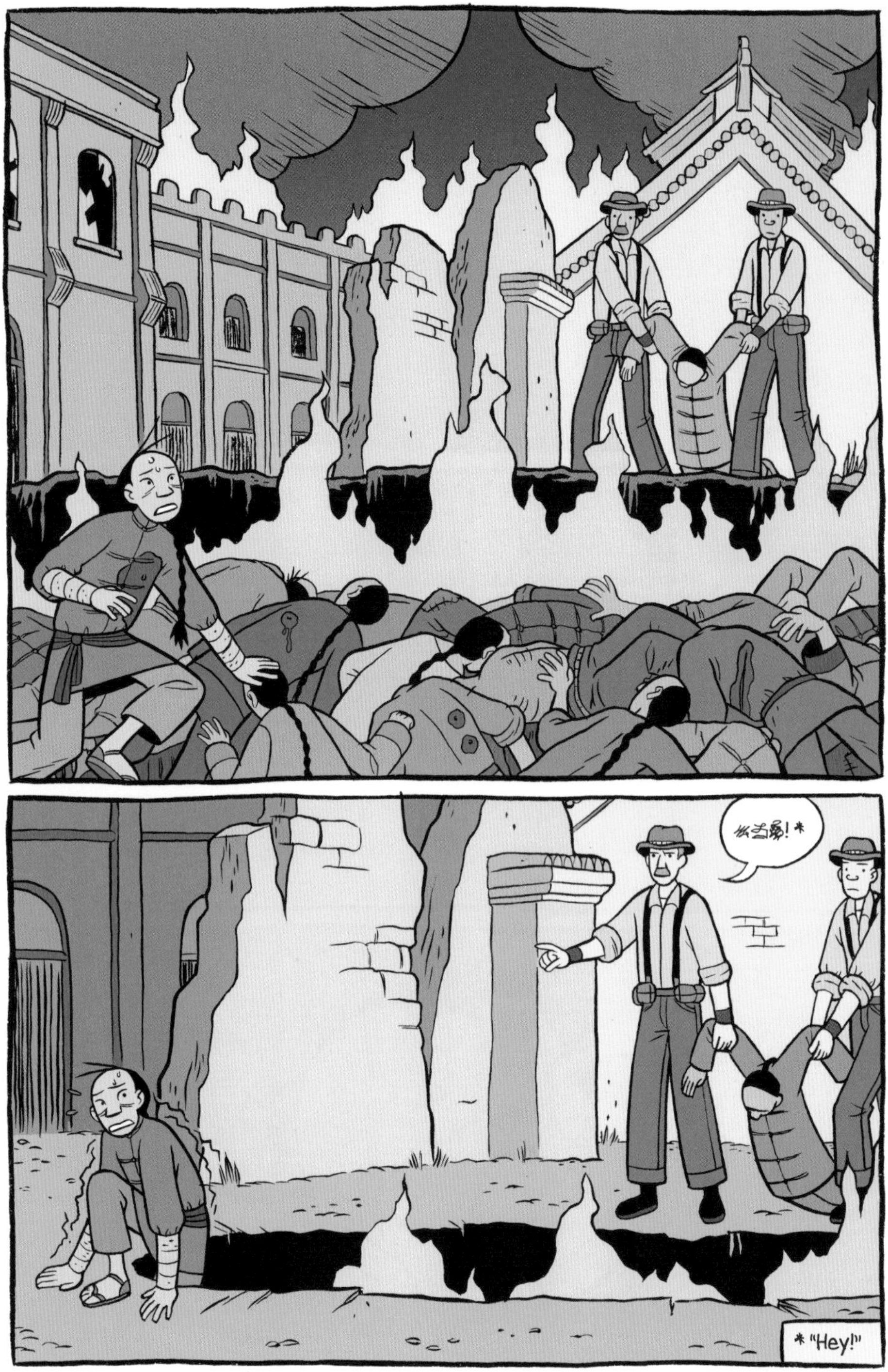
* "Hey!"

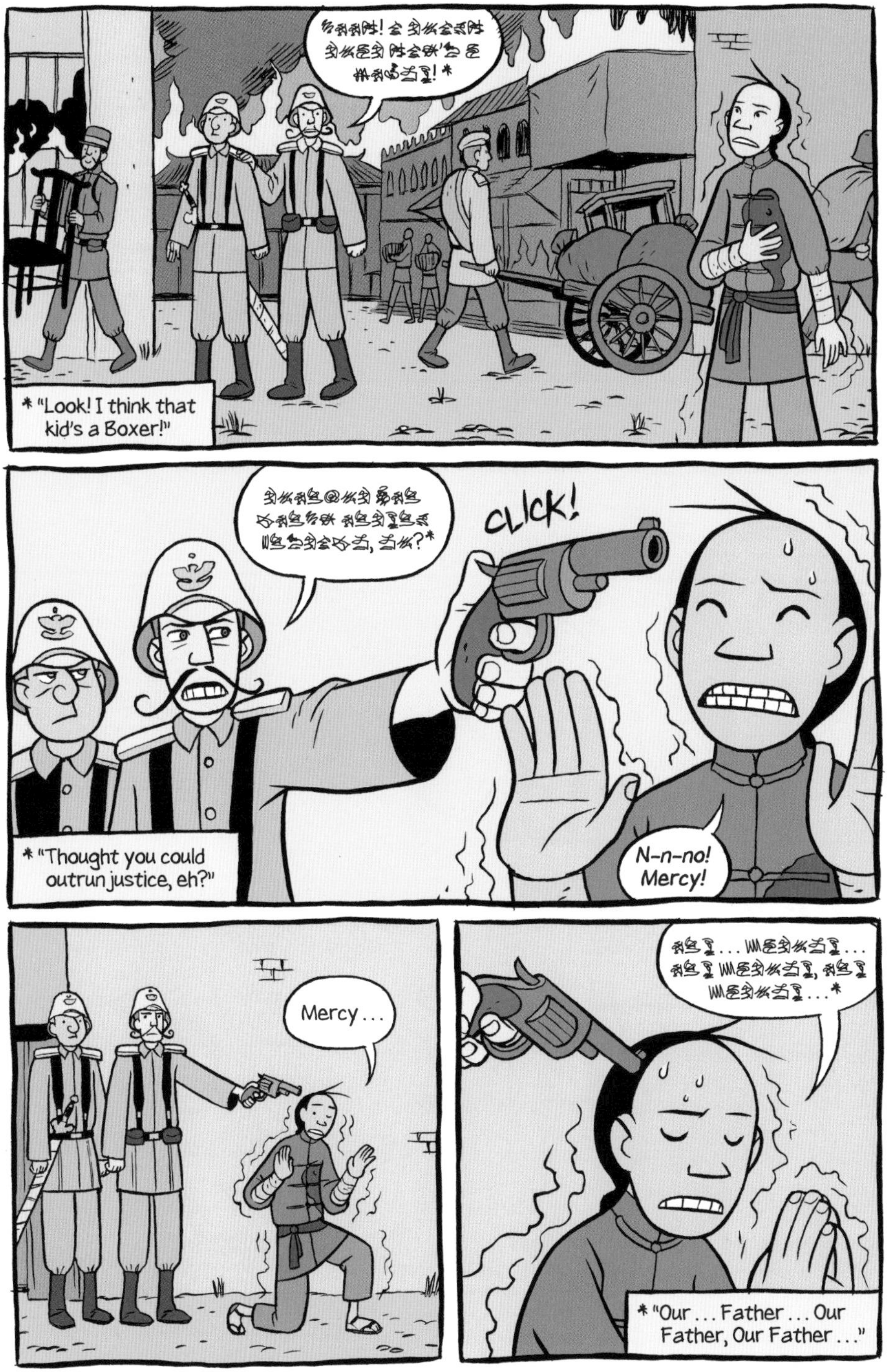
* "Look! I think that kid's a Boxer!"
CLICK!
* "Thought you could outrun justice, eh?"
N-n-no! Mercy!
Mercy...
* "Our ... Father ... Our Father, Our Father ..."

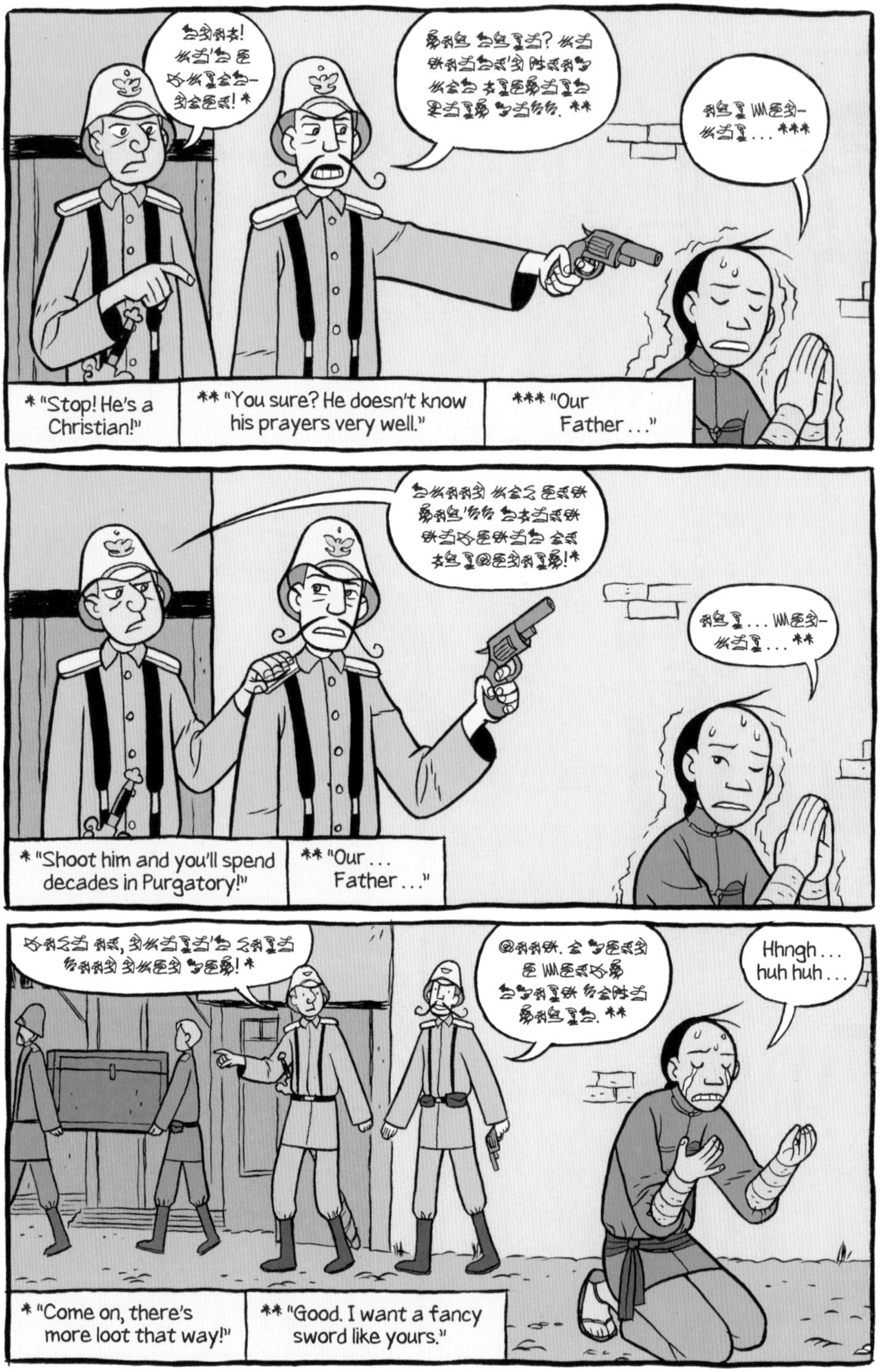
* "Stop! He's a Christian!"
** "You sure? He doesn't know his prayers very well."
*** "Our Father . . ."
* "Shoot him and you'll spend decades in Purgatory!"
** "Our . . . Father . . ."
Hhngh . . . huh huh . . .
* "Come on, there's more loot that way!"
** "Good. I want a fancy sword like yours."

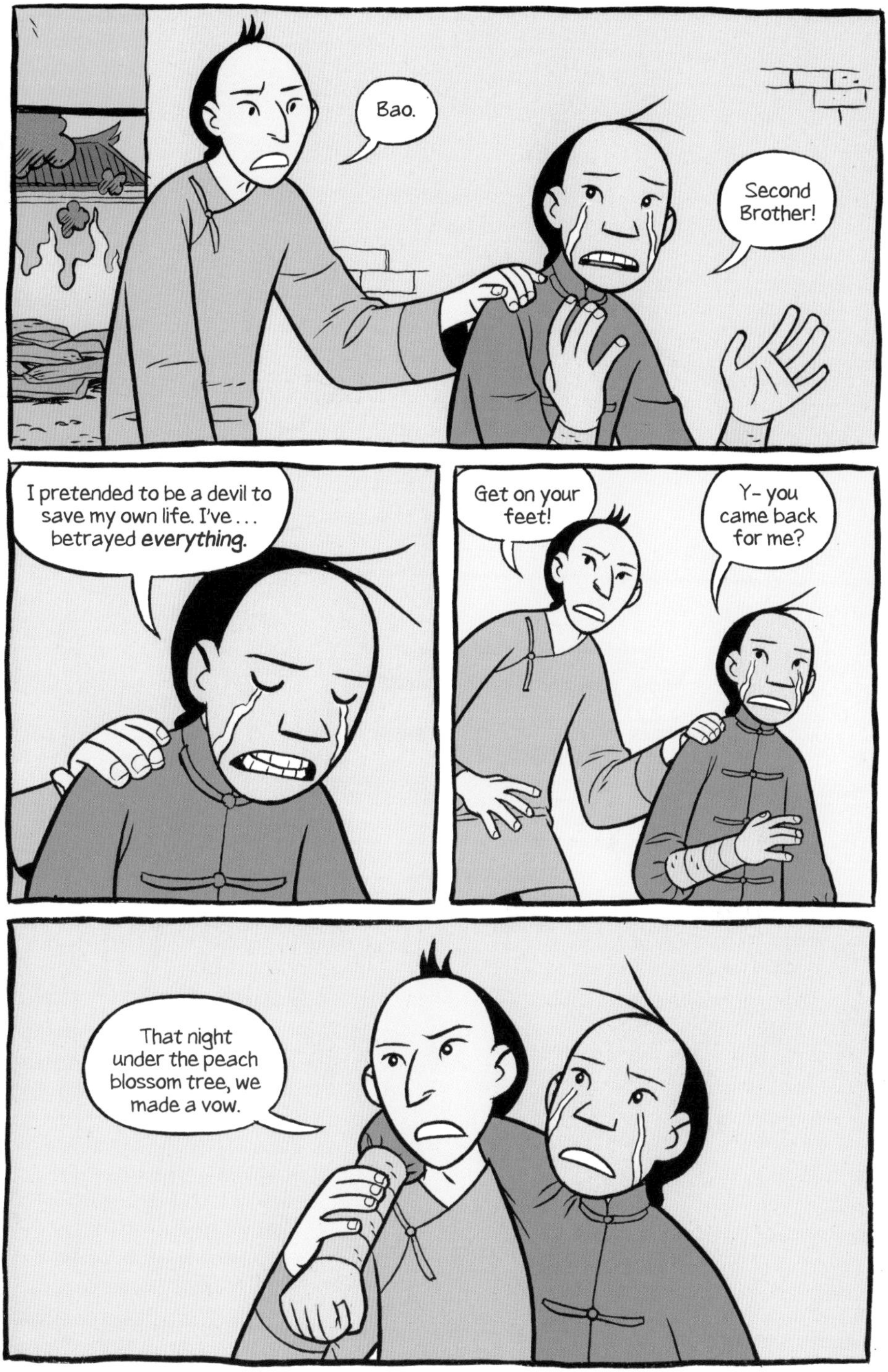
Bao.
Second Brother!
I pretended to be a devil to save my own life. I've . . . betrayed **everything**.
Get on your feet!
Y- you came back for me?
That night under the peach blossom tree, we made a vow.

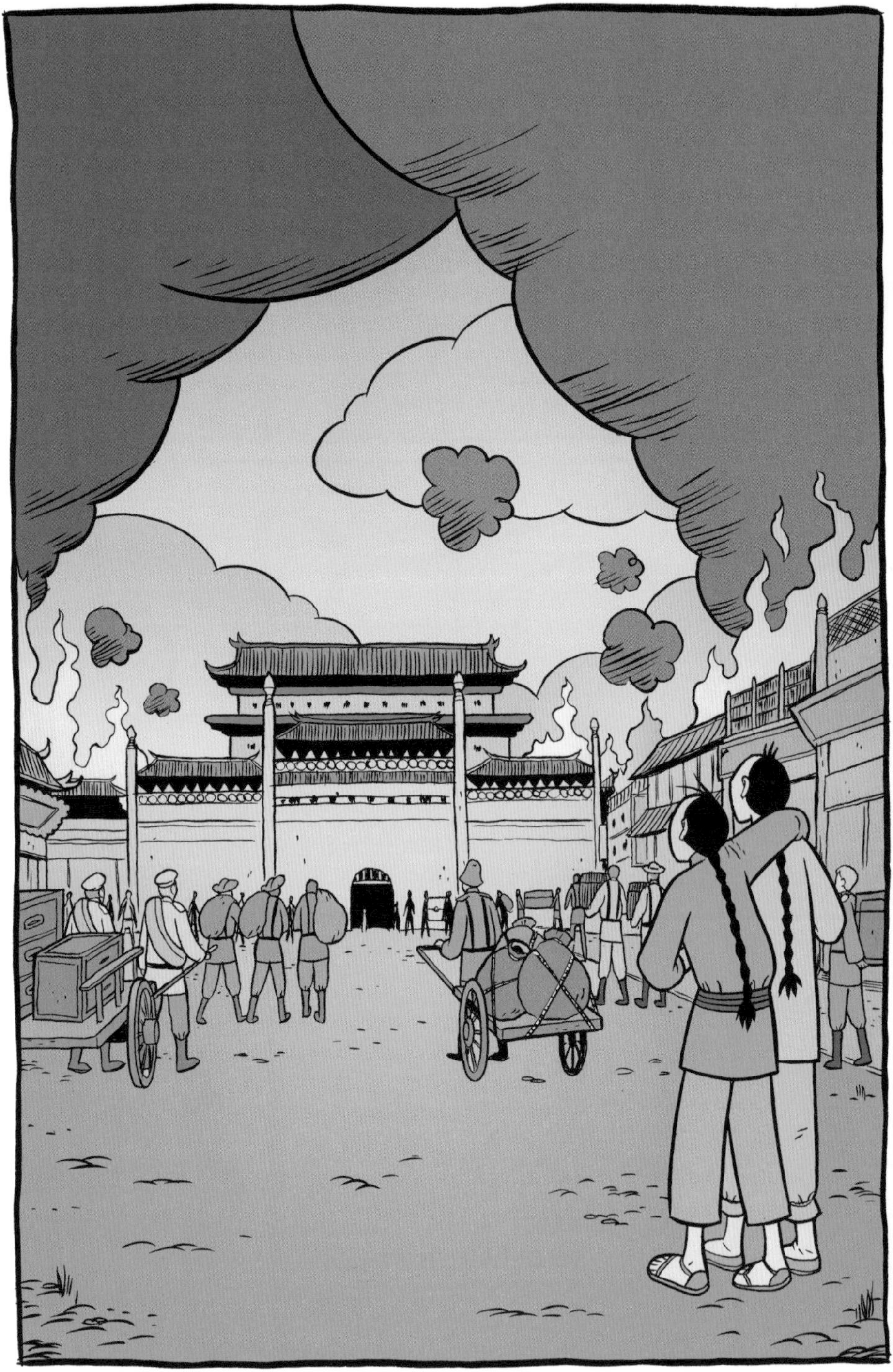

FURTHER READING

THE ORIGINS OF THE BOXER UPRISING by Joseph Esherick, University of California Press, 1988

THE BOXER REBELLION: THE DRAMATIC STORY OF CHINA'S WAR ON FOREIGNERS THAT SHOOK THE WORLD IN THE SUMMER OF 1900 by Diana Preston, Berkley Books, 2001

HISTORY IN THREE KEYS: THE BOXERS AS EVENT, EXPERIENCE, AND MYTH by Paul A. Cohen, Columbia University Press, 1998

ENCOUNTERS WITH CHINA: MERCHANTS, MISSIONARIES AND MANDARINS by Trea Wiltshire, Weatherhill, 1999

CHINA ILLUSTRATED: WESTERN VIEWS OF THE MIDDLE KINGDOM by Arthur Hacker, Tuttle Publishing, 2004

THE BOXER REBELLION (MEN-AT-ARMS) by Lynn Bodin and Chris Warner, Osprey Publishing, 1979

PEKING 1900: THE BOXER REBELLION (PRAEGER ILLUSTRATED MILITARY HISTORY) by Peter Harrington, Praeger Publishers, 2005

CHRISTIANS IN CHINA: A.D. 600 TO 2000 by Jean-Pierre Charbonnier, Ignatius Press, 2007

AS WINE POURED OUT: BLESSED JOSEPH FREINADEMETZ SVD MISSIONARY IN CHINA 1879–1908 by Fritz Bornemann, Divine Word Missionaries, 1984

THANK YOU

Theresa Kim Yang	Lark Pien	Lynn Tang Lee
Ellen Yang	Mark Siegel	Hank Lee
Henry Yang	Calista Brill	Shauna Olson Hong
Jon Yang	Gina Gagliano	Albert Olson Hong
Kolbe Yang	Colleen AF Venable	Fr. Edward Malatesta
Gianna Yang	Derek Kirk Kim	Fr. Joseph Kim
Suzanna Yang	Jason Shiga	Fr. Robert Bonfils
Elianna Yang	Jesse Hamm	The Jesuit Archives in Vanves
	Thien Pham	